MA
MYSTIC MESA

BY
CINDI MYERS

MILLS
BOON

First Published in Great Britain 2017
By Mills & Boon, an imprint of HarperCollins*Publishers*
1 London Bridge Street, London, SE1 9GF

© 2017 Cynthia Myers

ISBN: 978-0-263-92908-9

46-0817

Printed and bound in Spain
by CPI, Barcelona

Cindi Myers is the author of more than fifty novels. When she's not crafting new romance plots, she enjoys skiing, gardening, cooking, crafting and daydreaming. A lover of small-town life, she lives with her husband and two spoiled dogs in the Colorado mountains.

For Denise, the best sister-in-law ever.

Chapter One

"We've got another missing woman." Commander Graham Ellison tossed the photo of a smiling blonde in the middle of the table where the members of the Ranger Brigade had gathered for a morning briefing. The fresh-faced, blue-eyed young woman radiated vitality and happiness, jarring when compared to the stony visage of the commander. "Her name is Jennifer Lassiter, nineteen years old, from Denver," Ellison continued. "She was one of a group of archaeology students working in the area."

"That makes two missing women in the past month." One of the officers seated around the table—the only woman, whose nametag identified her as Carmen Redhorse—glanced at the photo and passed it down the table.

"Three." Officer Ryan Spencer spoke from the doorway of the room. The rest of the team swiveled to stare at him. Not exactly the entrance he had wanted to make on his first day at his new job. He ignored the stares, strode to the table and pulled out the only empty chair, at the end opposite the commander.

"Who are you?" a sharp-nosed, lean man who

sat behind an open laptop—Simon Woolridge—demanded.

"This is Ryan Spencer, with Customs and Border Protection," Commander Ellison said. "Our newest team member."

Ryan sat. "Sorry I'm late," he said. The drive from Montrose had taken longer than he had anticipated, partly because he had gotten behind a caravan of RVs making their way into Black Canyon of the Gunnison National Park, where the Ranger Brigade task force's headquarters were located. But he didn't bother to mention that. As his dad had always told him—never make excuses.

"What do you mean three women are missing instead of two?" The man to the commander's left spoke. He was the picture of a rugged outdoorsman—dark eyes and hair, olive skin, a hawk nose and strong chin. His nametag read Michael Dance.

"I got a bulletin this morning from my office," Ryan said. "My former office." Though he was technically still an officer with United States Customs and Border Protection, Ryan's current assignment made him a member of the multiagency task force whose job it was to prevent and solve crime on the vast network of public lands in southwestern Colorado.

He took out his phone and pulled up the message. "Her name is Alicia Mendoza and she's from Guatemala. Part of a group of illegal immigrants who were traveling through this area on their way to work in Utah. When they were picked up last night, one of them reported that Alicia had disappeared two days ago, near the national park."

Simon snorted. "Nice of them to let us know."

"You know now." Ryan pocketed his phone and looked around the table.

"Don't mind Simon." The man on Ryan's left offered his hand. "He's our resident grouch. I'm Randall Knightbridge. BLM."

"Pleased to meet you." Ryan shook hands with the Bureau of Land Management ranger, then turned to the man on his right.

"Ethan Reynolds," the man said. "I'm new, too. Only been with the Rangers a couple of months. I came over from the FBI."

"We'll finish the introductions later." The commander consulted a sheaf of papers in his hand. "Back to the matter of the three missing women. Jennifer Lassiter's fellow archaeology students report that she took a break early yesterday afternoon. A little while later, they noticed she was missing. Her friends searched the area for several hours but could find no sign of her. They notified park rangers and the county sheriff, who brought us in this morning."

"Where was she last seen?" Simon asked.

"Out near Mystic Mesa," the commander said. "The group is excavating an early Native American settlement."

"Daniel Metwater and his bunch are camped near there, aren't they?" Randall asked.

"They are." Simon tapped a few keys on the laptop. "They just received a new permit to camp near a spring out there. Their permit for their site near Coyote Creek expired last week."

"After the prairie fire they set near there, I'm surprised the park service renewed their permit," the woman said.

"The fire they allegedly set," a tall Hispanic officer who sat at the commander's right—Marco Cruz—said. "Fire investigators determined the wildfire was human-caused, but they have no proof anyone from Metwater's group was responsible."

"Except we know they were," Simon said.

Ethan leaned toward Ryan. "Daniel Metwater is a self-styled prophet who leads a band of followers around the wilderness," he explained. "There has been a lot of suspicious activity associated with his bunch, but we haven't been able to pin anything on him."

"The first young woman who went missing, Lucia Raton, was in Metwater's camp shortly before she disappeared," the commander said. "At first, he denied knowing her, but later we confirmed she had been in camp. She wanted to join his group, but he says he sent her away because she was underage."

"Later, we found a necklace that belonged to her buried about a mile from the camp, with a lot of things belonging to one of Metwater's 'family' members," the woman said.

"No body has been found and her family hasn't heard from her," Randall concluded.

"Interesting that this latest missing woman disappeared near Metwater's camp." Ethan tapped his pen on the conference table. "Where did the Guatemalan woman disappear?"

Ryan consulted his phone again. "It just says in the Curecanti National Recreation Area."

"That's forty-three thousand acres," Simon said. "You'll need to narrow it down a little."

"See if you can get some more specifics," the commander said. "Then you and Ethan follow up with the archaeologists, see what you can find out about Jennifer Lassiter."

"Maybe she got tired of digging in the dirt and decided to take a vacation with a boyfriend," Michael Dance said.

"For her sake, I hope that's the story," Carmen said.

"Moving on." The commander consulted his notes. "Lance, any update on the plant-smuggling case?"

Simon smothered what sounded like a laugh.

"What kind of plants?" Ryan asked.

"Expensive ones." Lance, a lanky young man, leaned back in his chair to address them. "The park rangers have found several places where the thief is digging up ornamental plants, some of which retail for hundreds of dollars. We've got a few faint tire tracks, but there's nothing distinct about them. No witnesses. Unless we catch this guy in the act, I don't think we have much of a chance."

"All right," the commander said. "We're almost done here. Just a little housekeeping to take care of." Ryan's mind wandered as Ellison shared some bulletins from area law enforcement, a heads-up about a controlled burn the Forest Service was conducting in the area, and construction updates in the park. The Ranger Brigade was an unusual force, comprised of officers from many different agencies, tasked with overseeing an expanse of public land the size of Indiana. Only a few hundred people occupied that land, but the potential for criminal activity, from smuggling to manufacturing drugs to theft of public property, was huge.

"All right, you're dismissed," Commander Ellison said. "Have a safe day."

Ryan pulled out his phone and sent a text to his former supervisor at Customs and Border Protection, asking for the specific location where Alicia Mendoza had been last seen. He hit the send button as the female officer approached. Her straight black hair hung almost to her waist, and her tawny skin and high cheekbones attested to a Native American heritage. "I'm Carmen Redhorse," she said. "Welcome to the team."

"Simon Woolridge." The agent with the laptop shook hands also. "I'm the tech expert on the squad. I've got lots of information on Daniel Metwater, if you need it."

"I'm Marco Cruz, DEA." The Hispanic agent from the Drug Enforcement Agency had a grip of steel, but a welcoming expression. "I hope you like working in the great outdoors, because we've got a lot of territory we cover, most of it pretty empty."

"Things can get exciting, though." Randall Knightbridge joined them, a cup of coffee in one hand, a fawn-and-black police dog at his side. "This is Lotte," he introduced the dog. "Another member of the team."

The last two officers he would be working with introduced themselves—Michael Dance was the rugged outdoorsman who had been seated at the other end of the conference table, and Lance Carpenter was the Montrose County Sheriff's Deputy who was heading up the stolen-plant investigation.

"Are you married?" Marco asked.

"No. The job hasn't given me much time for girlfriends."

"You might be surprised," Marco said. "But if you're not interested in a relationship, you might want to avoid drinking the water around here."

The others laughed, and, at Ryan's confused look,

Randall said, "A lot of us have gotten engaged or married recently. It's starting to look like it's contagious."

"But some of us are still immune," Simon said.

"Thanks for the warning," Ryan said. "I think." He hadn't come to the Rangers to find romance, but to jump-start a career that was beginning to feel stale.

Ethan clapped Ryan on the back. "Ready to talk to the archaeologists?" he asked.

"I am," Ryan said, grateful to have the conversation focused on the job once more. "Where are they located from here?"

"Come here and I'll show you." Ethan led the way to a map that took up much of one wall of the headquarters building. "We're here." He pointed to the national park entrance, then traced a path northeast to a flattened ridge. "And this is Mystic Mesa. The archaeologists have been excavating on the eastern side of the Mesa."

Randall, who had followed them, pointed to a draw Ryan guessed was about a mile from the archaeology dig. "Daniel Metwater and his followers are camped in here," he said.

"A prophet and his followers in the wilderness." Ryan shook his head. "That sounds so—I don't know— Old Testament."

"He isn't that kind of prophet," Randall said.

"What do you mean?" Ryan asked.

"No beard or robe in sight," Randall said. "He's the son of a wealthy industrialist and supposedly inherited the family fortune. Most of his followers are young people, searching for something."

"A lot of them are really beautiful young women," Ethan said.

"So you think he's killing some of them?" Ryan asked. "But it doesn't sound like the women who disappeared were part of his group."

"They weren't, but we know that at least one of them—Lucia Raton—had expressed an interest in Metwater's writings," Ethan said. "And it's a weird coincidence that she and Jennifer Lassiter were last seen near his camp."

Ryan's phone vibrated and he glanced at the screen. "This says Alicia Mendoza disappeared when the group she was traveling with stopped for water at a spring at the base of a mesa that ran north-south," he said. "The people she was traveling with didn't know a name and couldn't be more precise than that."

"Mystic Mesa runs north-south," Randall said. He pointed to a spot on the map. "And there's a spring right at the base of it. The only one for miles."

"That's only a stone's throw from Metwater's camp," Ethan said.

"Too much of a coincidence," Ryan said.

"Then I guess you know who else you need to talk to." Randall clapped Ryan on the shoulder. "Have fun," he said. "Metwater may or may not be a murderer, but he's definitely a pain in the backside."

JANA LASSITER GRIPPED the steering wheel of her Jeep and studied the barren landscape where her sister, Jenny, had disappeared. Red-rock chimneys and hoodoos jutted up from a flat plain of yellowed bunchgrass and dusty green piñon trees, their soot-gray trunks stunted and gnarled from years of fighting harsh winds and scorching sun. Dry washes and deeper canyons made fissures in the dusty surface of the land. Jenny had texted that she loved this place—that the remoteness and wildness of it made her feel so free. But the vast emptiness put Jana on edge. Compared to this great expanse, a single human was insignificant. With no signposts or roads or buildings, she already felt lost. Was that what had happened to Jenny? Had she wandered away from her group and simply forgotten where she was? Or had something more sinister taken her away?

Fighting a feeling of dread, Jana got out of the Jeep and was immediately buffeted by a stiff breeze. She held on to her straw sun hat and started toward the white pop-up canopy she had been told indicated the archaeologists' base of operations, dodging to avoid an honest-to-goodness tumbleweed and muttering a prayer that there be no snakes lurking behind the clumps of sagebrush she skirted.

A tall, graying man with a deeply pockmarked face looked up from a clipboard as she approached, his mouth turned down in a frown. She recognized Jeremy Eddleston, Jenny's supervisor. "I'm Jana Lassiter," she said, before he could order her away. "We met briefly at my sister's orientation."

His face relaxed, and he set the clipboard on the folding table in front of him and walked out to meet her, extending both hands. "Ms. Lassiter, it's good to see you again, though not under these circumstances. I'm so sorry for your loss."

She froze at his words, anger warring with panic in her chest. She opted for anger. "Is there some news I don't know about?" she asked. "Is my sister dead?" She had to force out the last word.

Eddleston's face turned the color of the iron-infused

sandstone around them. "Of course not. I mean, we don't know... I only meant..."

She decided to let him off the hook. "It's always difficult to know what to say in a situation like this," she said.

The stiffness went out of him, his shoulders slumping so that he appeared several inches shorter. "Exactly. We're all so terribly worried about Jenny. She was such a valuable part of our team, and so well liked. We can't imagine what happened to her."

"What did happen to her?" Jana asked. "That's what I came from Denver to find out."

"We don't know." Eddleston turned and gestured toward the mesa that rose up a quarter mile or so away, its slopes heavily pocked with large boulders and clumps of scrub oak and juniper. "We've been excavating in this area all summer. Jenny, as you probably know, joined us at the beginning of June. She was helping to sift through some of the material we had recently extracted and after lunch said she was going to take a short break to stretch her legs. Her friends thought that meant she was going to use the portajohn." He indicated the bright blue portable toilet under a tree to Jana's left. "Everyone was so engrossed in the work no one noticed she hadn't returned until the team began packing up for the day a couple of hours later. They called and looked everywhere, but she didn't answer and no one could find a trace of her."

"Why didn't you call the police right away?" Jana asked. "I understand they didn't get out here until this morning."

"There's no phone service out here," Eddleston said. "It's a ten-mile drive over rough roads to get a signal.

By the time anyone realized Jenny was missing, it was getting dark. As you might imagine, this place is almost impossible to find at night. There's only the Jeep trail we've made and no lights at all."

Jana shivered, trying not to imagine Jenny out here in that darkness, hurt and alone. But the images of her sister in danger rushed in anyway.

"I was away at a meeting I had to attend," Eddleston said. "But the rest of the team searched until they couldn't see their hands in front of their faces while others went for help."

"It's true." A young man who had been standing nearby joined them. "We shouted for her until we were hoarse. This morning the park rangers and the county sheriff brought out a search dog. They even flew a helicopter, searching for any sign of her. But they didn't find anything."

Jana scanned the area again. "I don't understand," she said. "How could someone just…vanish? Jenny isn't some flighty, irresponsible schoolgirl. She's smart and sensible. She wouldn't simply wander off."

Eddleston was nodding his head like a bobblehead doll. "I know. I've said the same thing myself. I wish I had answers for you, but I don't."

Jana opened her mouth to ask another question, but was silenced by the distinctive low crackling sound of a vehicle slowly making its way across the rocky track that passed for a road to the dig. She and Eddleston turned together to watch the approach of a black-and-white FJ Cruiser, light bar on top. The cruiser parked beside Jana's Jeep and two men in khaki uniforms and Stetsons exited.

The passenger was closest to Jana—a broad-shouldered, sandy-haired guy who would have looked right at home on a beach with a surfboard. He was clean shaven, and dark aviator glasses hid his eyes, but she had the sense he was checking her out, so she stared boldly back at him.

The driver, a slim, dark-haired man, spoke first. "I'm Officer Reynolds and this is Officer Spencer, with the Ranger Brigade. We're looking into the disappearance of Jennifer Lassiter and wanted to interview the people who were with her the day she disappeared."

"I'm Professor Jeremy Eddleston, lead archaeologist on this dig and Jennifer's supervisor." Eddleston stepped forward and offered his hand.

"Ma'am." The blond Ranger—Officer Spencer— touched the brim of his hat. "Did you work with Jennifer, also?"

"No. I'm her sister. I drove from Denver for the same reason you're here—to talk to people and try to find out what happened."

"When was the last time you talked to your sister?" Officer Spencer asked.

"We spoke the day before yesterday. She was in good spirits, enjoying her work and excited about some finds of pottery they had made." She glanced at Eddleston. "She said she liked the people she worked with."

"So she didn't mention anything that was troubling her?" Spencer asked.

"Nothing was troubling her, I'm sure," Jana said.

"Would you say you and your sister are close?" Spencer asked.

"Yes. We shared an apartment in Denver the first part of this summer, before she started the internship."

"Do you have any other siblings?" Spencer asked. "Parents?"

"Our mother and father both passed away some years ago," she said. Her mother had succumbed to cancer while Jana was still in high school, her father killed a few years later in a car accident on an icy road. "We don't have any siblings."

"And you're sure nothing was troubling your sister?" he asked again.

"Nothing was troubling her. If it had been, she would have told me. Why are you even asking these questions?"

Spencer glanced at his partner, who was deep in conversation with Eddleston. "We need to eliminate any obvious reason for your sister to walk off the job and disappear. Unfortunately, a certain percentage of missing persons are people who have chosen to run away from their responsibilities or even commit suicide. We look for things like depression, troubled relationships or financial difficulties as possible motivations. Once we eliminate those, we consider other explanations."

"Well, you'd better start considering those other explanations now. My sister wasn't depressed, she didn't have any debt, and she got along with everybody."

Spencer removed his sunglasses, the sympathy in his blue eyes catching her off guard. "What do you think happened to Jennifer?" he asked.

"I have no idea," she said. "You're supposed to find that out."

"Yes, but you knew her best. What do you think would have motivated her to leave the group? Would she want to be alone if she had had an argument with someone? Was she the type who would investigate an odd noise, or try to help an injured animal? Would she have left camp to check out an interesting rock formation, or maybe gone in search of a better cell signal?"

She relaxed a little. "I see what you're getting at." She looked around them, at the bright, windswept landscape. "I don't think she would have gone after an animal. She likes dogs and cats, but she's a little afraid of wild animals—like I am. There's apparently no cell service out here and she had been working out here long enough to know that, so there was no point in wandering around trying to find a better signal. I suppose it's possible she might have wanted some time alone if she had had an argument with someone."

"Then let's find out if that's the case." He moved to join his partner with Eddleston. "Did Jennifer have a disagreement with any of her coworkers that day?" he asked.

"Not at all," Eddleston said. "Jenny got along great with everyone."

"We'll want to talk to her coworkers and verify that," Reynolds said.

"Of course." The archaeologist squinted past them, obviously distracted. Jana turned and saw a dusty whirlwind on the horizon that drew nearer and morphed into a late-model, sand-colored Camry racing toward them. "I was wondering when he would show up," Eddleston said.

"Who is it?" Officer Spencer asked.

"Eric Patterson," Eddleston said. "He's a reporter with the Montrose paper."

Reynolds scowled. "We don't have time to talk to reporters."

"He's not just a reporter," Eddleston said. "And you probably do want to talk to him." He turned to Jana. "You, too."

"Why is that?" Jana asked.

Eddleston looked confused. "Because he's Jenny's fiancé. Didn't she tell you?"

Chapter Two

Ryan studied Jana's reaction to Eddleston's identification of the approaching visitor—shock, confusion and then anger played across a face that had the same fair beauty as her sister, but with a maturity that lent more angularity and sophistication to her features. Her eyes held more shrewdness than the photo of the missing young woman, as if she had learned the hard way to be skeptical of the promises people made.

The Camry stopped a short distance away in a cloud of red dust, and a slight young man with thinning blond hair and a boyish face stepped out. He assessed the quartet waiting for him with a glance and nodded, as if approving this welcoming party, then strode toward them and spoke in a loud voice, as if addressing a crowd. "I heard the Rangers had been assigned to the case," he said. "Now maybe we'll get some results. No offense to the local cops, but they don't have the resources and expertise you guys do."

Before either Ethan or Ryan could reply, Eric turned to Jana and seized her hand. "You must be Jana. Jenny has told me so much about you."

Jana pulled her hand away and didn't return Eric's smile. "Funny. She never mentioned you."

The wattage of his grin didn't lower. "We wanted to give you the news in person," he said. "We planned a trip to Denver to see you later this month. Jenny wanted it to be a surprise."

"So it's true—you're engaged?" Jana asked.

"Yes." He held up a hand like a cop halting traffic. "Now I know what you're thinking—Jenny is young and we haven't known each other that long—but when it's true love, I guess you just know."

"How long have you and Jenny known each other?" Ryan asked.

"Two months. We met when I was working on a story on this archaeological dig."

"Eric did a wonderful piece about our work that was picked up for the *Denver Post*," Eddleston said. "It was great publicity for our department."

"How long have you been engaged?" Ryan asked.

"Not long," Eric said. "We decided a couple of weeks ago, actually."

"It isn't like Jenny to keep something like this a secret from me," Jana said.

"Well, she isn't a little girl anymore, telling big sis everything," Eric said. "She wanted her own life."

Ryan felt Jana stiffen beside him. He didn't blame her. Patterson had all the subtlety of a steamroller. But an argument between the two of them wasn't going to help find Jenny. "When was the last time you spoke to Jenny?" he asked Patterson.

"We talked over breakfast at my place yesterday morning before she left to head out here for work." The way he said it—emphasizing the word *breakfast* and watching for Jana's reaction—made Ryan think he was bragging. He and Jenny had spent the night together and Patterson wanted to make sure Jana knew it. He was letting her know that he had been closer to her sister than she was.

Patterson turned to Eddleston. "I just came out to let you know I want to do anything I can to help," he said. "If you think more publicity in the paper would be useful, I'm your man."

"We'll certainly have questions for you," Ryan said before Eddleston could answer. "And we have a copy of the interview you gave the sheriff's office. Right now, we'd like to talk to some of the other people Jenny worked with."

"Of course." Eddleston gestured toward the base of the mesa, where half-a-dozen people milled about amid a grid of pink plastic flags. "Talk to anyone you like."

Ryan nodded to Jana and touched the brim of his hat. "Ma'am," he said, then followed Ethan across the rough ground toward the excavation.

When they were far enough away from the others that they couldn't be overheard, Ethan said, "Give me your impressions."

"The sister doesn't know as much about Jenny as she thought she did," Ryan said. "Eddleston is most concerned about making a good impression. The fiancé is too cocky and sure of himself and for some reason he's going out of his way to goad Jana."

"If Jenny was the only woman missing, I'd put him at the top of the suspect list," Ethan said. "But his name hasn't come up in our investigation of the first missing woman, Lucia Raton, and it seems unlikely he knew an illegal immigrant from Guatemala who just happened to be passing through."

"So he's a jerk but probably not a killer," Ryan said.

"Provided the women are dead," Ethan said.

"Right. We don't have any bodies, but we both know the stats." When young women went missing for no reason, too often they were eventually found dead.

"Maybe this case will be an exception to the norm," Ethan said.

For the next hour, the two Rangers questioned Jenny's coworkers, who all professed sadness and shock at her disappearance. They were able to establish a timeline for yesterday. No one had noticed anything unusual before she vanished. They all agreed she hadn't seemed depressed or afraid or anything like that. "Jenny was one of these really upbeat, look-on-the-bright-side kind of people," said a twenty-year-old archaeology major, Heidi. "I used to tease her about it sometimes. If she had a flat tire on the way in, she wouldn't complain about the tire, she'd talk about how amazing it was to be in such a beautiful setting with nothing to do but wait for something to come along and help."

"So even if something had happened that might upset most people, she wouldn't necessarily show any distress," Ethan said.

"I guess you could put it that way," Heidi said.

"What about her relationship with Eric Patterson?" Ryan asked.

Heidi slanted him a wary look. "What about it?"

"Was she happy? Excited about being engaged?"

"She never actually said anything about being engaged," Heidi said. "First I heard of it was after she disappeared and he came out with the local cops this morning and told everyone. He said they had agreed to keep it a secret until she had a chance to tell her sister."

"Did that strike you as odd—that she wouldn't have shared something like that?" Ryan asked.

She shrugged. "I don't know. I mean, it surprised me a little. I knew she had gone out with the guy a few times, but I didn't think it was that serious. I mean, they hadn't known each other long, but love makes people do crazy things sometimes, I guess."

"Tell me a little more about her mood yesterday," Ryan asked. "Did she mention anything at all about anything that had happened to upset her—an argument with someone, worry over finances, anything like that?"

Heidi shook her head. "Nothing like that. She was maybe a little quiet. When she took a break at about one, I didn't think anything of it."

"You thought she'd gone to use the restroom," Ryan said.

"At first, but then when she didn't come back, I figured she'd taken a walk. She did that sometimes, when things were slow. She was really interested in wildflowers and plants and stuff, and she liked to photograph the scenery."

"What was your first thought when you realized she was missing?"

She shrugged. "I wondered if she'd gone too far from camp and gotten lost." She swept her hand to indicate the surrounding landscape. "It's pretty empty out here. I know I get disoriented all the time. But we spread out and searched and none of us saw any sign of her. I wouldn't think she could have gone that far."

The rest of the students who had worked with Jenny shared Heidi's puzzlement as to what might have happened to Jenny. Ethan and Ryan finished their questions and headed back to the cruiser. Eric's Camry was gone and Eddleston had returned to his work, but Ryan was surprised to find Jana Lassiter waiting beside the cruiser.

"Could I speak with you a moment?" she asked as he approached. She glanced toward Ethan. "Privately?"

"I'll start filling out the reports," Ethan said, opening the driver's-side door.

Ryan walked with Jana about fifty yards, to the shade of a pile of boulders. "What's on your mind?" he asked.

"What do you know about Eric Patterson?" she asked.

"No more than you do," he said. "I've only been in town a week. I transferred to the Rangers from Grand Junction."

She hugged her arms around her stomach, as if she was in pain. "I didn't know about him—not just that he and Jenny were engaged, but I didn't even know he existed. That isn't like Jenny. Not that I expect her to tell me everything, but she always talks to me about the men in her life."

"Maybe she didn't say anything to you about Eric because this relationship was different from those others," he said. "More serious. Maybe she wanted to be more sure of her feelings before she shared them with you."

Jana shook her head. "That isn't her. And he's not her type at all. The men she dates are always funny and easygoing. Considerate. He's so cocky and full of himself. He isn't worried about her—he's basking in the attention her disappearance is bringing to him."

Ryan couldn't disagree with anything about her assessment of Eric Patterson. "People react differently to grief," he said. "Maybe he came off cocky just now because he was nervous about meeting you and trying to impress you."

She gave him a sharp look. "Do you always feel the need to play devil's advocate?"

"It's a cop thing. Questioning assumptions is sometimes a good way to find out new information."

She sighed and her shoulders slumped. "I suppose being disagreeable doesn't mean he had anything to do with Jenny's disappearance."

"We don't have a good enough picture of what happened to have any suspects yet," Ryan said. "We have more people to interview."

"Who?"

He didn't see any harm in telling her. "There's a group camped not far from here. We want to find out if any of them saw or heard anything."

"I don't understand why you don't have more people out searching for her," Jana said. "What about using dogs to track her? And what about her phone? Can't you find someone through their cell phone? Have you issued one of those alerts—an Amber Alert? Isn't that for missing persons?" With each new suggestion, she grew more agitated.

Ryan laid a gentling hand on her shoulder. "There are search and rescue teams combing the area right now," he said. "The sheriff's office has had a tracking dog out here and we've got people trying to trace her phone, but they're not getting any kind of signal. And Amber Alerts are only for children. Your sister hasn't been missing even twenty-four hours. There's still a chance she'll turn up unharmed. Maybe she just needed to get away for a while. She could have hitched a ride into town and be staying with a friend we don't know about."

She stared into his eyes, as if trying to read his thoughts and divine his intentions. "She wouldn't let me worry this way," she said. "If Jenny was with a friend, or anywhere she could make a call, she would let me know she was all right. I've tried calling and texting her dozens of times, but she isn't answering her phone. I'm really worried about her."

He took his hand from her shoulder and nodded. "From what you've told me, it does seem unusual for your sister to just walk away from everything. Right now, our best guess is that she is lost, so we'll continue the search efforts, including interviewing everyone who might have seen her."

She opened her purse and took out a business card. She scribbled something on the back, then handed it to him. "That's my cell number. I'm staying at the Columbine Inn. If you learn anything new, please call me."

He glanced at the number, then turned the card over. "You're a CPA?"

"You sound surprised."

His face felt hot. "It wouldn't have been my first guess."

"I get it. CPAs are supposed to be boring and plain. I hear librarians have the same problem."

"You aren't boring or plain." He slipped the card into his pocket. "I promise to keep in touch."

"I'm trusting you to do that." She met his gaze and he felt the pull of that look somewhere deep in his gut—a surprising but not wholly unpleasant sensation. "And just so you know, I don't give my trust very easily," she added, before turning and walking away.

JANA'S FIRST INSTINCT was to remain near the dig site, walking the desert and calling for her sister. But she had no idea where Jenny might go, and in the vast, mostly featureless terrain she was liable to end up lost herself. So she returned to Montrose, but not to the motel. Instead, she headed to the apartment Jenny shared with another young woman. April was a medical assistant at the local hospital, and she had told Jana to feel free to come in and look around.

She let herself in with the key Jenny had given her and stood for a moment surveying the living room. She had been here before, of course, on visits since Jenny had relocated here for the summer. But she had never been here without Jenny. Already the place felt alien without her sister's presence.

Steeling herself, she crossed the living room to Jenny's bedroom. She didn't know what she was looking for—what she might find that the police investigators wouldn't have uncovered. April had told her the police had already been there. They had made copies of Jenny's computer files and looked through her belongings, but shared no impressions of their findings.

Jana sat on the side of the bed and looked around, trying to see the room as an outsider might. The small space was as bright and sunny as Jenny herself—from the pink patchwork quilt on the bed to the paper flowers tacked to the bulletin board over her desk. Sophisticated cosmetics shared space with a stuffed pink bear. It was the room of a girl who was slowly transforming into a woman.

She swallowed hard against the lump in her throat. She refused to give in to tears, as if grieving would be disloyal. But the knowledge that her sister might not be all right, might in fact be dead, lurked at the edge of her consciousness, a horrible specter she wasn't yet willing to confront.

It's only been one day, she reminded herself. Jenny is young and healthy and smart. If she did get lost, she knows to stay put and wait for help. And she's got a lot of people working to find her. The memory of Officer Spencer's hand on her shoulder, a reassuring, comforting weight, returned and made her feel more settled. She believed he was doing everything he could to help her and Jenny. In the future, the sisters would look back on this time and laugh about the adventure.

She forced herself to stand and walk to the desk and power up the laptop computer. She knew the password—the same one Jenny had used for years—and soon was perusing her sister's files and email and Facebook page. Nothing seemed out of the ordinary. There was no journal detailing a secret worry or hurt, no anguished emails to friends, only the usual cheery greetings or gossiping about school or movies or weekend plans. She found a few emails from Eric Patterson, but they offered little insight into the relationship—invitations to dinner or confirmation of weekend plans. No words of love or secret scheming.

The sound of the front door opening startled her. "April, is that you?" she called. "I'm back here in Jenny's room."

"It's not April," came a man's voice, and a moment later Officer Ryan Spencer filled the doorway of the bedroom.

Heart thudding painfully, Jana stared at him, caught off guard. "What are you doing here?" she demanded.

"The sheriff's office gave us the information they had, but I wanted to see the place for myself." He came into the room, and the already-small space seemed to shrink around them. "I thought it would help me get a better feel for your sister."

Jana sank onto the bed again, fearful her shaking legs might not support her. Having the police here—in Jenny's private space—made the magnitude of her disappearance that much greater. "This room is just like Jenny," she said. She didn't elaborate—let him make of that what he would.

His gaze roamed around the room. She had the sense that he was analyzing everything he saw, putting each item into a bigger picture he was forming of her sister. At last his eyes came back to her. "Have you found anything I should know about?" he asked.

She glanced toward the desk and the open computer. "I don't know if it's anything important," she said. "But it's something that struck me as odd when I was looking through her social media."

"There are no pictures online of her with Eric Patterson," he said.

"Yes!" She stared at him, impressed in spite of herself. "She has pictures of herself with other friends on her Facebook and Instagram pages, and here." She indicated the bulletin board.

He nodded. "If you were engaged to someone, you would probably have lots of pictures of them." He walked over to the laptop and hit a few keys. "There's something else on this you ought to see," he said.

"Something I discovered looking at the copy of her hard drive the sheriff's office made."

"They made a copy of her hard drive?" She didn't know whether to be comforted by their thoroughness or alarmed that the investigation was moving so quickly.

"We've learned the hard way that we need to take these cases seriously from the start," he said. "There was a time when adults had to be missing for a while before law enforcement stepped in, but now we know the sooner we launch an investigation, the more likely we are to have a positive outcome."

She nodded. "That makes sense. So what did you find?"

"Come look."

Feeling steadier now, she stood and came to stand beside him, studying the screen, which showed a handsome, dark-haired man dressed in white, next to a blog post about the key to happiness. "What am I looking at?" she asked.

"It's a blog by a man named Daniel Metwater. He calls himself a prophet and preaches a kind of back-to-nature spirituality a lot of young people find very compelling. Jenny's browser history shows she had read quite a few of his posts and bookmarked his site."

"Why is that important?" Jana asked.

"Because Metwater and his followers are camped very near where Jenny disappeared."

Her stomach gave a nervous jump. "You mentioned wanting to question some people who were camped nearby. Did you mean this man, Metwater?"

"Yes, but I haven't talked to him yet."

"Why not?"

"I wanted to see what I could find out here first."

"I want to go with you when you talk to him," she said.

"No." The word held all the finality of a slamming door, but she intended to push that door open.

"I can help you," she said. "People will say things to me they won't say to a cop."

He shook his head, his jaw tense, blue eyes boring into her with an intensity that any other time would have been intimidating. But she had too much at stake to back down now. "If you don't take me with you, I'll go out there on my own," she said.

"I can't have you interfering with my case," he said.

"This may be your case, but she's my sister." She hated the tremor in her voice as she said the last words and fought hard to control it. "I will do everything in my power to find her. I'll talk to anyone and everyone who might have information that can help me find her, and you can't stop me."

"I could have you arrested for interfering with an investigation."

"You could. But would you really do that? When we met earlier today, you didn't strike me as a jerk."

He actually flinched at the word, as if she had slapped him. "Am I supposed to take that as a compliment?"

"Take it however you like." She lifted her chin and met his gaze, ignoring the tremor in her stomach as he leaned closer. She could smell the leather-and-starch scent of him, masculine and clean, and see the muscle jump along his jaw as he considered his answer.

"If I let you come with me, you can't take part in questioning Metwater," he said. "That has to be done by the book if we're going to get anything we might be able to use in court later."

"I understand. I thought I could mix with his followers. Find out if any of them know Jenny, or if she's been in the camp."

He rubbed his jaw, the scrape of beard against his palm sending another shiver of awareness through her. "You could talk to some of the women in the group," he said. "I don't expect them to be very cooperative with the police—they haven't made any secret of their dislike of law enforcement. But they might be more sympathetic to you."

She fought the impulse to throw her arms around him and kiss him—not so much because she thought he might object, but because she didn't trust herself to stop with one friendly kiss. This sexy cop got to her in a way that alarmed her. The last thing she needed now was that kind of distraction. "I won't get in your way," she said. "But we could work together."

His expression hardened again. "No offense, but I don't need your help. My job is to solve this case and find your sister."

She opened her mouth to argue, then thought better of it. He had agreed to what she wanted, so she might as well stay in his good graces—for now. "Do you think this man—Metwater—had something to do with Jenny's disappearance?" she asked.

"We don't know," Ryan said. "Right now, let's just say he's a person of interest."

"That means he's a suspect," she said, her heart beating faster again.

"I didn't say that. If you come with me, you can't do anything to interfere with the investigation and you can't share anything we see or do with reporters. Especially not with Eric Patterson."

She made a face. "I don't have any desire to talk to him. Maybe it's petty, but he rubs me the wrong way."

He nodded, as if he agreed with her. "When you meet Metwater, maybe you can tell us if he's someone who would have interested Jenny—would she have followed him into the wilderness?"

She swallowed past the sudden tightness in her throat. "And the more important question—if she did, why didn't she come back?"

Chapter Three

Daniel Metwater and his followers had set up camp in a shady grove near a freshwater spring at the base of Mystic Mesa. Ryan parked his cruiser next to a dilapidated pickup, and Ethan slid his vehicle in next to Ryan's. "I don't see anything," Jana said, climbing out of Ryan's vehicle and looking around. Though the sun was slipping toward the horizon, casting long shadows from the trees and boulders, there was still plenty of daylight left this time of year.

"It's up in the trees through here." Ethan pointed to a narrow path into the underbrush. He led the way, with Jana following and Ryan bringing up the rear.

They had only walked about ten yards when a shirtless man with blond dreadlocks stepped out in front of them. He carried a heavy wooden staff, which would have made an effective weapon. He took in the two uniformed officers and scarcely glanced at Jana, then settled on Ethan. "Is there a problem, Officer?" he asked.

"We have some questions for Mr. Metwater," Ethan said, and started to move past him.

Blondie stepped in front of them, holding the stick across his body. "I'm not supposed to let anyone into camp without permission?" His voice rose in a question at the end of the sentence and he looked doubtful.

"This badge means we don't need permission." Ethan stepped toward him again. Blondie glanced at Ryan, then moved off the path. The two officers and Jana filed by and entered a clearing around which were clustered a ragtag collection of tents, trailers and makeshift shacks. A dozen or more adults, most of them young women, and half-a-dozen small children milled around the area.

A tall man with a sharp, intelligent face looked up from a conversation with an attractive pregnant woman. Dark curls framed classically handsome features, but a scowl wrinkled his brow, and at the sight of the newcomers, everyone around him and the woman shrank away. "Hello, Mr. Metwater." Ethan addressed him. "Ms. Mattheson."

"Asteria, you may wait for me in the motor home," Metwater said. Ryan realized the blonde must be Andi Mattheson. According to the information Simon had given him, she was the daughter of a former senator and perhaps Daniel Metwater's most famous disciple. Without a second glance at the visitors, she slipped away.

"I thought we had reached an understanding that the Rangers were not to harass me and my family anymore," Metwater said. "Or did my attorneys not make that clear enough?"

Ryan pulled out his phone, woke it to display the photo of Jennifer Lassiter and turned the screen toward Metwater. "Have you seen this woman?" he asked.

Metwater peered at the image and shook his head. "No. Who is she?"

"How about this one?" Ryan scrolled to a photo of Alicia Mendoza.

"No." Metwater folder his arms over his muscular chest. "What is this about?"

"Do the names Jennifer Lassiter or Alicia Mendoza mean anything to you?"

Instead of answering, Metwater turned to Jana. "Who are you?" he asked. "You don't look like a cop."

"I'm Jana Lassiter," she said, pale but composed. "Jennifer Lassiter is my sister. She disappeared yesterday, from the archaeological dig near here."

Metwater turned back to the officers. "So of course you think I had something to do with this woman's disappearance, even though I've never met her or even heard of her."

Before Ryan or Ethan could speak, Jana stepped between them and Metwater. "Jenny had your blog bookmarked on her computer," she said. "She had been reading it right before she disappeared. We were hoping she came here to meet you."

Metwater's expression softened, and Ryan had a sense of the kind of charm that might persuade people that he had the answers they were seeking. "I'm sorry I can't help you," he said. "I never met your sister." He turned to the Rangers. "What about this other woman? Was she a fan of mine, also? I have many people who are interested in the message I have to share, but my aim is to help, not harm."

"Alicia Mendoza also disappeared very near here," Ethan said. "She was traveling through the area with a group of illegal immigrants. It's possible she became lost and sought refuge in your camp."

"Many things are possible," Metwater said. "But she never came here."

"What about Easy? Has he been around lately?" Ethan asked.

Ryan had to think a moment to remember who Ethan was referring to. Some notes from an earlier interview with the women in Metwater's camp had mentioned someone named Easy who had been seen with Lucia Raton when she left the Family's camp.

"I haven't seen him, no," Metwater said. "He's not a member of the Family."

"But he hangs out here sometimes, we understand," Ethan said.

"I don't require visitors to sign in and out."

"So it's possible Alicia Mendoza or Jennifer Lassiter were here and you didn't know about it," Ryan said.

"It's possible," Metwater said. "But not probable." He glared at them, defiant.

"If you hear anything about either woman—or about Easy—please let us know," Ethan said.

"We avoid mixing with the outside world as much as possible," Metwater said.

"Yet you welcome new members." Ryan looked around the camp—there didn't seem to be a shortage of people who wanted to join Metwater's group, despite the primitive living conditions.

"People come to me seeking a retreat from the false atmosphere of so-called civilized life," Metwater said.

Ryan eyed the motor home parked at the far edge of the clearing. The gleaming RV sported a solar array on the roof and was large enough to comfortably accommodate several people. While some of the Prophet's followers were roughing it, the man himself lived in wilderness luxury.

Metwater noticed the direction of Ryan's gaze. "I left a life of privilege to find a better way," he said. "The fact that my message resonates with so many people should tell you I preach the truth."

Plenty of charlatans and con artists managed to charm untold number of hapless victims. Until Ryan saw evidence to the contrary, he would assume Metwater fell into that camp.

"Mr. Metwater does speak the truth, at least about his background."

Ryan turned toward the new voice that had addressed them. "Hello officers, Jana," Eric Patterson said. "I was wondering when you would get around to showing up here."

"WHAT ARE YOU doing here?" Jana stared at the reporter. Had he decided to investigate Jenny's disappearance on his own? Or was her sister's supposed fiancé a member of Metwater's group?

"I invited him," Daniel Metwater said. "Eric is my special guest."

Eric's smile echoed Metwater's own. Jana thought they looked like two politicians posing for a photo op, their grins too large and not quite reaching their eyes. "I'm writing a profile of the Prophet for my paper," the reporter said. "We're privileged to have a figure of such national interest living in our area."

Jana glanced at Metwater. Was he really of national interest? She had certainly never heard of him, but then, she wasn't searching for meaning in her life or lost with nowhere to go, or any of the other things

Ryan had said attracted people to this remote camp. And neither was Jenny.

Maybe one of Jenny's friends had told her about Metwater, and she had been reading his blog out of curiosity. Jenny was always interested in new things, but that didn't mean she had decided to follow this false prophet into the wilderness.

"I thought you avoided mixing with the outside world," Ryan said. "Or don't newspapers count?"

"It's another way to spread his message," Eric said before Metwater could answer.

"I guess it's another way to solicit financial contributions, too." Ryan's eyes met Jana's, as if they shared an inside joke, and a jolt of pleasure shot through her. She did feel as if she and this cop were allies, that she wasn't alone in her longing to have Jenny returned to her safely.

"Cynics like you scoff, but I could tell you a dozen stories of people whose lives have been changed by my message," Metwater said.

"And I want to hear all of them," Eric said.

"Mr. Patterson," Jana began.

"Please, call me Eric," he said. "After all, we're practically related."

Jana clenched her teeth to keep from telling him they were definitely not related. She couldn't understand what Jenny saw in this man, but until her sister could confide in her, better to hold her tongue. "Did you know Jenny followed Mr. Metwater's blog?" she asked.

"Of course," he said. "Her interest in the Prophet led me to pitch his story to my editor." He turned to Metwater. "I'm only sorry my fiancée isn't here to meet you. She is a great admirer of yours."

"The loss is mine," Metwater said.

"You're sure Jenny never came here on her own or with you?" Ethan asked.

"I'm positive," Eric said. "We planned to come here together."

"Maybe she got curious, and knowing Metwater and his followers were camped so close, she decided to check things out on her own," Ryan said.

"I already told you, she hasn't been here," Metwater said.

"You told us the same thing about Lucia Raton," Ethan said. "Then we found out later she had been to see you."

Metwater pressed his lips together, but said nothing more.

"Jenny wouldn't have come here without me," Eric said. "We had planned to go together and she wouldn't dishonor those plans."

"What does honor have to do with it?" Jana asked, unable to contain her exasperation. "If Jenny wanted to do something, she did it. She didn't need your permission."

"Since you don't live here and aren't a part of Jenny's everyday life, you don't understand how close the two of us are," Eric said. "She wanted to share new experiences with me. When you truly love someone, doing things without them isn't as satisfying."

His patronizing tone set her teeth on edge. "Since when does getting engaged to someone mean you're joined at the hip?" she muttered.

"Now that we've established that you're wasting your time questioning me or my followers, I have an interview to conduct." Metwater put a hand on Eric's shoulder.

"We haven't established anything," Ryan said. But Metwater and Eric had already turned away.

Ryan started toward the pair, but Ethan stopped him. "We'll get back to those two later. In the meantime, let's talk to a few of the faithful." He nodded to Jana. "Mingle with the women and see what you can find out. Even if these people didn't have anything to do with your sister's disappearance, they might have seen or heard something."

"All right."

The two officers moved away, leaving her standing by herself. She tried to ignore the nervous flutter in her stomach and headed toward a group of women who stood in front of a large white tent near the motor home. At her approach, they all turned as if to retreat into the tent. "Please, don't leave," she called out. "I'm not a police officer. I just want to talk to you."

"You're with the police." A severe-looking woman with curly brown hair addressed her in a scolding tone. "You want to hassle us, the way they always do."

"I don't want to hassle anyone," Jana said. "I'm only trying to find my sister." She turned her phone toward them to show a recent photograph she had taken of Jenny, who was smiling broadly and looked so young and happy and alive. It didn't seem real that she could have simply vanished.

"We don't know her," the pregnant blonde who had been with Metwater when Jana and the others had arrived in camp said, not unkindly. "We can't help you."

"The archaeological dig where she worked is very

close to here," Jana said. "Did you know anyone else from there?"

The women exchanged glances. "We didn't know anyone," the oldest of the trio, with white-blond hair and pale eyes said.

"But you know something about them you're not telling me," Jana said. She hadn't missed the significance of the look between them.

"We visited them a few times," the pretty blonde said. "They showed us some of the pottery shards and other artifacts they found."

"Who showed you?" Jana asked.

"Not your sister," the brown-haired woman said. "We never talked to her."

Jana slumped, trying to hide her disappointment.

"We saw her, though," the older woman said. "She was with that reporter."

"Eric?" Jana asked.

"Yeah. That one." The brown-haired woman's sour expression left little doubt of her opinion of Eric Patterson. "They were arguing. Pretty loudly, too."

"What were they arguing about?" Jana asked.

The pretty blonde shook her head. "We couldn't tell, but she was pretty upset. At one point she shoved him."

"What did he do?" Jana asked.

"Nothing," the blonde said. "He was pretty calm about the whole thing, but she was really worked up."

"Did you overhear anything at all?" Jana asked. "Could you guess what she was upset about?"

All three women shook their heads. "They were standing too far away," the older woman said.

"I saw her one other time," the brown-haired woman

said. "I went by myself a few weeks ago to try to sell some stuff I had found to the head guy."

"What kind of stuff?" Jana asked.

"Some arrowheads and spear points, but he said the items I had weren't worth anything. A woman who looked a lot like the picture you showed us was with him when I got there. They looked pretty friendly." She smirked.

"What do you mean, 'friendly'?" Jana asked.

"They were kissing," the brown-haired woman said. "Going at it pretty hot and heavy, too," she said. "When I showed up they broke it off and the girl hurried away."

"But I'm sure Professor Eddleston is married," Jana said, trying to absorb this new information.

"He was wearing a ring," the brown-haired woman said. "So maybe instead of thinking the Prophet had anything to do with your sister's disappearance, you should check out her professor's wife."

Chapter Four

Ryan and Ethan's questions to Metwater's followers turned up nothing of interest. Most people the two officers approached turned away, disappearing into tents or trailers or slipping into the surrounding trees. Others were polite but responded to all questions with bland comments about the weather. No one would admit to having seen or heard of any of the missing women, or the mysterious Easy. "We're wasting our time here," Ryan said, turning away from an affable redhead who, when asked about the missing women, commented on the mild temperatures for this time of year.

"Metwater probably coached them on what to say to us," Ethan said. "Non-confrontational, but also completely unhelpful."

"I'd almost prefer confrontation." Ryan looked around and spotted Jana with a trio of women across the camp. As he and Ethan approached, the women hurried away. "Are you ready to leave?" he asked.

"Yes." Not waiting for a response, she turned and walked ahead of them to the parking area. She was standing by Ryan's cruiser when he arrived, and said nothing as they climbed into the vehicle and drove away.

"Something bugging you?" he asked, after another long minute of silence.

"Hmm?" She glanced at him, worry lines creasing her forehead.

"You're being awfully quiet. I thought maybe you were upset about something."

She looked away again, gaze fixed on the horizon. Ryan focused on the rough road, giving her time. He hoped she would trust him enough to share what was on her mind, whether it related to the case or not. "If you had asked me two days ago if I was close to my sister, I would have said yes. We were as close as two people could be," she said after a moment. "But now I feel like I was just lying to myself. I don't know Jenny at all. I'm asking people questions about her that I think I know the answers to, and the person they're describing to me is a stranger."

"Maybe it's not that you didn't know your sister, but that other people see her differently," he said.

"I didn't know about her engagement to Eric Patterson." She half turned to face him once more. "And just now, one of Daniel Metwater's followers told me she saw Jenny kissing Jeremy Eddleston."

That was a twist Ryan hadn't seen coming. "When did they see this? And where?"

"Last week. At the dig site. They said it was a very passionate kiss."

"Maybe they misinterpreted. Or even if they didn't, it's not that unusual for coworkers to become involved."

"Eddleston is married," Jana said. "And he's old enough to be Jenny's father. Why would she become involved with an older, married man—one of her professors?"

He tightened his grip on the steering wheel, her obvious distress making him want to reach for her— or to shake the person who had upset her so much. "From what little I've learned, your sister does strike me as smarter than that," he said. "But young people do make mistakes."

"She never said a word to me about being interested in Eddleston," she said. "But then, she wouldn't, would she? She would know I wouldn't approve." She faced forward once more, hands knotted in her lap. "Should I ask him about it? Or will I only make things worse if I confront him? Jenny would say I'm interfering— that it's none of my business."

"I'll take you back to your car, then I'll talk to him," he said.

"No. I want to go with you. I want to see his face when you confront him with this."

He stifled a groan. Did they have to go through this again? "I can't have you there when I question a poten- tial suspect," he said.

"Why not?" she asked. "He's more likely to let down his guard with me there, don't you think? And I've al- ready proved I can be useful to you, haven't I?"

"You're not an unbiased witness," he said.

"Are you? Aren't the police supposed to be on the side of the victim?"

"That's not the same as being related to her. You can't come with me."

"Fine. Then pull over."

"What?"

"Pull the car over. Now." She took hold of the door handle.

"What do you think you're doing?" he asked, alarmed.

"I'll walk from here to the dig site. I'll talk to Eddleston on my own and someone there can give me a ride back to my car."

"Don't test me," he said.

"And don't give me that line about arresting me for interfering with your case. I have every right to talk to the people who know my sister. If it was your sister wouldn't you do the same?"

Her stubbornness made him want to pull out his hair—but at the same time he admired her loyalty and determination to do everything in her power to find her sister. And she had proved she had a steady head on her shoulders and that people would talk to her. He eased the cruiser to the side of the road. "Don't get out," he said. "I'll take you with me. If I don't, you're liable to get us both in more trouble."

"I admire a man who can admit he was wrong," she said.

He made a growling noise in the back of his throat and headed the cruiser back in the direction they had come.

"If Eddleston and Jenny were involved, maybe he knows more than he's letting on about her disappearance," she said.

"Or maybe he was responsible," Ryan said. "Either directly or indirectly. Maybe they had a fight and she wandered off to calm down and got lost."

"The women I spoke with at Metwater's camp thought Eddleston's wife might have found out about the affair and done something to Jenny," Jana said.

"Why do they think that?"

"I don't know." She had been too stunned by the bombshell they had dropped to question them about it. "But it makes sense, doesn't it? A woman whose husband is cheating on her would be understandably angry with the other woman."

"Do you know his wife?"

"No. I don't even know Eddleston, really. I met him when Jenny started the internship. I assumed he's married because he wears a wedding ring." She hugged her arms across her chest. "But maybe that's what I get for making assumptions."

He keyed in his police radio. "Ethan, do you read me?"

"What's up?" Ethan's voice crackled over the radio. "I thought I lost you."

"I'm headed back to the archaeological dig. I have a few questions I need to ask Eddleston."

"Do you need backup?"

"No, thanks. I'll fill you in when I get back to headquarters."

"Ten-four."

"Will you question Eddleston's wife, too?" Jana asked.

"Probably."

"And then she'll know about Jenny. And her life will be ruined, too. What was my sister thinking?"

"I wonder if Eric Patterson knew about this," Ryan said.

"How could he not?" she said. "How is it even possible to be engaged to one man and carrying on an affair with another and not have them find out about each other?" She shook her head. "Maybe it's not even true. Maybe those women didn't see what they thought they saw. That's the only explanation that makes sense." The only explanation that fit with Jana's image of her sister.

Ryan parked the cruiser in front of the empty shade canopies at the dig site. In the distance, a group of people worked at the base of the mesa. Jana shaded her eyes with her hand and peered in that direction. "I think I see Eddleston," she said.

Ryan started walking toward the dig, Jana close behind him. His boots left deep imprints in the thick dust and heat shimmered off the rocks around them. He was very aware of the woman beside him, the floral scent of her perfume faint in the air around him, the soft pant of her breath as they labored up a small incline. Professor Eddleston looked up from examining a pottery shard with a magnifying glass as they approached. "Has there been some news about Jenny?" he asked.

"Not yet," Ryan said. "But I have a few more questions for you."

"Of course." Eddleston handed the shard and the magnifying glass to a young man and wiped his hands on the front of his khaki trousers.

"Let's move back into the shade." Ryan nodded toward the shade canopies.

"All right." Eddleston walked beside them toward the canopies. "We're really feeling Jenny's absence on the project," he said. "She's a hard worker and everyone here likes her."

"So you and she get along well?" Jana asked. Ryan didn't miss the edge in her voice, but Eddleston didn't seem to notice.

"We're a very cohesive team on this dig," he said. "Jenny fits in very well with the group."

They reached the shade canopies and Eddleston sat on the edge of one of the folding tables, his posture relaxed. "What do you need to know?" he asked.

"Another person we interviewed reported seeing you and Jenny Lassiter kissing passionately," Ryan said. "I want to know what that's about."

All the color left Eddleston's face. He stared at Ryan, mouth opened, and then the color returned, red flooding his cheeks. "Who told you that? When?"

Not a good sign that he didn't deny it. "So it's true? You were kissing her?"

"It wasn't what they thought. Jenny and I were friends. I…" He looked at Jana, who was glaring at him with open hostility.

"Were you having an affair with Jenny Lassiter?" Ryan asked.

Eddleston stared at the ground, mute.

"We're going to question the rest of the team about this," Ryan said. "Someone will know. It's impossible to keep relationships secret in a small group like this."

Eddleston made a choking sound. Ryan wondered if he was sobbing. After a long silence the professor cleared his throat. "Jenny and I went out a few times," he said. "My wife and I were separated. It was just for fun. It wasn't serious."

"Did Jenny know it wasn't serious?" Jana asked.

Eddleston glanced at her again. "Of course she did. Apparently, the whole time she was seeing me, she was also dating Eric Patterson. She was engaged to him—a fact I didn't even know until she disappeared."

"You didn't know Jenny and Eric were engaged?" Jana asked.

"I had no idea until he showed up at camp looking for her," Eddleston said. "I'd seen them together a few times, but I never dreamed there was anything serious between them. Frankly, she didn't even act as if she liked the guy that much."

"Does your wife know about the affair?" Ryan asked.

His face paled again. "No! And there's no need for her to. She and I are back together. We're trying to fix our marriage."

"Did Jenny know you and your wife were back together?" Jana asked.

"She did. And she was very cool about it. She wished me luck. That's how I know our relationship wasn't serious. We were both just having fun."

"Are you in the habit of seducing students?" Jana asked.

Eddleston drew himself up to his full height, his body rigid. "I did not seduce anyone," he said. "Jenny actually propositioned me. I'd be lying if I said I wasn't flattered, and surprised, too."

"Why were you surprised?" Ryan asked.

He grimaced. "Please, Officer, I know what I look like. I'm no movie star and Jenny is genuinely beautiful. She has no shortage of good-looking men her own age who would have been happy to date her. But she wanted to go out with me."

"Did she say why?" Ryan asked.

He let out a sigh and his shoulders slumped. "She said I made her feel safe. Not the greatest romantic declaration, but show me a man my age who isn't vulnerable to a young, beautiful woman's proposition and I'll show you a dead man or a saint."

"Safe from what?" Ryan asked. "Was she afraid of something—or someone?"

Eddleston shook his head. "I have no idea. I mean, she isn't a timid girl or anything like that."

"And you have no idea when she started seeing Eric Patterson, or when they got engaged?" Ryan asked.

"No."

Ryan studied him. So far, he had a sense Eddleston was telling the truth, but some people were better liars than others. "How did you feel when you found out?" he asked.

"I was upset." Eddleston shrugged. "While we were dating I thought we were exclusive. That's the impression I got." He turned to Jana. "Jenny didn't strike me as the kind of woman who keeps a lot of guys on a string. She's sweet. Kind of the girl-next-door type. But then this Patterson guy tells me they're engaged and I don't know what to think."

"What did you do when you found out about the engagement?" Ryan asked.

"There wasn't anything I could do. Jenny had disappeared. I was worried about her."

"Were you still seeing Jenny at the time of her disappearance?"

"We weren't dating anymore, no. We ended it a couple of weeks ago. I told her I wanted to try to fix things with my wife." He twisted the ring on his finger.

"Jenny was okay with that?" Ryan asked.

"I already told you she was."

"So the two of you didn't argue about it or anything?"

"No!" He leaned toward Ryan. "What are you getting at?"

"Breakups are usually rough," Ryan said. "Maybe she was upset you were going back to your wife. Or maybe you found out about Eric and were angry she'd been two-timing you. You had an argument, one thing led to another…" He let the sentence hang, the atmosphere heavy with the unspoken accusation.

"We didn't argue," Eddleston said. "And I didn't know she was engaged to Eric. I'm not even sure when they became engaged. It could have happened after we split."

"He says they've been engaged a couple of weeks," Jana said.

Eddleston compressed his mouth in a tight line but gave no answer.

"What do you think led Jenny to walk off the job yesterday afternoon?" Ryan asked. "Was it because she was upset?"

"I don't know anything about that," he said. "She wasn't upset with me." He turned to Jana. "I like your sister. She's a sweet girl and we had a good time. We were friends—we are friends. Neither one of us did anything wrong."

"Someone did something wrong," Jana said. "My sister is missing and no one can tell me what happened to her."

"If I knew, I would tell you," Eddleston said. "I hope you find her soon. And that she's safe."

"I'm going to have to talk to your wife, and to the rest of the archaeological team," Ryan said.

Eddleston's head dropped, but he nodded. "Do what you have to do. I'll say again—we didn't do anything wrong."

"If that's true, you don't have anything to worry about. But we may have more questions for you."

"I'll be here," Eddleston said. "I still have work to do, despite these unpleasant interruptions."

"Go back to work," Ryan said. "I'll be in touch."

He walked away, head bent, shoulders slumped. Ryan tried to figure what pretty young Jenny Lassiter had seen in the man. Jana walked over to stand beside him. "Do you think he's telling the truth?" she asked.

"Do you? Do you think Jenny would have propositioned him?"

The pain in her eyes made him ache for her. "I don't know. On one hand, Jenny always did have unconventional tastes in men."

"What do you mean, unconventional?"

"She didn't necessarily go for the classically handsome jocks. In high school, she dated geeks and outsider types. She liked artists and musicians and nerds. Looks really didn't seem to matter at all to her."

"What about her telling him he made her feel safe?"

Jana shook her head. "I don't know. She never mentioned being afraid of anything to me, and she wasn't a timid woman. She likes new people and adventures."

"And she never said anything to you about Eddleston or Patterson. Did she usually tell you about the men she dated?"

"Not every one of them, I'm sure, but certainly anyone she was serious about."

"According to Eddleston, that excludes him."

"Yes, and she might not have said anything about him because she knew I wouldn't approve."

"Because he was older?"

"Yes, and because he's married. I'm not a prude, but I draw the line at some things. I thought Jenny felt the same, but I guess not."

Impulsively, he reached out and squeezed her shoulder. "Don't beat yourself up over this," he said. "If your sister was keeping secrets from you, it was probably because she felt guilty or was afraid of disappointing you—not because she was trying to shut you out of her life."

"Thanks for saying that, even if I don't really believe it."

"Do you want to come with me while I talk to the others?"

She shook her head. "I've heard about all I can stand today. I need time to process it all."

"I need to speak to everyone now," he said. "Before Eddleston has time to influence what they might say."

"I understand. I'll wait for you in the cruiser."

Not pausing for a response, she began walking toward the vehicle. He'd noticed that when she made a decision, she acted on it without waiting for input from others. He couldn't decide if that was a sign of someone who was impulsive or a person who was confident in her own abilities.

She had warned him she didn't trust easily, but he found himself wanting more and more to earn that trust—to prove that she could be confident in his abilities as well.

JANA WAITED IN the passenger seat of the cruiser, a hot breeze bringing in the scents of dusty juniper and the almost musical ring of tools on rock carried from the dig site at the foot of the mesa. Despite the presence of the archaeological crew, the landscape looked empty—not a building or a fence or even a power line in sight. Jenny had raved about how beautiful the country was and how much she was enjoying exploring it with friends.

Was she out there in that vastness now, lost in a

remote box canyon, or lying injured at the bottom of a ravine? Jana pushed the disturbing images away and picked up her phone. She scrolled through her photos, many of her and Jenny together. Here they were at a restaurant in Denver, toasting the camera with twin glasses of iced tea. Here was a shot of Jenny in pajamas, her feet up on the balcony railing at Jana's apartment, sticking her tongue out at Jana because she hadn't wanted her picture taken.

She stopped on a photo of the two sisters mugging for a selfie taken not far from here—at one of the scenic overlooks in Black Canyon of the Gunnison National Park. Jenny had just landed the summer internship and Jana had come out for the weekend to help her celebrate. They had attended the welcome orientation where Jana had met Professor Eddleston, toured the national park, eaten at Jenny's favorite Mexican restaurant and spent the weekend doing what they did best—hanging out and enjoying each other's company.

Jana's eyes burned. She blinked rapidly and hurriedly scrolled to her text messages. Had there been anything there to indicate that Jenny was upset or worried—or in love with a man Jana hadn't even met? She scrolled back to the messages the sisters had exchanged since Jana's weekend visit.

First day was long and harder than I thought but so much fun. I am going to love this!

Jana read through the almost daily texts. The very ordinariness of the exchanges made her smile. Jenny got sunburned. She bought a straw hat. She ate at an amazing pho restaurant. She bought a new dress, went out with friends, flirted with a cute guy at the car wash. She was doing work she loved, having fun with friends—everything a nineteen-year-old could want.

No mention of any dates. That hadn't surprised Jana. The two sisters had each had long periods when they didn't date. They were too busy with work and friends to have time for one-on-one relationships with men. Yet, apparently, for most of this time period, Jenny had been dating Jeremy Eddleston and/or Eric Patterson.

Why had she kept these men a secret from Jana, when Jenny was so open about everything else in her life? Jana read through the rest of the messages, up until two days before—the last day she had heard from Jenny. She had practically memorized these last communications: Jenny was thinking about coming to Denver for Labor Day weekend. She needed to have the oil changed in her car. She wanted to take some more advanced archaeology classes this fall. She hoped she could get a part-time job waiting tables that wouldn't interfere with her class schedule.

Jana stilled, her finger poised over the screen, and stared at the last text from Jenny. One she knew she hadn't seen before.

Jana, I'm scared. I think I've made a big mistake and gone and gotten myself in big trouble.

Chapter Five

Several members of the archaeological crew had indicated that Heidi was closest to Jenny, so Ryan sought her out again. He found her kneeling beside a pile of rocks, carefully sorting through the fist-sized to head-sized chunks, separating them into piles. When his shadow fell over her, she looked up. "Hello, Officer." Her smile was warm. She tucked a lock of long blond hair behind one ear. "Nice to see you again."

He didn't have time to waste flirting with her. "Why didn't you tell me Jenny was involved with Professor Eddleston?" he asked.

She flushed a deep pink and sat back on her heels. "What…what are you talking about?" she stammered.

"You can't help Jenny by lying." He held out his hand. She took it and he pulled her to her feet. "Eddleston told me himself that he and Jenny dated. Why didn't you tell me?"

She bit her lower lip, a gesture that made her look even younger. "I didn't think it was important," she said. "I mean, she told me they had decided not to date anymore. He was going back to his wife and she was seeing Eric. So it was old news." She shrugged.

"Was the split amicable?"

"I guess. I mean, they seemed to get along at work and everything." She glanced over her shoulder, toward where the professor was bent over a rock ledge, examining something with a jeweler's loupe fitted to his eye. "You're not saying you think he had anything to do with her disappearance?"

He ignored the question. "So Jenny wasn't upset with Eddleston?"

"No!" She stared at him, eyes wide.

"Maybe she was jealous he had gone back to his wife."

"It wasn't like that with them." Another glance at Eddleston. "At least, I don't think so."

"It wasn't like what?"

"Serious. I mean, Jenny was gorgeous, right? And Eddleston, well, no offense, but he sort of reminds me of a plucked chicken."

Ryan bit the inside of his cheek to keep from smiling at the image, which did, indeed, resemble the professor. "Why did they date, then?" he asked. "Eddleston says she asked him out first."

"I know." Heidi sighed. "It's a mystery to me. I asked her once and she told me she needed someone safe."

Almost the same words Eddleston had used. Words that struck him as odd reasoning from a young woman with a stable life. "What did she mean by that?"

"I don't know. I asked her and she wouldn't explain."

"Do you think she was afraid of something? Or someone?"

"I don't know. Maybe?" She shook her head. "Jenny was always so upbeat, but sometimes—when people are like that all the time—I think maybe it's just a cover-up."

"What do you mean? What are they covering up?"

"They act all cheerful because it keeps people at a distance. Nobody asks too many questions if they think everything is always great. I hope that isn't the case with Jenny, but maybe it was. I mean, I'm her best friend. I should have seen if something was wrong. If I didn't, maybe it was because she was really good at hiding what was really going on."

"Her sister says she didn't pick up on anything, either, and I gather they were close," Ryan said.

"Yeah, they were tight. Jenny really looked up to Jana. But she didn't tell her everything." Her eyes met his, very green and guileless. "You don't, you know, when it's someone you really care about. I mean, I don't tell my parents when there's an accident at work, or a crime in my neighborhood. All it would do is upset them."

"So you think Jenny kept things like that from her sister?"

"Oh, sure."

"What did Jenny keep from me?"

Ryan turned to see Jana striding toward him, her phone in hand. The wind whipped her hair across her face, and she swiped at it with her free hand.

"Hello," Heidi said, the word almost inaudible.

"What was my sister keeping from me?" Jana asked.

"Nothing important, I'm sure," Heidi said. "She didn't want you to worry."

"Worry about what?"

"I don't know. Nothing that I can think of." She

looked to Ryan. "Can I go now? I have work I have to finish before we go home for the day."

"Go on," he said. He took Jana's arm and led her a short distance away.

"Did Heidi say Jenny was hiding something from me?" she asked, her expression clouded.

"We were just talking in general, about how people don't tell their loved ones everything because they don't want the people they care about to worry."

"Well, it doesn't work. I'm plenty worried." She thrust the phone at him. "I just found this."

He studied the message on the screen and adrenaline surged through him. "Did you just get this?"

"The date on the message is August tenth—yesterday. The day Jenny disappeared. But I swear, this is the first time I've seen it. It was marked as *read*."

"Did someone else have your phone?"

"No. It must be some glitch. Occasionally I get a message hours after it was sent, or my phone doesn't alert me to a new message. Maybe something like that happened. But look at what it says. She's in trouble. She was trying to tell me she needed help."

Jana was all but vibrating with anxiety, her voice high and strained. He put a hand on her shoulder to steady her. "Even if you had gotten this message when Jenny sent it, you were miles away in Denver," he said.

"Yes, but I could have texted back and asked her what was wrong. I could have called the police."

"Why didn't Jenny call the police?" he asked. "Maybe it wasn't that kind of trouble. Maybe this message doesn't even have anything to do with her disappearance."

She looked at him sharply, irritation replacing some of her agitation. "You don't really believe that, do you?"

"No." He pocketed the phone. "I need to keep this for a while. I'll have our tech guy take a look. Maybe we can determine where it was sent from."

"You can trace Jenny through her phone, can't you?" Her expression brightened. "I think I read something about pings. Have you tried that?"

"We have. But we're not getting anything from her phone."

"Maybe the battery is dead," she said.

"We're still trying everything to locate her." He tapped the phone. "Maybe this will help."

She glanced over her shoulder. "Did Heidi tell you anything useful?"

He hesitated. Discussing a case with a civilian went against all his training.

"I'm her sister!" She squeezed his arm. "I'm going crazy worrying about her. If you know anything that can help me, tell me."

If he knew anything that could take away her pain, he wouldn't hesitate to tell her, but the only thing that would do that was the news that her sister had been found. Still, some information was probably better than the feeling of being kept in the dark. "She confirmed that your sister and Professor Eddleston had a brief affair," he said. "They parted amicably and, according to Heidi, it wasn't a serious relationship."

"Why did she date the man at all?"

"Heidi said Jenny told her the same thing she told Eddleston—that he was safe, or that he made her feel safe."

"I reread all the text messages Jenny sent me since

I saw her last," she said. "None of them mentioned Eddleston or Eric Patterson. She didn't talk about dating anyone. And she never mentioned being afraid or unsure, or needing to be 'safe.'"

They reached the cruiser and he held the passenger door open for her. "I'll take a look at the texts, too," he said. "Maybe I'll see something. In the meantime, we'll get you a loaner phone."

She said nothing more until they were well away from the dig site. "I was so upset by the news that Jenny was having an affair with Eddleston that I forgot to tell you something else the women at Daniel Metwater's camp told me," she said.

"What was that?"

"They said they saw Jenny arguing with Eric Patterson. He was calm, but Jenny was apparently really upset."

He tightened his grip on the steering wheel. "When was this?"

"They didn't say. But not the same day one of the women saw Jenny kissing Eddleston." She turned to him. "Do you think it means anything?"

"Hard to say. Couples fight sometimes. I'll question the women again, see if we can put together a timeline. And I'll talk to Eric, too."

She crossed her arms over her chest. "I feel so helpless, sitting in that motel room, not doing anything. What can I do to help?"

His first inclination was to tell her there was nothing she could do—she had to let law enforcement do its job and she couldn't interfere. But he knew how he would react if someone told him that. "Make a list of every one of Jenny's friends that you know of," he said.

"Ask them if she talked about going hiking by herself or wanting to explore the area on her own. Find out if she was upset about anything or afraid of anyone."

"I can do that."

"In the meantime, Search and Rescue has a chopper flying the area, looking for any sign of her, and my team is talking to people and looking and putting the word out. If Jenny is out there, we'll find her."

She looked away, silent for a long moment as they left the dirt track and turned onto the paved highway. "Maybe she's not out there," she said softly. "Maybe she's dead."

"I hope that's not the case," he said.

"But when a young woman goes missing—a young woman who wasn't depressed or having money troubles or the type of person to disappear on purpose— when that happens, a lot of them never come back."

He chose his words carefully, not wanting to be dishonest, but also unwilling to upset her unnecessarily. "Cases like that are sometimes victims of violence. I don't know the exact statistics."

"Tell me about the other women you're looking for," she said. "Are they anything like Jenny?"

He didn't see how talking to her about the other women could hurt his case, and she might even have ideas that could help him. "Lucia Raton and Alicia Mendoza," he said. "They are near your sister's age— Lucia is eighteen and Alicia is twenty-five. They were last seen in this area—Lucia in a café a few miles up the road with a man we haven't been able to identify and Alicia with a group of illegal immigrants who were traveling through the wilderness area on foot. But other than that, they don't appear to have anything in common with your sister. Lucia was still in high school and Alicia didn't speak English."

"But three women disappearing within a few weeks in the same area looks like a pattern, doesn't it?" she asked.

"Yes, it does."

"Then it's more important than ever that we figure out what happened to Jenny," she said, her voice taking on a harder edge.

"Why is that?"

"If someone is purposely harming women, we have to stop him," she said. "If I can't save my sister, I have to try to save someone else."

Chapter Six

Jana spent a restless night in the motel, hoping against hope that the phone would ring with news that Jenny had been found alive and safe. The next morning, unable to bear another moment in her room, she retreated to the motel coffee shop. She ordered a cup of coffee, then sat with pen and paper, attempting to make a list of everyone Jenny knew, both here in Montrose and in Denver. After all, it was only a five-hour drive between the two cities, and it was possible someone there knew something that would help the case.

"Mind if I join you?"

A shadow fell across her notebook and she looked up to find Eric Patterson, his hand on the back of the chair across from her.

She opened her mouth to tell him she preferred to be alone, then thought better of it. This man was special to Jenny. She shouldn't miss the opportunity to get to know him better. Maybe one-on-one she would discover what it was her sister saw in him. "Please do," she said.

The chair scraped across the floor as he pulled it out and sat. He wore dark aviator glasses, which he removed and tucked into the neck of his peach-colored polo shirt. Despite not being classically handsome, he did have a kind of boyish appeal, though she found the self-important way he carried himself off-putting. "Any news about Jenny?" he asked.

She shook her head and closed the notebook.

"I haven't discovered anything, either," he said. "The paper asked me to do a story on Lucia Raton and Alicia Mendoza. They wanted me to include Jenny in that group—but I refused."

"Why?"

"Because, although at first glance it might seem that three women who disappear in the same area within a short period of time might be connected, Jenny's circumstances are completely different from the other two."

"I'm not sure I follow," she said.

"Both of the other women were engaged in risky behavior. Lucia was hitchhiking and Alicia was in this country illegally. Whereas, Jenny was working when she disappeared. She was an educated, smart young woman—not the type to strike up a conversation with a shady stranger or to let herself get into a dangerous situation. She once told me she was a good judge of character and I believe her."

He did seem to know her sister well. "What do you think happened to Jenny?" Jana asked. She leaned toward him, tensed for his answer.

"My first thought was that she wanted a break from work, decided to take a little walk and got lost."

Jana nodded. "That was my first thought, too. But searchers have combed the area around the dig site and they haven't found anything."

"Exactly." He pointed a finger at her, like a lecturer

making a point. "That led me to my second theory." He sipped his coffee, his eyes locked to hers, clearly waiting for her to ask about his theory.

If there was less at stake, she would have held her tongue to avoid satisfying his need for attention, but she didn't have time to waste on petty games. "What is your theory?" she asked.

"I think Daniel Metwater or one of his followers abducted her. It's one reason I'm eager to embed myself in the group. I could care less about writing a profile of the man—I want to find Jenny."

"Why do you think Metwater has something to do with her disappearance?" she asked. "You just said Jenny is smart and a good judge of character."

"Yes, but even smart people make mistakes sometimes. And our darling Jenny did have something of a blind spot when it came to the local prophet." He took another long sip of coffee. "You do know she regularly read his blog?"

"I saw it bookmarked on her computer."

"She really fell for all his talk of peace and harmony and living close to nature. I'll admit I teased her about it. It was one of the few things we ever disagreed about. When she found out he and his followers were camping near here, she was determined to see him, so I agreed to go with her."

"You told the Rangers she wouldn't have gone to the camp by herself."

"I didn't think so. But if Metwater or one of his followers came to where she was working and invited her to come with them..." He shrugged. "I'm hoping I can find out more as I research my article."

"I spoke to some women at Metwater's camp who

said they had visited the dig site—more than once," she said.

"See." Eric pointed at her again. "They could have struck up a conversation with Jenny and invited her back to camp, where Metwater got hold of her."

"None of her coworkers mentioned her talking to anyone else that day."

"Maybe they didn't see. The conversation could have happened when Jenny went for a walk out of sight of everyone else."

"The Rangers have already questioned Metwater and his followers," she said.

"Please! One thing anyone who has had much contact at all with Metwater's group knows is that they *hate* the Ranger Brigade. Daniel Metwater has a team of lawyers employed to file formal complaints and request restraining orders against the Rangers for harassing him and his followers. And the boys in brown have made a habit of blaming the Family for anything and everything that goes wrong in the park, though they haven't pinned a single crime on the Prophet."

"If Metwater or one of his people did abduct Jenny, what did they do with her?" Jana asked.

"I don't know." Eric's expression sobered. He pushed aside his coffee cup and grasped Jana's hand. "They may merely be keeping her prisoner, perhaps trying to brainwash her into joining their group. But we have to prepare ourselves for the possibility that she is no longer with us."

Jana wrenched her hand from his grasp. "You mean she might be dead."

He sat back. "It's what the Rangers think, even though they're too politically correct to say so."

Or too kind, Jana thought, remembering Ryan's sympathy. "If you learn something from Metwater that can help the Rangers in their investigation, will you tell them?" she asked.

"That depends on what I find out, and maybe on the timing. I wouldn't wait on the Rangers if I could rescue Jenny myself."

He would like that, wouldn't he, being the big hero? She pushed the uncharitable thought away. "I don't care who saves her, as long as she's safe," she said.

"Of course. That's what I want, too." He reached for her hand once more, but she leaned back, putting herself out of reach. He smiled. "The two of us didn't exactly meet under the best of circumstances, did we?" he said. "I would really like to get to know you better. When Jenny does return to us—and I'm not going to allow myself to think otherwise—I'd like her to know that the two people she loves most in the world are friends."

"Of course." She didn't know if she could ever be close to Eric, but for Jenny's sake, she wanted to be on good terms with him.

"Let me take you to dinner tonight," Eric said. "That will give us a chance to get better acquainted. I can tell you how Jenny and I met."

Yes, that was a story she would like to hear—though she would rather her sister had told her. "Dinner sounds good," she said. "And I am going a little crazy sitting around my motel room, waiting for something to happen."

"Which room is yours? I'll come for you at seven, if that's all right."

"I'll meet you in the lobby at seven."

He grinned. "You remind me so much of Jenny. Our first date she wouldn't let me come to her house, either, but met me at the restaurant."

She could have reminded him this wasn't a date, but why bother?

A movement at the front of the coffee shop caught her attention, and she looked up to see Ryan Spencer silhouetted in the doorway. Her heart sped up as he started toward them. "Looks like that Ranger is here to badger you again," Eric said. "I can get rid of him for you."

He pushed back his chair and started to stand. "Hello, Officer Spencer," Jana said. She made a point of smiling at the Ranger, sending the message that she didn't consider him a nuisance.

Ryan glanced from her to Eric. "Sorry to interrupt," he said.

"You weren't interrupting," she said. "I was just leaving, but you can walk me out." She stood and collected her purse.

"I hope you're not in too much of a hurry," Eric said, rising also and facing Ryan. "I have some questions for you about the missing women—Lucia Raton and Alicia Mendoza."

"I can't discuss details of an ongoing investigation," Ryan said.

"I'm not asking as a civilian. I'm working on a story for the paper."

Ryan looked him up and down. Nothing in his expression betrayed him, but Jana had the sense the reporter didn't impress the lawman. "I thought you were writing a profile of Daniel Metwater," the Ranger said.

"I can work on more than one story at a time. In fact, it's a requirement of the job."

"You're welcome to contact our media liaison," Ryan said. "I don't have anything for you." He stepped aside and motioned to Jana. "I'll walk with you a moment. I just had some news I wanted to share."

"What kind of news?" Eric said.

"The information is for Ms. Lassiter," Ryan said.

"If it's about Jenny, as her fiancé I have a right to know about it," Eric said.

The chill in Ryan's eyes could have frozen water. "The information I have is for Ms. Lassiter." He took Jana's arm. "We won't keep you any longer."

Eric glared at the lawman, hands fisted at his sides. He reminded Jana of a pug faced off against a Doberman. The newspaperman's bluster was no match for Ryan's quiet strength. After a tense moment, Eric turned to Jana. "I'll see you tonight," he said.

Ryan waited until Eric was gone before he spoke. "Do you want to stay and finish your coffee?" he asked.

"I'm done. There's a park on the corner. Could we walk there?"

"Of course."

Sun glared on the sidewalk and sparkled on the fountain in front of the motel. Ryan walked next to the street, matching his strides to Jana's, his quiet presence calming her. When they reached the park, they turned onto a shaded path. "Are you meeting Eric Patterson tonight?" he asked.

"I agreed to have dinner with him," she said. "I didn't really want to, but I felt I should make an effort to be friendly with him, for Jenny's sake."

"He's going to pump you to find out what I had to say to you," he said.

She stopped and faced him. "What *do* you have to say to me?"

"I wanted to return your phone." He took the smart-phone from his pocket and handed it to her.

She caressed the sleek silver case. "Did you find anything useful on it?"

"Not really. As far as we can determine, Jenny sent that last text to you from the dig site the morning of the day she disappeared."

"I thought there wasn't any service out there."

"Phone calls don't go through. Most of the time text messages don't, but in a few spots there's enough of a signal to send one. Have you thought any more about what she meant, when she said she had made a mistake?"

Jana shook her head. "I haven't a clue." She opened her purse to drop in the phone and spotted the list she had been making and took it out. "I wrote down the names of people Jenny knows, both here and in Denver. But I don't know how much help it will be to you." She tore off the page and handed it to him.

He studied the names, then folded the paper and tucked it into his shirt pocket. "I'll have someone check these out. Maybe we'll get lucky and one of these people will know something."

"Do you mind if we walk?" she asked. "I think better when I'm moving."

He fell into step beside her. "The aerial survey of the area didn't turn up anything," he said. "I'm sorry."

"Eric thinks Daniel Metwater or one of his follow-ers abducted Jenny."

"I thought he was a fan of the Prophet. He's writing about Metwater for the paper."

"He told me he's hoping to use his access to Metwater to find Jenny." She glanced at him. In profile he looked less like a carefree surfer and more forbidding, his face all strong planes and sharp angles. "He knew about her following Metwater's blog. He said Jenny was anxious to meet the Prophet, and though they agreed to visit the camp together, if someone from the camp came to the dig and invited her to go back to the camp with them, she would have accepted the invitation. That sounds like Jenny, and we know the women I talked to had visited the dig site at least twice. Maybe they came back the day Jenny disappeared and persuaded her to go with them."

"And what does Eric think happened then?"

"He suggested Metwater was holding her, trying to brainwash her into joining their cult." She pressed her lips together, then forced out the rest of the thought. "Or that she's dead."

"I'll have to review his interview with the sheriff to see if he mentioned any of this to them," Ryan said. "He didn't mention it when we questioned him."

"Maybe he just thought of it," Jana said.

"We're continuing to investigate Metwater, in relation to all the missing women," Ryan said. "We'll certainly question the women you spoke with. I can't say more."

"Eric told me Metwater hates the Rangers—that he thinks they harass him."

"Mr. Patterson knows a lot about the situation."

"He does have a personal interest in the case, and

I imagine his job gives him access to a great deal of information."

"Tell him if he finds out anything that could help us, he needs to let us know."

"I already did, though I get the impression he'd like to find Jenny himself and be the hero."

"If she's found safe, I won't complain."

"No ego involved?"

"The day I start thinking an investigation is about me is the day I need to turn in my badge."

She put her hand on his arm, the muscle hard beneath her fingers. "I wasn't questioning your dedication. And I appreciate knowing you're working hard to find Jenny."

He looked down at her hand, then covered it with his own—his touch reassuring but sending a definite heat through her. "How long do you plan on staying in Montrose?" he asked.

"Until I know what happened to my sister."

"We try to solve cases quickly, but, realistically, it could take weeks, or months. Sometimes cases are never solved."

She bowed her head. "I know."

"Don't you have to get back to work?"

"I'm self-employed. I've been able to do some work remotely, but, yes, eventually I'll have to get back to my office or risk losing my clients." She stared out across the park, toward a playground where a trio of children raced about, laughing. "It's hard to concentrate on anything else while I'm so worried about my sister."

"You're entitled to a victim's advocate. I can put you in touch with one."

"What does a victim's advocate do?"

"They're volunteers who liaison with law enforcement and crime victims or their families. They can also put you in touch with counseling and support groups."

Her shoulders sagged. "So you really think this is a crime?"

"There's still the possibility that your sister wandered off and got lost, but the odds of that seem slim, especially with two other women missing." His grasp on her tightened.

She thought about statistics she had read in the newspaper or heard repeated on television—that the longer a missing person remained unfound, the more likely it was that they were dead. Despair threatened to overwhelm her, but she refused to give in. Instead, she focused on Ryan—on the caring in his eyes and the strength in his grasp. "I want to stay here awhile longer," she said. "And I want to do whatever I can to help."

"Maybe this list will help," he said. "I'll let you know what we find."

His phone rang and he released her. "I need to take this call," he said, and stepped away.

She turned toward the playground again and was reminded of racing Jenny to the top of the slide at the park down the street from the house where they had grown up. Jenny was always the bolder of the two, running faster, climbing higher, teasing Jana with taunts of "slowpoke" and "fraidycat." Jana, though older, had always sought safety, order and control. It was probably why accounting appealed to her. Jenny had always craved adventure, so archaeology was a natural fit.

Had that sense of adventure and daring gotten Jenny into trouble now? Or was she simply the unlucky victim of some nameless evil? She hugged her arms across her middle, trying to ward off the chill that traveled through her despite the warm sun. She had faced some hard things in her life, including the deaths of her parents, but losing Jenny would be the hardest yet.

"Jana?"

She turned at the sound of Ryan's voice, alarm sweeping over her as she registered the distress in his eyes. "What is it?" she demanded. "What's wrong?"

"I'd better go now. I'll talk to you soon."

"I can tell from your expression something bad has happened. Tell me. I promise I won't get hysterical, but I need to know."

He gripped her arms, holding her up. "A road crew found a woman's body near the wilderness area."

Chapter Seven

Ryan led Jana to a bench, afraid she might collapse at any moment. She trembled in his arms, but made it to the bench and sank onto it. "We don't know yet if it's Jenny," he said.

"But it could be," she said, the words coming out in a moan.

"Don't assume anything until we know for sure," he said.

She sucked in a deep breath, fighting for control, and nodded. "What did the caller say?"

"Just that they'd found a body. They're taking it to the coroner's office."

"When will they know who it is?"

"I don't know." He didn't tell her that the body had been found in a shallow grave beside the road, that it had been partially unearthed by animals. The coroner would assess the remains and compare them to the descriptions of the missing women, as well as descriptions of the clothing they had been wearing when last seen.

Jana clutched at his hand. "Don't leave me," she said.

"I won't." He sat beside her. One of the mothers on the playground stared at them. She was probably wondering what he had said to upset Jana so. "Do you want to go back to your room?" he asked.

"Yes. It's too bright out here." She stood.

He didn't ask what she meant by that. Maybe bad news was harder to take on a beautiful, sunny day. He put his arm around her, and together they walked slowly back to the motel and around the side to her room. She fumbled with her key card, so he took it from her and opened the door.

"Can I get you anything?" he asked, as he followed her inside.

"On television, they're always giving people stiff drinks when they've suffered a shock," she said. "But I'm not much of a drinker." She sat on the side of the bed and he took the room's only chair, beside the front window.

He searched for something to distract her and noticed yarn and knitting needles on the nightstand. "What are you working on?" he asked, nodding toward it.

She cradled the ball of soft blue yarn. "I'm knitting a sweater," she said. "I usually find it relaxing, but I don't think I could concentrate on it now." She looked around the room, which was decorated in a country theme, with a floral bedspread and prints of tractors in cornfields on the wall. "What do we do now?" she asked. "Just wait?"

"There's a lot of waiting in my job," he said. "Results rarely happen as quickly in real life as they do on TV."

"I shouldn't keep you," she said. "You have work to do." She smoothed her hands down her thighs. "I'll be fine on my own. And you said you have to go."

He had only said that because he knew if he stayed with her he would tell her the news about the body. Since that cat was already out of the bag, there was no harm in remaining until he was sure she was okay. "I'll stay a little longer." He liked sitting here with her—not the circumstances that had brought them together, but he appreciated the opportunity to be alone with her, to enjoy looking at her. Despite her distress, she was beautiful—not the calendar-girl, cheerleader beauty of her sister, but a more mature, riper attractiveness that drew him.

"Tell me how you became a cop," she said.

He wondered if she was really interested or only searching for distraction. "I did a stint in the army right out of high school, hoping to earn money for college," he said. "After I was discharged, I enrolled in Colorado State University, studying business. At a job fair my senior year I stopped by a booth for Customs and Border Protection. They were looking for officers, and I thought it sounded more interesting than sitting in an office all day."

"And is it? More interesting?"

"Most of the time, yes. I mean, there's a lot of paperwork and waiting for things to happen. It's not all chasing criminals and solving big cases. But I enjoy the variety. And I feel like I'm making a difference."

"What does your girlfriend—or wife—think of the job?"

"I'm not married, or involved."

The corners of her mouth tilted up for the space of a breath. "I wasn't getting a married or involved vibe from you, but you never know."

His gaze met hers and he could almost see the sparks

arcing between them. "What kind of vibe are you getting?" he asked.

"One that makes me wonder how often you get involved with women who are part of a case you're working on."

"Never." He continued holding her gaze. "But there's a first time for everything, with the right woman."

She looked away, lamplight playing across the curve of her cheek and the smooth column of her neck. He fought the urge to kiss her there. "This may be the definition of bad timing," she said.

"Probably," he said. "But if everyone waited for life to be perfect no one would ever fall in love or get married or have children or start a new business or take a new job or any of the dozens of big decisions that add up to a full life."

"Yes, but do I feel this attraction to you because there's something between us, or because you're something steady I can hold on to while I'm reeling from my sister's disappearance?"

"I think the only way we're going to learn the answer to that question is to stick around and find out," he said. He stood and came over to sit on the bed beside her. He wasn't going to push her, but he wasn't going to hide his feelings, either. He took her hand. "It depends on what you want."

"I think, right now, I'd like you to kiss me."

"With pleasure." Cradling her cheek in one hand, he covered her lips with his. She tasted faintly of tea and honey, her mouth warm and silken. She slid her hand along his arm and then his shoulder, fingers playing across his skin as if memorizing the shape of him. When he angled his mouth to deepen the kiss, she slid closer, pressing her chest to his, soft curves against hard muscle, quickening his breath and heating his blood.

She opened her mouth beneath his, and he accepted the invitation, the welcome intimacy banishing his last doubts that they might be making a mistake. Her hand slid to the back of his neck and her tongue tangled with his, sending a new wave of pleasure through him. Moments ago, in the park, she had seemed fragile and helpless, but in his arms now she was strong and confident, a woman who knew what she wanted.

The knowledge that she wanted him filled him with desire and more than a little awe.

His ringing phone jarred them apart. Heart pounding, he groped for the cell, fighting to come out of the fog she had put him in. "Spencer."

"We have a positive ID on the body." Commander Graham Ellison's voice was calm and steady.

Ryan turned to Jana, who sat back, fingers pressed to her lips, eyes fixed on him. "Yes?"

"The coroner confirms it's Alicia Mendoza. She was wearing a locket with her name on it, and the clothes fit the description we got from the people she was traveling with."

"Alicia Mendoza," Ryan repeated.

Jana let out a sob and covered her eyes, her shoulders shaking though she made no other sound.

Ryan stood, walked to the window and peered out through a gap in the closed drapes. "Do we know the cause of death yet?"

"She was strangled. Probably at another location, then buried in the shallow grave by the roadside. We'll know more later, but the best estimate right now is that she died within hours of her disappearance."

"I'll be in the office within the hour," Ryan said.

"I want you to meet Simon and Ethan out at Metwater's camp. We've got a warrant to take the place apart."

Ryan felt the familiar jolt of a case gaining momentum. "What are we looking for?" he asked.

"Anything that ties Metwater to Alicia Mendoza or the other missing women. Alicia's hands were bound with white linen fabric, like those shirts and pants Metwater always wears."

RYAN MET ETHAN and Simon at the turnoff for the rough track that led around Mystic Mesa to Metwater's camp. From there they proceeded in two vehicles to the parking area. As soon as they exited their cruisers a beefy young man with a shaved head stepped out to greet them. He hefted a thick wooden walking stick in one hand. "What is your business in our home, officers?" he asked.

"We're here to speak with Daniel Metwater," Simon said.

"The Prophet doesn't allow weapons in the camp," the guard said. "If you'll leave them in your vehicle, I'll be happy to escort you to the Prophet."

"Not happening." Simon shoved past him.

"You don't have to escort us," Ethan said, as he, too, moved past the young man. "We know the way."

Brandishing the walking stick, the young man hurried after them. "The Prophet isn't free to see you right now," he said. "He's in an interview."

Ryan turned to the young man. "You need to put down that stick," he said. "Somebody might get the wrong idea and think you were threatening us with a weapon."

The guard reddened. His gaze flickered to the gun at Ryan's side, then he lowered the walking stick. "The Prophet doesn't like to be interrupted," he said, his tone almost pleading.

"Too bad."

Ryan joined the others at the bottom of the steps leading up to Metwater's motor home. Though the camp seemed deserted, he sensed people watched them from the tents and trailers all around them. Alert to possible danger, he kept one hand near his duty weapon as Simon knocked hard on the aluminum-clad door of the motor home.

He had lifted his hand to knock a second time when the door eased open and Andi Mattheson, aka Asteria, peered out. "The Prophet can't see you right now," she said. "He's in a meeting."

Simon wedged his foot in the narrow opening and pressed his shoulder to the door. "You need to let us in," he said, his voice surprisingly gentle. "Then you should leave. We don't want to see you hurt."

"I don't—" she started to argue.

"Trust me on this." Simon pushed the door open wide enough that he could put both hands on her shoulders. Then he steered her out the door and down the steps. "Wait for us in your tent," he said.

Scowling, she moved past the other two officers and down the steps. "Who knew you had such a way with women?" Ethan said as he and Ryan followed Simon into the motor home.

Metwater sat at the dining table with Eric Patterson

across from him. "What are you doing here?" Metwater rose to face them. "Get out of my home."

"Daniel Metwater, we have a warrant to search these premises." Simon laid the warrant on the table in front of Metwater.

"Search for what?" Metwater asked. "By what authority?"

Eric picked up the paper and scanned it. "By the authority of the Seventh Judicial District Court," he said. "It looks official."

"Mr. Patterson, what are you doing here?" Ryan asked.

"I'm interviewing the Prophet for the profile of him I'm writing," he said.

"You'll have to finish the interview some other time," Simon said. "You need to leave now."

"Oh no," Eric said. "I need to stay. Things are just about to get interesting."

"Leave, or I'll detain you for interfering with an investigation," Simon said.

"Mr. Metwater is entitled to have someone with him as a witness," Eric said. He turned to Metwater. "You want me to stay, don't you?"

"You're making that up," Simon said. "There's no requirement for a witness."

"I'm sure I read it somewhere," Eric said. "What if you're wrong and I'm right? The Rangers don't need any more bad publicity, do they?" He sat back and folded his arms. "Besides, if you end up charging Mr. Metwater with something and the case goes to trial, I'm an outside witness who can testify to what you find. That would look good to a jury, don't you think?"

The tips of Simon's ears were bright red, and Ryan

could practically see the irritation radiating from him. Ethan put a hand on Simon's shoulder. "Quit wasting time with him," he said. "Let's get on with the search."

Simon shrugged off Ethan's hand and turned back to Metwater. "Do you know Alicia Mendoza?" he asked.

"I've never heard of her," Metwater said.

"Alicia is the Mexican woman who went missing near here," Eric said. "You remember I was telling you about her."

Metwater glared at him.

"She was from Guatemala, not Mexico," Ryan said. He took Eric's arm. "You and Mr. Metwater need to wait outside."

"I want to talk to my lawyer," Metwater said.

"Go right ahead." Simon took his arm. "You can call him from Ms. Mattheson's tent, provided you can get a cell signal out here. I don't think you can, but you're welcome to try."

Metwater shook him off, but stood and started toward the door.

"You have to leave, too," Ethan told Eric.

"I could stay and help you," Eric said. "If you tell me what you're looking for."

"Out," Simon said. He waited for the reporter to move past him, then fell into step behind him. "I'll keep an eye on these two and Ms. Mattheson," he said. "Let me know if you find anything interesting."

When they were alone, Ethan turned to Ryan. "You want to take Metwater's bedroom? I'll look in here, then we'll hit the other rooms."

Ryan pulled on a pair of latex gloves and went to work. Starting to the left of the bedroom door, he circled the room clockwise, opening every drawer, feeling along every surface, riffling through books and looking behind pictures. He stripped the bed and searched between the mattress and box spring, then emptied the drawer of the bedside table. Metwater had a good supply of condoms and an assortment of sex toys in these drawers. His reading material was a mix of investment advice and the writings of eastern mystics. Maybe he was copying ideas for his blog posts from them. A notebook was filled with notes made in an almost indecipherable handwriting. Ryan bagged and tagged this to be reviewed at Ranger headquarters.

The dresser held a collection of white cotton or linen trousers and shirts, some silk pajama pants, underwear and socks. The closet held half-a-dozen expensive-looking suits and as many pairs of shoes. Ryan was about to shut the door and move on to another room when something white at the very back of the space caught his eye. He squatted and played his flashlight across the floor of the closet. A heap of white fabric, like a shirt that had slipped from a hanger, lay wadded in the very back corner of the space. Ryan pulled it out and stared at what once had been a shirt, but was now little more than a rag. The fabric had been cut and torn, so that long strips hung from the shoulders, and about half of it looked to be missing.

"Ethan!" he called. "Come take a look at this."

His fellow Ranger appeared in the doorway. "What have you got?" he asked.

Ryan held up the torn shirt. "I think we've found what we were looking for."

Chapter Eight

Jana couldn't believe Eric Patterson had stood her up. She had waited in the lobby of her motel from five minutes before seven until seven thirty and the reporter never showed. By that time she had read every brochure in the tourist-information rack by the door and played fourteen games of solitaire on her phone. He hadn't even had the decency to call and cancel. What had Jenny seen in the guy?

Starving and furious, she drove to a sandwich shop and placed an order to go, then took it to Jenny's apartment. If Eric did decide to finally show up at the motel, she was in no mood to talk to him. She called Jenny's roommate, April, from the parking lot. "I'm sorry to bother you," Jana said. "But would it be okay if I came up for a while?"

"Uh, sure," April said, sounding very unsure. "I have to leave in a little bit to meet a friend for drinks, but you still have a key, right?"

"I do. And thanks. I promise I'll be gone by the time you get home."

She followed April into the apartment and sat in a chair while April settled on the couch. She was a petite Asian American with short black hair streaked with purple. "Any word on how the search is going?" April asked.

"Nothing yet." She started to tell April about Alicia Mendoza's body being found, but why put worry about a connection between the missing Guatemalan woman and Jenny in April's head if it wasn't already there? "I know the Rangers are working hard to find her," she said, instead.

"They're bound to turn up something soon, right?" April said.

"April, did Jenny seem upset about anything in the days before she disappeared?" Jana asked.

"The cops asked me the same thing. But, no, Jenny wasn't upset." She smoothed her hands down her thighs. "We didn't really see each other that much, you know. We were both really busy with work and studies and stuff."

"Did you know Jenny was dating two different guys?" Jana asked.

"I knew she had a pretty active social life, but she didn't talk about her dates, much. Well, except I knew Eric. He was over here pretty often."

"Did you know he and Jenny were engaged?"

"He told me one day when he came to pick up Jenny, while she was in the bathroom getting ready. But he said it had to be a secret until they had a chance to tell you."

"Were you surprised?" Jana asked.

April wrinkled her nose. "A little. I mean, I didn't really think Jenny was that into him. I was going to ask her about it the next time we were alone, but I never got the chance."

There were so many things Jana wanted to ask her

sister, too. The thought of never having that opportunity was a constant dull ache in the pit of her stomach.

April stood. "I have to go now. But you can hang out as long as you like."

"Thanks," Jana said. "Sometimes it helps being here, where I feel a little closer to her."

After April had left, Jana retrieved her supper from the car and carried it up to the apartment. Bypassing the living room and kitchen, she went to Jenny's room. At the desk, she switched on Jenny's laptop, and arranged her food beside it. The screen saver popped up—a picture of a smiling Jenny, Eric standing next to and slightly behind her. Jana stared at the image. She would have sworn it hadn't been there two days ago when she was here. She and Ryan had both commented on the lack of photos of Jenny and Eric on the computer.

She clicked on the icon for Jenny's photo album. The page filled with thumbnails of her sister—alone, with friends—and with Eric. Enlarging one image, Jana studied a picture of Eric with his arm around a solemn-faced Jenny. The shot had been taken out of doors, possibly at the dig site. Though Eric was grinning broadly, Jenny looked unhappy about something.

Other images in the file were of Eric by himself. One looked like the kind of headshot that might run with a newspaper column while others resembled selfies taken in front of local landmarks, such as the painted canyon walls in Black Canyon of the Gunnison National Park. But none of these images had been on Jenny's laptop when Jana had looked two days before.

She was trying to puzzle this out when her cell

phone rang. The number was local, but not one she knew. "Hello?" she answered, cautious.

"Jana, it's Eric. I'm sorry I couldn't make dinner tonight. I would have called earlier, but I was out at Daniel Metwater's camp, with no cell service. I swung by the motel to apologize in person, but you weren't there."

"I'm sure your story on him was more important than dinner with me," she said, hoping he noted the sarcasm in her voice.

"It wasn't that. I planned to finish up in plenty of time to meet you, but the Rangers showed up and I didn't dare leave."

"The Rangers? Which Rangers?"

"Ryan Spencer and a couple of others. They had a warrant to search Daniel Metwater's motor home. I was in the motor home with Metwater when they arrived."

"And they asked you to stay?"

"No, but I would have been crazy to leave. Good thing I didn't, or I would have missed out on the biggest story of my career."

He sounded so excited—gleeful, even. "What happened?" she asked.

"The Rangers have arrested Daniel Metwater—for murder."

"Whose murder?" She had to force out the words, her tongue frozen along with the rest of her.

"For the murder of the woman whose body they found this afternoon—the one from Mexico or Guatemala or wherever it was. Apparently, Metwater killed her."

"The Rangers *think* he killed her," Jana clarified.

"Right. But they wouldn't have arrested him if they

didn't think they had pretty solid proof. I hope this isn't too upsetting for you. Where are you?"

"I stopped by Jenny's apartment."

"Are you there by yourself? You probably shouldn't be alone at a time like this."

A time like what? "I'm fine," she said.

"That's good to know. I have to go now. I have to write up this story and get it in tomorrow's edition. I'm thinking front page. This is big!"

The call ended before she could say another word. Jana stared at her phone, trying to absorb this news.

With shaking fingers, she punched in Ryan's number. He answered on the fourth ring. "Hello, Jana," he said, his voice warm and friendly, as if he was pleased to hear from her.

"Did you really arrest Daniel Metwater for Alicia Mendoza's murder?" she asked.

"Who told you that?" he asked, all the warmth vanishing from his voice.

"Eric Patterson called me."

He muttered what might have been a curse. "Yes, it's true," he said.

"Have they found anything to link Metwater to Jenny?"

"Nothing so far. I'm sorry, I have to go. I'll talk to you later."

The contrast between the two men struck her—Eric so energized and gleeful at the news of Metwater's arrest, Ryan weary and maybe a little sad. "Try to get some rest sometime," she said.

"You, too."

The call ended, and Jana sat, the silence of the empty apartment closing in around her. She thought of so many questions she should have asked Ryan. The Rangers thought Daniel Metwater had murdered Alicia Mendoza. Did they believe he had something to do with Jenny's disappearance, as well? Could they force him to tell them what had happened to Jenny? Was this the break they needed to find her sister?

If they found Jenny, would she still be alive? Every hour that passed without hearing from her seemed to increase the probability that Jana would never see her sister alive again.

She pushed the thought away and shut down Jenny's computer. Time to get out of here. At the motel she would take a long hot shower, then find a movie to stream—something cheerful and unchallenging, to take her mind off all the things around her over which she had no control.

She cleaned up the remains of her supper, wrote a note for April thanking her for letting her hang out in Jenny's room for a while, then left, making sure to lock up behind her.

It was almost ten o'clock, and clouds had moved in to obscure the moon. The parking lot was so dark that Jana thought about pulling out her phone and turning on the flashlight app. But she only had to walk a few yards to her car and didn't want to take the time to fumble with her phone. Instead, she took out her keys and clicked the button to unlock her car.

The headlights winked at her and she relaxed a little. She'd have no trouble making her way safely to the car now. Walking quickly, she moved toward the driver's-side door. What movie should she watch tonight? Was she in the mood for a comedy, or was a good love story the best thing to distract her?

She was reaching for the door handle when a pair of strong arms encircled her, crushing her ribs and lifting her off the ground. Then pain exploded at the back of her head and the world went black.

RYAN STUDIED THE man who sat across from him in the interview room at the Montrose police station. Ranger headquarters had no facility for holding prisoners, so they had brought Metwater here for questioning and detainment until he was either bailed out or held over for trial. Metwater didn't so much sit in the chair as balance there, like a panther readying himself to pounce. A pulse throbbed at his temple, and the muscles along his jaw knotted. His long, elegant fingers curled and uncurled into fists.

Ethan tossed the torn shirt onto the table in front of Metwater. "Does this belong to you?" he asked.

Metwater scarcely glanced at the garment. "It's a rag. It could belong to anybody."

"We found it in your closet. Check the label."

"I want my lawyer. I refuse to do anything without counsel present."

"Suit yourself," Ethan said. "I'll read the label to you." He lifted the collar of the shirt and squinted at the label. "Balenciaga. The same label as six other shirts like this that we found in your motor home."

Metwater stared at them, silent.

"You're living pretty large for a humble prophet," Ethan said. "I did a little research and these shirts retail for over two hundred dollars each. Not the kind of thing most guys have in their closets."

Metwater remained stone-faced.

Ethan glanced at Ryan, who had been leaning

against the doorjamb. Ryan straightened and joined
his partner at the table. "Highway workers found Alicia Mendoza's body this afternoon," he said. "She was
strangled with strips of fabric cut from a shirt like this.
We're pretty confident tests are going to show the fabric was cut from this shirt. They'll probably have your
DNA in them. Why don't you make it easier on yourself and tell us now what happened."

Metwater continued to glare at them. If it were possible for a gaze to burn through someone, Ryan would
be full of smoldering holes from Metwater's laser stare.

"Maybe Alicia came to your camp because she was
curious, or because she needed help," Ethan said. "You
invited her in. You wanted to get to know her better.
One thing led to another and maybe she refused your
advances, or maybe things got a little rougher than
you intended. Maybe it was an accident. Whatever, she
ended up dead, and you did the only thing you could
do—you got rid of the body."

"If I killed her, why would I be stupid enough to
leave evidence like this shirt lying around?" Metwater asked.

"You were probably pretty upset and stressed-out,"
Ryan said. "You forgot. It could happen to anyone."

"It didn't happen," Metwater said.

Ryan leaned over Metwater. He could smell the
sweat beneath the expensive cologne. "Alicia is dead,"
he said. "Someone killed her. Who would do that—
with your shirt?"

Metwater looked away, shutting them out.

Ryan straightened. "Put him in the cell until his
lawyer gets here," he said.

An officer cuffed Metwater and led him away. As

he was leaving, Ranger commander Graham Ellison slipped into the interview room. "His lawyer is going to fight us hard on this one," he said.

"Even the best lawyer can't explain away that shirt," Ryan said. "The fabric used to strangle Alicia Mendoza is going to match, I'm sure of it."

"The shirt looks significant, but it may not be enough to hold him," Graham said. "We haven't been able to get anyone to admit to seeing Alicia in Metwater's camp, and half a dozen of his followers swear he never left the camp the day she disappeared and was supposedly killed."

"What about his car?" Ethan asked. "Alicia's body got to that ditch in a vehicle. Maybe we could find DNA evidence in Metwater's car."

"He doesn't have a car," Graham said. "When he needs to go somewhere, someone else drives him. And, again, everyone swears he never left the camp."

"Have we found anything to link him to Lucia Raton or Jennifer Lassiter?" Ryan asked.

"We know Lucia was in his camp at one point, and Jennifer followed his blog," Ethan said. "A jury might see that as significant."

"I can guarantee a defense lawyer would argue it isn't," Graham said.

"What about the three women themselves?" Ethan asked. "Any connections between them?"

"None," Graham said. "Though it seems as if three women who go missing from the same area in the same brief period of time would be connected, we don't have anything concrete to tie them together."

Ryan's phone buzzed. He checked the screen, but the number didn't look familiar, so he silenced it. "We should put some pressure on Andi Mattheson," he said. "She's closest to Metwater. If he's involved in these missing women, she'll know."

"She's completely loyal to him," Ethan said. "I don't think she's likely to betray him."

"We could play up the jealousy angle," Ryan said. "No matter how loyal she is, she won't like it if he's hitting on other women." His phone buzzed again.

"Maybe you'd better take that call," Ethan said.

"Go ahead," Graham said. "Then go home. I don't think there's anything more we can do here tonight."

"Maybe we'll catch a break tomorrow," Ethan said.

Ryan moved into the hallway and pulled out his phone. The screen showed the same unfamiliar number. "Hello?"

"Officer Spencer?" The female voice sounded young and nervous.

Ryan tensed. "Yes."

"This is April Pham. Jenny Lassiter's roommate. Jana Lassiter asked me to call you."

Ryan gripped the phone so hard his fingers ached. "Is something wrong?"

"Someone attacked Jana outside my apartment tonight," April said, her voice wavering. "I came home in time to scare them away. She's here at the hospital."

Ryan didn't need to hear more. He pulled out his keys and ran toward the door. "I'm on my way."

Chapter Nine

Jana squinted in the glare of the bright light overhead and tried not to think about how much her head ached. The sharp odor of antiseptic stung her nose and she shivered in the blast from the air-conditioning, despite the blanket a nurse had spread over the gurney. "Paging Dr. Kitten. Paging Dr. Kitten." The announcement cut through the low-level emergency-room chatter, and Jana fought back an unexpected giggle. Was it tough to gain respect from your patients and colleagues when your name was Dr. Kitten? Or maybe Dr. Kitten was warm and approachable, in keeping with the name.

The doctor who had examined Jana was brisk and businesslike. Jana had a concussion and some bruising. "You should be fine in a few days, maybe a few weeks. Follow up with your primary-care doctor as soon as possible," he said, before hurrying away to his next patient.

The curtain around Jana's cubicle rattled as it slid back, and she turned toward the sound, regretting the movement as soon as she made it. She winced at the fresh stab of pain and Ryan hurried to her side. "Is something wrong?" he asked. "Should I call someone?"

"I'm fine." She managed a weak smile—it really

didn't do justice to how glad she was to see him. "What are you doing here?"

"April Pham called me."

"I didn't mean for her to get you out so late. What time is it?"

"Almost one. How are you doing?" He gripped the edge of the gurney.

"I'm okay. Well, except for a headache." She reached out her free hand—the one without the IV—and grasped his fingers.

His grip was strong and somehow managed to convey both his concern and his relief. "Do you remember anything about what happened?" he asked.

"Not much. I was leaving Jenny's apartment, walking to my car, and I guess someone hit me on the head. I blacked out. The next thing I knew, I woke up in the ambulance. I still don't know how I ended up here."

"April told the officers on the scene that when she arrived home, she heard a woman cry out, then saw a man and woman struggling. She shouted at them and pulled out her phone, and the man fled. She ran over and was surprised to find it was you."

"Thank God she showed up when she did. I don't even want to think about what might have happened if she hadn't."

He squeezed her hand more tightly. "Did you get a look at the guy at all?" he asked.

"No. He came up from behind me. I never saw him at all. Did April see anything?"

"No. It was too dark. What were you doing at Jenny's apartment?"

She grimaced, even though the movement intensified the throbbing in her head. "Eric Patterson and

I were supposed to have dinner," she said. "He stood me up and I was annoyed. So I went to Jenny's place. If she had been there, we would have laughed about the whole thing. Instead, I had to settle for being in the place where I feel closest to her." She tried to blink back the tears that filled her eyes, but one slipped down her cheek.

Ryan wiped the tear away gently. He didn't say anything, but the gesture spoke volumes and brought forth a fresh flow of tears.

She was doubly grateful when he pretended not to notice. "Eric was at Daniel Metwater's camp this afternoon," he said.

"He told me later when he called. That's the excuse he gave for missing dinner with me—that he had to wait to see what the Rangers found when they searched Metwater's motor home." She sniffed and wiped at her eyes with her fingers. He handed her a tissue and she smiled her thanks. "I still can't believe you arrested Metwater," she said. "Do you really think he killed Alicia?"

"We have evidence that suggests that, but nothing that links him to Jenny."

The fact that he even mentioned her sister told Jana he had been thinking along those lines. "I found something a little odd on Jenny's laptop when I was there this evening," she said. "Nothing that relates to her disappearance, I don't think, just something that struck me as strange."

"What was that?"

"Do you remember we talked about how it was weird that she didn't have any pictures of Eric on her computer or her social-media pages, even though they were engaged?"

"Yes."

"I didn't check her social media, but now her computer has all kinds of pictures of Eric—with her and by himself. I'm sure they weren't there the other night."

"I didn't see any pictures of him when I examined the computer."

"Do you think April could have put them there?" she asked. "But why would she do that?"

He pulled out his phone. "Why don't we ask her?"

Ryan put the phone on speaker so Jana could hear the conversation. After answering April's questions about Jana, Ryan told her the reason for his call. "Did you put any pictures onto Jenny's laptop in the last couple of days?" he asked.

"I haven't touched her laptop," April said, clearly shocked by the idea. "I mean, I would never mess with a roommate's belongings. Why are you asking?"

"Jana was looking at the laptop tonight and found some pictures that she hadn't seen on there before—pictures of Jenny and Eric, and some of Eric by himself."

"I didn't put them there," April said.

"Do you have any idea how they might have got there?" Ryan asked.

"I don't know," she said. "I mean—he was her fiancé. Maybe they were there all along and Jana just didn't see them before. Maybe she didn't open that file or something."

"The police didn't find any of these pictures when we went over the unit, either," Ryan said.

"Weird," April said. "I'm sorry I can't help you."

"Has anyone else—besides you and Jana—been in Jenny's room in the last couple of days?" Ryan asked.

She hesitated. "Well, Eric stopped by here yesterday morning. He said he needed to get a jacket he had left in Jenny's closet. The police told me they were through with the room, so I thought it would be all right to let him go in there."

"You didn't do anything wrong," Ryan reassured her. "Did he get the jacket?"

"He said he couldn't find it."

"How long was he in the room?" Ryan asked.

"Not long. A few minutes, maybe. I was watching TV and I didn't time him or anything."

"Thanks, April," Ryan said. "I appreciate your help." He ended the call and pocketed the phone.

"Why would Eric bother to add pictures to Jenny's computer?" Jana asked.

"I'm going to ask him," Ryan said. "And I'm going to find out where he was this evening after he left Metwater's camp."

"When he called me, he said he was working on his story about Metwater's arrest," she said. "He said he had a deadline to meet to get the story in tomorrow's— well, I guess now it's today's—paper. He sounded really excited about it."

"I still want to know where he was." His grim expression made her glad she wasn't Eric Patterson. Then a chill ran through her. "Ryan, you don't think Eric Patterson attacked me, do you? Why would he?"

"I don't know. But someone attacked you and I want to find out who. Patterson seems a logical place to start."

Nothing about this whole situation seemed logical to

Jana, but knowing Ryan was looking out for her made her emotional all over again. She was grateful when a nurse bustled into the room. "Now that your ride is here we can see about discharging you," she said. "I have some instructions for you." She turned to Ryan. "She's not to be left alone tonight. And call and report if you see anything unusual—slurred words, blurred vision, unsteady gait, things like that."

"I'll stay with her," he said. "And I'll call if there are any problems."

"Ryan, I can't ask you to do that," Jana protested.

"I'm staying." His tone told her there was no use arguing.

"Thank you," she said, as he helped her sit up.

She listened to the nurse's instructions, signed the papers she was handed, then was left alone long enough to change back into her clothes. A few minutes later, Ryan wheeled her out of the emergency department to his cruiser. "I could have walked," she said as he helped her stand.

"But you didn't have to." He saw her into the passenger seat and handed her her purse. She stared at the bag in her lap. "Do you think it's strange the guy who hit me didn't take my purse?" she asked.

"Maybe April scared him off before he could grab it." He walked around the vehicle and slid into the driver's seat. "Or maybe he wasn't interested in the purse."

"Which means what? He was interested in me?"

"Three women have mysteriously disappeared in this area in the past three weeks." Ryan started the cruiser. "And we know one of them is dead."

Her stomach lurched and she bit the inside of her

cheek, trying to regain her composure. "I don't think this is related," she said. "How could it be?"

"It may not be, but part of my job is looking at a case from every angle."

"Right." She folded her hands in her lap and stared straight ahead. Her head still throbbed, but less than it had earlier. Mainly, she felt exhausted. She wanted to crawl into bed and forget about all of this for the next ten hours or so.

Sleep. Where was Ryan going to sleep? Her motel room didn't have a sofa. It wasn't even a very large room. "Maybe you should take me to Jenny and April's apartment," she said. "I could stay there tonight. I'm sure April wouldn't mind."

"I'm taking you to my place," he said. "I want you where I can keep an eye on you."

"Oh." She wanted to object that he didn't need to go to so much trouble, but the thought of spending the night alone held no appeal. "Thank you," she said, instead.

"I'll swing by the motel so you can get your things," he said.

Right. She would need "things"—toiletries, her night gown and a change of clothes. Trying to think of everything made her head hurt.

She closed her eyes and surrendered to the soothing hum of tires on pavement, until the cruiser slowed for the turn into the motel parking lot. "My room's around back," she said. "Number 118."

"I remember."

Right. How could she have forgotten he had been in her room? Though the kiss they had shared now seemed so long ago.

He pulled into a vacant space across from her room and they climbed out of the car. She made no objection when he took her arm. Whether from shock and pain or the late hour, weariness dragged at her. She fumbled in her purse and found her key card. Her fingers brushed against her car keys. "My car—"

"We'll see to it in the morning," he said. "Don't worry about it now. Let me see your room key."

She handed him the card and he started to insert it in the slot, then stopped.

"What is it?" she asked. "What's wrong?"

"This lock has been tampered with." He shifted so that more light fell on the door, and pointed to gouges around the key slot and the knob. He took a handkerchief from his pocket and tried the knob. It turned easily and the door swung open. "Let me go in first," he said.

She nodded, too stunned to speak. He drew his weapon and eased around the door while Jana held her breath. A few moments later he emerged. "It's all right," he said. "It doesn't look as if anyone has been in here."

She moved past him into the room, which looked the same as when she had left it. Ryan took her suitcase from the closet and opened it on the bed. "Pack everything," he said. "You're not coming back here."

She didn't have the strength to argue, and she moved to the dresser and began emptying everything into the suitcase. Ryan disappeared into the bathroom and emerged with her makeup case and hairbrush. "I'll call in a report once I have you settled," he said. "And I'll notify the motel management and get someone out to question staff and guests, in case anyone saw anything."

When she had packed everything, he stashed her suitcase in the back of the cruiser, then helped her into the passenger seat. She willed herself not to think about what had happened, though the image of the violated door played in a loop in her head.

Ryan lived in one of a row of duplexes on the north side of Montrose. The house was plain but clean and comfortable. He led her to a bedroom at the back and set her suitcase on the floor. "The bathroom is across the hall. I'll get some sheets for the bed." He turned to go, but she put out a hand to stop him.

"Don't leave me just yet," she said.

"Of course."

She hesitated, then moved into his arms. "Just hold me," she said. "I don't feel as frightened when you hold me."

His arms encircled her, warm and strong. No one could get to her here—not the man who had attacked her in the parking lot or whoever had vandalized her motel room door. She closed her eyes and rested her head on Ryan's shoulder, and she was too tired and weak to hold back the sob that rose in her throat.

"It's okay," he murmured, and smoothed his hand over the back of her head. "You're safe now."

"I'm so scared," she said. "I could have died tonight."

His arm tightened around her. "You didn't die. I'll find whoever did this. I won't let him hurt you."

She raised her head to look at him, the compassion in his eyes bringing on a fresh flood. "I'm not only scared for myself," she said between sobs. "I'm beginning to think I'm never going to see Jenny again. What if she's dead?"

He cradled her head in his hand. "You'll get through it," he said. "It will be awful, but you'll get through it. I'll help you."

She nodded. He couldn't bring back her sister or lessen the pain news of her death would bring, but she believed he would stay with her, and, for now, knowing that was enough.

"Do you want to come with me to get the sheets for your bed?" he asked.

"I don't want sheets for my bed," she said. "I want to stay with you tonight. I just… I don't want to be alone."

"All right." He picked up her suitcase. "I won't leave you."

He led the way to his bedroom, a larger room furnished with a king-size bed. "You can change in there," he said, indicating a door that led to a large master bath.

She found her nightgown in the suitcase and changed out of her clothes in the bathroom. The sight of a brown stain on her blouse made her stomach heave when she realized it was her own blood. She balled up the blouse so the stain didn't show and focused on washing her face and brushing her teeth, without looking too long at herself in the mirror. The glimpses she allowed showed a pale woman who hardly looked like herself.

She returned to the bedroom to find Ryan already in bed. Weariness overcoming awkwardness, she crawled under the covers. He switched off the light and she lay still, her back to him. Then he moved toward her and his arm came around her. "Is this all right?" he asked.

"Yes." She settled against him, her head cradled in the hollow of his shoulder. "It's more than all right." For tonight, at least, being with him was going to hold back the fear and pain that threatened to overtake her.

Chapter Ten

Ryan lay awake for a long time, too aware of the feel of Jana against him, the softness of her body and the scent of her hair to sleep. He wanted her, but her very vulnerability held him in check. She needed his protection now more than she needed his passion.

He rose early and left her sleeping. Staying with her until she woke would be too much of a temptation. He was in the kitchen drinking his first cup of coffee when she came in, dressed but pale, anxiety haunting her eyes. "How are you feeling this morning?" he asked, as he took another cup from the cabinet by the stove.

"A little steadier." She accepted the cup, but avoided looking directly at him. "I'm sorry I was so clingy last night," she said.

"I have no complaints."

Her cheeks flushed pink, and he wanted to gather her into his arms and kiss away her embarrassment. But now wasn't the time. "While you were changing last night I called in a report on the forced lock on your motel room," he said. "We'll check it for fingerprints, but I'm not expecting we'll find much."

"This morning, I just want to get my car back," she

said. "Can you take me by Jenny's apartment before you go in to work?"

"I'll do that. But for now, I don't want you driving anywhere by yourself," Ryan said.

She opened her eyes and looked him in the eye for the first time that morning. "The doctor didn't say anything about not driving."

"No. But the vandalism of your room makes me think the attack on you last night wasn't random. Someone is targeting you. I'm not going to give them a chance to get to you."

"Who would want to hurt me?" she asked.

"I don't know. But until we find out, I don't want you going anywhere alone." He dumped the dregs of his cup in the sink and set the cup on the drain board. "I'll take you by to get your car, then I have to go in to work, but I've called a friend to come and stay with you this morning."

She frowned. "Another cop?"

"No. But she's married to a cop." He turned his back to her and opened a cabinet. "Do you want some breakfast? I've got cereal or frozen waffles."

"I don't really feel like eating," she said. "I just want to get my car."

He turned back to her and pulled her close. "I know it's a lot to take in," he said. "I wish I could make it easier for you."

"You make it easier just by being here."

They stood that way for a long moment, arms wrapped around each other. He breathed in the floral scent of her hair and savored the feel of her against him. He wished he could prolong this interlude, but every minute counted in the hunt for a killer, so after a while, he reluctantly pulled away. "Let's get your car," he said. "Then you can meet Emma."

"Emma?"

"Emma Ellison. You two can hang out today. You'll like her, I think."

Jana was grateful Ryan didn't press her to make conversation on the drive from his place to Jennifer's apartment. Her head ached and her stomach churned as she tried to process everything that had happened in the last twelve hours. The attack had been awful enough when it had seemed like a random mugging, but seeing the damage to the lock on her hotel room had shaken something at her core. She had never in her life not felt safe. Now, nothing about her life felt dependable.

She glanced over at the man in the driver's seat of the cruiser. Except Ryan. She could depend on him, she was sure of it. She wasn't sure she liked relying so heavily on someone else, but she was more than grateful that he was with her now. Last night, lying in his arms, she had felt so protected and safe. So...cherished.

Sleeping together might have led to more, but the timing had been all wrong. Too many bad things were happening—how could they help but color anything good that might happen between her and Ryan?

After today, she would be better, she told herself. She would spend the day with this Emma person and regain her equilibrium. Maybe Ryan would find out what happened to Jenny. Even if it was bad news— terrible news—at least she would know. That would be better, right?

She blinked back tears. Who was she kidding? How could anything but finding Jenny safe and alive be better?

Ryan pulled into the parking lot of the apartment building. "I'm parked over there," she said, indicating a group of visitor's spaces on the far side of the lot.

He parked in an empty space and they got out of the cruiser. "Which car is yours?" Ryan asked, taking her arm.

Something in his voice made her tense and look around. She gasped as her gaze fell on her Jeep, parked a few spaces over and behind them. The front windshield was shattered. "Oh no," she moaned.

Ryan released his hold on her and strode toward the vehicle. She followed, a fresh wave of shock rocking her as she saw that the driver's-side window was broken, as well, and someone had slashed the upholstery, stuffing spilling from the deep cuts. She steadied herself with one hand on the hood. "Who would do this?" she whispered.

Ryan scanned the lot. "I don't see any other cars damaged," he said.

She swallowed hard, a sour taste in her mouth. "You mean someone targeted *my* car," she said.

He took her arm again, and at the same time pulled out his phone. "I'll get a team over here right away to go over the car," he said. "Maybe we'll get lucky and find something."

"He must have come back, after the ambulance took me away, and done this," Jana said. She stared at the damaged car, icy fear spreading through her. The broken windshield was traumatic enough, but the slashed seats felt much more personal. There was anger behind those cuts—hatred.

Ryan ended one call and made another, then turned back to her. "We'll canvass the people in the apartments," he said. "Maybe someone saw or heard something. In the meantime, Emma is on her way over to pick you up."

Jana nodded, numb. Ryan put his hand on her shoulder and looked her in the eye. "I know this is rough," he said. "But you have to pull yourself together. Don't let this guy defeat you. Stay strong—for Jenny."

She nodded and took a deep breath. "Right." She couldn't afford to fall apart now. "Whoever did this hurt my car, but they didn't get me," she said. "I won't let them beat me." Instead of sitting around feeling sorry for herself, she would do whatever she could to try to find the man responsible for this—who maybe was linked to Jenny's disappearance. She wouldn't let him get away without being punished.

EMMA ELLISON WAS the kind of woman who couldn't help but make an entrance. Over six feet tall in heels, her formfitting jeans and sweater accentuated her generous curves. Add in a mane of white-blond curls and rhinestone-trimmed sunglasses and she looked more like an A-list star than a cop's wife. When Ryan had called Commander Ellison last night to report the attack on Jana and her car, Emma had insisted on staying with Jana while Ryan was at work, and her husband had seconded the suggestion, making it all but an order— an order Ryan was happy to follow.

She sped into the apartment parking lot in a bright red sports car and everyone in the area stopped what they were doing and watched her step out of the car. "Hello, Ryan," she said, sweeping past him on a wave of floral perfume. "And you must be Jana. I'm Emma." She thrust a tall paper cup into Jana's hand. "I hope you like caramel lattes. It's my personal favorite. Oh, and I brought muffins." She waggled a white paper bag. "None of these bachelors ever have anything very appetizing for breakfast."

"Thanks." Jana's smile almost reached her eyes.

"Emma is married to my commander, Graham Ellison," Ryan said. "She's a reporter."

"I cover the Western Slope for the *Denver Post*," Emma said. She waved at Ryan in a dismissive gesture. "You can go to work now, Officer. Jana and I have things to discuss."

"What things?" he asked.

Emma widened her eyes. "We're going to talk about you, of course."

RYAN'S GOODBYE WAS BRIEF, perhaps because Emma had her gaze fixed on him. Jana wanted to throw her arms around his neck and kiss him, and maybe thank him again for all he had done for her, but she had to settle for a brief squeeze of his hand as he murmured, "See you later."

When he was gone, she let Emma lead her to the car. Emma settled her drink in the cup holder, fastened her seat belt, and regarded Jana thoughtfully. "Let's take a drive out toward the lake first, enjoy our breakfast and get to know each other better, then we'll come up with a plan for the day."

"I appreciate your taking the time to come get me," Jana said. "But really, I'll be fine on my own. If you could just take me by Ryan's to get my things, then maybe some place to rent a car?" She couldn't keep the note of doubt out of the last words, despite her best efforts.

"I could do that," Emma said. "But then I'd have to go shopping and to lunch by myself, and we'd both miss out on making a new friend. Not to mention we'd have to listen to my husband and Ryan rake us over the coals when they found out I had left you alone, and that's just tiresome." She lowered her sunglasses to look Jana in the eye. "You don't really want to do that, do you?"

Jana gave a shaky laugh. "Well, when you put it that way."

"Terrific." Emma put the car in gear and headed out of the parking lot. Jana resisted the urge to look back at the officers swarmed around her car and instead sipped the coffee. It was hot and sweet—and maybe exactly what she needed.

"How's your head this morning?" Emma asked. "I heard you were knocked out."

"It doesn't hurt as much as it did last night." She sipped the coffee. "Thanks for the latte. Ryan made coffee, but…"

"But it was strong enough to put hair on your chest." Emma laughed. "Cop coffee. They're more interested in caffeine than taste. You'll get used to it."

"Oh, I…" Jana let her voice trail away, not sure what kind of answer to give.

"Have a muffin." Emma passed her the bag and a napkin. "Let me guess—part of you wants to protest that you're not going to stick around long enough to form an opinion about Ryan's coffee one way or another. But another part of you thinks the studly single cop is pretty darn interesting—am I right?"

Jana peeled the paper back from her muffin and pinched off a bite, then nodded. When she had woken up this morning to find herself alone in Ryan's bed, she'd been disappointed. The more time she spent with Ryan, the more her attraction for him grew. Their timing was lousy—any sensible person would tell her that getting involved with a man when her emotions were in such turmoil over Jenny's disappearance was a bad idea, but her heart wasn't paying attention to sense.

"Graham and I got together when some thug took a shot at me and Graham appointed himself my bodyguard," Emma said. She took a bite of muffin and chewed, cherry-pink lips curved in a half smile. "I thought he was the most insufferable, overbearing, bossy man I had ever met—and also the sexiest, smartest and most fascinating."

"Now isn't exactly the best time to start a relationship," Jana said.

"Honey, it is never the right time for a relationship with a cop," Emma said. "But don't let that stop you. For what it's worth, I think Ryan is definitely interested in you."

"What makes you say that?" There she went, blushing again.

"Are you kidding? He couldn't keep his eyes off you just now."

But maybe that was only because he thought she was going to lose it any minute. Certainly, the whole time she had known him she had been upset about one thing or the other—her sister or being attacked or having her car destroyed. Time to change the subject. "You said you're a reporter. Do you know Eric Patterson?"

Emma signaled for the turn onto the highway. "I know who he is," she said. "We've run into each other a couple of times, but we're not friends or anything."

"What's your impression of him?"

"You meet a lot of guys like him in my business—maybe in any business. He's ambitious. A little narcissistic. He has a reputation as something of a ladies' man."

Emma wouldn't have guessed that last one. "He does?"

"Well, he's the kind of smooth talker who seems to think every woman should fall under his spell." She shrugged. "That type never impresses me, but some women seem to go for it."

"He was engaged to my sister," Jana said.

"So I hear."

"But Jenny wasn't the type to fall for a smooth operator. She liked more—I don't know—self-effacing guys. Easygoing, athletic maybe, but with a good sense of humor." She ran through the list of men Jenny had dated seriously—a singer/songwriter, a computer-technology major, a rodeo cowboy—none of them at all like Eric Patterson.

"Maybe your sister was attracted to Eric because he was so different from her usual type," Emma said. "Or maybe she was going through a phase where she was experimenting with different things. Some people do that in college. You know, they find religion or they become obsessed with a band or start reading philosophy or dressing like a 1950s pinup girl. It's part of growing up."

"Maybe. Jenny was into different things lately. She never said anything to me, but apparently she'd been reading a blog written by Daniel Metwater."

"Ah, our local prophet." Emma nodded. "Your sister wouldn't be the first young woman to fall under his spell."

Jana leaned forward. "What do you know about Metwater and his followers?" she asked. "They seem like some throwback hippie cult or something to me."

"They are that, in a way." Emma took another drink of coffee. "Metwater is actually a really interesting guy. He's the son of a wealthy industrialist. He and his brother inherited the family fortune, but the brother got into a lot of trouble, embezzling money from the family business. He ended up dead—supposedly murdered by the mob, though that was never proven. As far as I could determine, that case is still open. Anyway, supposedly the shock of his brother's death led Daniel to renounce his capitalist roots and turn to spiritual pursuits. He preaches a lot about living apart from society, being at one with nature, et cetera."

"Do you think he's sincere?" Jana asked.

"His followers have to sign over all their worldly possessions to him when they join his so-called Family," she said. "That doesn't sound like someone who's really committed to living a nonmaterialistic life. And for all he preaches peace, he's had a pretty antagonistic relationship with the Rangers."

"Do you think he had anything to do with the women who have been disappearing?" Jana asked.

"It doesn't matter what I think," Emma said. "But I can tell you the Rangers think there's a lot more going on out there at his camp than an innocent gathering of peace-loving nature worshippers."

RYAN WAS ON his way to Ranger headquarters when Simon called and asked him to pick up the mail. "It comes to a PO Box and the admin who's supposed to collect it forgot," Simon said. "Just flash your badge and they shouldn't give you any trouble about getting it."

Twenty minutes later, Ryan stepped into headquarters carrying a large plastic tub filled with letters and packages. "Simon, there's a thick envelope for you from the Chicago police department," he said.

"Great." Simon snagged the envelope and tore open the flap.

Ryan leaned over his shoulder to study the cheaply bound volume of what looked like police reports.

"It's a copy of the files the Chicago police had on Daniel Metwater and his brother." Simon tossed the thick book on the corner of his desk. "I got curious about what they thought might have happened."

"What did happen?" Ryan asked. This was the first he had heard of Metwater having a brother.

"The brother, David, was murdered," Simon said. "We had always heard local police suspected a mafia hit, but I wanted to see for sure."

"Not a bad idea." Ethan joined Ryan and the others by Simon's desk. "Maybe you'll find something interesting." He turned to Ryan. "Anything for me?"

"Nope. And not for me, either." He turned toward Carmen. "I have a package for you, though." He hefted the large cardboard box. "From a Wilma Redhorse. Is that your sister?"

"My mother." She took the box and carried it to her desk.

"Your mother sends you packages at work?" Simon followed her to her desk.

"Did she send you cookies?" Ethan asked. "Because I'm getting kind of hungry."

"I don't know what's in here." She took a pair of

scissors from her desk drawer and began snipping at the thick layers of packing tape all around the box. "And she sends them to me here because she's convinced that if I'm not home and the carrier leaves the box on the front porch, someone will steal it."

"It happens." Ryan sat on the corner of her desk. "Maybe it is cookies."

She snipped the last of the tape and pulled back the flaps on the box. Then she pulled out a large ball of tissue paper. "She sent you a soccer ball," Ethan said.

"That's a lot of paper," Randall said. "Maybe it's a crystal ball and she doesn't want it to get broken."

"Why would my mom have a crystal ball?" Carmen asked. She began unwinding the many layers of tissue paper, then stopped, a look of horror stealing over her face. "Oh, no."

"Oh, no what?" Ryan stood. Beneath her normally tanned complexion, Carmen had gone very white.

She shook her head and started to stuff the tissue wad back into the box, but Simon intercepted her. "You can't bring us this far, then just stop," he said. "We all want to know what your mom sent."

She pulled away from him, but reluctantly removed the rest of the paper and scowled at the item in her hand.

Simon stared. "Is it a crown?"

Ryan looked in the box. "There's a sash in here, too." He held it up and read the gold lettering across the red satin. "Miss Northern Ute."

Ryan looked at Carmen, who was very red now. "You were a beauty queen?"

"Don't sound so shocked." She snatched the sash from him and stuffed it and the crown back into the box. "Not another word," she said, and tucked the box under her arm and left the room.

"What's wrong with her?" Randall asked. "If I were ever a beauty queen, I'd be proud of it."

"I can't tell you how grateful I am to live in a world where you are not a beauty queen," Simon said.

"Speaking of beauty queens, Andi Mattheson will be here any minute," Ethan said. "Marco and Michael are bringing her in for questioning."

"Call her Asteria if you want her to cooperate," Simon said. "Though I have my doubts we'll get anything out of her. Metwater has her thoroughly brainwashed." He turned to Graham. "I want to be in on the interview."

"Fine," Graham said. "But I want Ryan and Ethan there, too. They don't have the history with Metwater the rest of us do. She might let her guard down with them."

"Yes, sir," Ryan said. "And thanks again for sending your wife over to stay with Jana."

"I don't send Emma anywhere," the commander said. "She does what she wants and she didn't think Jana should be left alone right now. And, despite her glamour-girl looks, she knows how to take care of herself. Jana will be safe with her."

Maybe. But Ryan wouldn't rest until he caught whoever was terrorizing her and put a stop to it. He had to put those concerns aside, however, when Marco and Michael arrived, Andi/Asteria between them. The young woman wore a loose white gauze dress that flowed over her pregnant belly, and her blond hair was loose and hung almost to her waist. Only the coldness in her eyes when she looked at the officers belied her otherwise angelic appearance.

Marco and Michael led her to the conference room, and Ryan and Ethan followed them inside. The first two officers left and Ryan sat across from her. She had the kind of polished blond beauty that had kept her picture in the magazines, newspapers and on online gossip sites from the time she was a teenager. Though she had given up her designer gowns and expensive haircuts for peasant blouses and long, straight hair, she was still gorgeous, but Ryan thought there was something brittle about her beauty—push her too hard and she would crack open to reveal something ugly within.

Of course, that was exactly what the Rangers hoped to do today—to question Andi Mattheson until she cracked and gave them something that would link Daniel Metwater to the deaths of Alicia Mendoza and possibly two other women. "Thank you for coming in today to speak with us," Ryan began. He might as well get started, though Simon had yet to make an appearance.

"I didn't really have a choice, did I?" she said, fixing him with that cool gaze that made him feel about two feet tall.

"Can we get you anything before we begin?" Ethan asked. "Coffee or water?"

"No."

The door to the conference room opened and Simon stepped in. He handed Andi a bottle of water, then sat in the chair beside her, ignoring the other two officers. "Miss Mattheson, you live with Daniel Metwater, is that correct?" he asked.

"My name is Asteria." She gave him a frosty look

worthy of a star accustomed to dealing with imperti-
nent paparazzi.

"All right, Asteria," Simon emphasized the name,
his voice just short of a sneer. "You live with Daniel
Metwater in his motor home."

"I do not," she said. "I have my own tent."

"But you spend a great deal of time with him,"
Simon said. "You've answered the door almost every
time Rangers have visited Mr. Metwater in his motor
home."

"I act as the Prophet's personal secretary," she said.

"His secretary," Simon repeated.

"Why shouldn't I? I have a degree from Brown.
Where did you go to school, Officer?"

"Tulane."

This information surprised Ryan. Tulane University wasn't Ivy League, but it was certainly a presti-
gious university.

Simon's gaze never left Andi's face. He had a particularly intense expression at the best of times, eyes
so dark they were almost black, boring into the object
of his attention, as if daring the other person to blink
first. "You and Daniel Metwater are close," he said.

"If you're asking if I'm sleeping with him, that is
none of your business," she said.

"Fine." Simon looked away, his normally sallow
complexion flushed.

Ryan decided it was time for him to step in. "As Mr.
Metwater's personal secretary, you keep track of his
schedule, is that correct?" he asked.

"I log any appointments he might have on his cal-
endar," she said. "But I don't account for his move-

ments every minute of the day. I'm his assistant, not his minder."

She's been coached, Ryan thought. Someone—Metwater or his lawyer—had told her not to admit to knowing Metwater's whereabouts around the times the three women disappeared. "Were you with Mr. Metwater on July 22?" Ryan asked.

"I have no idea," she said. "That was weeks ago."

"What about August tenth?" Simon asked. "That was only four days ago."

"I was probably with the Prophet. I spend most days with him."

Simon leaned toward her and she shifted, leaning away from him, and put one hand protectively over her pregnant belly, which swelled the front of her loose cotton dress. "Tell me about a day you didn't spend with Daniel Metwater," Simon said.

She frowned. "Which day?"

"Any day recently that you haven't spent with the Prophet," Simon said.

"I… I've spent every day with him for the last— well, for at least the last month," she said.

"Do you mean you've spent all of every day in Metwater's company for the past month?" Simon asked.

"Yes."

"You haven't left to—for example—go to a doctor's appointment?" Simon stared pointedly at her belly.

She rubbed her hands together. "I'm very healthy. I don't need to see a doctor."

"No problems with blurred vision? I noticed you keep rubbing your hands. Are they numb or tingling? Have you been thirsty more lately?"

"I'm fine." She pushed back her chair. "Why are you wasting my time like this?"

Simon put his hand out to stay her. "I only want to know why you haven't left the camp in the last month," he said. "Before that you would go into town with the other women to shop and do laundry. I've seen you there."

"Yes, but we thought it was best for me to stay closer to camp."

"Who is we?" Simon asked. "Was this your idea or Metwater's?"

"We decided together."

"Why? What prompted the decision?" Simon's voice was sharp.

Too sharp, Ryan thought. "We're only concerned for your well-being and that of your baby," he said, trying to de-escalate the situation.

Andi didn't even glance at him, her gaze fixed on Simon. "I don't need to go into town," she said. "I have everything I need at the camp, and I'm safe there."

"Why wouldn't you be safe in town?" Ryan asked, before Simon could speak.

Andi smoothed her dress over her belly, her hand rubbing back and forth. "The Prophet offered to send one of his personal bodyguards with me if I wanted to go into town," she said. "But there's really nothing I need there."

"The other women don't have bodyguards," Simon said. "Why would you need one?"

She looked away, but not before Ryan caught the troubled expression in her eyes. "Did something happen to frighten you?" he asked, keeping his voice gentle.

"A man tried to grab me as I was coming out of

the grocery store rather late at night," she said, her head down so that he couldn't see much of her face. "I screamed and kicked at him. I kicked him in the groin and when he doubled over, I ran."

"Why didn't you report this to the police?" Simon asked.

"Because we don't involve the police in our affairs." She raised her head and glared at him. "If you knew anything at all about us, you would know that. We're a family. We take care of our own."

"So your response to this attack was to simply stay home?" Simon asked.

"I stayed where I knew I would be safe."

"Did you get a look at the man who grabbed you?" Ryan asked.

"No. It was dark and he was behind me. I was terrified he was going to hurt my baby."

Ryan could hear the terror in her voice still. The method the man had used was so similar to that used by Jana's attacker it made the hair on the back of his neck stand up. "What grocery store was this?" he asked.

"The City Market on the north side of town," she said. "I parked around by the Dumpsters because I dropped off some of our trash there."

The store was only a couple of miles from Jenny Lassiter's apartment, where Jana had been attacked, but it still might be only coincidence. "Have any of the other women in the Family been attacked?" Ryan asked.

"No." She swallowed. "The man knew me. He called me by name."

"He called you Andi?" Simon asked.

"No, he called me by my name now. He called me

Asteria." She pressed her hands over her eyes, as if trying to shut out whatever visions were replaying in her head. "He said he had been watching me and he knew I was perfect for his next victim."

Simon grabbed her wrist and gently lowered her hand. "You're sure those were his words?" he asked. "His next victim?"

She nodded. "I was so terrified. And when I heard about those other women going missing, I wondered..." Her voice trailed away and she shook her head.

"What did you wonder?" Ryan prompted.

"I wondered if I would have died that night if I hadn't gotten away," she said. "Would I have ended up buried by the side of the road like Alicia Mendoza?"

"WHERE ARE WE HEADED?" Jana asked, after she and Emma had finished their coffee and muffins and Emma turned the car back toward town.

"Have you been to The Boardwalk since you've been in town?" Emma asked.

"I haven't been much of anywhere lately," Jana said.

"Of course you haven't. So you definitely need a break. Do you like antiques?"

"Sure."

"How about rustic art, jewelry and old signs?"

Jana laughed. "Jewelry, yes. I don't know anything about the other two."

"The Boardwalk is a collection of antiques and junk shops on the south end of town," Emma said. "I'm in the process of redecorating the house Graham was living in when we married, giving it a more local vibe, if you will. I'm always on the lookout for interesting things to add to my collection. So if you'll indulge me…"

"It sounds perfect," Jana said. A few hours focused on rusting farm implements and old furniture was just the distraction she needed. "But could we swing by my motel first? I meant to call them this morning and forgot. I still need to check out."

"No problem. And when we're done shopping, I know a great place for lunch."

Ten minutes later, Emma pulled the convertible beneath the portico for the Columbine Inn. She followed Jana inside. "Not that I think you really need a bodyguard," she said, linking her arm with Jana's. "But let's humor Ryan. It's kind of sexy sometimes when a guy goes all protective on you, don't you think?"

Ryan Spencer was sexy pretty much all the time, Jana thought. But maybe she was a tiny bit prejudiced. What was it about the man that got to her so?

The desk clerk greeted Jana by name and accepted her key card. "We hope you enjoyed your stay with us," she said.

Except for the part about someone trying to break into my room, Jana thought. Then again, Ryan would have already notified them about that. "It was fine," she said.

She accepted the receipt the clerk handed her and turned to go. She and Emma were almost to the door when a familiar voice hailed them. "You are just the woman I've been looking for!"

Eric Patterson jogged up to them, out of breath. "Are you okay?" he asked.

"I'm fine." She knew he was just being nice, but something about him always rubbed her the wrong way.

"I heard about what happened," he said, taking her hand. "You could have been killed."

Thanks for pointing that out, she thought. "How did you hear about it?" she asked, pulling her hand away.

"I read the police report. And your Jeep, too." He shook his head. "I wouldn't recommend playing the lottery if I were you," he said. "You've had a run of really bad luck."

"I think being hit over the head and having your car destroyed qualify as more than bad luck," Emma said.

"Hello, Emma," Eric said, his manner more subdued.

"Hello, Eric. You really do get around, don't you?"

"What do you mean?"

"Well, I understand you were with Daniel Metwater when the Rangers arrested him yesterday and you still had time to read the police blotter this morning. When do you sleep?"

His expression grew stormy. "I was at the local cop shop this morning checking on the disposition of Daniel Metwater's case and asked a cop I know there if anything interesting had happened overnight. That's what makes me a good reporter. I'm always on the lookout for my next scoop."

"What is the disposition of Daniel Metwater's case?" Jana asked.

"He was released on bail this morning," Eric said.

"Really?" Emma asked.

"Would I lie?" He grinned. "And I've got a statement from his lawyer that he doesn't expect the grand jury to indict. The Rangers don't have enough evidence linking him to that woman's murder."

"But Ryan said they had evidence," Jana said.

"They have a shirt," Eric said. "It's not enough. But you can believe the Rangers will be keeping a very close eye on him. If he strikes again, they'll be on him like that." He snapped his fingers.

"So you think he's guilty?" Emma asked.

"Oh yeah," Eric said. "I mean look at the guy— handsome, smooth talker, irresistible to women—we're talking Ted Bundy all over again."

Jana felt sick to her stomach. "So you think he not only killed Alicia Mendoza, but Lucia Raton and Jenny, too?"

"I'm hoping I'm wrong, but we have to prepare ourselves for the worst." He took her hand again, and this time she didn't pull away. She needed every bit of her strength to remain standing against the fear and grief that rocked her. "You need to be careful yourself," he said.

"Why is that?" she asked.

"Because you don't want whoever attacked you last night to try again." He leaned forward and kissed her cheek, his voice gentle. "I may have lost Jenny, but I don't want to lose you, too."

Chapter Eleven

"Andi Mattheson swears the man who attacked her was not Daniel Metwater." Simon wrote this information on the whiteboard in the conference room, the marker squeaking above the buzz of the fluorescent lights. Marco and Michael had returned Andi to the Family's camp and the Rangers had convened to review the case.

"Daniel Metwater was in the Montrose jail when Jana and her car were attacked," Ryan said.

"The lab confirms that the material used to strangle Alicia Mendoza came from the shirt we found in Daniel Metwater's closet," Ethan said. "We're still waiting on the DNA results to prove that Metwater wore the shirt, but it matches the other shirts in his closet."

"But we don't have anything to place him away from his camp when Alicia, Lucia or Jenny went missing," Graham said.

"We've got half-a-dozen witnesses or more who will swear Metwater never left camp during those time periods," Marco added.

"We only have Andi's word that she was attacked," Graham said. "She could be making up the story to bolster Metwater's case."

"Maybe," Ryan agreed. "But she sounded genuinely terrified to me."

"Terrified of Metwater, maybe," Simon said. "He's been practically holding her prisoner."

"And we know Jana isn't making up her story," Ryan said. "And Metwater was definitely with us at that time."

"Maybe he had one of his disciples carry out the attack," Marco said.

"Maybe," Graham said. "The problem with our case is we have too many maybes."

"What if we're looking at this wrong?" Ethan said. "What if Metwater isn't the killer and by focusing on him, we're letting the real culprit go free?"

"Who else is a likely suspect?" Graham asked.

"There's the mysterious 'Easy.'" Ethan tapped his pen on the notebook in front of him. "When the women in Metwater's camp were interviewed shortly after Lucia Raton went missing, they mentioned seeing her with someone named 'Easy.' Now when we ask about him, everyone denies having seen him."

"The waitress at the café by the lake mentioned seeing Lucia having coffee with a man," Ethan said. "That was the last time anyone saw her. Maybe it was this 'Easy' fellow."

"That's all we've got?" Ryan asked. "Easy?"

"That's what the people in camp called him," Marco said. "The woman who first gave us the information said he wasn't a member of the Family, but he ran errands for Metwater sometimes."

"So we see if we can find out more about Easy," Graham said. "Circulate his description again, see if we get any hits."

"That still leaves the shirt," Ryan said. "How do you explain it?"

"Someone could have planted it to implicate Metwater," Ethan said.

Graham nodded. "Who has access to Metwater's closet?"

"Probably almost any of his followers," Simon said.

Marco sat back, arms across his chest. "So what do we do now? Go back to the camp and start questioning everyone?"

"We haven't gotten anywhere doing that so far," Graham said.

"I think we should lean on Eric Patterson," Ryan said.

The others turned toward him. "Why Patterson?" Marco asked.

Ryan sat up straighter. "Lean on him was probably a poor choice of words. I think we should ask him for his help. He's doing this newspaper story on Metwater—he has access to the camp and seems to be on good terms with everyone there. Maybe he's learned something that will help us."

"Asking the press for help is asking for trouble," Simon said.

"I used to feel that way," Graham said. "Before I married a reporter." He nodded to Ryan. "Approach Patterson. See if he's got anything for us." He turned back to the whiteboard. "One problem is that we don't know for sure that these cases are connected. We've got three missing women—one we know is dead—and two assaults. They're all young women and they all happened in this general area, but, beyond that, we don't have any link."

"They all knew the killer," Ethan said.

"Maybe," Simon said. "But maybe they were random targets. Maybe the only link is that the killer knew them."

"Or maybe there isn't a link," Marco said. "They're unrelated cases and we're wasting our time trying to connect them."

"Then find something to either prove or disprove the connection," Graham said.

"It might help if we knew what happened to the two missing women," Ethan said.

"Maybe looking at what we know about Alicia's death can help us," Graham said. He moved to the whiteboard and took the marker from Simon. "So what do we know?"

"She was killed soon after she disappeared," Ethan said. "Within hours."

"She was strangled," Ryan said. "And the body buried in a shallow grave on the side of the highway, in an area where there had been recent road construction."

"The killer was in a hurry," Simon said. "He had a car or truck or van, pulled over and dumped the body."

"He was lazy," Marco said. "He didn't want to work hard digging a grave, so he looked for a place where the ground was already disturbed."

"Maybe that's a pattern," Simon said. "We look for other shallow graves in disturbed ground and/or near roads. He wants to get in and out quickly, with as little trouble as possible."

Ryan made a note of this on his tablet. "Why kill an immigrant in the middle of nowhere?" he asked. "She hadn't been in the country long enough for him to stalk her, and she wasn't anywhere where very many people would have seen her."

"Metwater would have seen her if she came to his camp," Simon said. "If she got lost and went looking for help."

"Or one of his men would have," Ethan said.

"Who else?" Graham asked.

Ryan sat up straight, heart pounding. "One of the archaeologists. Their site was near there. They would have known about Jenny Lassiter, too." Why hadn't they thought of that before? They had been so focused on Daniel Metwater they might have overlooked the real killer.

"Go back and ask questions there," Graham said. "Find out if any of the men working at the dig site knew Lucia Raton. And run some backgrounds. Find out if any of them have priors for sexual assault, domestic violence, stalking—anything that raises flags."

"I'll take the archaeologists," Ethan said.

"I'll go with you," Ryan said. "I can talk to Eric Patterson when we're done at the dig site."

"Simon, you and Marco run down everything you can on Easy." Graham set aside the marker and stood back to study the whiteboard. "We're going to get this guy. We have to do it before he strikes again."

JANA ALL BUT ran to Emma's car and was already buckled into her seat when Emma joined her. "Let's get out of here," Jana said. She glanced toward the motel lobby, where she could just see Eric standing inside the door.

"On our way." Emma started the engine. "Are you okay?"

"Just a little creeped out." Jana shuddered. "What

did Eric mean, saying he didn't want to lose me? He never had me."

"Maybe he's one of those overly friendly guys—they don't get the concept of boundaries. Or maybe he's doing it on purpose because he can see it freaks you out."

"I am officially freaked-out." She rubbed her hands up and down her arms. "And I feel like I need a shower." She turned to Emma. "Do you think I'm overreacting?"

"No." She turned onto the highway. "But instead of a shower, why don't we try a little retail therapy to help you feel better?"

Jana would have thought she wasn't in the mood for shopping, but Emma's relentless good humor pulled her out of her funk. The two women explored every inch of the half-dozen shops in the collection of eclectic buildings beside the highway. Emma purchased an old metal gas-station sign that promised You Can Trust Your Car to the Man Who Wears the Star.

"It's perfect for Graham's birthday," she said. "We can hang it on the back deck, by the barbecue grill."

In a boutique Jana bought a bracelet made of wire-wrapped glass beads, and a key fob of hammered brass and leather. "Ooh, that looks nice," Emma said, leaning over Jana's shoulder to admire the piece. "Who's it for?"

Jana pretended to search for something in her purse. "I thought, maybe, when this is all over, I'd give it to Ryan to thank him for all the help he's given me," she said.

"You mean, like a going-away gift?" Emma asked.

"I do have a job and home in Denver to go back to."

"We have jobs and homes in Montrose, too," Emma said, her tone teasing. "If, you know, you decide to stay for some reason."

"I can't decide anything until I know what's happened to Jenny," Jana said. If it turned out her sister was dead, could she bear to stay in the town where she had died?

After lunch at a tea shop and more shopping, the women headed back to Ryan's duplex in the late afternoon. "Look who's home," Emma said as they turned the corner. Ryan's cruiser sat in the driveway. Emma parked behind it and as the women climbed out of the car, the front door opened.

"I was getting ready to call and check in with you," Ryan said, stepping onto the front porch.

"We went shopping, had lunch and did more shopping," Emma said. She hugged Jana. "I hope I see you again."

"I hope so. And thanks for everything."

Emma waved away the thanks. "I didn't do anything."

"But you did." Jana squeezed her hand. "You listened, and you did your best to distract me. That means a lot."

"Good luck," Emma said. "I hope you find your sister soon." She waved and headed back to her car. Jana waited until she'd left, then followed Ryan into the house.

"I'm making dinner," he said. "I hope you like grilled chicken."

"It sounds good." She dropped her purse and her packages on the end of the sofa and followed him into the kitchen. He had changed out of his uniform and wore jeans and an Old 97's T-shirt, his feet bare. This more laid-back version of Ryan was even more appealing than the cop in uniform who had first captured her attention.

"Did you have a good time today?" he asked.

"Emma was a lot of fun." She leaned back against the counter and he opened a cabinet and began pulling out bottles of spices. "I'm still trying to picture her married to your commander. He seems so severe and she's anything but."

"He's not severe around her. Maybe that's the secret." He glanced back at her. "How's your head?"

"It's not hurting anymore." She touched the lump on the back of her head and winced. "At least not much. I went by and checked out of my motel."

"Good. I meant to remind you this morning and forgot." He began measuring different spices into a bowl.

"A kind of strange thing happened while I was there."

He set down the measuring spoons and turned to face her, giving her his full attention. "What was that?"

"Eric Patterson was there—in the motel lobby. He said he'd been looking for me. He told me Daniel Metwater was released on bail."

"Yes."

"He also told me Metwater's lawyer thinks you don't have enough evidence to get the grand jury to indict him."

"At this point, he may be right. Without a stronger case, we have to remain open to the idea that Metwater may not be the man responsible for these crimes. Or maybe not all of them. It could be that he attacked

Alicia Mendoza, but not the other women. We're expanding our investigation to look at other suspects."

"What other suspects?"

"I can't tell you that." His voice was gentle but firm.

Of course he couldn't. She gripped the edge of the counter and looked down at her shoes. "Eric knew what had happened to me, and to my Jeep," she said. "He said a police officer friend of his told him."

"Is that what has you so upset? The prospect of Daniel Metwater out of jail?" He closed the gap between them and rested his hands on her shoulders. "I promise you'll be safe here with me."

She nodded. "I feel safe with you. And that isn't what upset me—or at least not the main thing."

He squeezed her shoulders gently. "What is it, then?"

She raised her head to look into his eyes. The tenderness and concern she found there steadied her. "When Eric left, he kissed my cheek and told me to be careful. He said he had already lost Jenny, and he didn't want to lose me, too. The way he said it, as if I really meant something to him, creeped me out. I hardly know the man. I don't even like him."

"He rubs me the wrong way, too," Ryan said. "But maybe he really does care about you, as his fiancée's sister. You're a link for him to her."

"Maybe. Emma said he has a reputation as a ladies' man. The smooth-operator type."

"I can see that."

"But I can't see Jenny with a man like him. It's so frustrating."

"It is. And it's frustrating not to know what happened to your sister." He gave her shoulders a final squeeze and turned back to his cooking. "We're working every angle we can think of, believe me."

"What did you do today?" she asked as he mixed the seasonings.

"I pulled at threads to see where they would lead." He took a plate of chicken breasts from the refrigerator.

"And where did they lead?"

"Nowhere so far." He sprinkled the seasoning mixture over the chicken. "But tomorrow is a new day and we have some new leads to follow. Maybe that will lead us somewhere constructive. Right now, let's grill this chicken so we can eat."

She followed him onto the back deck and sat in a lounge chair while he grilled the chicken, the scent of cooking meat mingling with the perfume of flowers that grew along the fence around the backyard. It was such a relaxing, domestic scene. Jana felt guilty for enjoying it so much while her sister was missing. Shouldn't she be doing something to try to find her? But what?

Jana would have said she wasn't hungry, but she ate every bite of the grilled chicken and vegetables Ryan prepared, accompanied by a glass of crisp white wine. "You're spoiling me, waiting on me like this," she said when her plate was empty.

"You've had a rough time of it. You deserve a little pampering." His eyes met hers across the table and she felt warmed through. The tenderness she had seen earlier was still there, but heightened by a wanting that echoed her own desire. Last night her injury and shock had been an unacknowledged barrier between them, but now she had no such shield to hide behind. Nor did she want to hide.

She slipped off her shoes and propped one foot on his knee. His hand caressed her instep, then began massaging her toes. She let out a low moan. "I'll give you an hour and forty-five minutes to stop that."

He continued massaging, working his way up her calf to her knee, leaning forward to reach her thigh. He stilled, eyes locked to hers. "Why are you stopping?" she asked.

"I'm not sure how far you want this to go."

She could be coy and pretend she didn't know what he was talking about, but she was past playing those kinds of games, amusing as they could be. She slid from his grasp, stood and walked around the table to him.

He leaned back, his expression guarded, until she took his chin in her hand and kissed him. "Why don't we see how it feels to go a little further?" she asked.

Ryan pulled Jana into his lap and kissed her, a long, drugging kiss that started at her lips and reverberated through her whole body, leaving her flushed and tingling and wanting more. "I'm thinking we should take it a lot further," she said, and slid her hand under his T-shirt, the warm muscles of his stomach trembling at her touch.

"Are you sure?" he asked, his voice husky.

"Right now, it's the only thing I *am* sure of." She kissed his throat, sweeping her tongue across his pulse. "I want to be with you."

Chapter Twelve

Ryan stood and led Jana toward the bedroom. Standing beside the bed, they undressed each other slowly, pausing often to kiss a bare shoulder or run a hand across a newly exposed expanse of skin. Anticipation trembled between them, both eager for completion but determined to savor the moment, to indulge in the sweet torture of prolonging the experience as much as possible.

When they were both naked, they lay side by side on the bed, continuing their exploration of each other's bodies. She reveled in the feel of him, and in the sensations he created in her. To find such joy in the midst of her sorrow over Jenny moved her almost to tears, but she pushed them away. Tonight was a gift, and she intended to wring every bit of pleasure from it.

He began kissing his way down her torso, lingering over first one breast and then the other until she was panting and arching toward him. He moved farther down, pressing a hand to her belly, steadying her, and the tension within her coiled even tighter. When his lips found her sex she cried out, not in pain but in pleasure, and felt him smile against her.

He rose on his knees, opened the drawer in the bedside table and took out a condom packet. After he had sheathed himself, she reached for him, no longer content to wait. She welcomed him into her, wrapping her body around his and moving with him in a rhythm that was both familiar and brand-new. He caressed her hips, guiding her, then slid one hand down between them to stroke her, his sure touch bringing her quickly over the edge.

She gripped him ever tighter as he reached his own climax, and she pressed her forehead to his shoulder, grounded by the feel of muscle and bone. So many relationships in her life had been built on what she and her partner could give to each other or do for each other. When had she ever been so content to simply be with a man? When had the mere fact of his presence meant so much to her?

RYAN HAD NO need to lie awake that night. He slept with Jana's body pressed to his and woke early to make love to her again. Getting involved with the sister of a crime victim complicated matters—that went without saying. But in his experience every relationship involved negotiating complications of one kind or another. He couldn't be sorry something good had come out of one of the most perplexing cases of his career.

"I need to go back out to the dig site this morning to talk to Jeremy Eddleston," he said as he and Jana finished a breakfast of coffee and waffles. "I stopped by there yesterday afternoon, but he wasn't around. One of his workers said he would be back this morning."

"Why are you questioning Eddleston again?" she asked. Her hair curled around her face, still damp from her shower, and she was no longer deathly pale, her cheeks warmed by a pink flush that he liked to think he could take credit for.

"We just had a few things we needed to clear up. I'd like you to come with me. You can wait in the cruiser while I talk to Eddleston, then we'll swing by Ranger headquarters."

"I should see about renting a car today," she said. "You don't have to babysit me."

"Don't think of it as babysitting." He rinsed his coffee cup and set it on the drain board. "Think of it as keeping myself from being distracted worrying about you."

"You can't keep me with you twenty-four hours a day forever," she said. "What if it takes weeks to solve this case? What if you never find out who attacked me?"

She was right, of course. It wasn't practical or fair to her to keep her under lock and key for long. "Stay with me today," he said. "We'll figure something out."

"Fair enough." She pushed back her chair and stood. "Let me grab my laptop so I can get some work done while you're on the job."

When Ryan and Jana arrived at the dig site an hour later, he was surprised to see a rental moving truck parked with the other vehicles. "Are they delivering something or hauling it away?" Jana asked.

"That's something I'll find out." He left her in the car and walked out to the base of the mesa, where he found Jeremy Eddleston surrounded by wooden packing crates.

"Good morning, Professor," Ryan said.

Eddleston looked up. "What are you doing here?" he asked. "As you can see, I'm very busy."

"Moving?" Ryan studied the stenciling on the box nearest him. Department of Archaeology, Colorado Mesa University.

"We're shutting down the site for the season and sending our equipment and the artifacts we've recovered back to the university, where they will be cataloged, cleaned and studied."

"I won't keep you," Ryan said. He took out his phone and pulled up the picture of Alicia Mendoza. "Do you know this woman?"

Eddleston leaned forward to squint at the image on the phone screen. "No," he said, and straightened.

"You're sure you haven't seen her around here, maybe near here?"

Eddleston shook his head. "I would particularly remember anyone trespassing on the dig site," he said. "We do get the occasional hiker or nosy tourist coming around and I quickly send them on their way." He lowered his sunglasses and peered over the top of them at Ryan. "I shouldn't have to tell you that antiquities theft is a serious crime—and a particular problem in remote sites like this one."

It was true that the Rangers had dealt with a case involving important Native American artifacts stolen from federal lands only last summer. "What about this woman?" Ryan scrolled to the photo of Lucia Raton.

Eddleston removed his sunglasses and studied the photo. "She looks familiar," he said. "Who is she?"

"She's another young woman who went missing in this area, a couple of weeks before Jenny Lassiter disappeared."

Eddleston replaced the sunglasses. "Then I must have seen her on the news."

Ryan pocketed his phone once more. "Can you tell me anything more about the day Jenny disappeared?" he asked.

"I've told you everything I know," Eddleston said.

"Maybe we should go over it again, in case you left anything out," Ryan said. "What was her mood that morning? Had the two of you argued?"

"Her mood was the same as always. Jenny was a normally cheerful person. We didn't argue. We didn't have anything to argue about."

"She wasn't upset you had decided to dump her to get back together with your wife?"

"I already told you, Jenny understood my decision. We were both adults, not two jealous kids."

"Adults have feelings. It wouldn't be unreasonable for her to feel hurt that you chose your wife over her."

"She wasn't upset." He slammed his hand down on one of the crates. "I don't have any more time to talk with you. Goodbye." He turned his back and strode toward the shade canopies, where a trio of students were boxing up more artifacts.

Ryan returned to the cruiser, frustration chafing at him. He slid into the driver's seat and slammed the door behind him. Jana looked up from her laptop. "What's wrong?" she asked.

"This case." He shoved the key into the ignition and started the engine. "We're not getting anywhere."

"I know you're trying," Jana said. "And I appreciate that. I hope the other families do, too."

"The problem is we don't have enough information. Which is why we have to keep digging."

He headed back to the highway but turned away from town. "Where are we going now?" Jana asked.

"I thought we might have a cup of coffee."

She gave him a puzzled look. "All right."

The Lakeside Café sported a vintage neon sign by the road and a carved wooden trout over the door, the once-bright pink-and-green paint on the fish faded by years of sun and wind. A cowbell hung on the back of the door and jangled when Ryan pushed it open. A curly-haired blonde with prominent front teeth looked up from behind the cash register. "Have a seat anywhere," she said.

Ryan led the way to a booth to the left of the door. The red leatherette seats sported several silver duct-tape repairs, and a plastic-coated placard on the Formica tabletop advertised the Friday night all-you-can-eat catfish. "You folks need menus?" The blonde approached their table.

"Just coffee for me," Ryan said. He looked across the table at Jana.

"Coffee for me, too," she said. "With cream."

"Do you want some pie with that?" the waitress asked. "We've got peach and cherry."

"It sounds wonderful, but I'll pass," Jana said.

"Thanks, but I'll pass, too," Ryan said.

"Is there a particular reason we stopped here?" Jana asked when they were alone again.

"This is the last place Lucia Raton was seen alive before she died," he said. "She was with a man we haven't been able to identify yet."

The waitress returned with two mugs, a cream pitcher and a coffeepot. "Sweetener is there by the salt and pepper," she said as she filled the mugs.

"Not very busy this time of afternoon," Ryan said as he accepted his cup.

"We'll pick up for dinner," she said. "All the fishermen will come off the lake and be hungry." She laughed. "Usually for anything besides fish."

"Have you worked here long?" Ryan asked.

"Ten years." She looked around the room, with its battered booths and mismatched chairs. "I can hardly believe it. Who would want to hang around this place that long?"

Ryan laid his credentials open on the table. "Mind if I ask you a few questions?"

She lowered herself to the edge of the seat beside Jana. "I don't know if I have any answers, but go ahead."

He pulled up Lucia's picture on his phone and checked the waitress's name tag. "Mary, do you remember seeing this young woman in here?"

She looked at the photo and nodded. "She's the girl who disappeared a few weeks back. I remember the sheriff's department had someone in here asking about her. I saw her, with a guy who was maybe a little bit older than her. They stopped in for coffee, like you two."

"Would you recognize the man if you saw him again?" he asked.

"I think so. I have a pretty good memory for faces." She chuckled. "Don't ask me to remember any names, though."

He scrolled to another photo, Jeremy Eddleston's university ID image. "Was this the man with Lucia that afternoon?"

Mary leaned forward to study the image, then shook her head. "That wasn't him. He's too old, and I'd remember that pockmarked face. This was a younger guy. He wore a ball cap and sunglasses, but I still think I'd recognize him. At the time I thought maybe he was her older brother. He acted kind of, I don't know, protective of her. She had been crying, I could tell, and he seemed to be trying to comfort her."

Ryan scrolled to a photo of Daniel Metwater. "Was it this man?" he asked.

Mary checked the photo and shook her head again. "I know him. He's that preacher guy who was in the paper. Here, I'll show you." She jumped up and hurried to the cash register and returned with that day's issue of the *Montrose Daily Press*. She pointed to a picture of Daniel Metwater below the fold on the front page, accompanying an article with the headline A Voice in the Wilderness—Prophet Leads His Followers on Local Pilgrimage. The byline was Eric Patterson.

"He's a good-looking young fellow," Mary said. "So I would remember if he'd been in here, but he hasn't been."

"Have you seen the man who was with Lucia in here since that day?" Ryan asked.

"No." The bell on the door jangled and two men entered, fishermen judging by the canvas vests and caps they wore. "I'm sorry I wasn't more help to you," Mary said, and hurried to greet the newcomers.

Jana sipped her coffee and studied him across the table. "What?" Ryan asked after a moment.

"I'm debating whether or not to ask you if Jeremy Eddleston is a suspect in my sister's disappearance and the murder of those other women."

"Officially, Daniel Metwater is our only named suspect." He sipped his coffee.

"But you're not so sure he did it," she said.

"Let's just say I like to be thorough in my investigation."

His pulled out his wallet to pay their tab and his phone rang. "You need to get out to the old logging site on Red Creek Road," Randall Knightbridge said as soon as Ryan answered. "Some hikers have found another body."

Chapter Thirteen

Jana knew something was wrong when Ryan went rigid. The knuckles of the hand that gripped the phone turned white. "I'm on my way," he said, and ended the call. He dropped the phone into the console and shifted the cruiser out of Park.

"What is it?" she asked as he sped onto the highway.

"I have to drop you off at my place," he said. "Wait for me there."

"If there's an emergency, why not take me with you?" she asked. "I can stay in the car like I did this morning."

He shook his head. "You can't."

"Why not? It's a waste of time—not to mention gas—to drive me all the way back to your place if your business is in the park."

He said nothing, his jaw clenched.

"Ryan, tell me what's wrong," she said. "Don't shut me out."

He glanced at her before fixing his eyes once more on the road. "They've found another body," he said.

Her heart lurched, as if someone had reached out and squeezed her chest. She gripped the armrest and tried to force herself to breathe normally. "Can they tell—?"

"I don't know who it is," he said. "But you see why you can't be there."

"In case it's Jenny." She said the last word on a sob and tried to swallow down the emotion. *Keep it together*, she commanded herself. "If it is her, you'll have to tell me sooner rather than later," she said. "You might even need me to identify her." The thought made her stomach lurch.

"No," he said. "We don't ask family members to identify the body at the scene."

"Thank you," she said, her voice scarcely above a whisper. She breathed deeply through her nose, fighting for calm. "I can go with you. I can stay in the car. I promise not to interfere or get hysterical."

"Not a good idea," he said.

"It isn't a good idea to delay any longer than necessary," she said. "And what am I supposed to do at your place while you're gone? Do you think I won't go crazy wondering what is going on? And do you think I really want to be alone when you call to tell me what you've found?"

He said nothing, but stomped on the brakes and swung the cruiser around to face the other direction. "You'll stay in the vehicle and you won't say a word," he said. "You'll pretend you aren't there."

"I will," she agreed, relief flooding her, along with a new fear. What if she had lied and she wasn't able to keep it together, especially if the body did turn out to be Jenny? *Don't think that*, she reminded herself. *Don't borrow trouble.*

The cruiser sped down the highway, wind whipping up choppy waves on the surface of the lake to her right. Sun sparkled on the water and small fishing boats bobbed in the distance like children's bathtub toys. Ryan braked and turned the cruiser onto a dirt road that led away from the lake, up a steep grade into a thick growth of forest that contrasted sharply with the barren land closer to the water. The temperature felt twenty degrees cooler and the scent of pine came in through the air vents.

They bumped along for several miles, the woods growing thinner as they climbed, giving way to areas full of jutting stumps and scattered limbs. Jana spotted a trio of vehicles parked ahead: a faded red Jeep, a mint-green Forest Service truck and a black county sheriff's SUV. Ryan pulled in behind the SUV. Without a word, he climbed out and strode toward the three men and one woman standing beside the vehicles.

Jana studied the group. She decided the woman, and the one man not in uniform, must be hikers. They had probably found the body and called it in. They would have had to hike to the road to make the call, then maybe the sheriff or Forest Service ranger had given them a ride back up here so they could point out their find. They were young—early twenties, she guessed. Not much older than Jenny. The woman looked as if she had been crying. The man stood with one arm around her shoulder and nodded solemnly as Ryan spoke.

Then Ryan and the other officers turned away and started walking up the hill, leaving the couple alone. The man looked over at Jana, then walked toward her, the young woman at his side. Jana opened the door of the cruiser as they approached. "Hello," she said.

"Are you a cop, too?" the young man asked, with the hint of a Southern drawl.

"No," she said. She knew Ryan expected her to pretend to be invisible and not say anything, but she wasn't going to pass up this chance to learn information he probably wouldn't tell her. "Are you the ones who called in the...the find?" She couldn't bring herself to say "body." Further proof, if any was needed, that she would have made a lousy law-enforcement officer.

The girl nodded. "We were climbing over some fallen limbs, trying to find the trail, and I tripped and fell." She shuddered and chafed her hands up and down her arms. "I landed right on top of it."

The young man pulled her close. "It's okay, Rennie," he said. He looked back at Jana. "I thought it was an animal at first—you know, a deer or something. But then I saw the skull. It had long hair. And I knew it was a person."

"What color was the hair?" Jana asked. She had to force out the words and held her breath, anticipating the answer.

"Dark," the man said. "Though it was hard to tell much. I mean, it looked like it had been up here awhile and animals..." His voice trailed away. "Well, you know."

She closed her eyes and let out a long breath. Jenny's hair was blond. Surely this corpse could not be hers.

"We had to hike all the way to the road to get enough signal to call nine-one-one," the woman said. "Then waited forever for someone to get here. I told Brian we should just leave once we'd made the call, but he said that wouldn't be right, and the cops would just trace us by our phone anyway. Can they really do that?"

"I don't know," she said. "But thank you for waiting. And for calling it in."

The sound of tires on gravel drew their attention and a second Ranger cruiser pulled in behind Ryan's. Officers Simon Woolridge and Ethan Reynolds got out and walked over to Jana and the young couple. "What are you doing here?" Simon asked Jana.

"I was with Ryan when he got the call," she said. "It was quicker to come straight here instead of dropping me off somewhere."

Simon grunted and headed up the hill, Ethan following. Halfway up, they met Ryan and the other two men making their way down. The men stopped and talked, and Simon handed Ryan a printout of some kind. Ryan scanned it, then looked down toward the cruiser.

He frowned when he saw the crowd gathered around his vehicle and began walking faster, quickly outpacing the other two. "Was I right?" Brian asked. "Is it a person?"

Ryan glanced at Jana. "We should talk somewhere else," he said.

"You can talk in front of me," she said. "I think I have a right to know."

Ryan studied the dirt between his feet. "You were right—the body is human. A female, shallow grave, maybe even just dumped in the ruts from the logging equipment they had up here in the spring. Looks like she's been up here awhile—maybe a few weeks, maybe longer."

"Any identifying clothing or jewelry?" Ethan asked.

"Dark hair," Ryan said. "Some animal depredation, but the clothes we found nearby were a denim skirt and jacket."

"That fits the description for Lucia Raton," Ethan said.

Ryan glanced at Jana. "Yeah, it does. We'll know more when we get the autopsy."

"Any idea how she was killed?" Simon asked.

Ryan shook his head. "We'll have to wait for the postmortem for that." He held up the phone. "I got some preliminary shots, but we'll want to get a forensics team up here, along with the coroner. I'll drive down and make the calls while you secure the scene." He moved around to the driver's side of the cruiser.

Jana didn't say anything until they reached the highway once more and Ryan had made his calls. Finally, he replaced the phone in his pocket and glanced at her. "Are you all right?" he asked.

She nodded. "Part of me is so relieved it wasn't Jenny," she said. "Does that make me a horrible person?"

"It makes you human." He pulled the cruiser back onto the highway and headed toward Montrose. "I'm taking you back to my place."

"All right." She knew he had work to do, even though the prospect of spending the evening alone with her doubts and worries troubled her. "I'm really glad that wasn't Jenny's body back there, but I'm frustrated that we still don't know what's happened to her," she said.

"We can't be sure Alicia's and Lucia's deaths are related," Ryan said. "Or if your sister's disappearance is part of this case."

"But you can't rule out a connection, either," Jana said.

He nodded. "We have to look at all the angles."

"What happens now?" she asked.

"The coroner will examine the body to determine cause of death, and we'll try to confirm the identity. If it is Lucia, we'll look for anything about her death that matches Alicia's murder. Sometimes patterns are clues about the murderer."

"Have you found any patterns so far?"

He glanced at her. "Jana, there are things you don't need to know."

She looked away. "Why do you get to decide what I do and don't need to know? We're talking about my only sister."

"The more people who know about evidence, the more likely it is to become compromised. And what are you going to do with the information anyway, but worry over it, trying to make connections where there aren't any?"

"How do you know there aren't any connections? Maybe I'll see something you don't."

"Or maybe there comes a time when you need to get on with your life and let us worry about solving the crime."

She felt the sting of his words as if he had slapped her. "Are you saying I need to go back to Denver and pretend none of this has happened?" *That you and I never happened?*

He slid his hands up and down the steering wheel. "When I came walking down that hill and saw you seated in the cruiser talking to that couple, all I could think was that you didn't belong there. You had no place at a crime scene and it wasn't right for me to bring you there."

"I wanted you to bring me there," she said. "I hate sitting around being helpless. I want to be involved."

"But you can't be involved." He slammed one hand down on the steering wheel, making her jump. "Did you ever think that the reason you were attacked two nights ago is because whoever did this saw you with me? The closer you get to this case, the more you put yourself in danger. I can't take that risk."

She couldn't believe the words she was hearing. Her heart pounded painfully and she struggled to keep her voice even. "What are you suggesting I do?" she asked.

"Go back to Denver," he said. "I'll make sure you're assigned a victim's advocate, who will keep you informed of anything you need to know about the case."

"So I won't see you again?" She had to force the words past her lips.

"That would be safest," he said.

"Ryan, what's going on?" she asked. "You can't make love to me this morning and then push me away this afternoon."

"We got the forensics report back on your car," he said. "Ethan gave it to me just now."

"The printout he handed you," she said, remembering. "What did they find?"

He blew out a breath. "There was a note in it, on the floorboard. We didn't see it because it was buried under a bunch of windshield glass. It was probably written by whoever vandalized your car."

"What did it say?"

He was silent so long she was ready to demand that he pull over so she could reach out and shake the words out of him. Finally, he said, "The note said, 'I saw you with that cop. I won't let him have you because you're mine.'"

She swallowed hard. "That's not a very specific threat."

"It's still a threat. I won't put you in danger."

"I think I'm safer with you than I am alone."

"You'll be safe in Denver. We can ask the police there to keep an eye on you. You'll be away from the killer."

"I'll be even farther away from my sister." *And away from you.* She wouldn't say the words out loud, afraid they made her too needy. She sat up straighter. "I won't go back to Denver," she said. "Not yet. If you want me to leave your house, I'll find another motel."

He said nothing, and her spirits sank. But she wouldn't give him the satisfaction of letting him see how hurt she was. She would wait until she was alone. Then she'd cry and swear and rant about a man who could steal her heart and so casually hand it back to her.

As soon as Ryan pulled into the driveway of his duplex, Jana got out of the car and headed up the walk toward the front door. He caught up with her, grabbing her hand. "Where are you going?" he demanded.

"I'm going to pack."

"No."

"Why not? You said you wanted me away from here—that you didn't want to be responsible. Fine, then. I'll find someplace else to stay."

"No." He pulled her against him and kissed her, a crushing kiss that both seared and soothed. When at last they broke for air, he pushed the hair back from her face. "I was an idiot to think I could let you go."

"You were trying to be noble," she said.

"You didn't think that when I was making my pitch for you to leave. You thought I was a jerk."

"A noble jerk."

He kissed her again. "Stay," he murmured against her lips. "I'll do my best to protect you."

"I know." She pulled back far enough to smile at him. "And remember, I've got your back, too."

"I feel better already."

"Watch it with the sarcasm, buddy."

"No, I mean it. And you know what would make me feel even better?" He pulled her closer against him.

"Mmm." She nuzzled his neck. "I'll bet I don't need three guesses."

"I love a woman with brains and beauty."

"Come on inside before we embarrass the neighbors." She turned and, giggling, raced inside. Her emotions felt as fragile and unsteady as a soufflé fresh from the oven, but she was determined to stick out this roller-coaster ride. She wasn't going to give up the best thing she had ever had because she had found it in the midst of the worst experience ever.

Chapter Fourteen

"I want to talk to Eric Patterson," Jana announced the next morning over a breakfast of cold cereal and coffee. "I think I'll call him today and try to set up a lunch date."

"What do you want to talk to him about?" Ryan asked. His first instinct was to tell her not to go anywhere near the reporter, but was that his cop sense nudging him—or plain old-fashioned jealousy? After all, Eric had told Jana he didn't want to lose her.

"I'm going to ask him if he's learned anything about Daniel Metwater that might help your case," she said. "After all, he's been spending a lot of time out there at the Prophet's camp."

"I'd planned on setting up an interview with him soon to ask him the same thing," Ryan said. "So you don't need to bother."

Jana set down her coffee cup with a loud *thunk*. "I have to do something," she said. "Besides, Eric owes me a date, and he'll probably tell me more than he would the cops."

"What makes you think that?" Ryan asked.

"No offense, but being interviewed by the police is nerve-racking. And remember I told you I thought he wants to be a hero? So he might withhold information that could lead to the Rangers solving the case before he does. But he might not be able to resist the urge to brag about his knowledge to me."

Ryan couldn't argue with her reasoning. "Be careful," he said. "Don't go anywhere alone with the guy."

She looked troubled. "Are you saying he's a suspect in the case?"

"I don't trust him, that's all."

"Neither do I. I figure I'll ask him to meet me someplace downtown—someplace public and crowded. I want information, not an intimate discussion. Though I'd like to know if he put those photos on Jenny's computer, and why."

"Be careful," Ryan said. "If he gets angry, he won't want to help you."

"Provided he knows anything—and that there's anything to know."

"All right. I have to go into work." He pushed his chair back. "I still don't like leaving you alone, but I get that I can't keep you prisoner."

"My new rental car is being delivered this morning," she said. "And I'll be fine. I promise to be careful."

After a passionate kiss goodbye that could have easily led to more, she locked the door behind him and called Eric Patterson. "Jana!" He sounded pleased to hear from her. "How are you this morning?"

"I'm good, Eric. How are you?"

"Great. The Rangers found Lucia Raton's body yesterday."

"I knew they found a body. Have they definitely identified it as Lucia's?" She was certain Ryan hadn't known this when he left this morning.

"I just got a look at the medical examiner's report. I'm writing up the story right now."

"Do you think you'll have time to break for lunch?" Jana asked. "Considering we couldn't get together the other night."

"That sounds like a great idea. I know your car is out of commission, so let me pick you up. Where are you staying?"

"I'm getting a rental car this morning. Why don't I meet you at Thai Fusion about twelve thirty?"

"Good. And I won't stand you up this time."

She hung up the phone, feeling better about the man. Maybe he was just the type to overreact in certain situations. After all, he was grieving for her sister, too, and she knew well enough that grief could play havoc with a person's emotions.

"You look like something the cat dragged in." Randall greeted Ryan when he arrived at Ranger headquarters. "Rough night?"

"Nothing coffee won't help," he said as he filled his cup.

Between making love with Jana and rehashing the events of the previous day, Ryan hadn't slept much. The lovemaking had been wonderful—the rehashing painful. He had handled things badly with her, and he wasn't certain she had completely forgiven him yet. The note in her car had sent him into a tailspin, and he hadn't been thinking clearly.

They had compromised this morning. Jana would stay at his duplex, awaiting the arrival of her new rental car. If she went anywhere, she would let him know of her plans, and she would be sure to stick to public places with other people around. It wasn't an ideal situation, but it was the best he could hope for.

He gathered with the rest of the team in the conference room. "What's first on the agenda?" Simon asked.

"Let's take another look at the note found in Jana's car." Graham indicated the wrinkled note pinned to the bulletin board. "Is it related to the case or not?"

"I'm assuming 'that cop' is you," Simon said, looking at Ryan.

Ryan ignored the dig. "Whoever wrote that note is watching Jana—or was watching her. Is it our killer?"

"Or maybe a jealous boyfriend?" Randall suggested.

Ryan shook his head. "No boyfriend."

"No prints, no DNA, nothing distinctive about the paper," Graham said. "We'll add it to the file, but don't focus on it for now." He turned to the whiteboard. "We have a positive ID on the body they found yesterday. It is Lucia Raton. She was strangled, though in this case there was no sign of the ligature with the body. The ME suspects some kind of cord or thin rope. Maybe clothesline."

"Same pattern of disposal as Alicia's body," Ethan said. "A shallow grave easily accessed from the road, not much digging involved. Not many people go up there, so not much chance of discovery."

"So odds are the two are related," Ryan said. "What's their connection to the killer?"

"Maybe no relation," Ethan said. "They could be random victims."

"He chose them for some reason," Graham said. "They don't look alike. They aren't the same age, or even the same ethnic background. So what attracted him?"

"They were alone and helpless," Simon said. "That's enough for some predators."

Ryan had left Jana alone. But she wasn't helpless. She wasn't out in the wilderness, far from other people and safety, the way Alicia and Lucia had been. The way Jenny had been.

"How are the background checks on the archaeologists going?" Graham asked.

"So far everyone is clean," Simon said. "No criminal records. A few speeding tickets. Eddleston had a DUI five years back, but he's been clean since. The story about getting back with his wife checks out, too. They're in counseling. Do we focus on Metwater's group next?"

Graham shook his head. "Metwater's lawyers have blocked our access to him and are screaming harassment. The DA wants us to back off until the furor dies down."

"We're federal. We can overrule the DA," Simon said.

"I got a phone call this morning from my boss at the Bureau and he's ordered no fishing expeditions. The only way we can approach Metwater or one of his people is if we have something concrete that links them to the case and warrants our checking them out."

"Are you saying Metwater got to the FBI?" Simon asked.

"He obviously has friends in high places," Graham said. "Let's not forget—before he was a traveling prophet, he was from a rich, powerful family."

"We have to be free to investigate the case," Simon said. "And someone needs to check on Andi Mattheson."

"Why is that?" Ethan asked.

"I think she's at risk for gestational diabetes. She rubs her hands a lot and tingling or numbness in the hands and feet could be a symptom, though the only way to know for sure is with a blood test."

"And you know this how?" Marco asked.

"I volunteered at my uncle's medical clinic when I was a teenager," he said.

"You never cease to amaze me," Marco said.

"Bite me."

"What about the idea to follow up with Eric Patterson to see if he's uncovered anything?" Graham asked.

"I'm working on that," Ryan said. Or rather, Jana was working on it. Maybe Ryan could find out where they planned to have lunch and just happen to drop by.

"That's all we've got this morning," Graham said. "Let's see if we can't do better today."

Ryan moved out of the conference room to his desk. Once there, he booted up his computer and pulled up the file on Jeremy Eddleston. What had a pretty young girl like Jenny seen in a man who was as plain as dry toast? He appeared to have no interests outside of archaeology. He even spent his weekends giving seminars to area high school students.

Ryan froze and zeroed in on the schedule the university had provided. On July 15, Jeremy Eddleston had given one of his Introduction to Archaeology talks to students at Montrose High School.

The school Lucia Raton had attended.

One week before she died.

Jana accepted the keys to the rental car provided by her auto insurance from the delivery driver and signed the paperwork. The green compact sedan wasn't as flashy as Emma's convertible or as fun as her own vandalized Jeep, but it would get her around town until her car had been repaired, a process her insurance company estimated would take ten days to two weeks now that the impound lot had released the vehicle.

In the meantime, she hoped her lunch with Eric would yield some useful information. She got to the restaurant early and was surprised to find him already waiting by the front door. "So good to see you," he said, hugging her close and kissing her cheek.

She fought the urge to push him away. "Hello, Eric," she said, taking a step back. "Good to see you, too. Why don't we go inside?"

The hostess seated them at a table in the back and presented them with menus. Jana pretended to study hers. "How's work going?" she asked him.

"I am on fire right now," he said. "My editor is loving the stories I'm giving him. Next week I'm going to hit him up for a raise. If I don't get it, I'll walk. With the credits I have lately, I shouldn't have any problem getting a position with a bigger paper. I could be the new Western Slope correspondent for the *Denver Post*."

"I thought Emma Ellison had that job," Jana said.

"She does now, but if someone better came along, she could be out the door." He grinned. "That's how things work in journalism."

The waitress took their orders and Eric settled back in his chair. "How have you been?" he asked. "How's your head?"

"It's better. Thanks for asking. I saw your profile of Daniel Metwater in the Montrose paper. You did a great job."

"I did, didn't I?" He laughed. "The guy is such a narcissist. All I had to do was ask one question and he was off and running, telling me more than I ever wanted to know about his so-called Family and mission and everything."

She leaned over the table and lowered her voice. "Did you pick up any clues that might point to his involvement with the murders or Jenny's disappearance?" she asked.

"I've got some really incriminating stuff." He sat back as the waitress set their meals in front of them. "I'm not ready to share it yet, but when I do, it will blow the case wide open."

"What did you find out?" she asked, trying—and failing—to rein in her eagerness.

"I can't tell you. Not that I don't want to, but it would be too dangerous."

"Dangerous?"

His eyes met hers, bright and intense. "Metwater has money and connections." He lowered his voice to a whisper. "Some people even say he has ties to the mob. In fact, organized crime may be involved in this case."

"What could organized crime have to do with those two women who died—or with Jenny going missing?" she asked.

"I think they probably saw something at Metwater's camp that they shouldn't have." Eric dug into his Thai basil shrimp. "Metwater didn't have any choice but to eliminate them. Of course, he may not have done the killing himself in every case, but I'm sure he was directing all the action."

Jana felt queasy. "Are you saying he ordered a hit on my sister?"

"I don't have all the proof I need yet, but it's shaping up that way," Eric said. "Of course, we won't know for sure until we find her, so it's important we keep looking. But something tells me these mob guys know how to hide a body where it will never be found."

The mob? It seemed so...surreal.

"Is something wrong with your food?" he asked. "You aren't eating."

She pushed the plate away. "I guess I'm too upset about Jenny."

He nodded and continued forking up shrimp and vegetables. "It is upsetting," he said around a mouthful of shrimp.

How could her sweet, funny, smart sister have ended up with a guy like this? Jana could barely contain her loathing. "Jenny's roommate tells me you stopped by her apartment the other day," she said.

"What, have you been checking up on me?" His smile was lopsided and not convincing.

"I mentioned to her that I had seen a bunch of photos of you and Jenny on Jenny's laptop—I'm sure they weren't there the other day. I thought maybe you had added them."

He shook his head, gaze focused on his meal. "Jenny has always had a lot of pictures of us," he said. "Her screen saver is a shot of us together, if I remember right."

"Eric, those photos weren't there the other day. The Rangers confirmed they weren't there."

"You mean *Ranger*, don't you? I noticed you and Ryan Spencer are getting pretty tight."

"Don't change the subject," she snapped. "What is going on here, Eric?"

"What do you mean, what's going on?"

"Everyone I talked to seemed as surprised as I was to hear of your engagement to Jenny. Professor Eddleston said he didn't know about it until after Jenny disappeared."

"I told you, we wanted to keep it a secret until Jenny had a chance to tell you." He tapped his fork on the table between them. "We were doing it for you. You should be grateful, not suspicious."

"Jenny's friend Heidi and her roommate, April, say they never heard Jenny say anything about being engaged to you," Jana said. "In fact, April said she didn't think Jenny was that into you."

"They're all liars!"

His shout echoed in the sudden silence. Jana leaned back in alarm. "You need to calm down," she said.

He grabbed his glass of water and downed half of it, his gaze fixed on her, the rage in those eyes frightening her. He set the glass down and wiped his mouth with the back of his hand. "I loved Jenny," he said, his voice even. "It hurts to hear anyone suggest otherwise."

"I didn't say you didn't love her." Jana tried to keep her voice low and non-confrontational. "But maybe the engagement announcement was a little premature? Maybe you intended to ask Jenny to marry you and you never got the chance."

"We were engaged," he said. "I'm sorry if that upsets you, but it's true."

"I'm just trying to figure everything out," she said. "I didn't mean to insult you."

"Jenny means the world to me," he said. "If she's gone, I'll probably never get over her."

Why couldn't she get past the feeling that he said

the words like lines in a play? He was playing the part of the grieving lover, but it just didn't ring true.

They finished the meal in silence and Eric claimed the check. "I'll put it on my expense account," he said as he counted out bills. "They can't object to me interviewing the sister of the missing woman, can they?"

He took her arm as they headed toward the parking lot. It took everything in her not to wrench away from him and run to her car. She sagged with relief when she recognized a familiar black-and-white cruiser parked next to her rental. Eric dropped her arm. "What is he doing here?"

Chapter Fifteen

Ryan got out of the cruiser as Jana and Eric approached. Seeing him standing tall and lean in his brown uniform, mirrored sunglasses hiding his eyes, sent a thrill through her. She hurried toward him. "What a nice surprise," she said. Then more softly, "How did you know I was here?"

"The car rental receipt was on the counter at my house, so I kept my eye out for it." He turned to Eric. "How are you, Patterson?"

"Shouldn't you be off investigating something?" Eric asked. "Working the case?"

"I'm always working the case." He kept his focus on Eric until the reporter looked away. Jana had to admit that the sunglasses only added to Ryan's ability to intimidate.

"I have to go," Eric said. "I'll talk to you later, Jana. I'll let you know if I find out anything pertinent."

Ryan watched the reporter until his car turned out of the parking lot. "How did lunch go?" he asked Jana.

"It went pretty much like all my interactions with him," she said. "Odd."

He removed the sunglasses and his eyes met hers,

the steady blue gaze instantly settling some of the butterflies in her stomach. "Odd in what way?"

"He thinks Daniel Metwater ordered mob hits on the missing women because they saw something at his camp that they shouldn't have. I'd think he was crazy, except that Emma told me Metwater's brother was supposedly murdered by the mob."

"Supposedly. But nothing points to Metwater's own involvement in organized crime."

"I can't tell if Eric seriously believes the story or if he was making it up for my benefit," she said.

"Did he offer any proof?"

"No. He said he was still gathering his evidence."

"Which means he probably has nothing."

"That's what I thought." She folded her arms under her chest and studied the gravel parking lot. "I asked him about the photos on Jenny's computer, too. He said he didn't put them there, that they've always been there."

"We know that's not true," Ryan said.

She worried her lower lip between her teeth.

"What aren't you telling me?" he asked.

"I may have gone a little too far," she said.

"In what way?"

"I told him I didn't believe he was really engaged to Jenny. I explained how no one seemed to know about the engagement until after she disappeared, and that people who knew Jenny best were surprised by the news. He got really angry."

"You called him a liar. Most people don't respond well to that."

"But what if he is lying?" she asked. "Wouldn't that be important?"

"It would," Ryan agreed. "Which is why we're keeping an eye on him. And we'll dig deeper—try to find out where he was and what he was doing when the other women disappeared."

"When will you know the answers to those questions?" she asked.

"It probably won't be today. We're stretched pretty tight," he said. "I was on my way out to interview Jeremy Eddleston again when I got a call to come into town and talk to a suspect in that plant-theft case Lance has been investigating. I decided that, as long as I was here, I'd see how things were going with you."

"I'm glad you did, seeing you got rid of Eric faster than I probably would have been able to on my own."

"What are your plans for the rest of the afternoon?" he asked as he walked with her to her car.

"I think I'll go back to your place and work," she said. "Maybe dealing with tax accounts will take my mind off Jenny for a little while at least."

"Better you than me." He bent and kissed her gently on the lips. "See you later?"

"I'll be looking forward to it."

That she could have anything to look forward to at a time like this amazed her, but she would take her blessings wherever she could find them and not complain. She had no doubt she could have dealt with Eric Patterson on her own, but she was glad she hadn't had to.

THE NEXT MORNING, Ryan and Ethan headed back to the dig site to question Jeremy Eddleston about his connection to Lucia Raton. "It's a pretty tenuous link," Ethan said as the cruiser bumped along the rutted road to the foot of Mystic Mesa. They had decided to leave

Ryan's cruiser at the turnoff so that they could plan their strategy on the way in. "We're still trying to get hold of the registration records for the seminar. Maybe Lucia wasn't even there."

"I still think there's something the professor isn't telling us," Ryan said. "Something about his manner— it's evasive."

"Cops make some people nervous. You know that."

"And some people have reason to be nervous."

When they reached the parking area, the moving truck was gone, and only two cars remained in the lot. The two Rangers left their vehicle and made the trek to the foot of the mesa. "Where is Professor Eddleston?" Ryan asked the two students they found there.

"He...he left about half an hour ago," a young man with a long blond ponytail said.

"You must have passed him on the way out," said his companion, a short young woman with cropped pink hair.

"We didn't pass anyone," Ryan said. He looked to Ethan.

"Hard to miss anyone on these dirt roads," Ethan said. "Though he could have seen us coming and turned onto a side road to wait for us to pass."

"Where was he headed?" Ryan asked.

"Back to the university, I guess," the girl said, wide-eyed.

"Or maybe home," the young man said. "He didn't say. And we didn't ask. He just told us to clean up here and we could leave."

"What's this about?" the girl asked. "Is the professor in some kind of trouble?"

Eddleston was going to be in a lot of trouble when

Ryan got hold of him. If it turned out he was the murderer—the man who had attacked Jana—Ryan would do everything in his power to see that he went to prison and never came out. Abruptly, he turned and headed back to the cruiser.

"What do you think?" Ethan asked.

"We could radio the others to search for him," Ryan said.

"But all we know is that he didn't tell us about teaching at Lucia's school," Ethan said. "We don't know if she was in the seminar. Even if she was, he may not have noticed her."

"Why didn't we see him on our way in here?" Ryan stared across the prairie, wondering if Eddleston was sitting in his car out there somewhere, waiting for them to leave.

"Even if he's avoiding us, that just makes him a person of interest," Ethan said. "It doesn't make him guilty."

"But what if he is guilty?" Ryan asked. "What if Lucia was in that seminar and Eddleston noticed her—and that's why she ended up dead?"

JANA WANTED TO get out of the duplex for a while. Being there with Ryan was one thing—he did a good job of distracting her from her circumstances. But being in this unfamiliar place alone made her restless. She still stung from how quickly he had been ready to send her back to Denver two days before. He said he wanted to protect her, but she wasn't some fragile flower or caged bird he could keep under lock and key.

At least he hadn't insisted she stay home today. He had wanted to—she could tell by the way his mouth had tightened when she had told him of her plans for the day, which included getting her hair done and buying a few groceries. Not that she didn't like frozen waffles and cereal, but she wouldn't say no to yogurt for breakfast, and he didn't have a single piece of fruit in the house.

But his mouth tightening had been his only sign of disapproval. Maybe he would relax after she managed to return home tonight unharmed.

She had found a salon that could work her in that morning, so she settled in for some much-needed pampering—a shampoo and trim, and a manicure. She tried not to think of the last time she had visited her sister in Montrose, when she and Jenny had gone together for mani-pedis, talking nonstop about anything and everything as they sat side by side in massage chairs. Every day was full of that kind of memory—eventually, she hoped she would experience them with fondness instead of this aching grief.

After the salon, she headed for the grocery store. While browsing the aisles, she spotted a special on pork loin and decided to make dinner for Ryan. Half an hour later, she headed to her car with four bags of groceries. But rather than go back to the duplex to unload them right away, she turned onto the highway leading out of town. She would take a quick drive to clear her head, then head back and maybe get some work done before she started dinner.

She passed the turnoff to the national park and wondered if Ryan was at Ranger headquarters, or out in the field conducting interviews or tracking down a lead. Her hands tightened on the steering wheel. She hated feeling so powerless to do anything to help. She was the person who knew Jenny the best and loved her the most, yet she had to stand by and let others search for her.

She passed the sign for the Curecanti National Recreation Area and slowed at the turnoff for Mystic Mesa. She could talk to Professor Eddleston again, but she didn't think he was likely to tell her anything he hadn't already told the Rangers.

She could visit Daniel Metwater's camp, maybe pretend to be interested in his teachings. She quickly dismissed the idea as foolish. She was no amateur detective, and snooping where she didn't belong would only get her into trouble.

Instead, she continued on to the lake. Sunlight shimmered on the expanse of blue water, orange cliffs reflected in its mirror-smooth surface. After a few miles she pulled over in a picnic area on the shore. The cluster of tables under metal awnings was deserted, so she sat on one of them and stared out at the water, breathing in the scents of fish and the sagebrush that grew along the rocky shore.

She remembered a boating expedition with her father when she was about twelve and Jenny was six. He liked to fish and would take them out with him, even though they squealed at the idea of baiting hooks with worms and made so much noise they scared all the fish away. He never seemed to mind and said he enjoyed spending time with his girls.

She wished he were with her now. Then again, maybe it was better he hadn't lived to endure the pain of his younger daughter gone missing.

Maybe dead. She drew in a deep, shuddering breath. Was it a betrayal of Jenny to admit that she was very likely gone now? The pain of the idea pierced her, but she forced herself not to shy away from it. For all Ryan's words after they had found Lucia's body had angered her, he had been right that at some point she would need to move on with her life.

Could that be any worse than being caught in this limbo, unable to hope or to mourn?

Another car pulled into the rest area, a tan Camry. She turned and was surprised to see a familiar figure emerge from the vehicle. "What are you doing here?" she asked, annoyed at having her peace disturbed.

"I was looking for you."

"Why?" Maybe the question was rude, but she had no interest in being polite to this man. If she ever did see her sister again, she would ask her why she had ever gotten involved with him.

"We need to talk." He moved around the picnic table toward her. He wore khaki trousers, hiking boots and a blue windbreaker that billowed around him in a gust of wind off the lake. Sunglasses hid his eyes from her.

"We don't have anything to talk about." Something about his manner—the swagger in his walk, perhaps—made her stand and move away. But he was much quicker than she had expected. He lunged forward and grabbed her, yanking her toward him.

"Let go!" she yelped, struggling. "You're hurting me."

"You've hurt me." His fingers dug into her forearms, bruising her. He was much stronger than he looked, and when she kicked at him, he threw her to the ground and knelt on her chest, crushing her.

She stared up at him, terror squeezing her heart

and stealing her breath. "What do you want with me?" she gasped.

"I saw you with that cop." He leaned close, his hot breath smelling of onions. "How could you betray me that way?"

"I... I don't know what you're talking about." She heaved against him and tried to roll away, but his crushing weight held her. She arched her neck, searching for help. If only someone would decide to pull in for a break. But not a single car passed on this lonely stretch of highway, and all the boaters were too far away to hear her cries or see what was happening onshore.

"I have to punish you now," he said. He pulled a white cloth from his pocket and wrapped it around her neck. "Goodbye, dearest," he said as he pulled the fabric tight.

Chapter Sixteen

Ryan spent the rest of the morning at Ranger headquarters, trying to track down Jeremy Eddleston. "He's not answering his office or cell phones," he said. "I called the university and no one has seen or heard from him since yesterday morning. His wife insists she hasn't heard from him, either."

"Has she reported him as missing?" Randall asked.

"She said he's probably holed up somewhere in the bowels of the university, cataloging the artifacts from the Mystic Mesa dig," Ryan said. "She doesn't seem terribly concerned."

"I'd think she'd be a little worried if he didn't come home at all, or at least call," Ethan said.

"Apparently, this isn't that unusual," Ryan said. Mrs. Eddleston's exact words had been, "My husband and I may be married, but we are very independent people. If I called the police every time he decided to spend the night at the university or a dig site instead of coming home they would start labeling me a nuisance."

"You interviewed her already, right?" Ethan asked.

"Yes," Ryan said. "She's got a solid alibi for the afternoon Jenny disappeared—she was at a marriage counselor's office."

"Was she surprised to learn her husband was involved with Jenny?" Ethan asked.

"No. Her husband may have thought she was in the dark, but I got the impression there wasn't much he did that she didn't know about."

"Was he telling the truth about their reconciliation?" Ethan asked.

"I think so." She hadn't struck Ryan as the type who would cover up for her husband. "She didn't come right out and say it, but she certainly implied that most of the money in the marriage is hers. He probably doesn't want to give that up to live on a professor's salary."

"So where is our professor?" Randall asked.

"I think he's avoiding us," Ryan said. He swiveled his chair around and stretched. "But odds are he'll turn up at the university or home eventually, and we'll corner him. In the meantime, let's put him aside and focus on another suspect."

"Who?" Ethan asked.

"I want to dig a little deeper into Eric Patterson's background," Ryan said.

"He says he was working at the paper the afternoon Jenny disappeared," Ethan said. "No one there specifically remembers him being there that day, but no one will say he wasn't, either. Reporters are in and out of the office all day. His work computer does show he was logged in at the time."

"But computer records can be faked," Ryan said.

"He's got a definite link to Jenny Lassiter," Randall said. "But can we prove he knew Lucia or Alicia?"

"Maybe we should take a closer look at the articles he's written for the paper," Ethan said. "Maybe he did a story where he interviewed high school students."

"I don't see how he could have known Alicia," Ryan said. "And her killing feels more like a crime of opportunity—the wrong guy finds her lost in the desert and strangles her. Maybe because she refused his advances, maybe just for the thrill of it."

"Which brings us back to Daniel Metwater or Jeremy Eddleston," Randall said. "Both of them were in the area where Alicia became separated from her group."

"I hate cases like this," Ethan said. "After a while, everyone looks like a suspect."

"And we could be dealing with more than one suspect," Randall said.

"Where's a script writer when you need one?" Ethan said. "They always manage to tie everything up neatly on TV."

"Good to see you all so hard at work." Simon came in and dumped his backpack on his desk.

"We're brainstorming," Randall said. "You got any new leads for us?"

"Maybe." He took a file from his bag and carried it over to them. "We finally got hold of the roster for the Introduction to Archaeology Saturday seminar at Montrose High School," he said. "Luisa Raton is on it."

"Whoa." Randall grabbed the folder and scanned it. "So she and Eddleston did have contact."

"One of the teachers who was there tells me Lucia sat up front and asked a lot of questions," Simon said. "No way Eddleston could have missed seeing her."

"I think we need to pay another visit to Mrs. Eddleston," Ethan said. "Let's push a little harder and find out what she knows, and if she's heard from her husband."

JANA WOKE TO darkness and pain. Her throat ached so that it was agony to swallow. She was curled in a fetal position, jostled back and forth, some new misery blossoming with each movement. As her eyes adjusted to the dimness, she realized she was in a car trunk, her back pressed against the spare tire. She lay on something scratchy, maybe an old blanket. Just enough light seeped in around the trunk to show the direness of her situation.

Carefully, trying not to make any noise, she uncurled her body as much as possible and reached up to her throat. Something was wrapped around her neck but had loosened. She tugged, freeing a long strip of some lightweight fabric, and gasped, taking her first deep breath in who knew how long. Her throat still ached, but the knowledge of how close she had come to dying, yet had survived, sent a surge of adrenaline through her.

Think, she commanded herself. She needed to assess her situation. She was in the trunk of a car. It was traveling pretty fast and there wasn't a lot of road noise, so they were probably still on pavement—the highway, then. She didn't know how long she had been unconscious, but probably not very long. Her attacker had strangled her with the cloth, then dumped her in the car trunk. He hadn't bound her hands or feet, which told her he had probably assumed she was dead or dying. Now he was taking her where? To dispose of her body?

Horror at the thought sent a shudder through her, but she forced her mind back to the problem at hand. She could freak out later, but not now. Now she had to keep her wits about her. She studied the interior of the car trunk again. Hadn't she read that car trunks had interior releases, in case a child crawled inside and got stuck? She felt along the sides until she found a rough place that might have once been the latch, but it wasn't there. Had it broken accidentally—or had the driver of the car deliberately filed it off?

She felt faint at the thought and once again fought for control. She knew the man who had tried to strangle her was the murderer, and that he had probably killed Jenny. Her sister would have trusted him—would have probably willingly gone with him anywhere.

She blinked back tears and felt all about her for a weapon. Her fingers closed around a folding shovel—the kind people kept in their cars for digging out of snow. A tire iron would have been better, but maybe this was the kind of car with the tire tools tucked in a recess under the trunk floor. The shovel would have to do for now.

Her captor thought she was dead. When he opened the trunk, he wouldn't be expecting her to leap out. She would hit him in the face as hard as she could with the shovel, hopefully breaking his nose.

And then what? She had no idea where he was taking her. Running blindly into the woods wouldn't help her. Even if she ran to the road, she had no guarantee anyone would come by who would help her.

She would have to use this car to drive away. She would have to keep hitting the man until he was unconscious. Then she would take his keys—or maybe she would get lucky and he would have left them in the ignition—and she would try to find a main road and follow it to a gas station or somewhere with a phone. Then she would call Ryan. She wouldn't even mind if he said *I told you so*.

"I DON'T KNOW where my husband is, Officer." Melissa Eddleston was a slim blonde in her early fifties, with bright blue eyes and elegant features. The homely professor must have something going on, Ryan thought, to have landed yet another beauty. He'd been tagged with interviewing Mrs. Eddleston again, while Ethan and Randall headed to the university.

"I told you before, he's probably sitting in the basement somewhere, lost in cataloging his finds from the dig site," she said. "Have you looked for him there?"

"We have two officers there now," Ryan said. "But so far they haven't located him. He's not at the dig site, and he isn't answering his phone. He hasn't logged on to the computer at the university since yesterday morning."

"I'm sorry to say, Jeremy is the epitome of the cliché absentminded professor," Mrs. Eddleston said. "He often turns off his phone when he is involved in his work. Trust me, he's somewhere delighting in pottery shards and broken sandals."

Ryan looked around the living room of the spacious home on a private golf course. Twin white leather sofas flanked a brass-and-glass cocktail table. Gold-upholstered side chairs and gold-and-white lamps made the room look elegant and somewhat sterile. Not the kind of place where most men would be comfortable, he thought. "Where did the professor live while the two of you were separated?" he asked.

She pressed her lips together. "I don't know what that has to do with anything."

"I'm trying to think where else he might go."

"He had an apartment over on Fifth. It's the kind of cheap place filled with students and the newly divorced. He hated it. I'm sure he wouldn't go back there."

"Was your husband's affair with Jennifer Lassiter the first time he cheated on you?"

Her face paled and her nostrils flared. "I'm not sure you can call it *cheating* when a couple is legally separated," she said, the words crisp and clipped.

"Before you were separated, had he ever cheated on you?" Ryan kept his eyes on her, showing no mercy. He needed the answer to his questions, no matter how uncomfortable they made her.

"I don't see how that question is relevant."

"The fact that you don't want to answer makes me think your husband had strayed before," he said.

She bowed her head, some of the starch drained from her posture. "Once that I know of for sure," she said. "Though I suspected a couple of other times. It's why I wanted the separation. But Jeremy is older and wiser now. He's working with our counselor. I'm quite sure he is sincere in his desire to be faithful."

"Were his other lovers all young women like Jennifer?" Ryan asked.

"He's a professor. He's surrounded by young women. They throw themselves at him." She sniffed. "She certainly did."

"You're aware that Jennifer Lassiter is missing," Ryan said.

"I am. But I can promise you Jeremy had nothing to do with that."

"How can you be so sure?"

"Because he was with me the afternoon she went missing. He left the dig site early for our first counseling appointment."

"What time was the appointment?" According to Jenny's coworkers, she had gone for a walk about one o'clock.

"The appointment was from two to three in the afternoon. I told you this before."

"You told me you were at a marriage counselor's that afternoon. You didn't mention your husband."

"Didn't I?" She waved her hand dismissively. "It doesn't matter. He was there. We went for coffee afterward, then came home and stayed here the rest of the evening."

To make a two-o'clock appointment, Eddleston would have had to leave the dig site by one fifteen. The last time any of Jenny's coworkers could remember having seen her had been one o'clock. Not a lot of time to kidnap someone, perhaps kill them and hide the evidence.

"And your husband was with you the whole time, from two until the next morning?" Ryan asked.

She frowned, tiny lines radiating from the corners of her eyes.

"Mrs. Eddleston, I can bring you in for questioning if I feel you're withholding information," he said.

"He was late for our appointment," she said. "Not very—maybe twenty minutes. He said he got involved in his work. I believed him. I *believe* him. Why are you asking these questions?"

"Are you aware that another young woman—a high school student—went missing a couple of weeks before Jennifer disappeared? A girl named Lucia Raton?"

"I heard news reports about it, yes."

"Did you know that your husband knew Lucia?"

"What?" There was no mistaking her alarm. "How? A high school student? He wouldn't—"

"He taught a Saturday seminar, an introduction to archaeology, at her high school."

"He teaches many of those seminars. He enjoys introducing young people to archaeology."

"He never mentioned Lucia to you?"

"Why would he? He may have had a weakness for young women, but never a girl that young. Officer, we have two daughters!"

"What about Alicia Mendoza. Did he ever mention her?"

"No. I don't know that name."

"There's no need to badger my wife, Officer."

They both turned to find Jeremy Eddleston standing in the archway leading to the living room. His face was gray and drawn, and he looked at least ten years older than when Ryan had first seen him at the dig site. He took a step into the room. "I know you've been looking for me," he said. "I'm ready to tell you everything."

Chapter Seventeen

The car had turned onto a dirt road, the ride suddenly much slower and rougher. Jana tried to brace herself inside the trunk, but at every bump and curve she was thrown painfully against the sides. She gritted her teeth, trying not to cry out, terrified her captor would hear her and know she was still alive.

She rolled back toward the bumper and was wedged there. The car was climbing an incline. Were they headed back to the old logging site? Maybe the killer reasoned since the Rangers had found Lucia Raton's body, they wouldn't return there to look for another.

She didn't know how many minutes passed before the car stopped, but it seemed a long time. She grabbed the shovel and braced herself. The car door opened, then slammed shut, the sound hollow from inside the trunk. Footsteps moved around the side of the car, crunching in the gravel. She heard the scrape of the key in the lock and braced herself. The narrow band of light widened as the lid began to rise and she lifted the shovel, ready to strike.

"Oh, no, you don't!" The killer grabbed her with both hands and dragged her from the vehicle, forcing the shovel out of her grasp and banging her knees painfully against the edge of the trunk. She struggled against him, terror lending her strength.

He released one hand long enough to strike her, a hard blow to the side of the head that left her reeling and tasting blood where she had bit her lip. She struggled to steady herself and stared at him. Her mind raced with things she wanted to say to him—vile curses to hurl at him or horrible accusations. Instead, she said, "What did you do to Jenny? Where is my sister?"

He smiled, an expression that made her sick to her stomach. "I loved Jenny," he said. "But she wouldn't love me. I told her I would take care of her—that we could be together forever, but she said she couldn't be with someone like me."

"What did you do to her?"

"The same thing I did to Lucia and Alicia. The same thing I'm going to do to you."

He still held her with only one hand. She tried to pull away, but his fingers closed around her wrist even tighter, so that she feared her bones might snap. "Why did you kill them?" she asked.

"I had to make sure I did it right when it came time to take care of Jenny," he said. "So I had to practice. I picked up Lucia when she was hitchhiking. I was on my way to see Metwater and she was just leaving his camp, so I turned around and offered her a ride. I took her for coffee. She was unhappy and wanted to run away from home. I saw that I could help her. She's not unhappy anymore. She's not anything."

Jana's stomach lurched. Her throat and her wrist screamed in pain, but she fought to keep a clear head. The longer she kept him talking, the more time she was buying herself. "What about Alicia?" she asked.

"I wasn't planning on killing her, but I saw her walking along the road and decided it wouldn't hurt to try again—just to make sure I had perfected my technique." He frowned. "I had tried one other time, with Andi Mattheson—Daniel Metwater's pet—but she got away. I didn't want to risk that happening with Jenny."

She stared at him. Clearly he was insane, which made him all the more frightening. How did you reason with someone like that?

"I failed with Andi," he continued. "But she gave me the idea to frame Metwater. He thinks he's so superior, all those women fawning over him. The Rangers hate him anyway, so it was almost too easy to make them see him as the culprit. I planted that torn shirt in his closet and they went after it like dogs on a meaty bone. They never even thought to look at me. After all, I'm harmless." His laughter sent an icy chill through her. "You know another great thing about all of this?" he continued. "I'm getting some great newspaper stories out of it. I wouldn't be surprised if I didn't win at least one Associated Press award for my series on the serial killer who's terrorizing this sleepy little county. This could be the break I need to move on to a really great job with one of the major media outlets. I guess it's true what they say—the people who get ahead are the ones who help themselves."

His words made her physically ill, but she had to keep him talking. She had no idea what time it was, but if she could stall until Ryan returned to the condo, he would be alarmed that she was missing and would come looking for her. She knew the odds of him ever locating her on this deserted side road were slim, but it was the best chance she had of getting out of this alive.

"You attacked me that night at Jenny's apartment," she said.

"I was interrupted." He tightened his hold on her again. "But now I'm going to finish what I started."

"No!" she screamed, startling him. His grip on her weakened just enough for her to pull away. He lunged after her, his fingers grabbing at the hem of her shirt. She heard the fabric tear and stumbled with the forward momentum of the sudden release. Gravel bit into her palms as she shoved herself up again and started running, feet scrabbling for purchase, her pursuer's shouts sending shudders through her.

"You can't get away from me!" he screamed. "There's nowhere for you to run!"

JEREMY EDDLESTON SLUMPED onto one of the white leather sofas while Ryan took a seat on the other. Mrs. Eddleston perched on the far end of her husband's sofa, eyeing both men warily. "Were you aware I've been trying to reach you since yesterday?" Ryan asked.

"Yes." Eddleston's shoulders sagged further. "I saw the cruiser headed toward the dig site yesterday and I turned into a side canyon and waited until you'd passed. I figured you were coming for me—that you'd found out my secret. I've spent the past twenty-four hours driving around, trying to think what to do. I spent the night in my car, parked behind a deserted gas station somewhere in the middle of nowhere." He ran a hand over his unshaven chin. "I didn't sleep much. I knew if you talked to enough people, you'd eventually find out the truth. I decided I had better come clean before I dug my grave any deeper."

His choice of words sent a chill through Ryan. "What do you have to tell me?" he asked.

"I lied when I said I hadn't seen Jenny the afternoon she disappeared. I did see her."

Ryan waited. Silence often coaxed more from people than additional questions.

Eddleston looked sideways at his wife, who refused to meet his gaze. "I left work early that afternoon," he said. "Around twelve. I met a friend for lunch at the café out by the lake."

"A friend?" Mrs. Eddleston coated the words in ice.

"We were lingering over coffee when Jenny came in with Eric Patterson," Eddleston said. "She didn't look happy, and almost as soon as they sat down they began arguing."

Ryan tamped down the anger that surged in him. "Why didn't you tell us this before?" he asked.

Eddleston glanced at his wife again. "Because I knew if I did, word would get back to Melissa."

"Who was the woman this time?" Melissa Eddleston asked. "Another one of your students?"

"It doesn't matter," he said. "It's over between us. I promise."

"Your promises mean nothing to me anymore. Who was she?"

He pressed his lips together, bleaching them of all their color.

Ryan pulled out a notepad. "I'll need the name in order to corroborate your story," he said.

He sent his wife another pained look. "Lisa Cole. She's an adjunct history professor at the college."

Melissa gave a muffled cry, stood and fled from the

room. Eddleston stared after her. "I don't think she'll forgive me this time," he said.

"What happened with Jenny and Eric?" Ryan asked.

Eddleston dragged his attention back to Ryan. "They argued for ten minutes or so. She said something about how she wanted him to leave her alone. He kept saying he loved her and they belonged together. Finally, she shouted that she didn't love him and stormed out. He rushed after her."

"Did they leave together?" Ryan asked.

"I don't know. When Lisa and I paid our check and left about five minutes later, they were gone."

"What about Lucia Raton?" Ryan asked.

Eddleston blinked. "What about her?"

"She attended the Introduction to Archaeology seminar you presented at Montrose High School a few days before she disappeared."

"Did she? I'm sorry, I don't remember."

"She was a very pretty girl. She sat near the front and asked a lot of questions."

"Maybe…" He shook his head. "I do so many of those presentations. They all run together after a while."

"So you don't remember a pretty young girl who was fascinated by you and your subject matter?"

Eddleston shook his head. "I have my weaknesses, but children are not one of them."

"I'm going to ask you again—did you have any kind of encounter with Lucia Raton—did you see her or talk to her or have any idea what happened to her?"

"No. I promise I never laid eyes on her." He looked up at Ryan through his bushy brows. "I didn't hurt Jenny," he said. "She was my friend. I know you don't believe me, but it's true. And I tried to be a friend to her. She seemed to need that."

"Why did she need a friend?" Ryan asked. "Didn't she have friends her own age?"

"I don't know," Eddleston said. "But she said she liked being with me because she always felt safe." He sighed. "I don't like to believe this because it hurts my ego, but Jenny told me her father died when she was still quite young. Maybe she saw me as a kind of father figure."

Ryan put away his notebook and stood. "What happens now?" Eddleston asked.

"You probably want to find a good divorce lawyer," Ryan said.

"You're not going to charge me?" the professor asked. "I withheld evidence."

"You did, but I'm not going to charge you. And while infidelity is distasteful, it isn't against the law."

Back in the cruiser, Ryan telephoned Ethan. His fellow Ranger must have been out of cell-phone range; Ryan had to leave a message on his voice mail summarizing his interview with Eddleston. "I'm going to follow up with the girlfriend," he said. "But I have a feeling the professor is telling us the truth this time."

He ended the call and prepared to telephone the commander when his phone buzzed. He checked the screen and answered. "Simon, what's up?" he asked.

"Where are you?" Simon asked. "Where's Jana?"

"Jana's at my condo." She had mentioned doing some shopping that morning, but surely she was back by now. "Why?"

"You need to get hold of her. I think she's in danger."

Ryan started the cruiser and put it into gear, thoughts

racing. "Why is she in danger?" he demanded. "What have you found out?"

"I went out to Daniel Metwater's camp this morning," Simon said. "I talked to Andi Mattheson. She told me who Easy is."

"Easy?" Ryan turned the cruiser onto the highway, headed toward his duplex.

"The man who was seen with Lucia Raton before she died. Metwater had ordered his followers not to talk about him, but I persuaded Andi to tell me. Easy is Eric Patterson."

"What?"

"Easy is Eric Patterson. He isn't some reporter who just decided to do a profile of Daniel Metwater. He's been hanging around the camp for weeks now."

"Why do you think Jana is in danger?"

"Andi says Eric was never engaged to Jenny Lassiter. He bought her a ring but she wouldn't accept it. Andi saw them arguing about it one day a couple of weeks before Jenny disappeared. She said lately he's been talking about Jana the same way he used to talk about Jenny—about how they were meant to be together forever."

Ryan flipped the switch to activate his lights and siren and pressed down hard on the accelerator. "I'm going to find Jana," he said. "I hope to God we aren't too late."

JANA FELL, SLIDING down the steep slope, rocks tearing her jeans and ripping long gashes in her arms. "Give up now!" Eric shouted above her. "You'll never get away from me."

Shards of rock exploded to her left and she looked

back to see him standing at the top of the incline, a pistol in his hand. He raised it and aimed toward her.

Panicked, she levered herself up and ran to the side, into a tangle of twisted pines and juniper. She tripped on roots and rolled her ankles on rocks, but terror drove her forward. She had no idea where she was or how far behind her Eric was, but she had to keep moving. She wouldn't let him kill her. She wouldn't die.

After several minutes, though, she had to stop. Her lungs burned and every breath was a struggle. She pressed her back against the trunk of an ancient pine and studied the shadowed woodland for any sign of her pursuer. She saw nothing and heard nothing but her own ragged breathing. Not so much as a bird chirped in the stillness.

She felt for her phone in her pocket. Amazingly, it hadn't been crushed in her mad scramble. Unfortunately, the screen showed not a single bar of service. She pressed the 9-1-1 buttons anyway, hoping against hope that somehow the signal would make it through the ether. She had heard law-enforcement could track people by their cell phones. But in order to track someone, they would have to know a person was missing. As far as anyone knew, she was still happily shopping in Montrose. Who knew when Ryan would arrive home and find her missing? He might have to work late on the case, and by the time he missed her, it would be too late.

Would someone see her car at the picnic area and report an abandoned vehicle? How long would it take for that report to make its way to Ryan? She swallowed a lump in her throat. If he knew she was in danger, she was certain he would come to her rescue. If only he knew.

Chapter Eighteen

Ryan called up Jana's number on his phone and waited impatiently while it rang and rang. "You have reached the voice mailbox of..."

"Jana, it's Ryan. Answer me now. It's important."

No one picked up and he angrily ended the call and tossed the phone onto the console. Where was she? He pressed his foot to the floor, the siren wailing. He scarcely slowed for the turnoff to his condo, tires squealing as he braked for the approach to his drive-way. But he saw long before he arrived that the drive was empty. The green rental car she had gotten yesterday wasn't in the garage or parked on the street.

He made himself stop the cruiser, get out and go inside. "Jana!" he shouted, hearing the panic in his voice. "Jana, are you here?"

No answer. He raced back to his vehicle and called her cell again. When the voice-mail message came on, he ended the call and punched in the number of Ranger headquarters. "What's going on there?" he asked when Randall Knightbridge picked up the phone.

"Simon and I went by the newspaper office, hoping to surprise Eric Patterson," Randall said. "His editor said he hadn't been in that morning, even though there was a mandatory editorial meeting. We checked his apartment and he wasn't there, either."

Ryan swore. Of course, that would have been too easy.

"We've got an APB out on him," Randall said. "Simon and Marco headed back to Metwater's camp in case Patterson shows up there, and we've got people at the newspaper, and at his apartment."

"I'll head to the Lakeside Café," Ryan said. "Eddleston says Eric was with Jenny there the afternoon she disappeared. I'll see if I can get a positive ID on him as the man who was there with Lucia before she died. Has anyone heard from Jana?"

"Sorry, no. You haven't seen her?"

"No."

"We'll keep looking," Randall said. "Hang in there."

He didn't ask why Randall would say that. His feelings for Jana must have been obvious to his coworkers even if he hadn't found the courage to share them with Jana. If he saw her again—*when* he saw her again—he would tell her how much he loved her and how he never wanted her to leave him.

No cars sat in the café lot, though he spotted two vehicles around back, neither of them Eric Patterson's Camry. He parked and went inside. Mary looked up from a magazine as he entered. "Hello, Officer," she said. "Back for more of my coffee?"

"I'm looking for someone." He pulled up a photo of Eric Patterson and showed it to her. "Do you recognize this man?"

She tilted her head a little as she studied the photo, then nodded. "He could be the guy," she said.

Ryan's gut clenched. "What guy?"

"The one who was with that missing girl."

"And you're sure he hasn't been in here since then," Ryan asked.

She shrank back a little and he realized he had barked the question. He took a deep breath, telling himself to stay calm. "Someone else said they saw him in here a few days ago with a different young woman," he said.

"Oh, well, that would have been when I went to visit my sister over in Westminster," Mary said. "I was away for five days last week."

"Who worked while you were away?" Ryan asked.

"Bernadette came in two days and Shelly worked the other three," Mary said.

"I'll need their contact information," Ryan said. "I may want to talk to them." He glanced around the empty café. "You're sure the man in that photo hasn't been by here today."

"No, honey. Just the usual fishermen and a couple of campers and some highway workers." She began writing on the back of an order pad. "Here's how to get in touch with Bernadette and Shelly."

"What about this woman?" Ryan showed her a photo of Jana. "Have you seen her?"

Mary shook her head. "Not since she was here with you yesterday. She's pretty, isn't she? Is she a special friend of yours?"

"Yes." Jana was a special friend. He hoped he got the opportunity to tell her so.

He took the piece of paper Mary handed him with the waitresses' contact information and handed her one of his cards. "Call me right away if the man or the woman I showed you come in here," he said.

"Sure thing." She placed the card on the counter beside the register. "Hang on one second."

She left and returned shortly with a to-go cup. "You look like you could use some coffee for the road," she said. "No charge. And I hope you find your friend."

Ryan headed down the road, unsure what he was looking for. All he knew was that Eric Patterson had probably buried two other women in this area. Jenny Lassiter was most likely dead, also. Ryan didn't know if Eric had killed the women where he had found them, or brought them out here to do the deed—he hoped the latter. He needed to believe that Jana was still alive, that he still had time to save her.

He passed the turnoff that led up to the old logging site. A forensics team had searched the area and found no more graves. Eric had left Alicia Mendoza in a drainage ditch dug by highway contractors. Where else in the area would Ryan find disturbed ground that the killer might consider suitable for disposing of a body?

A flash of dark green caught his eye as he passed a picnic area and he braked hard and swung the cruiser into a sharp U-turn. He was calling in the plate on the vehicle before he had even come to a stop, but he already knew what the answer to his query would be. Phone to his ear, he climbed out and approached the car.

"That vehicle is registered to VIP Rentals," the woman on the other end of the phone said.

Ryan didn't need to hear more. He slipped the phone back into his pocket and hastily put on latex gloves. Then he tried the driver's door. The car was unlocked. Before he even had the door opened, he recognized Jana's purse on the front seat.

He checked the rest of the car. Four bags of groceries in the trunk. The meat was still cool to the touch, so it hadn't been sitting there too long. But how long?

Leaving the car, he walked toward the closest picnic table. He hadn't gone far before he saw the drag marks—parallel lines in the dust leading from the concrete pad for the picnic table to the parking lot. They ended abruptly, a couple of feet from faint tire treads. Ryan knelt to study the treads. He guessed they were passenger-car tires, though he was no expert. Whether they came from Eric Patterson's Camry he couldn't say, but he didn't like the odds that they weren't a match for Patterson's car.

He pulled out his phone again and called Ranger headquarters. This time fellow officer Michael Dance answered. "I found Jana's car," Ryan said. "It's at a picnic area by the lake. There are signs of a struggle in the parking lot and some tire treads. We need to get someone out here to take photos and measurements. And we need to start a search for her, right away."

"Carmen's free. I'll send her," Michael said. "And we'll get everyone we can to start searching. Where are you off to now?"

"I don't know. I'll let you know when I get there."

Ryan returned to his car and pulled out a Forest Service map. It showed all the roads, trails, rest areas and campgrounds in this area. He found a pen and circled the logging site where Lucia's body had been found and the stretch of road construction where the workmen had discovered Alicia. He studied the mass of roads, streams and contour lines between the two and zeroed in on a road marked Private, Admittance by Permit Only. He traced the road up a series of closely spaced contour lines until it ended at a pair of crossed pickaxes. The symbol for a mine.

His heart skipped a beat. A mine could mean an old adit or shaft. The perfect place to dispose of a body.

ERIC DIDN'T BOTHER trying to sneak up on Jana. He crashed through the woods with all the subtlety of a moose, crunching leaves and snapping twigs announcing his approach. "You won't get away from me," he said. "When I want something, I don't give up."

She didn't give up, either. She wasn't going to let fear or his bullying and threats make her surrender without a fight. She pushed off from the tree trunk she had been resting against and began running again. She hoped she was moving back toward the road. If she could get to the car before he did, she might have a chance of getting away.

She hadn't gone too far before she realized she could no longer hear Eric crashing through the trees behind her. And he wasn't firing in her direction. Had she been lucky enough to lose him? She slowed her pace to a trot, straining her ears for any sounds of approach. Glancing back over her shoulder, she saw nothing but the bleached trunks of aspen, jutting up from the ground like the quills of a porcupine.

She slowed more, still moving but allowing herself to catch her breath. If only she had a cell phone signal, she could use a mapping app to figure out where she was. Of course, if her phone worked, she could summon help and she wouldn't be in this fix.

She started forward again, but stopped abruptly, loose rock sliding from beneath her shoes, bounding and echoing as it descended into a deep canyon. She stared down at the sheer drop at her feet. Sun glinted on a narrow stream of water far below and sparkled on threads of quartz in the vertical rock slabs.

"Watch that last step, it's a big one."

She turned and saw the gun pointed at her, then the man behind it. Eric was close enough now that he wouldn't miss if he fired. He closed the gap between them and grabbed her arm. "I told you you wouldn't get away from me," he said, and tugged her back the way she had come.

"Where are you taking me?" she asked as she stumbled along beside him.

"I'm taking you to join your sister. You can be with her forever now. That's what you want, isn't it?"

His words, and the almost gleeful way he said them, made her knees weak. She stumbled and almost fell.

Eric yanked her upright and pressed the barrel of the gun into her side. "Don't try anything stupid," he said. "I don't want to have to kill you yet, but I will."

Which meant he would eventually kill her if she didn't escape from him first. He had already proved she couldn't outrun him. He apparently knew the area well. She pictured him exploring the area, planning his crimes. Planning to murder the woman he claimed to love.

Could she wrestle the gun away and turn it on him? She doubted it. His finger was too close to the trigger. One wrong move from her and he'd simply fire it. A bullet at this short range would be devastating.

She could try to trip him, but he held her so tightly he would only bring her down with him. She wished she knew judo or some other martial art, where she might have learned how to use an opponent's own weight against him.

It's hopeless, a voice whispered in her head.

No! she answered back. Everything she had read told her the people who survived against the odds were the ones who didn't give up. She wouldn't give up.

They left the woods and started up the rocky slope she had descended earlier. "Where are we going?" she asked.

"I told you, I'm taking you to join your sister."

"Yes, but where?" she said.

He chuckled. "You're just like her, you know? She was curious, too. Always asking me questions. What are you doing? Why are you doing that? Where are we going? It's one of the things I liked about her, actually. She was so smart and inquisitive. She would have made a good reporter."

Hearing him talk about Jenny this way made her stomach churn with rage. If she could have martialed her anger into a weapon, she would have engulfed him in flames. "So where are you taking me?" she asked again, hoping if she learned the answer it would help her plan an escape.

"Look down at your feet," he said. "Tell me what you see."

She looked down. "I see rocks." Her knees and arms still ached from falling on this jagged scree, some of the rocks the size of her fist, others as big as her head.

"It's mine waste," he said. "From the Molly May mine. They pulled a lot of gold out of here in the 1870s, but no one comes up here anymore."

"You're taking me to a mine?" Her spirits sank. Colorado was riddled with old mines from which men had extracted—some with more success than others gold, silver, copper, iron, coal and other minerals over the years. When the mines stopped yielding their riches they were abandoned, left to fill with water and debris. The more accessible were covered with iron barriers or grates to keep out unwary passing animals and people, but those higher in the mountains, off the beaten path, remained open.

The perfect place to dispose of a body. She swallowed a surge of nausea.

"Come on." Eric tugged on her arm. "I haven't got all day."

Weathered timbers came into view above them and proved to be a roughly framed hut that formed the entrance to the mine. She dug in her heels, holding back. "I don't want to go in there," she said.

She expected another outburst of anger, but Eric turned to her with surprising tenderness. "It's not far," he said. "Only about fifty yards in before we get to the first shaft. Jenny is waiting for you there. Won't you be happy to see her?"

Jana bit her lip, afraid she was going to cry. She didn't want to give him the satisfaction of knowing he had broken her. "I don't like the dark," she said, which wasn't a lie.

"You don't have to worry," Eric said. "I know the way."

"It's still dark." She hoped she didn't sound as pathetic as she felt.

He released his hold on her arm, but kept the gun pressed into her side, then reached into his pocket and pulled out a Mini Maglite. "See," he said. "I think of everything. Now come on."

RYAN GUNNED THE cruiser up the rough mining road, tires slipping and rocks ringing on the undercarriage. He kept his foot pressed to the accelerator, wrestling the steering wheel to keep the vehicle on the narrow track. More than once the SUV slid dangerously close to the drop-off beside the road, but he somehow kept going. Now wasn't the time for caution; he only prayed he wasn't too late.

He'd called for backup from the picnic area, then headed for the turnoff, lights and siren off in case Eric was close enough to see or hear and be alerted to his approach. He wasn't sure how he was going to deal with Patterson, but he would assess the situation when he found the murderer.

Sun glinted off metal ahead. Ryan slowed as he recognized Eric Patterson's Camry. The trunk was open, a yellow plastic snow shovel on the ground in front of it. Ryan parked behind the Camry, angling the cruiser sideways to block it in. He shut off the engine and studied the scene. A footpath led up the slope away from the car, probably to the mine, though he had no idea how far away that might be.

A soft breeze rustled the trees that had grown up close to the little clearing, bringing in the scent of pine and the music of birdsong. Under other circumstances, this would have been an idyllic scene. But a sense of dread colored the atmosphere with gloom.

Ryan drew his Glock and eased over to the cover of the trees. Moving as swiftly as possible yet trying not to make any noise, he began climbing the slope. After five minutes of climbing, the modest entrance to a mine adit emerged from the side of the mountain, the opening a black mouth framed by silvered timbers.

He crossed the gap between the trees and the mine opening on a run, ducking around the side of the timbers for cover. Waiting for his breathing to slow, he strained his ears to listen.

The low murmur of voices, too garbled to make out words, drifted from the opening. Heart pounding, Ryan ducked inside. He plastered himself against one side of the tunnel, damp seeping through the rocks soaking into his shirt. Carefully placing each step, he inched along the wall, toward a faint light that glowed in the distance.

The voices became clearer as he neared the light. "Stand there, with your back to the shaft," a man— Eric Patterson—said.

"What are you going to do?" Jana's voice trembled with fear. Ryan forced himself not to react. He inched closer, weapon raised.

"I'm trying to make this easy for you," Eric said. "If you cooperate this will be a much better experience."

"You're going to kill me," Jana said. "How can that in any way be a good experience?"

"Look, if you don't cooperate, I'll just push you in and you can starve to death down there. Would you like that better?"

Ryan didn't need to hear any more. "Eric Patterson, freeze!" he shouted, and rushed forward to the end of the corridor. Patterson turned and fired, his bullet striking the rock wall beside Ryan's right shoulder, sending granite shards flying.

Jana screamed and dropped to the ground on one side of the open shaft. Eric turned and aimed his weapon not at Ryan, but at her. "Come any closer and I'll kill her," he said.

"Then you'll die, too," Ryan said. "Is that what you want?"

"You should never have interfered," Eric said. "If you hadn't tried to take Jenny from me I never would have had to resort to this."

"I didn't know Jenny," Ryan said.

"Don't lie to me!" Eric barked, and shifted the gun to aim at Ryan. "First it was that professor—what did she ever see in that ugly old man? I thought I had fixed that. I made it to where she could never leave me again. Then you came along and I saw you kissing her. It made me sick. You should have left well enough alone."

"Put the gun down," Ryan said. "You won't solve anything by killing anyone."

"Don't come any closer!" Eric leveled the pistol at Ryan, who dived for the ground as the shot exploded in the small space, the sound reverberating painfully in his ears, the smell of cordite stinging his nose. He rolled on his side and saw Eric stumble backward, Jana clutching his ankle with both hands.

Patterson shifted the weapon to aim at Jana, but he never got off the shot. Ryan's bullet caught him square in the chest, sending him crashing backward, down into the shaft, his scream rising over the echo of gunfire.

Ryan crawled to Jana's side. She lay face down on the ground, her shoulders trembling. He gathered her into his arms. "Are you hurt?" he murmured, stroking her hair. "Did he hurt you?"

She raised her head to look at him, tears streaming down her cheeks. "He killed Jenny," she sobbed. "She's down at the bottom of that shaft. He shot her and left her alone down there."

He cradled her head on his shoulder while she sobbed. Nothing he could say would soothe her grief, so he let her cry. When her tears at last subsided, he kissed the top of her head. "I'm glad he didn't kill you, too," he said.

She nodded, and he helped her to stand. "Thank God you came," she said. "I told myself if I could hang on long enough, something would happen. I had to keep trying. I wouldn't give up."

"That's what I love about you." He turned her to him and kissed her again, on the lips. She melted against him, her hands threaded in his hair. It was a kiss of desperation and relief and more than a little passion— emotion heightened, he knew, by all they had been through. But that didn't mean his feelings for her were any less real.

"I know this isn't a good time," he said. "And I'm not asking anything of you. I just want you to know I love you."

"I love you, too," she said. "In spite of everything else, I love you. It's crazy and not at all what I expected, but I can't seem to help myself."

"Police! Ryan? Are you there?" A man's voice echoed off the rock walls of the tunnel.

"We're down here!" Ryan shouted.

Footsteps thundered down the tunnel. Moments later, Ethan, Simon and the rest of the Ranger Brigade appeared in the opening. "Eric Patterson is dead at the bottom of the mine shaft," Ryan said. "Along with Jennifer Lassiter."

"How are you, Officer Spencer?" Graham asked.

"I'm fine now, sir. Just fine." The Rangers stepped aside to let Ryan and Jana pass.

"What happens now?" she asked, when they emerged from the mine.

"I'm taking you home," he said.

"I mean, what happens with Eric, and Jenny?"

"They'll retrieve the bodies. You'll need to decide what to do. If you want a funeral or some kind of memorial service I'll help you with that. Or we can assign you a victim's advocate."

"Poor Jenny." She leaned against him. "If only I had known what she was going through, I could have helped."

"She didn't want to worry you," he said. "And she thought she could handle Eric herself. I talked to Professor Eddleston earlier and he said she liked being with him because he made her feel safe. I think she came on to Eddleston as a way of getting rid of Eric. She thought if he knew she was involved with someone else, he'd leave her alone."

"He wasn't sane," Jana said. "You heard the way he talked in there—as if Jenny and I were the same person." She raised her head, eyes wide. "I almost forgot—he told me he did murder Lucia and Alicia. And he attacked me that night at Jenny's apartment. He said he did it to practice before he killed Jenny." She covered her mouth with her hand and choked back a fresh sob.

"We'll need a statement from you later," Ryan said. "But not now. You don't have to think about it now."

"I have to tell you before I forget something," she said. "He said he put the shirt in Daniel Metwater's closet, to try to frame him. Oh, and he attacked Andi Mattheson, too, but she got away."

Ryan nodded. So the Rangers had been right to think all these assaults and disappearances were connected. "We'll get your statement tomorrow," he said. "For now, let's get you home."

She studied him. "But your place isn't my home," she said.

"It can be if you want it to be." He led her around to the passenger side of the car. "Is that what you want?"

"I want to stay with you," she said. "Not just now. I don't want to go back to Denver, except to close out my business there and give up my apartment. I don't want to leave you."

"I want you to stay with me, too." He kissed her again, gently, as if she were made of spun sugar. She seemed so fragile and precious to him now, though he knew she was strong as steel. She had to be, to have endured all she had today.

She smiled through a fresh wave of tears. "Do you think we can make this work?" she asked. "We aren't starting out under the best of circumstances."

"Things will only get better from here," he said. "And whatever happens, we'll get through it together. If that's what you want."

"It's what I want." She threw her arms around him and pulled him close. "I don't give up. You know that, don't you?"

"As long as you don't give up on us."

"Believe it," she said.

"I do." It wasn't a wedding vow, but with luck and time it would be. Now that he had found this woman, he didn't intend to let her go.

* * * * *

"I will get you out of here, Gabriella. But I need to do my job, too."

Jaime leaned forward, his mouth so close Gabriella inhaled sharply, drowning a little in his dark eyes, wanting to get lost in the warm strength of his body.

He pulled his face away from hers, shaking his head. "I shouldn't—"

But Gabriella didn't want his "shouldn'ts" and she didn't want him to pull away, so she tugged Jaime closer and covered his mouth with hers.

Her tongue traced his mouth and she sighed against him. Melting, leaning. Crawling under all the defenses he wound around himself. False identities. Badges and pledges. Weapons and uniforms and lies. Even having dreamed of it, even in the midst of allowing it to happen in the here and now, Jaime knew it was wrong. Kissing Gabriella, drowning in it, was like taking advantage of her. It flew in the face of who he was as an FBI agent, as a law enforcement agent.

He should pull away. He should stop this madness. But he didn't stop. Couldn't. Because while it went against all those things he was, it didn't go against who he was. Deep down, this was what Jaime wanted…

STONE COLD UNDERCOVER AGENT

BY
NICOLE HELM

First Published in Great Britain 2017
By Mills & Boon, an imprint of HarperCollins*Publishers*
1 London Bridge Street, London, SE1 9GF

© 2017 Nicole Helm

ISBN: 978-0-263-92908-9

46-0817

Our policy is to use papers that are natural, renewable and recyclable products and made from wood grown in sustainable forests. The logging and manufacturing processes conform to the legal environmental regulations of the country of origin.

Printed and bound in Spain
by CPI, Barcelona

Nicole Helm grew up with her nose in a book and the dream of one day becoming a writer. Luckily, after a few failed career choices, she gets to follow that dream— writing down-to-earth contemporary romance and romantic suspense. From farmers to cowboys, Midwest to *the* West, Nicole writes stories about people finding themselves and finding love in the process. She lives in Missouri with her husband and two sons and dreams of someday owning a barn.

The first romance novel I ever read was a romantic suspense, and I never thought I'd be able to write one. Thank you, Helen and Denise, for helping me prove past me wrong.

Chapter One

Gabby Torres had stopped counting the days of her captivity once it entered its sixth year. She didn't know why that was the year that did it. The first six had been painful and isolating and horrifying. She had lost everything. Her family. Her future. Her *freedom*.

The only thing she currently had was…life itself, which, in her case, wasn't much of a life when it came right down to it.

For the first four years of her abduction, she'd fought like a maniac. Anyone and anything that came near her—she'd attacked. Every time her captor got up close and told her some horrible thing, she'd fought in a way she had never known she could.

Maybe if the man hadn't so gleefully told her that her father was dead two years into her captivity, she might have eventually gotten tired of fighting. She might have accepted her fate as being some madman's kidnapping victim. But every time he appeared, she remembered how happily he had told her that her father had suffered a heart attack and died. It renewed her fight every single time.

But the oddest part of the eight years of captivity was that, though she'd been beaten on occasion in the midst of fighting back, mostly The Stallion and his men hadn't ever forced themselves on her or the other girls.

For years she'd wondered why and tried to figure out their reasoning...what their *point* was. Why she was there. Aside from the random jobs The Stallion forced her and the other girls to do, like sewing bags of drugs into car cushions or what have you.

But she was in year eight and tired of trying to figure out why she was there or what the point of it was. She was even tired of thinking about escape.

She'd been the first girl brought to the compound and, over the years, The Stallion had collected three more women. All currently existing in this boarded-up house in who knew where. Gabby had become something like the den mother as the new girls tried to figure out why they were there, or what they had done wrong, or what The Stallion wanted from them, but Gabby herself was done with wondering.

She had moved on. After she'd stopped counting every single day at year six, the past two years had been all about making this a reality. She kept track of Sundays for the girls and noted when a month or two had passed, but she had accepted this tiny, hidden-away compound as her life. The women were as much of a family as she was ever going to have, and the work The Stallion had them doing to hide drugs or falsify papers was her career.

Accepting at this point was all she could do. If sometimes her brain betrayed her as she tried to fall asleep, or one of the girls muttered something about escape, she pushed it down and out as far as it would go.

Hope was a cancer here. All she had was acceptance.

So when just another uncounted day rolled around and The Stallion, for the first time in all of those days, brought a man with him into her room, Gabby felt an icy pierce of dread hit her right in the chest.

Though she'd accepted her fate, she hadn't accepted *him*. Perhaps because no matter how eight years had passed, or how he might disappear for months at a time, or the fact he never touched her, he seemed intent on making her *break*.

Quite honestly, some days that's what kept her going. Making sure he never knew he'd broken her of hope.

So, though she had accepted her lot—or so she told herself—she still dreamed of living longer than him and airing all his dirty laundry. Outliving him and making sure he knew he had never, *ever* broken her. She very nearly smiled at the thought of him dead and gone. "So, who are you?"

The man who stood next to The Stallion was tall, broad and covered in ominous black. Black hair—both shaggy on his head and bearded on his face—black sunglasses, black shirt and jeans. Even the weapons, mostly guns, he had strapped all over him were black. Only his skin tone wasn't black, though it was a dark olive hue.

"I told you she was a feisty one. Quite the fiery little spitball. She'll be perfect for you," The Stallion said, his smile wide and pleased with himself.

The icy-cold dread in Gabby's chest delved deeper, especially as this new man stared at her from somewhere behind his sunglasses. Why was he wearing sunglasses in this dark room? It wasn't like she had any outside light peering through the boarded window.

He murmured something in Spanish. But Gabby had never been fluent in her grandparents' native language and she could barely pick out any of the words since he'd spoken them so quickly and quietly.

The Stallion's cold grin widened even further. "Yes. Have lots of fun with her. She's all yours. Just remember the next time I ask you for a favor that I gave you exactly what you specified. Enjoy."

The Stallion slid out of the room, and the ominous click of the door's lock nearly made Gabby jump when no sounds and nothing in her life had made her jump for nearly two years.

While The Stallion's grin was very nearly…psychotic, as though he'd had some break with reality, the man still in her room was far scarier. He didn't smile in a way that made her think he was off in some other dimension. His smile was… Lethal. Ruthless. *Alive.*

It frightened her and she had given up fear a very long time ago.

"You don't speak Spanish?" he asked with what sounded almost like an exaggerated accent. It didn't sound like any of the elderly people in her family who'd grown up in Mexico, but then, maybe his background wasn't Mexican.

"No, not really. But apparently you speak English, so we don't have a problem."

"I guess that depends on your definition of problem," he said, his voice low and laced with threat.

What Gabby wanted to do was to scoot back on the bed as far into the corner as she possibly could, but she had learned not to show her initial reactions. She had watched The Stallion get far too much joy out of her flight responses in the beginning, and she'd learned to school them away. So even though she thought about it, even though she pictured it in her head complete with covering her face with her hands and cowering, she didn't do it. She stayed exactly where she was and stared the man down.

He perused the bedroom that had been her life for so long. Oh, she could go anywhere in the small, boarded-up house, but she'd learned to appreciate her solitude even in captivity.

The man opened the dresser drawers and pawed through them. He inspected the baseboards and slid his large, scarred hands up and down the walls. He even pulled at the boards over the windows.

"Measuring for drapes?" she asked as sarcastically as she could manage.

The man looked at her, still wearing his sunglasses, which she didn't understand at all. His lips curved into an amused smile. It made Gabby even more jumpy because, usually, the guards The Stallion had watching them weren't the brightest. Or maybe they'd had such rough lives they didn't care for humor of any kind. Either way, very few people, including the women she lived with, found her humor funny.

He was back to his perusal and there was a confident grace about him that made no sense to her. He wasn't like any of the other men she'd come into contact with during her captivity. He was handsome, for starters. She couldn't think of one guard who could probably transfer from a life of crime into a life of being a model, but this man definitely could.

It made all of her nerves hum. It gave her that little tingle that mysteries always did—the idea that if she paid enough attention, filed enough details away, she could solve it. Figure out why he was different before he did her any harm.

She'd begun to wonder if she hadn't gone a little crazy when she noticed these things no one else seemed to. She was pretty sure Tabitha thought she was out of her mind for having theories about The Stallion's drug and human trafficking operations. For coming up with a theory that he spent three months there and split the other seasons at three other houses that would ostensibly be just like this one.

She'd been here for eight years and she knew his patterns. She was sure of it. Things puzzled together in her head until it all made sense. But the girls all looked at her like she was crazy for coming up with such ideas, so she'd started keeping them to herself. She'd started trying to stop her brain from acting.

But it always did and maybe she had gone completely and utterly insane. Eight years ago her life had been ripped away from her, but she didn't even get to be dead. She had to be here living in this weird purgatory.

Wouldn't that drive anyone to the brink of insanity? Maybe her patterns and theories were gibberish.

Finally the man had looked through everything in the room except her bed where she was currently sitting. He advanced on her with easy, relaxed strides that did nothing to calm the tenseness in her muscles or the heavy beating of her heart. She couldn't remember the last time in her captivity she'd felt so afraid.

He didn't say anything and she couldn't see his eyes underneath the sunglasses, so whatever he was thinking or feeling was a blank-expressioned mystery.

Finally, after a few humming seconds, he lifted a long finger up to the ceiling. She frowned at him and he made the gesture again until she realized he wanted her to get off the bed.

Since most of the guards' preferred way of getting her to do something was to grab her and throw her around, she supposed she should feel more calm with this man who hadn't yet touched her.

But she wasn't calm. She didn't trust him at all.

She did get up off the bed and, instead of scurrying away, tried to measure her steps and very carefully move to the farthest corner from him.

The man lifted every single blanket on her bed and then, in an easy display of muscles, the heavy mattress and box spring, as well. He got down on all fours and looked under the bed and, finally, she realized he was searching for something in particular.

She just had no idea what on earth he could be looking for.

"No bugs?"

She stared at him. What, did he have some weird fear of ladybugs or ants or something? Then she realized the intensity with which he was staring at her and recalled how carefully he had looked through every inch of this little room. Yeah, he wasn't looking for insects.

"I've been here for eight years. As far as I know, he's never bugged or videotaped individual rooms."

The man raised his eyebrows. "But he films other rooms?"

Gabby trusted this man almost less than she trusted The Stallion, which was not at all. She offered a careless shrug. The last thing she was going to do was to share all of her ideas and information with this stranger.

"Tell me about your time here."

There was a gentleness to his tone that didn't fool her at all. "Tell me who you are."

He smiled again, an oddly attractive smile that was so out of place in this dire situation. "The Stallion told me you'd be exactly what I was looking for. I don't think he knew just how perfect you'd be."

"Perfect for what?" she demanded, trying to keep the high-pitched fear out of her voice.

"Well, he thinks you'd be the perfect payment. A high-spirited fighter—the kind of woman who would appeal to my baser instincts."

This time Gabby couldn't stop herself from pushing back into the corner or cowering. For the first year she'd been held captive, she'd been sure she'd be sexually assaulted. She'd never heard about an abduction that hadn't included that, not that she'd had any deep knowledge of abductions before.

But no one had ever touched her that way and she'd finally gotten to a point where she didn't think it would happen. That was her own stupid fault for thinking this could be her normal.

The man finally took off his sunglasses. His eyes were almost as dark as his hair, a brown that was very nearly black. Everything about his demeanor changed; the swagger, the suave charm, gone.

"I'm not going to hurt you," he said in a low voice.

Maybe if she hadn't been a captive for eight years, she might have believed him. But she didn't, not for a second.

"You're just going to need to play along," he continued in that maddeningly gentle voice.

"Play along with what?" she asked, pushing as far into the corner as she could.

"You'll see."

Gabby wanted to cry, which had been an impulse she'd beaten out of herself years ago, but it was bubbling up inside her along with the new fear. It wasn't fair. She was so tired of her life not being fair.

When the man reached out for her, she went with those instincts from the very first time she'd been brought there.

She fought him with everything she had.

JAIME ALESSANDRO HADN'T worked his way up "The Stallion's" operation by being a particularly *nice* guy. Undercover work, especially this long and this deep, had required him to bend a lot of the moral codes he'd started police work with.

But thus far, he'd never had to beat up or restrain a

woman. This woman was surprisingly agile and strong, and she was coming at him with everything she had.

He was very concerned he was going to have to hurt her just to get her to stop. He could stand a few scratches, but he doubted The Stallion was going to trust him with the next big job if he let this woman give him a black eye—no matter how strong and "feisty" she was.

God, how he hated that word.

"Ma'am." He tried for his forceful FBI agent voice as he managed to hold one of her arms still. He didn't want to hurt the poor woman who'd been here eight years—a fact he only knew because she'd just told him.

He shouldn't have been surprised at this point. He'd learned very quickly in his undercover work that what the FBI had on Victor Callihan, a.k.a. The Stallion, was only the tip of the iceberg.

If he thought about it too much, the things The Stallion had done, the things Jaime had done to get here… Well, he didn't, because he'd had to learn how to turn that voice of right and wrong off and focus only on the task at hand.

Bringing down The Stallion.

That meant if she didn't stop flailing at him and landing some decent blows, he was going to have to restrain her any way he could, even if it caused her some pain.

Though he had her arm clamped in a tight grip, she still thrashed and kicked at him, very nearly landing a blow that would have brought him to his knees. He swore and, though he very much didn't want to, gave her a little jerk that gave him the leverage he needed to grab her from behind with both arms.

She still bucked and kicked, but with his height advantage and a full grip on her upper body, he could maneuver her this way and that to keep her from landing any nasty hits.

"I'm not going to hurt you. I'm going to help you, I promise."

She spat, probably aiming for him but missing completely since he had her from behind. It was only then he realized he'd spoken in Spanish instead of English.

He'd grown up speaking both, but his work for The Stallion and the identity he'd assumed required mostly speaking Spanish and pretending he struggled with English.

It was slipups like that—not realizing what language he was speaking, not quite remembering who he was—that always sent a cold bolt of fear through him.

He needed this to be over. He needed to get out. Before he lost himself completely. He could only hope that Gabriella Torres would be the last piece of the puzzle in getting to the heart of The Stallion's operation.

"I'm not going to hurt you," Jaime said in a low, authoritative tone. Certain, self-assured, even though he didn't feel much of either at this particular moment.

"Then let go of me," she returned, still bucking, throwing her head back and narrowly missing head-butting him pretty effectively.

He tried not to think about what might have happened to her in the course of being hidden way too long from the world. It was a constant fight between the human side of him and the role he had to play. He wouldn't lose his humanity, though. He refused. He might have to bend his moral code from time to time, but he wouldn't lose the part of him that would feel sympathy. If he lost that, he'd never be able to go back.

Jaime noted that though Gabriella still fought his tight hold, she was tiring.

"Be still and I'll let you go," he said quietly, hoping that maybe his outer calm would rub off on her.

She tried to land a heel to his shin but when that failed she slumped in his arms. "Fine."

Carefully and slowly, paying attention to the way she held herself and the pliancy of her body, Jaime released her from his grip. Since she didn't renew her fight, he took a few steps away so she could see he had no intention of hurting her.

When she turned and looked at him warily, he held his hands up. Her breathing was labored and there were droplets of sweat gathered at her temples. She had a pretty face despite the pallor beneath her tan complexion. She had a mass of dark curls pulled back and away from her face, and he had to wonder how old she was.

She looked both too young and too world-weary all at the same time, but he couldn't let that twist his insides. He'd seen way worse at this point, hadn't he? "I'm not going to harm you, Gabriella. In fact, I want to help you."

She laughed, something bitter and scathing that scraped against what little conscience he had left.

"Sure you·do, buddy. And this is the Taj Mahal."

Yeah, she'd be perfect for what he needed. Now he just had to figure out how to use her without blowing everything he'd worked for.

Chapter Two

Gabby was wrung out. Physically. Emotionally. It had been a long time since she'd had something to react so violently against. Her breathing was uneven and her insides felt scraped raw.

She wanted to cry and it had been so long since she'd allowed herself that emotional release.

She couldn't allow it now. Not with the way this man studied her, intently and far too interested. She had become certain of her power in this odd world she'd been thrust into against her will, but she didn't believe in that power in the face of this man.

She closed her eyes against the wave of despair and the *need* to give up on this whole *surviving* thing.

"Gabriella. I know you have no reason to trust me, but I'm going to say it even if you don't believe it. I will not hurt you."

The worst part was that she was so exhausted she *wanted* to believe him. No one had promised her safety in the past eight years, but just because no one had didn't mean she could believe this one.

"I guess it's my lucky day," she returned, trying to roll her eyes but exhaustion limited the movement.

"I know. I know. I do. Don't trust me. Don't believe. I just need you to go along with some things."

"What kind of things? And, more important, *why*?" She shook her head. Questions were pointless. The man was going to lie to her anyway. "Never mind. It doesn't matter. Do whatever you're going to do."

"You fought me."

"So?"

He stepped forward and she stumbled away. He shook his head, holding his hands up again, as if surrendering. "I'm sorry. I won't. I'm not going to touch you." He kept his hands raised as he spoke. Low, with a note to his voice she couldn't recognize.

Panic? No, he wasn't panicked in the least. But there was something in that tone that made her feel like time was running out. For what, she had no idea. But there was a *drive* to this man, a determination.

He had a goal of some kind and it wasn't like The Stallion's goals. The Stallion had a kind of meticulous nature, and he never seemed rushed or driven. Just a cold, careful, step-by-step map in his head to whatever endgame he had. Or maybe no endgame at all. Just... living his weird life.

But *this* man in her room had a vitality to him, an energy. He was trying to *do* something and Gabby hated the way she responded to that. Oh, she missed having a goal, having some *fight* in her. The weary acceptance of the past two years had given her less and less to live for. Helping the other girls was the only thing that kept her getting up every morning.

"What do you want from me?"

"Just some cooperation. Some information. To go along with whatever I say, especially if The Stallion is around."

"Are you trying to usurp him or something?"

He released a breath that was almost a laugh. "N—" He seemed to think better of saying no. "Who knows? Right now, I need information."

"Why should I give you anything?"

He seemed to think about the question but in the end ignored it and asked one of his own. "Is it true…?" He trailed off, giving her a brief once-over. "They haven't touched you while you've been here?"

She stared hard at the man. "One time a guard tried to touch my chest and I knocked his tooth out."

The man's full mouth curved a little at that, something so close to humor in his expression it hurt. Humor. She missed…laughing. For no reason. Smiling, just because it was a nice day with a blue sky.

But she couldn't think about all the things she missed or her heart would stop beating.

"What happened to the guard?"

Gabby shrugged, hugging herself against all this *feeling*. Thoughts about laughter, about the sky, about using her mind to put the pieces of the puzzle together again.

You gave that up. You've accepted your fate.

But had she, really, when the fight came so easily and quickly?

"I don't know. I never saw him again."

"Was it only the one time?"

Gabby considered how much information she wanted

to give a stranger who might be just as evil as the man who held her captive. She could help him boot The Stallion out…and then get nothing for her trouble. She wasn't sure if she preferred to take the risk. The devil you knew and all that.

But there was something about this man… He didn't fit. Nothing about his demeanor or mannerisms or his questions fit the past eight years of her experience. What exactly would be the harm in telling him what she knew? What would The Stallion do? He'd been the one to leave her with this man.

"As far as I know, they can knock us around as long as they don't break anything or touch our faces. If they go overboard, or get sexual, they disappear."

The man raised an eyebrow. "How many have disappeared?"

Gabby shrugged, still holding herself. "It was more in the beginning. Five the first year. Three the second. Only one in the third. Then five again the fourth. Two the fifth, then none since."

Both his eyebrows raised at this point, his eyes widening in surprise. "You remember it that specifically?"

Part of her wanted to brag about all the things she remembered. All the specifics she had locked away in her brain. All the patterns she'd put together. None of the girls had ever appreciated them. She had a feeling this man would.

But it would be showing her hand a little too easily for comfort. "Not a lot to think about in this place. I remember some things."

"Tell me," he said, taking another one of those steps

toward her that made her want to cower or run away to whatever corner she could find. But she stood her ground and she shook her head.

If she told him, it would be in her own time, when she thought telling might work in her favor in some way.

He stood there, opposite her, studying her face as though he could figure out how to get her to talk if he simply looked hard enough.

So she looked right back, trying to determine something about *him*.

He had a sharp nose and angular cheekbones, a strong jaw covered liberally with short, black whiskers. His eyes looked much less black close up, a variety of browns melding to the black pupil at the center.

He had broad shoulders and narrow hips and even the array of weapons strapped to him didn't detract from the sexy way he was built. Sexy. Such an odd thing. She hadn't thought about sex or attractiveness or much of anything in that vein for eight long years.

She didn't know if she was glad she could still see it and recognize it or if it just made everything more complicated. Far more lonely.

The eerie click of a lock interrupted the moment and he looked back at the door, then at her. His expression was grave.

"I'm not going to hurt you," he whispered. "But this may scare you a little bit. That's okay. Fight back."

"Fight ba—"

He reached out and grabbed her by the shirt with both large hands. She screeched, but he had her shirt ripped in two before she landed the first punch.

JAIME PRETENDED TO laugh as Gabby pounded at him. He glanced at The Stallion, doing his best to stand between the man and his view of Gabby. He'd tried not to look himself, but he needed the illusion of a fight. A sexual one.

He couldn't let his disgust at that show. *"Senor?"* The Stallion always got some bizarre thrill when Jaime called him that, so he'd done it with increasing regularity. Being the egomaniac that he was, The Stallion never got tired of it. "An hour, no?"

"I'm sorry to interrupt, but I need you immediately. Your hour will have to wait."

Jaime scowled. He didn't have to fake it, either. He wanted more information from Gabriella. If the woman had remembered how many guards were dismissed every year…who knew what other kind of information she might have.

Jaime inclined his head as if he agreed, though he didn't at all. He wanted to get information out of Gabriella as soon as possible. The more he got and the sooner he got it, the less he'd have to do for The Stallion.

He gave her a fleeting glance. Those big, dark eyes were edged with fury, and she crossed her arms over her chest. The bra she wore was ill-fitting and he couldn't help but notice the way her breasts spilled over the fabric even under her crossed arms.

He quickly looked back at The Stallion. He handed Gabriella the remains of her shirt. *"Perdón,"* he offered, making sure he didn't sound sorry in the least.

The Stallion chuckled as Jaime walked to meet him at the door. "You could be so much better at your job if you weren't so easily distracted," the man said, clapping him on the shoulder in an almost fatherly manner as he pulled the door closed, leaving Gabby alone in the room.

He didn't lock the door this time and Jaime was surprised at how much freedom he allowed the women he kept there. Of course, the front and back doors were chained and locked even when The Stallion was inside, and all the windows were boarded up in a permanent, meticulous manner.

There were no phones in the house, no computers. Absolutely no technology of any kind aside from kitchen appliances. But even that was relegated to a microwave and a refrigerator. No stove and no knives beyond dull butter ones.

He wondered if the women inside knew that only a couple of yards away, in a decent-size shed, The Stallion kept all the things he denied the women. Computers and phones and an array of weapons, which was where The Stallion was leading Jaime now.

"We have a situation I want you briefed on. Then you may go back to our Gabriella and finish your..." He trailed off and shook his head as he locked and chained the back door they'd exited into an overgrown backyard. "Sex is such a *base* instinct, Rodriguez. Women are a worthless expense of energy. I'm fifty-three, for over half my life I have searched for the perfect woman and failed time and time again. Though, I will admit the women I've kept are of exceptional quality. Just not quite there..."

The man got a far-off look on his face as they walked through the long grass toward his shed. It was the kind of far-off look that kept Jaime up at night. Void of reason or sense, completely and utterly…incomprehensible.

The Stallion patted his shoulder again, tsking. "I know this is all going over your head. You really ought to work on your English."

Jaime shrugged. It suited his purpose to be seen as not understanding everything that went on because of a language barrier, and at times it had been hard to remember he was supposed to barely understand.

But when The Stallion started going on and on about women, Jaime never had any problems keeping his mouth shut and his expression confused. It was broken and warped and utter nonsense.

The Stallion unlocked the shed and stepped inside. Two men were sitting on chairs around The Stallion's desk, which was covered in notes and technology. The man strode right to it and sat on his little throne.

"Herman's gone missing," he said without preamble, mentioning The Stallion's most used runner in Austin. "He didn't deliver his message today, and so far no one has figured out where he disappeared to. Wallace, I'm giving you the rest of today to find him. He can't have gone too far."

The fair-haired man in the corner nodded soundlessly.

"If he *somehow* gives us the slip that long…" The Stallion continued. "Layne, you'll take him out."

Layne cracked his knuckles one by one, like he'd seen too many mobster movies. "Be my pleasure. What happens to him if Wallace finds him, though? I wouldn't mind getting some information out of him."

The Stallion's mouth curved into a cold, menacing line that, even after two years, made Jaime's blood run cold. "Rodriguez will be in charge if we find him. I'd like to see what he can do with a…shall we say, recalcitrant employee. *¿Comprende?*"

"*Sí, senor.*"

"Wallace, you're dismissed. Report every hour," The Stallion said with the flick of his wrist. "Layne, have the interrogation room readied for us, please."

Both men agreed and left the shed. Jaime stood as far from The Stallion as he could without drawing attention to the purposeful space between them. The man steepled his hands together, looking off at some unknown entity Jaime was pretty sure only he could see.

Jaime stood perfectly still, trying to appear detached and uninterested. "Did you need me, *senor*?"

The Stallion stroked his forehead with the back of his thumb, still looking somewhere else. "Once we figure out what's going on with Herman, I'll be moving on to a different location." His cold, blue gaze finally settled on Jaime. "You'll stay here and hold down the fort, and Ms. Gabriella will be yours to do whatever you please with her."

Jaime smiled. "Excellent." He didn't have to fake his excitement about that, because Jaime was almost certain Gabriella had exactly the information he'd need to pull the sting to end this whole nightmare of a job.

And then Jaime could go back to being himself and figuring out…who that was again.

Chapter Three

Gabby considered taking a nap in lieu of lunch. Her little *visit*, which she couldn't begin to understand, however, had eradicated any appetite she'd had.

That man had acted like two different people. Even the way he talked when The Stallion was present and when he wasn't was different. His voice, when he'd spoken with her, had only the faintest touches of Mexico, reminding her of her parents' accents—a sharp, hard pang of memory.

But when he spoke to The Stallion, it was all rolled R's and melodic vowels. Even his demeanor had changed. That goal or determination or whatever she thought she'd seen in him just...disappeared in the shadow of The Stallion. He was someone else. Something more feral and menacing.

But, despite the very disconcerting shirt-ripping, and the way his gaze had most definitely lingered on her chest, he had been honest with her thus far.

He hadn't hurt her, but he'd let her hurt him. Blow after blow. Considering she'd gotten into the habit of exercising to keep her overactive mind from driving her crazy, she wasn't weak. She had punched him with everything she had, and though he hadn't made too much of an outward reaction, it had to have hurt.

She shook away the thoughts, already tired of the merry-go-round in her head. If she couldn't nap or eat, she'd do the next best thing. Exercise until she was too exhausted to think or to move or to do anything but sleep.

She rolled to the ground, then pushed up, holding the plank position as she counted slowly. It had become a game, to see how long she could hold herself up like this. The counting kept her brain from circling and the physical exertion helped her sleep better.

A knock sounded at the door, which was odd. No one here knocked. Except the girls, but that was rare and only in case of emergency.

Before she could stand or say anything, the door squeaked open and in stepped the man from earlier.

She scowled at him. "I only have so many clothes, so if you're going to keep ripping them, at least get me some duct tape or something."

He pulled the door closed as he stepped inside. "I won't rip your clothes again…unless I have to." He studied her arms, eyebrows pulling together. "You're awfully strong."

"Remember that."

"It could definitely work in our favor," he muttered. "Now, where were we?"

She pushed into a standing position. "You don't want to go back to where we were. I'll hit you where it *re-*

ally hurts this time." Why he smiled at that was completely beyond her.

"You might literally be perfect."

"And you might literally be as whacked as Mr. Stallion out there."

He shook his head in some kind of odd rebuttal. "Now—"

"You act like two very different people."

He froze, every part of his body tensing as his eyes widened. "What?"

"You act like two completely different people. In here alone. With him. Two separate identities."

He was so still she wasn't even sure he breathed.

"Two separate identities, huh?"

"Your accent is different when he's not here. The way you hold yourself? It's more...relaxed when he's with you. Rigid with me. No...almost..." She cocked her head, trying to place it. "Military."

She knew she was getting somewhere at the way he still didn't move, though he'd carefully changed his wide-eyed gaze into something blank.

Yeah, she was right. "You were military."

"No."

"Police then?"

"You're an odd woman, Gabriella." He said her name with the exaggerated accent, and it reminded her of her long-dead grandfather. He hadn't been a particularly nice man or a particularly mean man. He'd been hard. Very formal. And while everyone else in her family had called her Gabby, he'd been the lone holdout.

He'd never appreciated the "Americanization" of his family, even though he'd immigrated as a young man.

"I'm right. You're…" Her eyes widened as she put it all together. Him not hurting her. Him gathering information. Being someone else with The Stallion.

He gave a sharp head shake so she didn't say anything, but she did step closer. "But you are, aren't you?"

"No," he returned easily, nodding his head as he said it.

Her heart raced, her breathing came too shallow. He was an undercover police officer. She had to blink back tears. "Tell me what it means, that you're here. Please."

He let out a long breath and stepped toward her. This time she didn't scurry away. She needed to know more than she was afraid of him. He'd checked the room for bugs before, and she knew they were safe to talk in there, but she also understood how a man like him would have to be inordinately careful. *Undercover.* What did it mean? For her? For the girls?

He inclined his mouth toward her ear, so close she could feel his breath against her neck. "I can't promise you anything. I can only tell you that I am trying to end this, so whatever information you can give me, whatever you can tell me, it'll bring me closer to finishing out my job here."

He pulled back, looking at her, his gaze serious and that determination back in his dark eyes.

She tried to repeat those first five words. *I can't promise you anything.* It was important to remember, to not get her hopes up. Just because he was an undercover police officer…just because he wanted to take

The Stallion down…it didn't mean he *would*. Or that he'd get her out in the process.

"How did you put it all together?" he asked. "I'm not…"

"You're very good. Very convincing. I'm probably the only person you let your guard down for, right?"

He nodded, still clearly perplexed and downright worried she'd figured it out.

"I don't know, ever since I got here… I remember things, and I can see…patterns that no one else seems to see. I thought I was going crazy. But… I don't know. I was always good at that. Observing, remembering, figuring out puzzles and mysteries. It just works in my head."

"Clearly," he muttered. "Hopefully you're the only one around here with that particular talent or I'm screwed."

"How long?" she asked. Was he just starting out? He was so close to The Stallion, surely…

"Two years."

She let out a breath. "That's a long time."

"Yes," he said, a bleak note in his voice that softened her another degree toward him. He'd voluntarily held his own identity hostage, separated himself from his life. He'd probably had no idea the things he'd end up missing or wanting.

God help her, she hadn't had a clue in that first day, week, month, even year. She'd had no idea the things that would grow to hurt her.

She felt a wave of sympathy for the man and, even if it was stupid or ill-advised, she had to follow it. She had to follow this first possibility in *ages* that there might be an end to this. "How can I help?"

"So, you trust me?"

"I don't trust anyone anymore," she returned, feeling a little bleak herself. "But I'll try to help you. Because I believe you are what I think you are."

"That'll work. That'll work. But there's something you have to understand. Being a different person means being a *different* person. The ripping-your-shirt thing..."

"It was for him to think that you were...having your way with me." She shuddered a little at the thought, at how close they might have to come to...proving that.

"Yes. There may be times I have to push that a little bit. Because he is..." He cleared his throat. "What do you understand about your position here? Is there a reason you were kidnapped? Is there a reason he's kept you girls...untouched?"

"I'm not really sure. I have no idea why I was taken. I was waiting at my dad's work for him to get off his shift and all of a sudden there were all these people and men talking and I was grabbed and thrown into a van with some other people. They took us somewhere that I don't know anything about. It was all dark and sometimes we were blindfolded or there were hoods put on our heads."

Gabby felt ill. She didn't relive the kidnapping anymore. She'd mostly gotten beyond *that* horror and lived in the horror of her continual imprisonment. Going back and thinking about coming here brought up all sorts of horrible memories.

How awful she'd been to her mother that night when

she'd had to cancel her date to pick up Dad. All that fear she hadn't known what to do with or how to survive with when she'd been taken, moved, inspected. But she had. She had survived and lived, and she needed to remind herself of that.

"Eventually, after I don't know how long… Actually that's not true." She didn't have to lie to this man about her memory or pretend she didn't know exactly what she knew like she did with so many people. "It was two days. It was two days from the time they took me and put me in the van to the time they took me to this other place, kind of like a warehouse. They took me—and all the people from that first moment—there and then we were sorted. Men and women went to different areas. And then The Stallion came."

"Keep going," he urged, and it was only then she realized she'd stopped because she could see it. Relive every terrifying detail of not knowing what would happen to her, or why.

"I didn't know that's who he was at the time, but he walked through and he asked everyone if we knew who he was. One woman in my group said yes and she was immediately taken away."

"Did he say his name or offer any hints about who he was beyond The Stallion?"

"No. I've gone over it a million times in my head. He must've…he must be someone, you know? He had to be someone with some kind of profile?"

"Yes, he is."

"He is?" She stepped toward the man who could mean freedom, a scary thought in and of itself. "Who?

What's his name? Why is he doing this?" she demanded, losing her cool and her calm in an instant.

"I can't answer those questions."

She grabbed his shirtfront, desperate for an answer, a reason, desperate for those things she'd finally given up on ever getting. "Tell me right this second, you miserable—"

"I'm sorry," he said so gently, so *emotionally*, she could only swallow a sob.

"He kidnapped me. He brought me here. He separated me from my family for eight years, and you can't tell me who he is?" she demanded, her voice low and scratchy but measured. She was keeping it together. She would keep it together.

"Not now. There are a lot of things I can't tell you, because everything you know jeopardizes what I'm doing here. You deserve the answers, you do, but I can't give you what you deserve right now. But if you help me, you'll have the answers, and you'll have your *life* back."

Odd *that* prompted a cold shudder to go through her body. "You can't promise me that."

"No, I can't, but I promise to put my life on the line to make it so."

She didn't know what to do with that or him, or any of this, so she turned away from him, hugging herself, trying to calm her breathing.

There were no promises. There were no guarantees. But she had a *chance*. She had to believe in it. She had to *fight* for it. With everything she had. If not for herself, for the three girls she shared this hell with. For their family's, and hers, even if they probably thought she was dead.

She owed it to a lot of people to do what this man said he would do: put her life on the line to make it so.

GABRIELLA WAS CLEARLY BRILLIANT. The way she described remembering things and figuring out patterns no one else did, to the point she thought she was crazy… It sounded like a lot of the analysts he knew. Because when you saw things no one else saw, it was very easy to convince yourself you were wrong.

But she wasn't wrong, and she had *so* much information in that pretty head of hers… Jaime was nearly excited even though she now had the power to end his life completely.

He didn't care because he was so close now. So damn close to the end of this.

She might be brilliant, but he was a trained FBI agent, after all. He wasn't going to let her figuring him out be the end. No way in hell.

"Tell me about what happened after the woman who knew who he was disappeared."

Gabriella nodded. "She was taken away from the room. She had no chance to say anything at all. After that, the rest of us women were separated into groups, and I tried to find a rhyme or reason for these groups, but I really couldn't. Except that all of the women in my group were young and reasonably fit. Dark hair, though none of the same shade—it ranged from black to light brown."

Jaime thought back to The Stallion's odd statement

about searching half his life for the perfect woman. He couldn't make sense of it, but that had to be connected to this.

"At that point, it was just six of us. The Stallion lined us up and, one by one, he inspected us."

"Inspected you how?"

Gabriella visibly shuddered, and Jaime hated that she had to relive this, but she did. If they were going to put The Stallion away, she'd probably have to relive it quite frequently.

"He touched our hair and...smelled it." She audibly swallowed, hugging herself so tightly he wished he could offer some comfort, some support.

But he was nothing to her.

"He had one of his cronies measure us."

"Measure you?"

"You know, like if you've ever been measured for clothes?" She turned to face him again, though her dark eyes were averted. But she gestured to her body as she spoke. "Shoulders, arms, chest, hips, legs, inseam, and the guy yelled out each number and The Stallion wrote it all down on this little notepad."

She was quiet for a few seconds and instead of pushing this time, he let her gain her composure, let her take the time she needed.

Time wasn't on his side, but he couldn't...lose the humanity. That was his talisman. *Don't lose your humanity.*

"He dismissed everyone except me."

Jaime didn't know how to absorb that. He could picture it too easily after everything he'd done with and for

The Stallion. The fear she must have felt having been taken for no reason, having been chosen for no reason that she understood.

It was dangerous to fill her in on the things he knew. But he had already entered dangerous territory when he had allowed himself to behave differently enough with her for her to figure out who he was. *What* he was.

"He's a sick man," Jaime offered.

"A sick man who is very, very smart or very, very lucky since he hasn't gotten caught in eight years. Probably more than that."

"Yes. Listen, there are a lot of things The Stallion does. But this thing you're involved in… He told me something just now about how he spent over half his life looking for the perfect woman. That women are basically stupid and you shouldn't dirty yourself with them unless you find this perfect specimen."

"Oh, how lovely. I'd love to show him how *stupid* I can be. With my fists."

He smiled at the irritation in her tone because it was *life*. A spark. It wasn't that shaky fear that had taken over as she had relived her kidnapping experience.

"Let him have his delusions. They might get us out of this mess." He wanted to reach out and take her shoulders or…something. Something to cement this partnership, but he was still a strange man in her room who'd ripped her shirt. He had to be careful. Human. "Between what you said and he said, I think that's what he's been doing with this arm of things. Searching for the perfect woman."

"So that's what the measuring was, then. He has

a perfect size, I just bet." Gabriella rolled her eyes. "Disgusting pig. And then when we got here he, like, tested me. He would ask these questions, and I never answered. I only fought. For weeks, every time he opened his mouth, I'd just attack. I thought maybe that's why..."

She took in a shaky breath, still hugging herself. Jaime hadn't been lying when he'd said she might be perfect. She was smart, she was strong—not just physically. Strong at her core.

"I thought for sure I would be raped, but I never have been, and I've never understood why."

"He thinks women are dirty. At least, in this context of looking for the perfect woman. I can't rationalize a madman, but the point is that you were brought here because he thought you *could* be the perfect woman. The fighting, I guess, proved to him that you weren't."

"I thought that for the longest time, but that isn't it. Jasmine—she was brought here my second year—she didn't fight him at all. She told him she'd do whatever he wanted as long as he would let her go. I was the only one who fought, but he hasn't touched any of us. No matter what our reactions were, he found us lacking in some way, I guess."

Gabriella shook her head. "So, he brought us here because we were a possibility, then he tests us and decides we're not perfect, but then why does he keep us?" She looked up at him for answers.

Jaime hated that he couldn't give them to her—and that hate kept him going. Because at least he still had a conscience. He'd started to worry. "That's where I come in. I've been working my way up to get close to figuring out who he was. When I did that, it was decided I'd stay and get enough information on him that we can arrest and prosecute."

"And you don't have that yet?"

"Not to the extent my superiors would like. Which is why we came up with a plan."

"Let me guess. You can't tell me about the plan."

"Actually, this one I can. A little. You're a gift to me."

She physically recoiled and he could hardly blame her.

"Excuse me?"

"I've slowly become his right-hand man and as I learned about the girls he keeps locked up… I wanted to get close to one of you to figure out how I could get you out. How we could all work together to get you out. So I convinced him that a woman would be better payment than drugs or money. I mean, I get paid, too, bu—"

"Of course you do. I'm sure you get money and a horse and forty acres of land. The payment of a woman is simply pocket change, right?"

"Gabriella."

She began to pace the tiny room, her irritation and anxiety so *recognizable* to him he started to feel the same build in his chest.

"This is insane," she muttered. "This is so impossible. These things don't happen! They don't happen to people in my family. They don't happen to people! This is movie craziness."

"No. It's your life," Jaime returned firmly. He needed her to focus, to get past the panic. "There's one of his compounds that has the most evidence on his whole operation, and it's the only one that I don't know where it's located. So, as I work with him right now, that's what I'm trying to figure out. If you've been watching, paying attention, listening…you might have the answer. But we have to pretend like…"

"Like I'm the gift to you. And you can do whatever you want with me," she said flatly.

"Yes. But the key here is that it's pretend. I'm not going to hurt you. I've done a lot of things that will stick with me for a very long time." He stopped talking for a few seconds so he could regain his composure. He didn't like to think back at some of the chances he'd had to take or some of the people he'd had to hurt. Though he hadn't actively killed anyone, he had no doubt some of the things he'd been involved in had led to the death of someone else.

There were a lot of terrible things you could do to a person without killing them.

He had to get hold of himself, so he did. He forced himself to look at Gabriella. She was studying him carefully, as though she could see the turmoil on his face.

To survive, he had to believe this was a very special woman who could see things no one else could. Because if she could see these things and other people could, as well, they would probably both end up dead.

"I know it sounds crazy," she said carefully, "but I know what it's like. I've helped hide drugs that I'm sure have killed people. I've had to dig holes that I think were…so he could bury people. I've had to do terrible things, and sometimes I'm not even sure that I had to. Just that I did."

"No." He took a step toward her and though he knew he had to be careful so he didn't startle her, he very slowly and gently reached out and took her hand in his. He gave it a slight squeeze.

"We've done what we had to do to survive. In my case, to bring this man to justice. We have to believe that. Above everything else."

She looked down at their joined hands. He had no idea what she saw or what she felt. It had been so long since he'd been able to touch someone in a kind way, in a gentle way, it affected him a bit harder than he'd expected.

Her hand was warm and it felt capable. She squeezed his back as though she could give him some comfort. This woman who'd been abducted from her family for eight years.

When she raised her gaze to his, he felt an odd little jitter deep in his stomach. Something like fear but not exactly. Almost like recognizing something or someone, but that didn't make sense, so he shook it away.

Chapter Four

Gabby looked at her hand, encompassed by a much larger one. She wondered if the small scars across his knuckles were from his undercover work or if he'd got them before.

What would he have been like before his assumed identity?

And what on earth did *that* matter?

She forced her gaze back to him, his dark brown eyes somehow sure and comforting, when nothing in eight years had been *comforting*. It shouldn't be potent. It was probably part of his training—looking in charge and compassionate.

She'd never been too fond of cops, though that may have been Ricky's influence. Her first serious boyfriend. A poster child for trouble. Gabby had been convinced she could change him, that everyone saw him all wrong. Her parents had been adamant that she could *not* change what was wrong with that boy.

They'd barred him from their house. Insisted Gabby live at home through her coursework at the community college, and had been making noise about her not trans-ferring to get her bachelors.

It had all seemed like the most unjust, unfair fate. They didn't have enough money, they didn't have any trust. The world had seemed cruel, and Ricky had been nice...to her.

She was twenty-eight now and that was the only re-lationship she'd ever had. A boy, really, and she'd only been a girl.

This man holding her hand was no *boy*, but she wasn't sure what she was. Except a little off her rocker for having this line of thought.

She cleared her throat and pulled her hand away. "So. What is it you need from me?"

He was quiet for a moment, studying his hand, which he hadn't dropped—it still hovered there in the air be-tween them.

"My main goal is to find the last compound," he fi-nally said, bringing his hand down to his side. "It's the one he's the most secretive about. So much so, I'm not sure he takes any of his employees there."

"I don't know if I can help with that. I did have this theory..." She trailed off. "I wish I had something to write on," she muttered. She searched her room for something...something to illustrate the picture in her head.

She opened one of her drawers and retrieved her brush, pins and ponytail holders, some of the few "ex-tras" The Stallion afforded her. A giddy excitement jum-bled through her and maybe she should calm it down.

But this was something. God, *something* to do.

Something real. Something that wasn't just pointless fighting but actually working toward a *goal*.

Freedom.

She settled herself at that word. It had come to mean something different in eight years. Or maybe it had come to mean nothing at all.

She shook those oddly uncomfortable thoughts away and looked around for a place to create her makeshift map. "I can't explain it without props," she said, setting a brush on the center of the floor.

"Let's do it on the bed instead of the floor, so if anyone comes in we can…" He rubbed a hand over his unkempt if short beard. "Well, cover it up."

Right. Because to The Stallion she was a *gift*. No, that was too generous. She was a thing to be traded for services. She shuddered at the thought but…the man kneeled at the bed. The man who hadn't used her as payment but was using her as an informant.

The man whose name she didn't know.

"What should I call you?" she asked suddenly. Because she was working with this man to free—no, not to free anything, but to bring down The Stallion—and she hadn't a clue as to what to call him.

He glanced at her and she must be dreaming the panic she saw in his expression because it disappeared in only a second.

"They call me Rodriguez," he said carefully. "But my name is Jaime A— I…" He shook his head as he focused, as he seemed to push away whatever was plaguing him. "Call me Rodriguez. It's safest."

She knelt next to him, biting back the urge to repeat

Jaime. Just to feel what his name would sound like in her mouth.

Silly. "All right, Rodriguez." She placed the brush at the center of the bed. "This is Austin. The bed is Texas. I don't have a clue…" She trailed off, realizing this man would know where they were. He hadn't been blindfolded or hooded. He actually *knew* if they were still in Texas, if they were close to home.

She breathed through the emotion swamping her. "Where are we?" she whispered.

"An hour east of El Paso. Middle of nowhere, basically. Only a few small towns around."

She blinked. El Paso. She'd had theories about where they could be, and El Paso had factored into them, but theories and truths were…

"Take your time," Jaime said gently.

"But we don't have much time, do we?" she returned, staring into compassionate eyes for the first time in eight years. Because as much as all the girls felt sorry for each other, they felt sorry for themselves first and foremost.

Jaime nodded toward the bed. "Technically, I don't know how much time we have. I only know the quicker we figure it out, the less chance he has of hurting people. More people."

She took a deep breath and returned her focus to the bed. "The brush is Austin. I get the feeling that's something like…the center. I don't know if it's a head-quarters or…"

"Technically, he lives in Austin. His public persona, anyway."

His public persona. Though it fit everything she knew or had theorized, it was hard to believe The Stallion went about a normal life in Austin and people didn't see something was wrong with the man. Warped and broken beyond comprehension.

"So, we've got his personal center at Austin," Jaime continued for her, taking one of the rubber bands she'd piled next to her. He reached past her, his long, muscular arm brushing against her shoulder. "And this is the compound close to El Paso."

"Right. Right." She picked up another rubber band. "He seems to work by seasons, sort of. I started wondering if he had a place in each direction. If this is west, he has a compound in the north, the south and the east. Unless Austin is his east." She placed rubber bands in general spots that represented each direction, creating a diamond with Austin at the somewhat center.

"He has a compound in the Panhandle. Though I haven't been there, he's talked of it. I've been to the one on the Louisiana border. I didn't think he had women there, but… Now that I've seen this setup, maybe he did and I just didn't know about it."

The idea that there'd been women to help and he hadn't helped them clearly bothered him, but he kept talking. "But south… He's never mentioned any kind of holdings in the south of Texas." He tapped the lower portion of her bed. "It has to be south."

"It would make sense. The access to drugs, people."

"It would make all the sense in the world, and you, Gabriella, are something of a miracle." He grinned over at her.

"It's… Gabby. Everyone, except *him*, calls me Gabby."

His grin didn't fade so much as morph into something else, something considering or…

The door swung open and the next thing Gabby knew, she was being thrust onto the bed and under a very large man.

JAIME HADN'T HAD a woman underneath him in over two years, and that should not at all be the thought in his head right now. But she was soft underneath him, no matter how strong she was…soft breasts, soft hair.

And a kidnapping victim, jackass.

"Rodriguez. Boss wants you." Layne's cruel mouth was twisted into a smirk, clearly having no compunction about interrupting…well, what this looked like, not so much what it was.

Damn these men and their interruptions. He was getting somewhere, and he didn't mean on top of Gabriella.

Gabby.

He couldn't call her that. Couldn't think of her like that. She was a tool, and a victim. Any slipups and they could both end up dead. He glanced down at her, completely still underneath him, and it was enough of a distraction that he was having trouble deciding how to play things in front of Layne.

She blinked up at him, eyes wide, and though she wasn't fighting him, he'd scared her. No matter that she understood him, his role here, he didn't think she'd be trusting him any time soon. How could he blame her for that?

Wordlessly he got off Gabby and the bed and straightened his clothes in an effort to make Layne think he was more rumpled than he really was.

"We'll finish this later," he said offhandedly to Gabby, hoping it sounded to Layne like a hideous threat.

Jaime sauntered over to the door, not looking back at Gabby to see what she was doing, though that's desperately what he wanted to do. He grabbed his sunglasses from his pocket and slipped them on his face as he stepped out into the hallway with Layne.

"Awfully clothed, aren't you?" Layne asked.

Jaime closed the door behind him before he answered. "Still trying to knock the fight out of her. Wouldn't want to intimidate her with what's coming." Jaime smirked as if pleased with himself instead of disgusted.

"It's a hell of a lot better when there's still a little fight in them," Layne said, glancing back at Gabby's door as they walked down the hall.

Jaime's body went cold, but he reined in his temper, curling his fingers into fists, his only—and most necessary—reaction.

"Do you think *senor* would be pleased with that world view?" he asked as blandly as he could manage.

Layne's gaze snapped to Jaime and his threat. The man sneered. "Not every idiot believes your Pepe Le Pew act, buddy."

Jaime flashed his most intimidating grin, one devoid of any of the *humanity* he was desperate to believe he still had. "Pepe Le Pew is French, *culo*."

"Whatever," the man said with a disinterested wave. "You know what I mean."

"I know a lot of things about you, *amigo*," Jaime said, enjoying the way the man rolled his eyes at every Spanish word he threw into the conversation.

Layne didn't take the hint. "Maybe you want to pass her around a bit. Boss man's been pretty strict about us getting anything out of these girls but you—"

Jaime stopped and shoved Layne into the wall. What he really wanted to do was punch the man, but he knew that would put his credibility in jeopardy, no matter how much dirt he had on Layne. He wrestled with the impulse, with the beating violence inside him.

No matter what this man might deserve, he was not Jaime's end goal. The end goal was to make this all moot.

So, he held Layne there, against the wall, one fist bunched in the man's T-shirt to keep him exactly where he wanted him. He stared down at the man with all the menace he felt. "You will not touch what is mine," Jaime threatened, making his intent clear.

"You've already stepped all over what's mine," Layne returned, but Jaime noted he didn't fight back against Jaime's hold—intelligence or strategy, Jaime wasn't sure.

"I ran this show before he brought you in," Layne growled.

"Well, now you answer to me. So, I'd watch your step, *amigo*. I know things about you I don't think The Stallion would particularly care to hear about. A hooker in El Paso, for starters."

Layne blustered, but underneath it the man had paled. This was why Jaime preferred everyone think of him as muscle who could barely understand English. They underestimated him. But Jaime hadn't walked in here blindly. He knew The Stallion's previous head honchos wouldn't take the power share easily. So he'd collected leverage.

Thank God.

"Now, are you ready to keep your disgusting tongue and hands to yourself?" Jaime asked with an almost pleasant smile. "Or do I have to make your life difficult?"

Layne ground his teeth together, a sneer marring his features, but he gave a sharp nod.

"Muy bueno," Jaime said, pretending it was great news as he released the piece of garbage. "Let's proceed, then." He gestured grandly down the hall to the back door.

Layne grumbled something, but Jaime was relieved to see concern and fear on the man's face. He could only hope it would keep the man in line.

They exited the house and Jaime waited while Layne chained everything up. The late summer sun shimmered in the green of the trees, and if Jaime didn't know what lurked in the shed across the grass, he might have relaxed.

As it was, relaxing wasn't happening any time soon.

Jaime let Layne lead the way to the shed. He preferred to touch as little as possible in that little house of horrors.

Both men stepped in to find The Stallion pacing, hands clutched behind his back, and Wallace looking wary in the far corner.

The Stallion looked up distractedly. "Good. Good. We've gotten news of Herman before Wallace even got anywhere." The man's hands shook as he brought them in front of him in fists, fury stamped across his face. The usual calm calculation in his eyes something darker and more frenzied. "With the Texas Rangers and a hypnotist." The Stallion slammed a fist to the desk that made the creepy-ass dolls on the shelf above shake, their dead lifeless eyes fluttering at the vibration.

Jaime forced himself to look away and stare flatly at his boss. *Fake boss*, he amended.

"Luckily, Mr. Herman doesn't know enough to give them much of a lead, but he certainly represents a loose end." The Stallion took a deep breath, plucking one of the brunette dolls from the shelf. He cradled it like a child.

It took every ounce of Jaime's control and training to keep the horror off his face. Grown men capable of murder cradling a doll was not…comforting in the least.

"I've sent a team to get rid of Herman. Scare the hypnotist. I don't think I want to extinguish her yet. She might be valuable. But I want her *scared*." He squeezed the doll so tight it was a wonder one of its plastic limbs didn't break off.

"There we are, pretty girl," The Stallion cooed, re-settling the doll on the shelf and brushing a hand over its fake hair.

Jaime shuddered and looked away.

"Until this mess is taken care of, you are all on lock-down. No one is leaving the premises until Herman is taken care of."

"Then, boss?" Layne asked a little too hopefully.

The Stallion smiled pleasantly. "And then we'll decide what to do about the hypnotist."

Lockdown and death threats. Jaime tried to breathe through the urgency, the failure, the impossibility of saving this man's life.

He'd try. Somehow, he'd try. But he had the sinking suspicion Herman was already gone.

Chapter Five

Gabby couldn't sleep. It wasn't an uncommon affliction. Even in the past two years, exercising herself to exhaustion, giving up on things ever being different, avoiding figuring out the pieces of The Stallion puzzle, insomnia still plagued her.

Because no matter how she tried to accept her lot in life, she'd always known this wasn't *home*.

But what *would* be home? Her father was dead. Her sister would be an adult woman with a life of her own. Would Mom and Grandma still live in the little house on East Avenue or would they have moved?

Did they assume she was dead? Would they have kept all her things or gotten rid of them? The blue teddy bear Daddy had given her on her sixth birthday. The bulletin board of pictures of friends and Ricky and her and Nattie.

Her heart absolutely ached at the thought of her sister. Two years apart, they hadn't always gotten along, but they had been friends. Sisters. They'd shared things, laughed together, cried together, fought together.

Tears pricked Gabby's eyes. She hadn't had this kind

of sad nostalgia swamp her in years, because it led nowhere good. She couldn't change her circumstances. She was stuck in this prison and there was no way out.

Except maybe Jaime.

That was not an acceptable thought. She could work with him to take down The Stallion, and she would, but actually thinking she could get out of there was... It was another thing altogether.

She froze completely at the telltale if faint sound of her door opening. And then closing. She closed her hands into fists, ready to fight. She couldn't drown that reaction out of herself, no matter how often she wondered if giving in was simply easier.

"Gabby."

A hushed whisper, but even if she didn't remember people's voices so easily, she would have known it was Jaime—*Rodriguez*—from a man calling her Gabby.

Gabby. She swallowed against all of the fuzzy feelings inside her. Home and Gabby and what did either even mean anymore. She didn't have a home. The Gabby she'd been was dead.

It didn't matter. Taking The Stallion down was the only thing that mattered. She sat up in the dark, watched Jaime's shadow get closer.

The initial fear hadn't totally subsided. She wasn't *afraid* of him per se or, maybe more accurately, she wasn't afraid he would harm her. But that didn't mean there weren't other things to be afraid of.

She had sat up on the bed, but he still loomed over her from his standing position. She banked the edgy nerves fluttering inside her chest.

He kneeled, much like he had earlier today when they'd been putting together her map. Except she was on the bed instead of her makeshift markers.

"Do you have any more ideas about the locations? Aside from directions?" he asked, everything about him sounding grave and…tired.

"I have a few theories. Do we…do we need to go over all that tonight?"

"I'm sorry. You were sleeping."

"Well, no." She had the oddest urge to offer her hand to him. He'd taken her hand earlier today and there had been something… "Is something wrong?"

He laughed, caustic and bitter, and she didn't know this man. He could be lying to her. He could be anyone. Then there was her, cut off from normal human contact for *eight* years. The only place she had to practice any kind of compassion or reading of people was with the other girls, and she'd been keeping her distance lately.

So she was probably way off base to think something was wrong, to feel like he was off somehow.

But he stood, pacing away from the bed, a dark, agitated shadow. "It doesn't get any easier to know someone's going to die. I tried…" He shook his head grimly. "We should focus on what we can do."

"You tried what?" Gabby asked, undeterred.

"I tried to get a message to the Rangers, but…" He kneeled again and she couldn't see him in the dark, found it odd she wanted to.

"But?"

"I think it was too late."

Gabby inhaled sharply. Whether she knew him or

not, whether she'd lost all ability to gauge people's emotions, she could all but *feel* his guilt and regret as though it were her own.

She didn't know what the answer to that was...what he might have endured in pretending to be the kind of man who worked for The Stallion. Gabby couldn't begin to imagine... Though she'd ostensibly worked for the man, she'd never had to pretend she liked it.

"If we're an hour west of El Paso, I would imagine each spot would be likely the same distance from the city in its sector," she said, because the only answer she knew was bringing The Stallion down.

It couldn't bring dead people back, including herself, but it could stop the spread. They had to stop the spread.

She kept going when he said nothing. "He's very methodical. Things are the same. He stays here the same weeks every year. He eats the same things, does the same things. I would imagine whatever other places he has are like this one. Possibly identical."

In the dark she couldn't see what Jaime's face might be reflecting and he was completely and utterly still.

"Jaime..."

"Rodriguez. We have to...we can't be too complacent. There's too much at stake. I am Rodriguez."

"Okay," she returned, and she supposed he was right, no matter how much she preferred to call him something—anything—other than what The Stallion called him.

"But you're right. The eastern compound was around an hour west of Houston. I wonder... He is methodical, you're right about that. I wonder if the mileage would be exactly the same."

"It wouldn't shock me."

"Have you seen the dolls?"

Gabby could only blink in Jaime's shadow's direction. "Dolls?"

"He has a shelf of dolls in his office. They sit in a row. I'd always thought they were creepy, but today…" Jaime laughed again, this one wasn't quite as bitter as the one before, but it certainly wasn't true humor. "You should get some rest. I didn't mean to interrupt you. We can talk in the morning." He got to his feet.

She didn't analyze why she bolted off the bed to follow him. Even if she gave herself the brain time to do it, she wouldn't have come up with an answer.

He was a lifeline. To what, she didn't know. She didn't have a life—not one here, not one to go back to.

"I wasn't sleeping." She scurried between him and the room's only exit. "What about the dolls?"

He was standing awfully close in his attempt to leave, but he neither reached around her for the door nor pushed her out of the way. He simply stood there, an oppressive, looming shadow.

Gabby didn't know what possessed her, why she thought in a million years it was appropriate to reach out and touch a man she'd only met today. But what did it *matter*? She'd been here eight years and worrying about normal or appropriate had left the building a long time ago.

So she placed her palm on his chest, hard and hot even through the cotton of his T-shirt. Such a strange sensation to touch someone in neither fight nor comfort. Just gentle and…a connection.

"Tell me about the dolls," she said in the same tone she used with the girls when she wanted them to listen and stop whining. "Get it off your chest."

HIS CHEST. WHERE Gabby's hand was currently touching him between the vee of straps that kept his weapons at hand. Gently, very nearly *comfortingly*, her hand rested in the center of all that violent potential.

Jaime was not in a world where that had happened for years. His mother had hugged him hard and long that last meal before he'd gone undercover, and that had been it. Two years, three months and twenty-one days ago.

He had known what he was getting himself into and yet he hadn't. There had been no way to anticipate the toll it would take, the length of time and how far he'd gotten.

That meant bringing The Stallion to justice was really the only thing that could matter, not a woman's hand on his chest.

And yet he allowed himself the briefest moment of putting his hand over hers. He allowed himself a second of absorbing the warmth, the proof of beating life and humanity, before he peeled her hand off his chest.

"He cradled the doll like a baby. Talked to it. Damn creepiest thing I've ever seen—and I've seen some things." He said it all flippantly, trying to imbue some humor into the statement, but it felt good to get it out.

The image haunted him. A grown man. A doll. The threat on a man who would most certainly be dead even if Jaime's secret message to his FBI superiors made it through.

Dead. Herman, a man he'd never met and knew next to nothing about, was dead. Because he hadn't been able to stop it.

"Dolls." Gabby seemed to ponder this, and though her hand was no longer on his chest, she still stood between him and the door, far too close for anyone's good.

"If there are identical dolls in every compound, I'll never be able to sleep again after this is all over."

Even in the dark he could see her head cock, could *feel* her gaze on him. "Do you think of after?"

"Sometimes," he offered truthfully, though the truth was the last thing they should be discussing. "Sometimes I have to or I'm afraid I'll forget it isn't real."

"I stopped believing 'after' could be real," she whispered, heavy and weighted in the dark room of a deranged man's hideout.

He wanted to touch her again. Cradle her small but competent hand in his larger one against his chest. He wanted to make her a million promises he couldn't keep about *after*.

"I... I can't think about after, but I can think about ending him. If we're an hour west of El Paso, give or take, and the western compound is an hour west of Houston, then what would the southern compound be? San Antonio?"

"If we're going from the supposition it's the closest guarded one because it's closest to the border, I think it'd be farther south."

"Yes." She made some movement, though he couldn't make it out in the dark. Likely they could turn on the lights and no one would think anything of it, she had been a gift to him, after all, but he found as long as she didn't turn on the lights, he didn't want to, either.

There was something comforting about the dark. About this woman he didn't know. About the ability to say that a man's life wasn't saved probably because of him. Because who else could he express that remorse to? No one here. No one in his undercover life.

He finally realized she had moved around him. She wasn't exactly pacing, but neither was she still in the pitch-black room.

He couldn't begin to imagine how she'd done it. This darkness. This uncertainty. For eight years she had been at someone else's mercy. As much as he sometimes felt like he was at someone else's mercy, it was voluntary. It was for a higher purpose. If he really wanted to, if he didn't care about bringing The Stallion down, he could walk away from all this.

But she was here and said she couldn't even think about after. Instead she lived and fought and puzzled things together in her head. Remembered things no one would expect her to.

She was the key to this investigation. Because she'd been that strong.

"Loredo, maybe?" she offered.

"It's possible," Jaime returned, reminding himself to focus on the task at hand rather than this woman. "Doesn't quite match the pattern of being close to bigger cities like Houston and El Paso."

"True, and he does like his patterns." She was quiet for a minute. "But what about the northern compound? There isn't anything up there that matches Houston or

El Paso, either. Maybe whatever town in the south it's near matches whatever town is north."

"I haven't been to the northern one, so I don't know for sure, but one would assume Amarillo. Based on what I know."

"Laredo and Amarillo would be similar. Was the place west of Houston similar to this?"

It was something Jaime hadn't given much thought to, but now that she mentioned it… "I never went in the house, but there was one. It didn't look the same from the outside, but it's very possible that the layout inside was exactly the same."

"If you didn't go in the house, where did you go there?"

It confirmed Jaime's suspicion that the girls didn't know anything about the outside world around them. "He has a shed for an office outside."

"It must be in the back. He had us dig holes in the front."

It shouldn't shock him The Stallion used the women he kidnapped for manual labor, and yet the thought of Gabby digging shallow graves for that man settled all wrong in his gut. "Did you ever see…?"

"We just dug the holes and were ushered back inside," she replied, her tone flat. Though she had brought it up yesterday when they'd first met, so clearly it bugged her. "It's the only time I've been out…" She shook her head. "The office shed. Is the one here the same as the one in the west?"

He wanted to tell her she'd make a good cop—focusing on the facts and details over emotions—but that spoke of an after she couldn't bring herself to consider. So he answered her question instead.

"The one he has here is a little bit more involved than the one he had there. And no dolls."

"The doll thing really bothers you, huh?"

"Hey, you watch a grown man cradle and coo at a doll the way a normal person would an infant and tell me you wouldn't be haunted for life."

Though it was dark and Jaime had no idea if his instincts were accurate without seeing her expression, he thought maybe she was teasing him. An attempt at lightening things a little. He appreciated that, even if it was a figment of his imagination.

"As long as I'm on lockdown, I can't share any of this information with my superiors. It would be too dangerous and too risky, and I've already risked enough by trying to warn them about..." He trailed off, that inevitable, heavy guilt choking out the words.

"If the man ends up dead, it has nothing to do with you," Gabby said firmly.

"It's hardly nothing. I knew. And I didn't stop it."

"Because you're here to bring down The Stallion. Doing that is going to save more men than saving one man. Maybe I wouldn't have thought about it that way years ago, but... You begin to learn that you can't save everyone, and that some things happen whether it's *fair* or not. I hate the word *fair*. Nothing is fair."

That was not something he could even begin to argue with a woman who'd been kidnapped eight years ago.

"Do you know who this man was?" she demanded in the inky dark.

"He delivered messages for The Stallion."

"Then I don't feel sorry for him at all."

"You don't?" he asked, surprised at her vehemence for a man she didn't know.

"No. He worked for that man, and I don't care who you are or how convincing he is in his real life, if you work for that man, you deserve whatever you get."

She said it flatly, with certainty, and there was a part of him that wanted to argue with her. Because he knew things like this could make you hard. Rightfully so, even. She deserved her anger and hatred and her uncompromising views.

But he could not adopt them as his own. He was afraid if he did that he would never find his way out of this. That he would become Rodriguez for life and forget who Jaime Alessandro was. It was his biggest fear.

He felt sorry for Gabby, but it made him all the more determined to make sure she got out. He would make sure she had a chance to find her compassion again.

"Until I can get more intel to my superiors, the next step is to keep gathering as much information as we can. The more I can give them when the time comes, the better chance we have of ending this once and for all."

"End." She laughed, an odd sound, neither bitter nor humorous. Just kind of a noise. "I'm not sure I know what that word means anymore."

"I'll teach you." That was a foolish thing to say, and yet he would. He would find a way to show her what endings meant. And what new beginnings could be about.

Because if he could show her, then he could believe he could show himself.

Chapter Six

Gabby was tired and bleary-eyed the next day. Jaime
had stayed in her room for most of the night and they
had talked about The Stallion, sure, but as the night
had worn on, they'd started to veer toward things they
remembered about their former lives.

She'd kept telling herself to stop, not to tell yet another story about Natalie or not to listen to another about
the birthday dinners his mother used to make him. And
yet remembering her family and the woman she'd been
years ago—which had never been tempting to her in
all these years—had been more than just tempting in a
dark room with Jaime.

She should think of him as nothing but Rodriguez.
She shouldn't be forming some odd friendship with a
man whose only job was to bring down The Stallion.
Knowing those things seemed to disappear when she
was actually in a room with him.

He was fascinating and kind. She missed kindness.
In a way she hadn't been able to articulate in the past
eight years. The other kidnapped girls were mostly nice.
Alyssa was a little hard, but Gabby had spent many a

night holding Jasmine or Tabitha as they cried. She had reassured them they wouldn't be hurt and hoped she wasn't lying. She had given them all kindness and compassion, but there was something about being the first—the older member, so to speak—that meant none of the girls offered the same to her.

Gabby was the mother figure. The martyr to them. Everyone thought she was strong and fine and somehow surviving this. But she wasn't. She was broken.

Jaime saw the victim in her, though. It should be awful, demoralizing, and yet it was the most comforted she'd felt in eight years.

But it would weaken her. It *was* weakening her. There was this war in her brain and her heart whether that weakening mattered.

Maybe she should be weak. Maybe she should lean completely on this strange angel of a man and let him take care of everything. If it all worked out in the end and The Stallion was brought down, and she was free—

She wasn't going to go that far. She'd save thinking about freedom for after.

So she sat at the kitchen table with Jasmine, Tabitha and Alyssa eating breakfast and wondering what Jaime would be up to this morning. Would he be as exhausted as she was? Would he be thinking of her?

Foolish girl. But it nearly made her smile—to feel foolish and stupid. It was somehow a comfort to know she could be something normal. Stupid felt deliciously normal.

At Jasmine's sharply inhaled gasp, Gabby glanced up from her microwaved oatmeal. All the girls were looking wide-eyed at the entrance to the hallway.

Jaime stood there in his dedicated black, weapons strapped against his chest. Those sunglasses on his face. Gabby wondered if there was a purpose to always wearing them. So no one could see the kindness in his eyes. Because even in the dark she had to think that kindness would radiate off a man like him.

Since the girls seemed scared into silence, she nodded toward him. "Rodriguez."

"You know him?" Jasmine squeaked under her breath.

"He's The Stallion's new right-hand man." She looked back at Jaime and tried to work on the sarcastic sneer she sent most of the guards. "Right?"

Jaime's lips quirked and she could almost believe it was in pride, but she saw the disgust lingering underneath it.

Was she the only one who saw that? Based on the way Jasmine scooted closer to her, as though Gabby could protect her from the man, Gabby wondered.

"Senorita."

It took everything in her not to roll her eyes at him and smile at that exaggerated accent.

"You're wanted privately, Gabriella," he said with enough menace she should have been scared. She didn't think the little fissure of nerves that went through her was *fear*.

"But, please, finish your *desayuno*. I am nothing if not gracious with my time."

Gabby began to push her chair back, the crappy packet oatmeal completely forgotten. But Jasmine's fingers curled around her arm and held on tight.

"Don't go, Gabby. Fight."

Gabby looked down at Jasmine, surprised that none of the women seemed to see the lack of threat underneath Jaime's act. But then, they didn't know what she knew. Maybe that made all the difference.

"It's all right. When have I ever not been able to handle myself?" She smiled reassuringly at... Sometimes she thought of the girls as her friends. Sometimes as her charges. And sometimes simply people she didn't really know. She didn't know what she felt today. But she patted Jasmine's arm before peeling the woman's fingers off her wrist. "I'll be back for lunch."

"Don't make promises you can't keep, *senorita*."

She shot Jaime a glare she didn't have to fake. He didn't have to make these women more scared. They already did that themselves.

She walked over to where Jaime stood in the entrance to the hallway. He made a grand gesture with his arm. "After you, Gabriella."

Again she had to fight to mask her face from amusement. He should go into acting once this was all over. The stage where his over-the-top antics might be appreciated.

As she began to walk down the corridor to her room, Jaime's hand clamped on her shoulder. Hot and hard and tight. She didn't have to feign the shiver or the wild worry that shot through her.

It wasn't comfortable that he could turn himself on and off so easily. It wasn't comfortable that, though she was intrigued by the man and convinced of his kindness, she didn't know him at all. Anything he'd told her so far could be lies.

When he acted like this other man, she could remember she shouldn't trust him. She couldn't believe everything he said. He could be as big a liar as The Stallion, and just as dangerous.

But they walked to her room with his hand clamped on her shoulder and somehow in the short walk it became something of a comfort. A calming presence of strength. She missed someone else having strength. True courage. Not the strength The Stallion or his guards exerted. Not that physical, brute force.

No, Jaime was full of certainty. Confidence. He was full of righteous goodness and she wanted to follow that anywhere it would lead.

She wanted to believe in righteous goodness again. That it was possible. That it could save her.

And what will happen after you're saved?

Jaime closed the door behind them, taking off his sunglasses and sliding them into his pocket. Immediately his entire demeanor changed. How did he do it? She opened her mouth to ask him but he seemed suddenly rushed.

"We don't have much time. There's a meeting in ten minutes and Layne will be sent to fetch me. I need… when he comes…"

She cocked her head because he didn't finish his sentence. He studied her and then he swallowed, almost nervously. "I'll have to, uh, do what I did the other day."

"The other day?"

"I'll try not to rip your shirt, but I'm going to need to…er, well, grab you."

"Oh." She let out a shaky breath, the white-hot fear of

that moment revisiting her briefly. "Right. Well, okay. But, uh, you know, not ripping my clothes would be preferred, if only because I don't have many."

His lips almost curved, but mostly something heavily weighted his mouth and him. She supposed he could play the part of Rodriguez easily enough in front of whoever walked through, but demonstrating the physical force expected of him? No. She couldn't imagine Jaime ever getting comfortable with that.

Maybe she was wrong. Maybe she was making everything up. Maybe he enjoyed scaring women and she was stupidly coping by turning him into a hero.

If a hero hadn't saved her in the past eight years, why would she think one would now?

"What do you know about his schedule? You said something about him staying certain times in certain places. Is he usually here, at this location, at this time?"

Gabby filtered through her memories. The ways she used to count days. Her many theories about The Stallion's yearly travel.

"Yes. He'd usually be here, but getting ready to leave." She tried to work out the days that would be left, but she'd stopped paying such close attention to the days and—

The thought hit her abruptly—a sharp blow to the chest as she met his intense brown gaze. "You know what day it is." She'd meant that to be a question, not the shaky accusation it had turned into.

He blinked down at her. Something in his face softened and then shuttered blank. "August 23, 2017."

She did the math in her head, trying to get through

the shaky feeling of knowing what day it was. What actual day. For so long she'd known, but in the past two years she'd let it slide to seasons at most.

It was 2017. She'd been here for the entirety of the 2010s.

"Gabby." He touched her shoulder again, not the hard clamp of a guiding hand but a gentle laying of his palm to the slope of her arm. It was weird not to flinch. Weird not to want to. She wanted to lean into the strong presence. To the way he seemed to have everything under control…even when he didn't.

"August twenty-third. I would say usually he leaves for the southern compound on the twenty-sixth. I think. Around there. Never quite at the end of the month, but close."

Jaime smiled down at her, clearly pleased with the information.

When was the last time she'd seen a smile that wasn't sarcastic? When had anyone tried to smile at her reassuringly in eight long years? It hadn't happened.

She quashed the emotional upheaval inside her. Or, at least, she tried. It must've showed on her face, though, because he moved his hand up to her cheek, a rough, calloused warmth against her skin.

She knew he wanted to fix this for her. To promise her safety. But she didn't want to hear it. Promises… No, she wanted nothing to do with those.

JAIME WAS LOSING track of time and it wouldn't do. But she looked so sad. So completely overwhelmed by the weight of her existence here. He wanted to do something, anything, to comfort her. To take the tears in her eyes away, to take the despair on her face and stamp it out. He wanted to promise her safety and hope and a new life.

But he could promise none of those things. This was dangerous business, and they could easily end up dead. Both of them.

No matter that he would do everything in his power to not let that happen, it didn't mean it wasn't possible. It would be worse to promise something he couldn't deliver than to fail his mission.

"That means we'll have to wait about three more days. If he has me stay here while he goes to the southern compound, it gives me the opportunity to get this new information to my superiors. If he wants me to go with him, then I'll know where it is. Either way, we win."

"We may win the battle but not the war," she stated simply, resolutely. He wondered if she was just a little too afraid of getting hopes up herself.

He brushed his thumb down her cheek, even though it was the last thing he should've done. But though she was probably more gaunt than she would have been had she been living her actual life, though she was pale when the rich olive of her complexion should be sun-kissed, she was soft. And something special.

Her eyebrows drew together, but she wasn't looking at him. She was looking at the door and she mouthed something to him, but he couldn't catch what it was. She didn't hesitate. She grabbed him by the shoulders and pulled him close, her big brown eyes wide but determined. She mouthed the words again and this time he thought he caught them.

The door. Someone was at the door. Behind the door. That meant there was only one thing he could do. He choked back his complicated emotions and dropped his mouth to her ear.

"I'm going to kiss you. It won't be nice. The minute the door opens, shove me away with everything you've got. Understand?"

Her eyes were still wide, her hands on his shoulders. As if she trusted him.

She gave a nod and all he could do was say a little prayer that this would not be…complicated. But if someone was listening at the door, he had to prove he was Rodriguez and nothing more. That meant not being nice. That meant taking what he wanted whether it was what she wanted. And then, somehow, not getting lost in that. Humanity. His calling card. To keep his humanity.

But first… First he had to be Rodriguez. That meant he could not gently lower his mouth to hers. He had to take. He had to plunder.

And he had to stop talking to himself about it and do it.

He slid his arm around her waist and pulled her to him roughly. It was both regret and something far darker he didn't want to analyze that twined through him. He crushed his mouth to hers if only to stop his brain from moving in this hideous circle.

He focused on the fact that it wasn't supposed to be nice or easy. It was supposed to scare and intimidate. If she trembled, he was only doing his job. He was proving to everyone that he was Rodriguez—awful and mean, a broken excuse for a human being.

He thrust his tongue into her mouth and tried not to commit her taste to memory. But when was the last time he'd tasted a woman? Sweet and hot. Uncertain, and yet, brave with it. She let his tongue explore her mouth and she did not fight him.

He scraped his teeth along her plump bottom lip and fought to remember who he really was. Not this man, but a man with a badge. A protector. A believer in law and order.

Gabby's fingers tensed on his shoulders and then relaxed. She did something that felt like a sigh against his mouth, and then he was being pushed violently back and away from sweet perfection.

He allowed himself two steps from the shove before stopping. He did everything to ignore the way his body trembled. Ignored the desperate erection pressing against his jeans. Ignored the inappropriate desire running through his blood. It was wrong and it was cruel but surely his body's natural reaction to that sort of thing after such a long absence.

Or so he told himself.

He didn't look at Gabby because it would surely unman him completely. Instead he turned to face the interruption with a sneer on his mouth.

Layne didn't need to know the hatred in his expression was for himself, not the interruption.

"You have the worst timing, *amigo*," he said, trying to eradicate the affectedness from his voice. "I grow weary of it."

Layne snorted. "You knew I was coming to fetch you at one. And here you are, yet again, clothed and being pushed around by a woman. Starting to question your strength, Rodriguez."

"Question all you want. Then test me. I'd love you to."

Layne merely crossed his hands over his chest. "Boss wants us now."

"Sí." Jaime strode to the door, making sure never to look back at Gabby. The only reason Jaime paused in the hallway instead of going straight to The Stallion was to ensure Layne left Gabby's room without saying a damn thing. Because if that man said something to her...

Jaime balled his hands into fists. He had to get his temper under control. He wasn't pissed off at Layne. The man had done exactly what he was supposed to.

Jaime was pissed at himself.

Much like the afternoon before, Jaime let Layne lead him down the hall and outside. When they entered the shed this time, The Stallion's demeanor was calm rather than the unhinged anger of yesterday. He was sitting at his desk all but smiling.

"You're late. I suggest you get that kind of impulse under control. I demand timeliness in all things, gentlemen."

"Sí, senor."

"Now that that's been taken care of, we have our next target."

"The hypnotist?" Wallace asked from the corner.

"Yes, but not just her. A Texas Ranger has taken it upon himself to protect this young woman. I sent two men to follow them and to bring her to me." The Stallion reclined in his chair, his smile widening.

"What about the Ranger?" Jaime asked.

"He's of no use to us. I want her," The Stallion said with a sneer. "I hate when law enforcement try to get in my way. Bunch of useless pigs. We'll get rid of him and take the girl. The girl is *very* important." The Stallion's empty blue eyes zeroed in on Jaime. "There is a message I want you to deliver to our Gabriella, Rodriguez."

Jaime tried to maintain a blank expression, but it was hard with the addition of Gabby into the conversation. That should be a warning in it of itself that he was letting himself get too wrapped up in this whole thing.

"The hypnotist has quite the interesting connection to our oldest guest."

"Connection?" Jaime repeated, hoping he covered the demand with enough confusion in his tone to make The Stallion think it was a language barrier issue.

"Natalie Torres is our hypnotist. Whatever Herman told her and this Ranger, I want to know it. But more, I want the girl." The Stallion turned his computer screen to face Layne and Jaime. "The resemblance. Do you see it?"

Jaime schooled himself into complete indifference. *"Sí."* The woman in the picture was more slight of build than Gabby and she had a softer chin and a sharper nose. But she had the same mass of curly black hair. The same big brown eyes.

"Tell our Gabriella her sister will be joining us soon. Make sure you mention how close she was to being the perfect woman. Perhaps her sister will fit the role she could not." The Stallion leaned back in his chair, smiling a self-satisfied smirk.

Jaime tried to match it, afraid it only looked like a scowl. But if he failed, The Stallion was too happy with himself to notice.

Chapter Seven

Gabby knew it was beyond foolish to wait in the dark and hope Jaime would come to her again. She'd answered the questions he'd needed answered and he probably had henchman things to do.

Besides, she didn't really want to see him. Not after that kiss, which was hardly fair to call a kiss since it wasn't real. Like her life. It was a shallow approximation of something else. No matter how his mouth on hers had rioted through her like some sort of miracle.

She was clearly delirious or crazy. Maybe it was some sort of rescue-fantasy type thing that all kidnap victims succumbed to. She didn't know, and it wouldn't matter. Because it had all been fake. It had been a show.

Layne was… Gabby didn't know if "suspicious" was the right word, but he clearly didn't like Jaime and that was going to be dangerous. Because he would be watching him and making sure that whatever moves he made matched up with the man he was supposed to be. Making enemies as an undercover agent had to be incredibly dangerous and Layne was clearly Jaime's enemy.

Maybe she should think up something that could

help Jaime in that regard. Surely there had to be something she'd witnessed or put together that would make all of this moot. Something he could tell his superiors that would make sure they felt like they had enough to prosecute.

Maybe if she told him the exact location of the holes she'd had to dig two summers ago, Jaime could find out what was buried there. Maybe that would be enough. Surely a dead body or two would be something.

If they could get through the next two days, and The Stallion left, surely Jaime could do a little figurative and literal digging.

She could make a map, like the one they'd made when trying to figure out the locations of the other compounds. But it would be difficult without paper. It would be difficult without being outside and working through landmarks. Maybe Jaime could sneak her out once The Stallion was gone.

She very nearly laughed at herself. Yes, after eight years she was going to sneak outside and bring The Stallion down with an undercover FBI agent. That was about as plausible as getting kidnapped, she supposed. But then what? She'd go back to her life? Eight years missing and she'd just waltz back into her old life? Twenty-eight with eight years of absolutely no education or work experience. Eight years without a *life*.

Maybe she could add digging shallow graves to her résumé. *Excellent seamstress. Know just where to hide the drugs.*

This was such stupidity. Why was she even going down this road? The future had never held any appeal, and it still didn't. Jaime was here to do a job, and she'd do whatever he needed, but she certainly wasn't going to allow fantasies about escaping. About helping him or saving him from his gruesome undercover work.

The door opened and Gabby's heart jumped to her throat. Not as it had the night before. That night, she'd been scared. This night she was anything but.

She scrambled into a sitting position. But instead of staying in the dark, or saying her name, Jaime turned on the light. She blinked against the sudden brightness.

"I apologize," he said, his tone strangely bland, maybe a little tense. "I should've warned you."

"It's all right," she replied carefully, trying to read the blank expression on his face. He was tense and not like she'd ever seen him before. Because this wasn't his Rodriguez acting, and it wasn't exactly the honest and competent Jaime, either.

"Is everything all right?" she asked after he stood there in silence for ticking seconds.

"I want you to know that it will be. But there is some uncomfortable information I have to share with you."

Her heart sank, hard and sharp. She realized who this Jaime was. FBI Agent Jaime. A little aloof, delivering bad news. Probably how he delivered the news to a family that someone was dead.

"Uncomfortable?" she repeated, because surely if another one of her family members was dead it would be more than *uncomfortable*.

"If I could spare you this, I would," he said, taking a step toward her, some of his natural-born compassion leaking through. "But I have to do what The Stallion asks right now."

A shiver of fear took hold of her, with deep awful claws, and she pressed herself into the corner of where her bed met the wall.

But this was Jaime, and he wasn't going to hurt her just because The Stallion told him to. She wanted to believe that. But for a moment she wondered if something in her would have to be sacrificed to take The Stallion down.

"It's just a message, Gabby," he said softly. "I won't hurt you. I promise. No matter what."

Part of her wanted to cry. Over the fact he could see through her so easily. The fact she could feel guilty over making him think that she thought he was going to hurt her. She wanted to cry at the unfairness of it all, and that was just...so seven years ago.

She straightened with a deep breath and fixed him with her most competent I-can-handle-anything expression. "Just tell me. Say it outright."

"The Stallion is after your sister."

Gabby thought she couldn't be surprised at what horrors The Stallion could do. After all, he'd gleefully informed her of her father's heart attack. Made it very clear she had been the cause. She knew The Stallion killed, and extorted, and hurt people.

He was after her sister. Her Nattie. There was no way to be calm in the face of it. She jumped off the bed and reached for Jaime.

"He doesn't have her," he said calmly. So damn calm.

"And she's with a Texas Ranger who will do everything in his power to protect her—that, I know for sure."

"But he's after her. He's after *her*. Purposefully. Why? Why?"

Jaime took her by the shoulders, looking her directly in the eye. She could see all of that compassion and all of the right he wanted to do. No matter how she told herself not to believe in it. No matter how she told herself it was a figment of her imagination and that he couldn't really be good, she felt it. She *believed* it and knew it. No amount of reason seemed to change the fact that she trusted him.

"She has something to do with the dead messenger. I don't know the whole story yet, but I think she knows something. She's a hypnotist working with the Rangers, and if she's with the police… This could be… It could be a positive development. I know it doesn't feel like that, but this could be a positive."

"Is she…is she looking for me?" Gabby asked, ashamed that her voice wavered. But Nattie, a hypnotist, working with the Rangers? It didn't make sense. And Gabby was afraid of whatever the answer would be. If Natalie was looking for her, Nat had wasted eight years of her life. If she wasn't and this was some cosmic coincidence…

Jaime's strong hands squeezed her shoulders. Comforting. Strong. "I don't know. I don't know why your sister was in that interrogation room with The Stallion's messenger. I don't know why…" He shook his head, regret and frustration in the movement. "I wish I knew more, but I don't. But The Stallion wants you to know he's after your sister because he wants to break you."

Maybe if it had been her and The Stallion alone delivering his message, it would have succeeded in breaking her. But something about having Jaime there, something about feeling his strength and his certainty that this could work out...

"He won't break me," Gabby said firmly.

Jaime's mouth curved, one of those kind smiles that tried to comfort her. It made her feel as though...as though there was hope. That was dangerous. Hope was such a dangerous thing here.

"You're an incredibly brave woman," Jaime said, giving her shoulders yet another squeeze.

The compliment warmed her far too much. Much more so than when the girls gave it to her. Then it felt like a weight, a responsibility, but when Jaime said it, it sounded like an *asset*.

"It's not exactly brave to survive a kidnapping. You don't get much of a choice." No, choice was not something she had any of.

"There is always a choice. And the ones you've made have made this possible, Gabby. The things you remember, the theories you've come up with... You're making this all the more possible. I know you don't believe in endings, or maybe you can't see the possibility of them, but I am going to end this. One way or another, we will end him."

We. It was that final straw, a thing she couldn't fight. To be a "we" after so long of feeling like an I. Like the only one who could do something or be something or fight something.

"I believe you," she whispered. *Too much.* She shouldn't feel it, and she shouldn't say it. She should feel none of the things washing through her at the way his face changed over her saying she believed him.

She shouldn't want to kiss this man she'd known for two days. She shouldn't want to feel what it would be like for him to kiss her for real. Without weapons and fake identities between them.

But there was something kind of beautiful about being a kidnap victim in this case. That she had no life to ruin, no self to endanger. Nothing to lose, really. There was only her.

What choices did she have? Jaime thought she had a choice, but he was wrong. She was nothing here. A ghost at best. What she did or didn't do didn't truly matter.

Even now, with The Stallion after Natalie, there was nothing she could do except hope and pray the Texas Ranger with her was a smart man, and a good man, and would protect Natalie the way Jaime was protecting Gabby right now.

Because no matter that he shouldn't, she knew that was the decision he'd made. He would protect her above himself.

Tentatively she touched her fingertips to the vee of his chest between the straps of guns. She could feel underneath her fingertips the heavy beating of his heart. A little fast, as though he had the same kinds of swirling emotions inside him that she had inside her. She glanced up at him through her lashes, trying to read the expression on his face. A face she'd memorized. A face she thought she would always remember now.

There was enough of a height difference that she would have to pull him down to meet her mouth.

It was such an absurd thought, the idea of wrapping her arms around his neck and pulling his lush mouth to hers. She smiled a little at the insanity of her brain. And he smiled back.

"Thank you for that," he said.

She had lost the thread of the conversation and had no idea what he was thanking her for. All she could think about was the fact he was stepping away from her. Letting her shoulders go and making enough distance that her fingers fell from his chest.

"I should let you sleep," he said, backing slowly away and toward the door.

Gabby should leave it at that. She should let him go and she should sleep. But instead she shook her head.

"Please don't go. Stay."

IT WAS WRONG. It would be wrong to stay. It would be wrong to let her touch him. It would be wrong to let her belief in him change anything. It didn't matter. All that mattered was doing his duty. His duty included protecting her, not...

"There are things I could tell you," Gabby offered, for the first time in all their minutes together seeming nervous without fear behind it. "More things to help with making sure we can end this."

It didn't escape him the way she halted over the word

"end." Like she still didn't quite believe a life outside these walls could exist, but she was trying to believe in one. For him? For herself? He had no idea.

He only knew that everything he should do was tangled up in things he shouldn't. Right and wrong didn't always make sense anymore, and it would take nothing at all for him to lose sight of the fact that anything more than a business partnership with her was a gross dereliction of duty. It was taking advantage of a woman who had already been taken so much advantage of.

But she wanted him to stay. She wanted him to stay. Not the other way around.

"I was just thinking before you got here that if I could tell you where the holes were that we dug two years ago, you might be able to connect it all together. If The Stallion does go in a few days, you'd be able to dig it up or something, and… Maybe that would be… Surely finding a body would be enough. Your superiors would want to press charges at that point, wouldn't they?"

The way she cavalierly talked about digging holes for bodies scraped him raw. It had always been hard to accept that there were people in the world who could hurt other people in such cruel and unusual ways. He'd always had a hard time reconciling the world as he wanted it—with law and order and good people—to the world that was with people who broke those laws and that order and had no good intentions whatsoever.

He didn't know what to do with the kinds of feelings that twisted inside him when he knew that nothing should have ever happened to her. She had been a normal girl, picking her father up from work, and she'd been kidnapped, measured and emotionally tortured into this bizarre world of being hidden away. Not touched, but put to work digging graves and hiding drugs.

"Don't you think?" she repeated, stepping closer to him.

She reached out to touch him and he sidestepped. He was too afraid if she touched him again, all of the certainty inside him would simply disappear and he would do something he would come to deeply regret. Something that would go against everything he'd been taught and everything he believed.

He was there to protect her, and that meant any deeper connection—physical or otherwise—was not ethical. It was screwing with a victim, and he wouldn't allow himself to fall that low. He had to keep a dispassionate consideration for her own good, not develop a passionate one.

"It's possible that evidence would be sufficient," he finally managed to say, his voice sounding raw. "But even if The Stallion goes to another compound, Layne and Wallace will still be here. Me doing any kind of digging is going to be hard to explain."

"Not if you told them that The Stallion ordered you to do it. He stays away for three months. So you'd have time before they'd tell him, wouldn't you?"

"I don't know how they communicate with him when The Stallion isn't here. I'm sure there'd be a way for them to keep tabs on me, and we both know that's exactly what Layne will be doing whether he's supposed to be or not."

"What about Wallace?" Gabby demanded.

Jaime scratched a hand through his hair. "I don't think Wallace is the brightest, but he's the most loyal. Layne is out to get me. Wallace will do whatever it takes to protect The Stallion. Either way, I don't think I have much hope of getting anything past them. At least, not anything tangible like digging."

Noticing her shoulders slump, he hurried on.

"But that doesn't mean it's not useful information. Maybe we can't use it right this second to shut this whole thing down, but every last shred of evidence we have when we finally get to that point is another nail in The Stallion's coffin. Men like him—powerful, wealthy men with connections... They're not easy to take down. We need it all. So it's still important."

"Right. Well. What else could I tell you that would help?" she asked hopefully.

A million things, probably, but he thought distance might do them both a bit of good. Too close, too alone, too much...bed taking up a portion of the room. "Don't you want to sleep?" Because he wanted to convince himself sleep was why he was thinking about beds.

She looked at him curiously. "I haven't had much to do in eight years except sleep. Day in and day out."

"Right, but..." He struggled to find a rebuttal and failed.

The curious look on her face didn't disappear and he couldn't exactly analyze why he suddenly felt bizarrely nervous. He'd been prepared for a lot of things as an undercover FBI agent, but not what to do with nerves over a woman.

A woman he'd known for all of two days. Who

knew his secret now, and was thus her own dangerous weapon, but even in his most suspicious mode, he couldn't believe she'd turn him in. They were each other's best hope.

"Is it hard to switch back and forth?" she asked earnestly.

"Switch back and forth?" He'd been so lost in his own thoughts he was having a hard time following hers.

"Between the real you and this character you have to play?"

"Are you sure they're so different?" He'd tried to say it somewhat sarcastically, or maybe even challengingly, but the minute it came out of his mouth, he knew what he really wanted to hear was that she could tell the difference. That she absolutely knew he was two separate people. Because if she could see it, if this stranger could see it, then maybe it was true. Maybe he really hadn't turned into someone else altogether.

"I've been nothing but Rodriguez for two years. You're the only one who knows any different. I don't know if it's easy. I only know that... This is the first time I've had to do it."

She stepped toward him again and he should sidestep again. He knew he should. Everything about Gabby called to him on a deep cellular level, though, and he didn't know how to keep fighting that call. There was only so much fighting a man could do.

She brushed her fingertips across his chest again. "Do you always wear these?"

Jaime looked down at the weapons strapped to his chest. "I try to. Not a lot of trustworthy men around."

Her fingertips traced the leather strap, which was strangely intimate considering the fact he never let anyone touch his weapons. It was a part of the persona he'd created. Slightly paranoid, always armed and always dangerous. No one touched his weapons.

Yet, he was letting her do just that. Touching them in ways she couldn't begin to understand he was touched.

"You could take them off in here." She looked up at him through the long spikes of her eyelashes.

It was tempting enough to lose his breath for a moment. "Wouldn't be smart," he rasped, surprised how visceral the reaction was to the thought of not being strapped to the hilt with guns and ammo. What would that feel like? He'd forgotten.

"Right. Of course not." She offered him a smile, something he supposed was an attempt at comfort, and that, too, was out of the ordinary. Something he didn't remember.

"I have to go."

"Why?"

He should lie. Tell her he had important henchman duties to see to, but the truth came out instead. "I can't stay in my own skin too long. It's too hard to go back otherwise."

Then she did the most incomprehensible thing of all. She rolled up on her tiptoes and brushed her lips across his cheek. His cheek. Soft and sweet. A soothing gesture. She came back down to be flat-footed and gave him a perilous smile.

"Then you should go. Good night, Jaime."

That, he knew, to be a challenge. He should correct

her. Tell her that she absolutely had to call him Rodriguez. Lecture her until she wished he'd never come into her room.

Instead he returned her smile and said, "Good night, Gabby," before he left.

Chapter Eight

Gabby didn't know the last time she'd felt quite so light. Probably never here. It was probably warped.

Maybe if Jaime had showed up in her first year, it wouldn't be quite so easy to fall into comfort or friendship or even pseudo-flirting. Maybe there would have been enough of the real world and non-ghost Gabby to keep her distance or to keep her head straight.

But she had been here eight years, and all of those things before ceased to exist. All she had was these past eight years, and they had been dark and dreary and horrible. It was nice to have something to feel *light* about.

It didn't mean she wasn't worried about Natalie. It didn't mean she was happy to be kidnapped. It didn't mean a lot of things, but it did give her the opportunity to feel somewhat relaxed. To breathe. To smile as she thought of Jaime's bristled cheek under her mouth.

She made breakfast for the girls, which she did every Sunday. Even after she'd stopped counting the days, she made sure to know what days were Sundays so she could do this for them. Give them something, if not to look forward to, something that felt like this was home and not just prison.

She didn't know if any of them still believed in home. She didn't. This was a prison no matter what, but sometimes it was nice to feel like it wasn't.

"We've been talking," Alyssa announced with no preamble, which was her usual way of broaching a subject. She had only been here for two years and one of the illuminating things about being imprisoned with other people was the realization that victims could be good and bad people themselves.

Alyssa was a bit of a jerk. Had been from the first moment, continued to be these two years later. She was too blunt and always abrasive, never kind to the softer girls. In real life, Gabby thought she might have ended up punching the woman in the nose.

But this wasn't real life.

"What about?" Gabby asked pleasantly, as if she cared.

"Rodriguez and his interest in you."

That certainly caught her off guard, but she feigned interest in her breakfast. "Interest?"

"He's traipsing in and out of your room at all hours."

Gabby slowly turned to face the trio of women in the exact same situation as her. They should be friends and yet all she felt like was an irritable babysitter. "Are you watching me, Alyssa?" Gabby asked, not bothering to soften the threat in her voice.

She wouldn't let anyone figure out what was going on, mostly because she didn't think the girls could hack it, but also because she didn't trust any of them. Perhaps same circumstances should have made them something like sisters, but when you were struck by senseless tragedy it was damn hard to remember to be empathetic toward anyone else.

"I've been watching *him*," Alyssa said with a sniff. "Are you sleeping with him?"

Gabby blinked. She couldn't tell if it was jealousy or fear or *what* that sparked Alyssa's interest. She only knew she was tired. Tired of navigating a world that didn't make any sense, and yet she barely remembered one that did.

She sighed. "The Stallion has *gifted* me to Rodriguez. I'm supposed to do whatever he wants." She almost smiled thinking about how surprised The Stallion would be to discover what Jaime really wanted.

Alyssa's eyes narrowed at the information but Jasmine gasped in horror and Tabitha looked frightened.

"Why you?" Alyssa demanded.

"I'm sorry, did you want to be offered up as payment for a job well done to any bad guy who walks through?" Gabby snapped.

Alyssa fidgeted, her expression losing a degree of its hostility. "Will it get you out?"

Gabby didn't know what to say. What little pieces of her heart that were left cracked hard for Alyssa thinking there was any possible way of getting out. And then there was the very fact that if anyone was ever going to get them out, it would be Jaime.

But not like Alyssa meant. "No," Gabby replied flatly. "Nothing we do for them gets us anything. We're things to them, at best. Certainly not people."

"What do we do then?" Jasmine asked, her voice wobbly and close to tears.

"We wait for him to die," Tabitha said morosely, lowering herself to a seat.

Jasmine sniffled and sat next to Tabitha, but Alyssa still stood, staring at the girls and then at Gabby. "Maybe we hurry that along."

Gabby's eyebrows winged up. It wasn't that she'd never wondered what it might take to kill The Stallion and escape on her own. It was just… She never thought the other women would have the same thoughts.

But Alyssa's face was grim and impassive, and the other girls were contemplatively silent.

"There's four of them, though," Tabitha offered in a whisper, as though they were plotting and not merely… thinking aloud.

"And four of us," Gabby murmured. A few days ago she would have shut this conversation down. She would have reminded them all that there was no hope and they might as well make the best of their fates.

She would have been wrong. Wrong to squash their hope, and their fight, like she'd been wrong to squash her own.

Jaime had brought it back, had reminded her that life did in fact exist outside these walls. Natalie, on the run. Blue skies. Freedom.

A dangerous kind of hope built in her chest. An aching, desperate need for that freedom she'd tried to forget existed. Even as Jaime had talked of ends and bringing him down, she had tried to fight this feeling away.

But it was all his fault she'd lost the reserves, because he'd appeared out of nowhere and trusted her in his mission. He'd somehow crashed into her world and opened her up *to* life again, not just existence.

"How would we do it?" Tabitha asked, her eyes darting around the kitchen nervously.

Alyssa eyed Gabby still. "Rodriguez wears a lot of guns, and if you are a gift, it means he gets awfully close to you."

"I couldn't steal his gun without him noticing."

Alyssa shrugged easily. "That doesn't mean you couldn't get it and shoot before he had a chance to notice."

The three women looked at her expectantly and she wondered if they hadn't all gone a little crazy. "Or, he stops me and shoots me first."

Alyssa raised a delicate shoulder. "Maybe it'd be worth the risk."

"Then you risk it," Jasmine said, surprising Gabby by doing a little standing up for her. "It was your idea, after all."

This time Alyssa smirked. "But Gabby is the one with access to his *guns*."

Gabby couldn't think of what to say to that. She had access to a lot of things, but she couldn't and didn't trust Alyssa with the information, and she wasn't sure she could trust Jasmine or Tabitha, either. All it would take was one woman to slip up or break and Jaime could end up dead.

It wasn't safe to let them into this, and it wasn't fair to refuse these women some hope, some power.

Leave it to Alyssa to make an already complicated, somewhat dangerous, situation even more twisted.

Gabby took a deep breath and tried to smile in some appropriate way. Scheming or interested or whatever, not irritated and nervous. Not…guilty. "I'll see what I can do, okay?"

"Don't put yourself in harm's way, Gabby," Jasmine said softly. "What would we do without you?"

Alyssa snorted derisively, but Gabby pretended she didn't notice and smiled reassuringly at Jasmine. "I'll be careful," she promised.

A whole lot of careful.

JAIME STOOD IN the corner of The Stallion's well-lit shed while the man paced and raged at the news Wallace had just delivered.

"How did they get away? How did my men get arrested? I demand answers." He pounded on his desk, the dolls shaking perilously, like little train wrecks Jaime couldn't stop staring at.

"I don't know," Wallace said, shrinking back. "I guess the Ranger tangled 'em up with the local cops."

The Stallion whirled on Wallace. "Who is this Ranger?"

"Er, his name's V-Vaughn Cooper. With the unsolved c-crimes unit. Uh—"

Jaime lost track of whatever The Stallion's sharp demand was at the name. Vaughn Cooper. He *knew* Vaughn Cooper. Ranger Cooper had taught a class Jaime had taken in the police academy.

Christ.

"Rodriguez." It took Jaime a few full seconds to engage, to remember who and where he was. Not a kid in the police academy. Not an FBI agent. Rodriguez.

"¿Senor?" he offered, damning himself for his voice coming out rusty.

"No. Not you. Not yet." The Stallion muttered, wild eyes bouncing from Jaime to the other men. "Wallace. Layne. You find them. You track them down. The girl, you bring to me. The Ranger, I don't give a damn about. Do what you will."

Layne grinned a little maniacally at that and Jaime knew he had to do something. He couldn't let Cooper get caught in some sort of ambush. He couldn't let a man who'd reminded them all to, above all else, maintain their humanity, get killed. Especially with Gabby's sister.

"Senor, perhaps you could allow me to take care of this problem." He smiled blandly at Layne. "I might be better suited to such a task."

The Stallion gave him a considering once-over. "Perhaps." He paced, looking up at his collection of dolls then running a long finger down the line of one's foot.

Jaime barely fought the grimace.

"No, I want you here, Rodriguez. We have things to discuss."

That wasn't exactly a comfort, though he did remind himself that as long as he was here, Gabby was safe. He wasn't so sure Layne would leave her be if Jaime wasn't around, even with The Stallion's distaste over hurting women.

Jaime assured himself Ranger Cooper knew what

he was doing, prayed he knew what he was up against. If the man had outwitted the first two of The Stallion's men, surely he could outwit Wallace and Layne.

"You have three days to bring her to me. The consequences if you fail will be dire. I would get started immediately."

The other two men rushed to do their boss's bidding, hurrying out of the shed, heads bent together as they strategized.

Jaime remained still, trying to hide any nerves, any concern, with cool disinterest.

The Stallion turned to him, studying him in the eerie silence for far too long.

"I hope you're being careful with our Gabriella," The Stallion said at last.

"Careful?" Jaime forced himself to smile slyly. He spread his arms wide, palms up to the ceiling. "Care was not part of our bargain, *senor*."

The Stallion waved that away. "No, I'm not talking about being gentle. I'm talking about being *careful*. Condoms and whatnot."

Jaime stared blankly at the man. Was he…giving him sort of a sex-ed talk?

"Women carry diseases, you know." The Stallion continued as though this was a normal topic of conversation. "And she's not a virgin, according to her."

"I…" Jaime couldn't get the rest of the words out of his strangled throat. The "according to her" should be some kind of comfort, but why had the man been quizzing her on the state of her virginity? Why did he think Jaime—er, Rodriguez, would care?

"Perfect in every way, save for that," The Stallion said, shaking his head sadly. "Oh, well, then there were her toes."

"Her...toes?"

"The middle one is longer than the big toe. Unnatural." The Stallion shuddered before running his fingers over his dolls' feet again.

Jaime knew he didn't hide his bewilderment very well, but it was nearly impossible to school away. What on earth went through this man's head? He ran corporations. Jaime doubted very much anyone in Austin knew Victor Callihan was really a madman. Perhaps eccentric, somewhat scarce when it came to social situations, but he was still *known*. Somehow he could hide all this...whatever it was, warped in his head.

"Regardless, if you are to be my right-hand man, and insist upon indulging in these baser instincts inferior men have, I expect you to keep yourself clean."

"I... *Sí*." What the hell else was there to say?

"Good. Now, I held you back because I have some concerns I didn't want to broach in front of Layne and Wallace. I think we've been infiltrated."

There was a cold burst of fear deep within Jaime's gut, but on the outside he merely lifted an eyebrow. "Where?"

"Here," The Stallion said grimly, tapping his desk. "I don't believe that Ranger was smart enough to outwit my men unless he was tipped off. This is why I sent Layne and kept you with me."

"I do not follow."

The Stallion sighed exhaustedly. "You're lucky

you're such a good shot, but I suppose I wouldn't want anyone too smart under me. How could I trust them to follow my lead?" He shook his head. "Anyway, if Layne and Wallace fail, I will be assured it's one of them, and they'll be taken care of. If they succeed, then I know my suspicions are wrong and we can carry on."

Jaime inclined his head and breathed a very quiet sigh of relief.

"If they fail, you will be in charge of punishing them suitably." The Stallion frowned down at his desk. "I don't like to alter my schedule..."

"If there's somewhere you need to be, I can be in charge here. I can mete out whatever punishments necessary, gladly."

The Stallion made a noise in the back of his throat. "This situation is priority number one. I need to do some investigating into this Ranger, and I want to be here for the arrival of Gabriella's sister to do my initial testing. For now, you're free to fill your time with our Gabriella. Get it out of your system before her sister gets here, if you would, please."

Jaime bowed faintly as if in agreement.

"You did give her my message, didn't you?" The Stallion asked, his gaze sharp and assessing.

"Sí."

"And how did she react? Were there tears?"

The Stallion sounded downright ecstatic, so Jaime lied. *"Sí."*

He sighed happily. "I should have done it myself, though I do like you telling her and then doing whatever it is you must do with her. Yes, that's a nice punishment for the little slut."

Jaime bit down on his tongue, hard, a sharp reminder that defending anyone wasn't necessary, no matter how much it felt it was.

"May I go, *senor*?" he asked through clenched teeth.

The Stallion inclined his head. "Do what you can to make her cry again. Yes, I like the idea of proud Gabriella crying every night. And when her sister comes... well, I'll bear witness to that."

All Jaime could think as he left the shed was *like hell he would.*

Chapter Nine

Gabby didn't see Jaime all day. She'd expected him—to pop into her room, to come into the kitchen at dinner, something. But she'd eaten with the girls nearly an hour ago and she'd been in her room ever since…waiting.

She shouldn't be edgy, yet she couldn't help herself. The more time she had alone—or worse, with the other girls—the more her mind turned over the possibility of actually killing a man.

Actually escaping.

But she had Jaime for that, didn't she? Alyssa's cold certainty haunted Gabby, though. Should she have thought of this before? Not just as angry outbursts, but as a true, honest-to-God possibility?

Of course, this was the first time in eight years Gabby'd had access to anything that might act as a viable weapon. If she could count Jaime and his guns as accessible.

Where was he? And what was he doing? Had The Stallion sent him on some errand? Was he gone for good?

Her heart stuttered at that thought. Somehow it had

never occurred to her that something might happen to him or that he might get sent elsewhere, but Layne and Wallace, and the other three men who sometimes guarded them were forever leaving for intervals of time. Some never to return.

Oh, God, what if he never came back and she'd missed all her chances? What if she was stuck here forever? What if all that hope had been a worthless waste of—

Her door inched open and Jaime stepped inside, sunglasses covering his eyes, weapons strapped to his chest. Strong and capable and *there*.

She very nearly ran to him, to touch him and assure herself he was real and not a figment of her imagination.

The only thing that stopped her was the fact that in three short days she'd come to rely on this man, expect this man, and in just a few minutes she'd reminded herself why she couldn't let that happen.

He could be shipped out. He could be executed. Any- thing—*anything* could happen to him and if she didn't make a move to protect herself and Jasmine, Alyssa and Tabitha…they'd all be out in the cold.

She tamped down the fear that made her nauseous. Jaime seemed to remind her of the best and worst things. Hope. Freedom. An end to this hell. Then how it could all be taken away.

"I have a bit of good news for you," he said, slipping his glasses off and into his pocket.

Some of the fear coiled inside her released of its own accord. It was so hard to fear when she could see his dark brown eyes search her face as if she held some answer for him. Some comfort.

"Okay," she said carefully, because she wasn't sure she had any for him.

"Your sister and the Texas Ranger she's with escaped The Stallion's first round of men."

"First...round."

"And I know the Texas Ranger she's with. He's a good man. A good police officer."

"But he's sending another round of men," Gabby said dully, because though she'd not spent a lot of time with The Stallion, she knew his habits. She knew what he did and what he saw. When he saw a challenge, he didn't back down.

"Layne and Wallace," Jaime confirmed, crossing to where she sat on her bed. He crouched in front of her and, after a moment, took her hands in his. "I tried to get him to send me, but he thinks Layne is leaking things to the cops."

Gabby jerked her gaze up from where it had been on their joined hands. "He thinks there's a leak," she gasped. That meant Jaime was in danger. That meant once The Stallion figured out it wasn't Layne, he'd figure out it was Jaime and then—

Jaime squeezed her hands. "I don't actually think he thinks that because of anything I've done. He thinks it too convenient that Ranger Cooper and your sister outwitted those men, but he's underestimating the Ranger."

"Maybe he's underestimating my sister."

Jaime smiled, and not even one of those comforting ones. No, this seemed closer to genuine. A real feeling, not one born of this place. It smoothed through her like a warm drink on a cold day, which she barely remembered as a thing, but his smile made her remember.

"Maybe that is it. He certainly underestimates you."

"But you don't." She touched his cheek, brushed her fingertips across his bristled jaw. Five seconds in his company and she'd forgotten all the admonitions she'd just made to herself. But in his presence—calm and strong and comforting—she forgot everything.

Her gaze dropped to the weapons strapped to his chest and she sighed. Well, not everything. Alyssa's words were still there, scrambling around in her brain.

She dropped her fingers from his face to his holster of weapons. She traced her hand over a gun. She didn't know anything about guns. He'd have to somehow teach her to fire one, and it wasn't as if she'd be able to practice anywhere.

But maybe one of the other girls knew how to shoot. If she got one to them...?

She sighed, overwhelmed. This was why she'd given up making a plan. Too many variables. She could analyze a problem, remember a million facts and figures, puzzle together disparate pieces, but when it came to all the unknown fallout of her possible actions...

It made her want to curl up in her bed and cry.

"What's wrong?"

She had to put it all away. Emotion had never gotten her anything in this place. Unless it was anger. Unless it was fight.

"Would they notice?" she forced herself to say

strongly and evenly. "If you gave one of these to me, would anyone notice it missing?"

His expression changed into something she didn't recognize. Into something almost like suspicion. "You want one of my guns?" he asked, moving out of his crouch and into a standing position. He folded his arms across his chest and looked down at her, and it was a wonder anyone who really paid attention didn't see the way his demeanor screamed *law enforcement*.

"What do you want to do with it?" he asked carefully, the same way she thought he might interrogate a criminal.

She wasn't sure what she'd expected, but she didn't like *that*. Trust was a two-way street, wasn't it? Didn't he have to trust her for her to trust him?

"What's going on, Gabby?"

She looked away from his dark brown gaze, from the arms-crossed, FBI-agent posture. She looked away from the man she didn't know. Hard and very nearly uncompromising.

She shouldn't tell him about the girls' plan. It felt like a violation of privacy, and yet, if she kept it from him he could just as easily be hurt, or accidentally hurt one of the girls.

It was a no-win situation, which should feel familiar. She'd been living "no win" for eight years.

Then his finger traced her cheek, so feather-light, before he paused under her chin, tilting her head up so she would look at him.

She was tired of hard things and no-win situations and *this*. But Jaime… It was as though he looked at her as neither just another kidnapping victim nor as the strong leader, not as anything but herself.

"What do you know about me, Jaime?" she asked, not even sure where the question came from but knowing she needed an answer. She needed something.

He cocked his head, but he didn't ask her to explain herself. Instead he pulled her up into a standing position, gripping her shoulders and staring down into her eyes. Everything about him intense and strong and just...*him*.

"I know you're brilliant. That you're beyond strong. I know you love your family, and it eats at you that you can't protect Natalie from this. I know you've been hurt, and you're tired. But I also know you'll endure, because there is something inside of you that cannot be killed. No matter what that man does. You're a fighter."

It was a torrent of words. Positive attributes she'd thought about herself, questioned about herself. All said in that brook-no-argument, no-nonsense tone, his gaze never leaving hers. She knew he had to be a good liar to have survived undercover for two years, and yet she couldn't believe this was anything but the truth.

Jaime saw who she was—not what she'd done or how long she'd been here. He saw her. In all the different ways she was.

"The girls want to—" Gabby swallowed. She had to trust him. She did, because he was her only hope, and because he saw her like no one else had in eight years. "They want me to try to get a gun from you, and then go after The Stallion."

Jaime's forehead scrunched. "They can't do that."

"Why not?" she demanded, something like panic pumping through her. She wanted to be out of there. She wanted a *life*. Even if it wasn't her old life, she wanted…

Him. She wanted him in the real world, and she wanted her.

"I'm here to take him down, Gabby. I'm here to make sure he goes to jail, not just for justice, but so we can put an end to all the evil this man is doing. We can't shoot him in a blaze of glory. That just leaves a power vacuum someone else can take."

"I don't care," she whispered, feeling too close to tears for even her own comfort. But she didn't care in the least. The Stallion was going after her sister and she just wanted him *dead*.

"I understand that. I do. But—"

"My freedom isn't your fight." She sat back down on the bed, slipping through his strong grasp. He could see her. Maybe he even felt some of the things she felt, but her fight was not his fight.

He crouched again, not letting her pull into herself. He took her hands and he waited, silent and patient, until she raised her wary gaze to his.

"It's part of my fight," he said, not just earnestly but vehemently, fervently. "It's a part I don't intend to fail on. I will get you out of here. I will. But I need to do my job, too. It is why I'm here."

A tear slipped out, and then another, and she felt so stupid for crying in front of him, but everything ached in a way she hadn't let it for a very long time.

He brushed one tear off with his thumb then he leaned forward, his mouth so close she inhaled sharply, drowning a little in his dark eyes, wanting to get lost in the warm strength of his body.

"Don't cry," he said on a whisper before he brushed his mouth against another tear, wiping it from her jaw with his mouth.

He pulled his face away from hers, shaking his head. "I shouldn't—"

But she didn't want his shouldn'ts and she didn't want him to pull away, so she tugged him closer and covered his mouth with hers.

HE'D DREAMED OF THIS. Gabby's mouth under his again. Not because he was trying to be someone else. Not because he was trying to convince *anyone* he was taking what he wanted.

No, he'd dreamed of her mouth touching his because they'd both wanted it, not from anything born of this place. On the outside. Free. Themselves. He'd imagined it, unable to help himself.

Even having dreamed of it, even in the midst of allowing it to happen in the here and now, he knew it was wrong. Not just against everything he'd ever been taught in his law-enforcement training, but against things he believed.

She was a victim. No matter how strong she was. No matter how much he felt for her. She was still a victim of this place. Kissing her, drowning in it, was like taking advantage of her. It was wrong. It flew in the face of who he was as an FBI agent, as a law-enforcement agent.

But he didn't stop. Couldn't. Because while it went

against all those things he was, it didn't go against who he was. Deep down, this was all he wanted.

Her tongue traced his mouth and she sighed against him. Melting, leaning. Crawling under all the defenses he wound around himself. False identities. Badges and pledges. Weapons and uniforms and lies.

He should pull away. He should stop this madness.

He curled his fingers into her soft hair. He angled her head so that he could taste her better. He ignored every last voice in his head telling him to stop. Because she was touching him. Tracing the line of his shoulders. Pressing her hand to his heart. She scooted closer, brushing her chest against his.

She whispered his name against his mouth. His real name. And he wanted to be able to be that. He wanted to be able to be the man who could give her everything she wanted and everything she deserved.

But he wasn't that man. Not here. Not now. He couldn't even let her have fantasies of ending The Stallion's life.

He mustered all of his strength and all of his righteous rightness. Somehow...*somehow* he did the thing he least wanted to do and pulled away from her.

Her breath was coming in heavy pants, as was his. Her dark eyes were unfathomably warm, her lips wet from his mouth. He wanted to sink himself there again and again until they thought of nothing but each other.

"Jaime," she said on a whisper.

"We can't do this. I can't..." He tried to pull away but her arms were strong around him.

"Do you know how long it's been since someone's kissed me? Since I *wanted* someone to kiss me?"

"Gabby," he returned, pained. Desperate—for her and a way this could be right.

"I know it isn't the time or the place. I know it isn't prudent or whatever, but I have lived here for eight years without anything I wanted. I survived here without anyone touching me kindly, comfortingly or wanting to. Without anyone seeing me as anything other than a *thing*. If I'm going to believe in an *end*, I have to believe I can go back to being something real, not just this…ghost of a person."

"Getting involved with the victim is not an acceptable—"

She pulled away from him quickly and with absolutely no hesitation. She turned her head away, shaking it. He'd stepped in it, badly.

"I know you don't want to see yourself as a victim," he began, trying to resist the impulse to reach for her. "But in my line of work—"

"I understand."

But she didn't understand. She was angry and she didn't understand at all. "I do know how you feel," he offered softly.

She rolled her eyes.

"It hasn't been eight years, but two years is a long time to go without anyone seeing you for who you are. There aren't a lot of hugs and nice words for the bad guy, Gabby. Even the *other* bad guys don't like me because I've been slowly taking them down so that I could be the one next to The Stallion. It isn't all fun and games over here."

"Are you asking me to feel sorry for you?" she asked incredulously.

"Of course not." He raked a hand through his hair, trying to figure out what he *was* trying to ask of her. "I'm saying that I understand. I'm saying that I would love to give you what you want. I would…"

"I'm just a victim. And you can't get involved with the victim. I get it."

"You don't, because if you thought it was that simple… I have never in my entire career even considered kissing someone who was involved with a case I was part of. I have never once been unable to stop thinking about a woman who had anything to do with *work*. I have never been remotely—*remotely*—tempted to go against everything I believe. Until you."

That seemed to dilute at least some of her anger. She still didn't look at him, which was maybe for the best. He wasn't sure if she looked at him that he'd be able to stay noble.

Because her soft lips tempted him. And the defiant look in her eyes… Everything about her was very near impossible to resist.

He hadn't been lying that he'd never wanted someone the way he wanted her. Even if he took the police part out of it. No woman, no matter how short or long a period of time they had been in his life, had made him feel the way Gabby made him feel.

He wondered if that wasn't why she was upset. Not

that he'd stopped the kiss, but that she thought he didn't see her the way he did.

She'd asked what he knew about her, and he'd been completely honest and open about all the things he *knew* she was. Maybe he shouldn't have been, but she was everything he'd said, and he knew being attracted to her, caring about her, wasn't as simple as whatever label a therapist would likely put on it.

It was Gabby, not the situation, that called to him. But the situation was what made everything far too complicated.

"I can't give you a weapon," he offered into her stubborn silence.

"All right," she said, and she didn't sound angry. She sounded tired. Very close to giving up. But then she straightened her shoulders and inhaled and exhaled slowly. Then she met his gaze, fierce and strong.

"I have to have a story for the girls... I have to... They want out, Jaime." Something in her face changed, a kind of empathetic pain. "I used to be able to tell them it wasn't any use to think about getting out, but we can't keep doing this. Alyssa is right. Staying here isn't worth being alive for."

"So what kept you alive for so long?" he asked because he couldn't imagine. He couldn't *fathom*.

"My family, I guess. Daddy died because of his guilt over me. The least I could do was still be alive. The least I could do was get back somehow." She looked down at her hands, clenched in her lap. "I thought I'd given up that hope, but I don't know. Maybe I just convinced myself I had."

He covered her clenched fists with his own. "I'm going to get you back to your family." God, he'd do it. Come hell or high water. If he had to *die* first, he would do it.

"Not so long ago you said you couldn't promise me that."

"Not so long ago I was doing everything by the book." He believed in the book, but he also…he also believed in this woman. "You're right. Things can't stand. It's been too long. We can't keep waiting around. We have to make something happen."

She finally looked at him, eyebrows raised. "Really?"

"As soon as we get word that your sister has escaped Layne and Wallace, we'll…" It was against everything he'd been taught, everything he was supposed to do, but he couldn't keep telling Gabby to wait when he could be getting her out.

"Once we know your sister is safe, we'll figure out an escape plan. You can't tell the others who I am but… Maybe you can tell them I'm sympathetic, if you trust them to keep that to themselves. Tell them that if you work on me for a few days, you might actually be able to get a weapon from me. If anything slips up to The Stallion or anyone else, I'll tell him it's part of my plan. If you get the girls to stand down a few days. I don't want to risk getting out and something happening to your sister."

"Why?" she asked, still studying him, her forehead creased.

"Because you love her."

Something in her face changed and he couldn't read it. But she moved. Closer to him. No matter that he should absolutely avoid it, he let her kiss him again.

Slow and leisurely, as if they had all the time in the world. As if it was just the two of them. Gabby and Jaime. As if that were possible.

And because the thought was so tempting, so comforting in this world of dark, horrible things, he let it linger far too long.

Chapter Ten

Gabby had kissed four men in her life. Ricky, of course. Corey Gentry on a dare in eighth grade. A guy at a frat party—she didn't know his name—and now Jaime.

In the past eight years she would've considered this part of her dead. The part that could care about kissing and touching. The part of her brain that could go from that to sex.

It was a miracle and a joy to still have the same kind of desire she'd had before. It was a miracle and a joy to be kissing Jaime, his lips so soft, his touch nearly reverent. As though she were something of a miracle to him.

Ricky had never kissed her like this and she'd been convinced she loved him. But he'd been a boy and she'd been a girl. They'd been selfish and Jaime… Jaime was anything but selfish. A good man. A strong and honorable man.

That somehow made the kiss more exciting, knowing he thought it was wrong but couldn't quite help himself. Knowing he felt the same simmering feelings and that he didn't think it was because of their situation. It was because of who they were.

Gabby. Jaime.

She thought she hadn't known who she was anymore, but she was learning. Jaime was showing her pieces of herself she'd forgotten. He was bending his strict moral code for her and that, above all else, spoke to a feeling most people wouldn't believe could happen in three days. She herself wasn't sure she'd believed something like this could grow in three days.

But here she was feeling things for a man that she'd never felt before. She wanted to be able to make sacrifices for him, and she wanted him safe, and she wanted him *hers*.

He pulled away slightly and it was another wondrous thing that every time he pulled away she could *feel* how hard it was for him to do so.

"I have a meeting with The Stallion," he said, his voice very nearly hoarse. "I can't be late again or things could get ugly." He tried to smile, probably to make it sound less intimidating, but it didn't work.

She clutched him harder. "Come back," she blurted. She said it spontaneously, but she still meant it. She wanted him to come back. She wanted more than a kiss.

"So we can…" He cleared his throat. "Plan, right?"

She smiled at him because it was cute he would even think that. "We can plan, too." She watched him swallow as though he were nervous. She didn't mind that the least little bit.

"Gabby."

"Come back tonight. Spend the night with me."

It was a wonderful thing to know he wanted to. That though he was resisting, something deep inside him wanted to or he wouldn't question it at all. It was so against his inner sense of right and wrong, but he wouldn't fight with that if he didn't truly want her.

"It wouldn't be right. To… It would be taking advantage," he said, as though trying to convince himself.

"You're worried about me taking advantage of you?" she asked as innocently as she could manage.

He laughed, low and rumbly. It struck her that this was the first time she'd heard it, possibly one of the very few times she'd heard nice laughter in *years*.

"Gabby, you've been through hell for eight years."

As if she needed the reminder. "I guess that's all the more reason to know exactly what I want," she said resolutely. She knew what she wanted and if she could have it… If she could have him… She'd do it now. She wouldn't waste time. "I want you, Jaime."

He inhaled sharply, but he didn't say anything. "I have to go," he said, getting to his feet.

She gave him a nod, but she thought he'd be back. She really thought he'd return to her. Because he felt it, too. He had to feel it, too. No matter how warped she sometimes felt, this was the most real she'd felt in eight years. The most honest and the most true. The most certain she could survive getting out of this hell. That she wanted to.

That settled inside her like some weird evangelical itch. She wanted to be able to give that same feeling to the other girls. They deserved something, too. Something to believe in. They hadn't spent as much time as her, no, but they had spent enough. They had all spent enough.

Jaime was willing to break the rules and get them there, as soon as Natalie was safe. Not because that helped him any, but because she loved her sister and he knew that meant something to her.

Gabby left her room. She didn't know where exactly Jaime had gone, but she wasn't after him quite now. First, she wanted to find Alyssa. She wanted everyone to know that she was on board, maybe not in the way they thought, but regardless. They were going to find a way out of this.

She walked into the common room, which was basically their workroom opposite the kitchen and dining area.

Tabitha and Jasmine were sitting on the dilapidated couch working on a project The Stallion had assigned them a few days ago. Gabby realized she'd forgotten all about the project and what her role in it was supposed to have been. But ever since Jaime had arrived, it hadn't even occurred to her. Then again, she supposed to The Stallion her job now was to be payment to Jaime. Though she was surprised the girls hadn't asked her for help.

Jasmine looked at her first, eyes wide. She looked from Alyssa, who was riffling through drawers frantically in the kitchen, back to Gabby.

"Did you...?" she whispered then trailed off.

Gabby nodded. "I didn't get a gun or anything, but I think I can. If you give me some time." There was hope. She needed to give them hope.

Alyssa slammed a cabinet door closed and stormed over to them. "What does that mean?" she demanded.

"It means I couldn't quite sneak a weapon off of him, but he seemed a little…sympathetic almost. Like if I keep feeding him our sob story he might…"

"What you really need to do is willingly sleep with him, not fight him off," Alyssa said flatly, giving her a once-over. "When he thinks you're not fighting him, it'll give you time to grab his gun and shoot him."

Gabby couldn't hide a shudder. Maybe if they'd been talking about any of the other men, she wouldn't have felt an icy horror over Alyssa's words. But this was Jaime. Still, she couldn't let even the other girls think he'd gotten to her.

She forced herself to look at Alyssa evenly. "And then what?"

"What do you mean and then what?" Alyssa demanded.

"There are at least three other men here almost at all times. What do you suggest I do after I shoot him? I'm pretty sure gunshots can be heard somewhere else in this little compound, then one of them is going to come running to shoot me. They've got a little more experience with guns and killing people than I do."

Alyssa pressed her lips together, neither mollified nor understanding.

"You just have to give me some time," Gabby said, trying for calm and in charge. "If not to convince him to give me a weapon, then at least time to find a way to sneak one off him without him noticing right away. We do this without a plan, without thinking everything through, then we're all dead. You can't just…"

Alyssa's face was even more mutinous, turning red

almost. Gabby tried for conciliatory, though it grated at her a bit. "I know we all want out." She looked at Tabitha and Jasmine, who were watching everything play out from where they sewed on the couch. "And I know once you start thinking about all of the things you could do once you got out of here that it builds inside you and everything feels... Too much. You start to panic. But if we are going to survive getting out of here, we have to be smart. Okay?"

"Does it matter if we survive?" Alyssa asked, all but snarling at Gabby.

Jasmine gasped and Tabitha straightened.

"Of course it matters," Tabitha shouted from the couch. She took in a deep, tremulous breath, calming herself as Jasmine patted her arm. "I'd rather be alive and here for the next *ten* years than die and never get a chance to see my family again." Her voice wavered but she kept going. "We have to have patience, and we have to do this smart. This is the first time any of us has access to a weapon, and we can't waste the chance. It won't happen again. At least, not for a very long time."

Alyssa scoffed, but she didn't pose any more arguments. "I'm going crazy in this place," she muttered, hugging herself.

"Why don't you help us work?" Jasmine offered. "I know it isn't any fun, but it'll at least keep your mind busy."

"You two can be his slave. I have no interest."

Tabitha and Jasmine exchanged an eye-roll and Alyssa stomped back to the kitchen. She riffled through the drawers again, inspecting butter knives and forks.

Gabby hoped Natalie and her Ranger escaped The Stallion's men once and for all, and quickly. Not just for her own sake, and for Jaime's, but because she wasn't certain Alyssa would last much longer.

If she didn't last, if she kept being something of a loose cannon, then they were all in danger. Including Jaime.

JAIME DIDN'T GO to Gabby that night. He knew it was cowardly to avoid her. He also knew it was for the best. For both of them. He wouldn't be able to resist what she offered, and it wasn't fair to take it. So he kept himself away, falling into a fitful sleep that was never quite restful.

The next day he busied himself outside. He fed The Stallion a story about wanting to come up with some new security tactics, but what he was really trying to do was to see if he could find any evidence of a shallow grave.

The Stallion was so obsessed with Layne and Wallace's progress in finding Ranger Cooper and Gabby's sister, Jaime felt pretty confident he could get away with a lot of things today.

Including going to see Gabby for only personal reasons.

He shook the thought away as he toed some dirt in the front yard. Unfortunately the entire area, especially in the front, was nothing but hardscrabble existence. Scrub brush and tall, thick weeds. It was impossible to tell if things had been dug, if things had grown over, if empty patches of land were a sign of a grave or just bad soil.

Being irritated with himself over his inability to find a lead didn't stop him from continuing to do it.

Until he heard the scream. A howling, broken sound. Keening almost. Coming from inside. From a woman.

"Gabby," he said aloud.

He forgot what he'd been doing and ran full-speed to the front door. He struggled with the chains on the doors and cursed them. It took him precious minutes to realize the door wasn't just locked and chained, it had been sealed shut with something. There was no possible way of getting to her through this door. He swore even louder and rushed around to the back.

Was The Stallion inside or in his shed? Was he hurting them? Jaime grabbed one of the guns from his chest. If he was hurting Gabby—if he was hurting any of them—this was over. Jaime wasn't going to let that happen. Not for anything. Not for any damn evidence to be used in a useless trial.

He'd just kill him and be done with it.

Nearly sweating, Jaime finally got all the locks and chains undone. He hadn't heard another scream and didn't know if that was a good or bad sign. He ran down the hall, looking in every open door. Gabby wasn't in her room and it prompted him to run faster.

He reached the main room and skidded to a halt at the sight before him. Gabby was standing there in the center of the room looking furious, blood dripping down her nose.

"What the hell happened?" he demanded, searching the room and only seeing the other women.

Gabby's gaze snapped to his and she widened her eyes briefly, as if to remind him he had an identity to maintain. It wasn't Demanding FBI Agent. *Or concerned...whatever you are.*

Either way, he'd forgotten. He'd let fear make him reckless. He'd let worry slip his mask. He very well could have ruined everything if not for that little flick of a gaze from Gabby.

He took a breath, calming the erratic beating of his heart. He moved his gaze from Gabby's bloody face, fighting every urge to grab her and pat her down himself to make sure she wasn't hurt anywhere else.

"Well, *senoritas*?" he demanded, rolling his R's in as exaggerated a manner as he could manage in his current state. He glared at the other three women. The two blondes were holding the brunette down on the couch.

The brunette was breathing heavily, her nostrils flaring as she glared at Gabby. Slowly, she took her gaze off Gabby and let it rest on him.

She sneered and then spat. Right on one of the girls holding her. The slighter blonde shrieked and jumped back, which gave the brunette time to throw off the other woman and jump to her feet.

It wasn't wasted on him that Gabby immediately went into a fighter stance.

"First shot was free, but you hit me again, I will beat you," she said, angry and menacing as the brunette stepped toward her.

Jaime stepped between them. "I will say this only

once more. What is going on?" He realized he was still holding his gun and gestured it at the angry brunette threateningly.

The girl who'd been spit on squeaked and cowered while the girl who'd been flung off the brunette turned an even paler shade of white.

"Let's have story time, Alyssa. Tell our captor here what you're after," Gabby goaded.

"I'm going to get out of here," Alyssa yelled, whirling from Jaime to the blondes. "I don't care if I kill all of you." She pointed around him at Gabby. "I am going to get the hell out of here."

Jaime didn't want to feel sorry for the girl considering she was clearly at fault for Gabby's bloody nose, but he looked at Gabby and watched her shoulders slump and the fury in her eyes dim.

Damn it. He couldn't blame the woman for losing her mind here. Not in the least. But it was the last thing they needed if they were actually going to put something in motion that might get them out.

"You would be dead before you killed anyone, *senorita*. Calm yourself."

She bared her teeth at him. "I can't do this anymore. I can't do this anymore. Shoot me." She lunged toward him. "God, put me out of my misery."

"Hush," he ordered flatly, tamping down every possible empathetic feeling rising up inside him. "I'm not going to kill you. And you are not going to kill anyone. You're going to calm yourself."

"Or what? What happens if I don't?" She got close

enough to shove him, even reached out to do it, but Gabby was stepping between them.

Jaime was certain the woman would throw another punch at Gabby and he would have to intervene, but Gabby did the most incomprehensible thing. She pulled the woman into a hug.

And the woman began to sob.

The others started, too. All four of them crying, Gabby with her nose still bleeding.

Jaime had to clench his free hand into a fist and pray for some kind of composure. It was too much, these poor women, taken from their lives and expected to somehow endure it.

"What is all this?" The Stallion demanded and Jaime was such a fool he actually jumped. Where had all his instincts gone? All his self-preservation? He'd lost it, all because Gabby had gotten under his skin.

Jaime steeled himself and turned to face The Stallion.

"Your charges were getting out of hand. I had to do some knocking around," Jaime offered, nodding at Gabby's nose. If any of the girls wanted to refute his story, it would possibly end his life.

But none of them did.

"She is mine, no?" Jaime continued, hoping the fact Gabby was a gift meant he'd forgive him for the supposed violence that had shed blood.

The Stallion was staring oddly at Gabby, and it took everything in Jaime's power not to step between them. In an obvious way. Instead he simply angled his body and hoped like hell it wasn't obvious how much he wanted to protect her.

"Crying," The Stallion said in a kind of wondering tone. "Well, I am impressed, Rodriguez. No one has ever gotten her to cry."

Gabby flipped him the finger and Jaime nearly broke. Nearly ended it all right there.

"I trust our friend has told you that your sister will be joining us soon," The Stallion said, watching her far too carefully no matter how Jaime tried to angle himself into the picture.

"And yet she isn't here yet. Why is that?" Gabby returned in an equally conversational tone.

Jaime might have fallen in love with her right there.

The Stallion, however, snarled. "You're lucky I don't want to touch your disease-ridden body. But I have found someone who will. Take her away from me, Rodriguez. I don't want to see that face until her sister is here. Make sure to lock her room once you're done with her. She's done with outside privileges."

"And these?" Jaime managed to ask.

The Stallion snapped his fingers. "To your rooms. Don't make me turn you into gifts, as well."

The girls, even the instigator, scattered quickly.

The Stallion squinted at Gabby and maybe it was her unwillingness to cower or to jump that made her a target.

If Gabby cared about that, she didn't show it. So Jaime took Gabby by the arms, as gently as he could while still appearing to be rough to The Stallion. "I will take good care of her, *senor*," he said, donning his best evil smile.

"I'm glad you're willing to soil yourself with this," The Stallion said. "I should have had someone do this long ago. I don't care what you have to do to make her cry. Just do it."

Jaime gave a nod since he didn't trust his voice. He nudged Gabby toward the hallway and she fought him on it, still staring at The Stallion.

"You're a disgusting excuse for a human being. You aren't a human being. You're a monster." And then, apparently taking a page out of Alyssa's book, she spit at him.

The Stallion scrambled away and then furiously scowled at Jaime.

"Are you going to let her get away with that?" he demanded, fury all but pumping out of him.

Oh, damn, Gabby and her mouth. How the hell was he going to get out of this one?

Chapter Eleven

Gabby had gone too far. She realized it a few seconds
too late. She'd wanted to make sure The Stallion didn't
think she was happy to go with Jaime. She wanted The
Stallion to think she hated Jaime as much as she hated
him, and she didn't know how to show it considering
she didn't hate Jaime even a little bit.

But she'd put Jaime in an impossible position. The
Stallion expected Jaime to hurt her now. In front of him.

And how could he not?

Jaime's jaw tightened and Gabby knew it wasn't because he was getting ready to hurt her. It was because
he didn't want to and he was having a hard time figuring out how to avoid it. But he didn't need to protect her.

She lifted her chin, hoping he would understand. "Hit
me with your best shot, buddy," she offered.

Much like when he'd come into the room, guns blazing, not using his accent at all, she gave him a little
open-eyed glance that she hoped would clue him in.

He had to hit her. There was no choice. She understood that. She wouldn't hold that against him. Besides,
he'd pull the punch. It'd be fine.

He raised his hand and she had to close her eyes. She didn't want the image in her head even if she knew he had to do it. She braced herself for the blow, but it never came.

Instead his fingers curled in her hair, a tight fist. Not comfortable, but still not painful, either.

"It appears you need to be taught some respect, *senorita*. Let's go to your room where I can give you a thorough lesson. I teach best one-on-one."

Gabby opened her eyes, ignoring the shaking in her body. She didn't dare look at The Stallion—she didn't want to know if he'd bought that ridiculous tactic or not. She couldn't look at Jaime, because she didn't want anything to give him or her away.

So she sucked in a breath as though Jaime's fingers in her hair hurt and stared at the floor as if he was forcing her. She stumbled a little as he nudged her forward, trying to make it appear as if he'd pushed her. She put everything into the performance of making it look like he was being rough with her when he was being anything but.

"I will come to give you a full report when I'm done, *senor*."

"Excellent." The Stallion sounded pleased with himself. Satisfied.

Jaime continued to nudge her all the way to her room, and she let out a little squeak of faked pain. When Jaime finally gave her a light push into her room, she could only sag with relief.

Jaime closed the door and flicked the lock. Before she had a moment to breathe, to say a thing, she was being bundled into his arms and gently cradled against his hard chest and the weapons there.

She relaxed into him, letting him hold her up. She was shaking more now, oddly, but it was such an amazing thing to be cradled and comforted after everything that had just happened, she couldn't even wonder over it.

"We need to get you cleaned up," Jaime said, his voice low and sounding pained.

She waved him away, wanting to stay right there, cradled against him. "Leave it. Maybe it'll convince him you were suitably rough with me if we let it bleed more."

"He's not going to see you again," Jaime said fiercely, his arms tightening around her briefly. "You're under lock and key now, and if he tries to come in here, I will kill him myself."

She looked up at him curiously. He was... He'd avoided her for days, and Gabby couldn't blame him because she knew he was trying to do something noble. Still, she didn't quite understand his anger.

Frustration or fear, maybe even annoyance, she might have understood, but the beating fury in his eyes, completely opposite to the gentle way he held her, was something she couldn't unwind.

"What was the other woman's problem?" he asked, studying her nose.

"She hit the two-year mark," Gabby stated with a tired sigh.

"What does that mean?"

Gabby sighed. "Oh, I don't know. It just seems that around two years in here you start to realize how stuck you are. How no one's going to come and save you. I think we all have a little bit of a meltdown at two years."

"Did your two-year meltdown include punching another woman in the face?"

"No. I was alone. I did try to use a butter knife to stab a guard," she offered almost cheerfully.

His mouth almost...almost quirked at that.

"I was desperate," she continued. "With that desperation comes a kind of insanity. Alyssa's hitting that same wall. Losing it. Wondering what it's worth being stuck in this horrible place. Of course, she has the worst possible timing, but what can we do? We just have to try and end it as soon as we can."

"You hugged her." Jaime's voice was soft, awe-filled.

Gabby turned away from him and his comforting, strong arms, uncomfortable with the way he said it as though she'd done something special. But she hadn't. Not really.

"You forget sometimes, when you're in here, that a simple hug can be reassuring. She needed someone to be kind. You...you reminded me of that. Humanity. Compassion. So, I did what you've done to me."

"You did it after she punched you in the nose," he pointed out.

"I let her punch me. I thought it would help her get some of the rage out of her system. I'm hoping getting some of it out will stop her from just...losing it completely."

"You are a marvel," he said, like she was some kind of genius superhero. It shouldn't have warmed her. She should tell him she wasn't.

But she wanted to believe there was something marvelous about her.

"I'm washing you up," he said, taking her arm and pulling her into the little nook that acted as a bathroom. There was a toilet and a sink, but no door, no privacy. Still, Jaime grabbed a washcloth from the little pile she kept neatly stacked in the corner.

He flicked on the tap and soaked the cloth in warm water. He squeezed it out before holding it up to her face gently. Ever so gently, he wiped away the blood that had started dribbling out of her nose after Alyssa had hit her.

"You're lucky she didn't break it," he muttered.

Gabby rolled her eyes. "I *let* her hit me, and I pulled back a bit. I'm a lot stronger than all that bluster."

He cupped her face with his hands, long fingers brushing at her hairline. "That you are," he said with a kind of fervency that had a lump burning in her throat.

"You've been avoiding me," she rasped.

"Yeah," he said. "I'm trying to do the right thing."

"What about instead of doing the right thing, you do what I want? How about you give me something I want?"

He sighed and shook his head. "I don't know how I ever thought I'd resist you." Then his mouth was on hers.

Potent and hot. Not quite so gentle. Gabby reveled in the fact that he could be both. That he could give her everything and anything she wanted.

"Tell me if I hurt your nose," he murmured against her mouth, never breaking contact. His hands trailing through her hair, his body pressed hard and tight against hers.

She could barely feel the ache in her nose. Not with Jaime's tongue sliding against hers. Not with the smell of him and leather and what might be outside if she even remembered what outside smelled like.

She realized whatever this was, it was frantic and needy. It was also something that could be temporary all too easily. The chances she'd have to touch him, to be with him…

She needed to grasp and enjoy and lose herself in this moment, in the having of it. She molded her hands against his strong shoulders, slid them down his biceps and his forearms. Everything about him was honed muscle, so strong. He could've been brutal with someone else's heart, but Jaime was anything but that.

His hands smoothed down her neck and, for the first time, he dared to touch more than just her face or her shoulders. The fingers of one hand traced across her collarbone over her T-shirt. His other hand slid down her back, strong as he held her against him.

She could feel him, hot and hard against her stomach. It had been a long time since she'd done this, and it was possibly the most inappropriate moment, but there wasn't time to think.

She didn't want to think. She wanted to sink into good feelings and let *those* take over for once.

She arched against him and the fingertips tracing her collarbone stilled. Then lowered. He palmed one of her breasts and she moaned against his mouth.

"We can stop whenever," he said, so serious and noble and *wrong*.

"I don't ever want to stop." She wanted to live in a

moment where she had some power. Where she had some hope. "Take off your guns, Jaime."

He stilled briefly and then reached up to the shoulder of the harness and unbuckled it. He pulled the strand of weapons off his body, his eyes never leaving hers. He hesitated only a moment before he laid the weapons down next to her bed.

He took a gun from his waistband she hadn't known was there and placed it on the little table next to her bed. Something almost resembling a smile graced his mouth as he reached to his boots and pulled a knife out of each.

There was something not just weighty about watching him disarm, but something intimate. She watched him strip himself of all the things he used to protect himself. All the things he used to portray another man. To do his job, his duty.

"I think that's all of them," he said in a husky voice.

She didn't have any weapons to surrender, so she grabbed the hem of her shirt and pulled it off. She moved her hands to unbutton her pants, but Jaime made a sound.

"Stop," he ordered.

She raised a questioning eyebrow at him.

He crossed back to her, a hand splaying against her stomach, the other sliding down her arm. "Let me."

She swallowed the nerves fluttering to the surface. No, nerves wasn't the right word. It was something more fundamental than that. Would he like what he saw? Would he still be as enamored with her when they were naked? When it was over?

She wanted to laugh at her momentary worry about

such things. But, like so many other thoughts, it was a comforting reaction—a real-life response. That she could still be a woman. That she could still care about such things.

His hands were rough against her skin. Tanned against how pale she was with no access to sunlight. She watched as he traced the strangest parts of her, as if fascinated by her belly button or the curve of her waist. But he was still fully clothed, though he'd surrendered all his weapons.

She gave the hem of his shirt a little tug. "Take this off," she ordered, because it was nice to order. More than nice to have someone obey. Power. Equality, really. He could order her and she could order him, and they could each get what they wanted.

He pulled his shirt off from the back, lifting it over his head and letting it hit the floor. He really was perfection. Tall and lithe and beautiful. He had scars and smooth patches of skin. Dark hair that drew a line from his chest to the waistband of his jeans.

She moved forward and traced the longest scar on his side. A white line against his golden skin.

"How did you get this?" she asked.

"Knife fight."

She raised her gaze to his eyes, but his expression was serious, not silly. "You were in a *knife* fight?"

He shrugged. "When I first started out as Rodriguez, I was doing some drug running for one of his lower-level operations. Unfortunately a lot of those guys try to double-cross each other. I was caught in the cross… well, cross-stabbing as it were."

He said it so cavalierly, as if that was just part of his

job. Getting stabbed. Horribly enough to leave a long, white scar.

"Did you go to the hospital?"

Again he smiled, almost indulgently now. "There was a man who did the stitching back at our home base."

"A man? Not a doctor?" she demanded.

"Doctors were saved from more…life-threatening injuries. Even then, only if you were important. At that point, I wasn't very important."

Gabby tried to make sense of it as Jaime shook his head.

"It's a nonsensical world. None of it makes sense if you have a conscience, if you've known love or joy. Because it's not about anything but greed and power and desperation."

She traced the jagged line and then bent to press a kiss to it. He sucked in a breath.

"I bet there was no one to kiss it better," she said, trying to sound lighthearted even though tears were threatening.

"Ah, no."

"Then let me." She raised to her tiptoes to kiss him. To press her chest to his. She still wore a bra, but the rest of her upper body was exposed and she tried to press every bare spot of her to every bare spot of him.

She tasted his mouth, his tongue, and she wanted the kiss to go deep enough and mean enough to ease some of those old hurts, some of that old loneliness.

For both of them.

THERE WERE THINGS Jaime should do. Things he should stop from happening. But Gabby's kiss, Gabby's heart, was a balm to all the cruelties he'd suffered and administered in the past two years. She was sweetness and she was light. She was warmth and she was hope.

At this point he could no longer keep it from himself, let alone her. She wanted this. Perhaps she needed it as much as he did. Regardless, there was no going back. There was only going forward.

Her skin was velvet, her mouth honey. Her heart beating against his heart, the cadence of a million wonderful things he'd forgotten existed.

Her fingertips were curious and gentle as they explored him, bold as though it never occurred to her she shouldn't.

All of it was solace wrapped in pleasure and passion. That someone would want to touch him with reverence or care. That he wasn't the hideous monster he'd pretended to be for two years. He was still a man made of flesh and bone, justice and right.

And despite her time here as a victim, she was still a woman. Made of flesh and bone. Made of heart and soul.

He smoothed his hands up and down her back, absorbing the strength of her. Carefully leashed, carefully honed.

He reached behind her and unsnapped her bra, slowly pulling it off her and down her arms. It meant he had to put space between them. It meant he had to wrestle his mouth from hers. But if anything was worth that separation, it was the sight before him. Gabby's curly hair tumbled around her face. Her lips swollen, her cheeks flushed.

The soft swell of her breasts, dark nipples sharp points because she was as excited as he was. As needy as he was. He palmed both breasts with his too-rough hands and was rewarded by her soft moan.

Of course this amazingly strong and brave woman before him was not content to simply let him look or touch. She reached out and touched him, as well, her hands trailing down his chest all the way to his waistband. She flipped the button and unzipped the piece of clothing with no preamble at all.

He continued to explore her breasts with his hands. Memorizing the weight and the shape and the warmth, the amazing softness her body offered to him. And it was more than just that. So much more than just the body. A heart. A soul. Neither of them would be at this point if it wasn't so much more than *physical*. It was an underlying tie, a cord of inexplicable connection.

She tugged his jeans down, his boxers with them. And then those slim, strong hands were grasping him. Stroking his erection and nearly bringing him to his knees.

He needed to find some sort of center. Not necessarily of control but of reason. Sense and responsibility. This was neither sensible nor responsible, but that didn't mean he couldn't take care of her. That didn't mean he wouldn't.

Gently he pulled her hand off him. "I need to go get something. I'll be right back."

She blinked up at him, eyebrows furrowed. Beautiful and naked from the waist up.

He pressed his mouth to hers as he pulled his jeans

up, drowning in it a minute, forgetting what he'd been about to do. It was only when she touched him again that he remembered.

"Stay put. I will be right back." When she opened her mouth, he shook his head. "I promise," he repeated, his gaze steady on hers. He needed her to understand, and he needed her to believe him.

She pouted a little bit, beautiful and sulky, but she nodded.

"Right back," he repeated and then he was rushing to his room, caring far too little about the things he should care about. If The Stallion was around... If the other girls were okay... But it hardly mattered with Gabby's soul entwined with his.

He went to his closet of a room and grabbed the box that had been given to him. The box was still wrapped and he had no doubt about the safety of its contents.

And he would keep Gabby safe. No matter what.

With a very quick glance toward the back door, Jaime very nearly *scurried* back to Gabby. That back door was clearly shut and locked. Surely The Stallion had disappeared into his lair to obsess over Layne and Wallace's progress.

Jaime entered Gabby's room once again, closing and locking the door behind him quickly. She wasn't standing anymore. She was sitting on the edge of her bed and she was still shirtless.

He walked over and placed the box of condoms on the nightstand next to his smaller gun. He watched her face carefully, something flickering there he didn't recognize as she glanced at the box.

"We still don't have to," he offered, wondering if it was reticence or something close to it.

Her glance flicked from the box to him. "Why do you have these?"

"If you haven't noticed The Stallion is a little convinced women have—"

"Cooties?" Gabby supplied for him.

Jaime laughed. "I was going to say diseases. But, yes, essentially, cooties."

"So he gave those to you?"

"When I convinced him that only female payment would do, he insisted I take the necessary precautions."

She frowned, puzzling over the box. He didn't know what to say to make her okay. But eventually she grabbed the box and ran her nail around the edge. Pulling the wrapping off, she ripped open the box and took out a packet.

She studied him from beneath her lashes and then smirked. "I think this is where you drop your pants."

He laughed again. Laughing. It was amazing considering he couldn't think of the last time he'd laughed. With Gabby he felt like he wasn't just a machine. He wasn't simply a tool to bring The Stallion down or a tool to help The Stallion out. He'd been nothing but a weapon for so long it was hard to remember that he was also real. Capable of laughing. Capable of humor. Capable of feeling.

Capable of caring. Perhaps even loving.

He'd never been a romantic man who believed in flights of fancy and yet this woman had changed his life. She'd changed his heart and he didn't have to know how she'd done it to know that it had happened.

He pushed his jeans the remainder of the way down, watching her the entire time. Her gaze remained bold and appraising on his erection.

She scooted forward on the bed, tearing the condom packet open before rolling it on him. Finally she looked up at him. Her gaze never left his as she lay back on the bed and undid the fastenings of her pants. She shimmied out of her remaining clothes and then lay there, naked and beautiful before him.

He took a minute to drink her in. Because who knew how much time they would have after the next couple of days. He would save her—he would do anything to save her—and he did not know what lay ahead. He did know he had to absorb all of this, commit it to memory, connect it to his heart.

He stepped out of his jeans and then crawled onto the bed and over her. She slid her arms around his neck and pulled his mouth to hers. The kiss was soft and sweet. An invitation, an enchanting spell.

He traced the curve of her cheek with one hand, positioning himself with the other. Slowly, torturing himself and possibly her, as well, he found her entrance. Nudged against it. Taking his sweet time to slowly enter her.

Joined. Together. As if they were a perfect match. A pair that belonged exactly here. How could he belong anywhere else when this was perfect? When she was perfect?

She arched against him as if hurrying him along, her fingers tightening in his too long hair.

"We have time, Gabby. We have time." He kissed her, soft and sweet, indulging himself in a moment where he was simply seeped inside of her.

A moment when he was all hers and she was all his. And she relaxed, melting. His. All his.

Chapter Twelve

Gabby had known sex with Jaime would be different for a lot of reasons. First and foremost, she wasn't a young girl sneaking around, finding awkward stolen moments in the back of a car. Second, he wasn't a little boy playing at being a hard-ass bad man.

He was a strong, good, *amazing* man, doing things her ex-boyfriend would have wilted in front of.

But mostly, sex with Jaime was different because it was them. Because it was here. Because it mattered in a way her teenage heart would never have been able to understand. Perhaps she never would have been able to understand if she hadn't been in this position. The position that asked her to be more than she'd ever thought she'd be able to be. Because the truth of the matter was, eight years ago she had been a young woman like any other. Selfish and foolish and not strong in the least.

She would never be grateful for this eight years of hell. She would never be happy for the lessons she'd learned here, but that didn't mean she couldn't appreciate them. Because whether she was happy about it or not, it had happened. It was reality. There was only so much bitterness a person could stand.

With Jaime moving inside her, touching her, caring about her, bitterness had no place. Only pleasure. Only hope. Only a deep, abiding care she had never felt before.

He kissed her, soft and gentle, wild and passionate, a million different kinds of kisses and cares. His body moved against hers; rough, strong, such a contrast. Such a perfect fit.

Passion built inside her, deep and abiding. Bigger than anything she'd imagined she'd be able to feel ever again. But Jaime's hands stroked her body. He moved inside her like he could unlock every piece of her. She *wanted* him to.

The blinding spiral of pleasure took her off guard. She hadn't expected it so quickly or so hard. She gasped his name, surprised at the sound in the quiet room. Surprised at all he could draw it out of her.

He still moved with her. Growing a little frantic, a little wild. She reveled in it, her hands sliding down his back. Her heart beating against his.

She wanted *his* release. Wanted to feel him lose himself inside her.

Instead of galloping after it, though, he paused, as if wanting to make this moment last forever. Satisfied and sated, how could she argue with that? She would stay here, locked with him, body to body forever.

He kissed her neck, her jaw. His teeth scraped against her lips and she moved her hips to meet with his. But he was unerringly slow and methodical. As though they'd been making love for years and he knew exactly how to drive her crazy. How to make her fall over that edge again and again. Because she was perilously close.

Aside from the tension in his arms, she would have no idea he was exerting any energy whatsoever. That spurred something in her. Something she hadn't thought she'd ever feel again. A challenge. And need.

She tightened her hold on his shoulders, slicked though they were. She sank her teeth into his bottom lip, pushing hard against him with her hips. He groaned into her mouth. She slid her hands down his back, gripping his hips, urging him on. One hand tightened on her hip, a heavy, hot brand.

She looked into his eyes and smiled at him. "More," she insisted.

He swore, sounding a little broken. That control he'd been holding on to, that calm assault to bring her to the brink, snapped. He moved against her with a wildness she craved, that she reveled in.

She'd brought him to this point, wild and a little broken. *She* could be the woman that did this to him, and that was something no one could ever take away. *She* was the woman who had made him hers. Maybe she wouldn't always have Jaime, but she'd always have this.

He groaned his release, pushing hard against her, and it was the knowledge she'd brought him there that sent her over the edge again herself. Pulsing and crashing. Her heart beating heavy, having grown a million sizes. Having accepted his as her own.

He lay against her, and she stroked her hand up and down his back, listening to his heart beat slowly, slowly, come back to its regular rhythm. He made a move to get off her, but she held him there, wanting his weight on her for as long as it could be.

"Aren't I crushing you?" he asked in her ear, his voice a low rumble.

"I like it," she murmured in return.

He nuzzled into her neck, relaxing into her. As though because she'd said she liked it he would give her this closeness for as long as he could. She believed that about him. That he would always give her whatever he could. Once they knew Natalie was safe, he'd agreed to get her out under any means possible, and she believed.

For the first time in eight years she believed in someone aside from herself. For the first time in eight years she had hope and care and pleasure.

She might've told him she loved him in any other situation, but this was no regular life. Love was… Who knew what love really was? If they got away, back into the real world, maybe…maybe she could learn.

JAIME SLEPT IN Gabby's bed. It was a calculated risk to spend the night with her. He didn't know how close an eye The Stallion was keeping on him with everything going on. In the end, perhaps a little addled by her and sex, he'd figured, if pressed, he'd explain all his time as making sure Gabby paid for her supposed lack of respect.

It bothered him to have to think of things like that. Bothered him in a way nothing in the past two years had. That he had to make The Stallion think he was hurting Gabby. It grated against every inch of him every time he thought about it.

So he tried not to think about it. He spent the night in her bed and the next day mostly holed up with her in her room. They made love. They talked. They *laughed*.

It felt as though they were anywhere but in this prison. A vacation of sorts. Just one where you didn't leave the room you were locked into. He wouldn't regret this time. It was something to have her here, to have her close.

They didn't talk about the future or about what they might do when they got out. Jaime would have some compulsory therapy to go through. A whole detox situation with the FBI, along with preparations for the future trial. Any further investigating that needed to be done would at least fall somewhat within his responsibility.

But he was done with undercover work. He'd known that before he'd met Gabby. These past two years had taken too much of a toll and he couldn't be a good law-enforcement officer in this position anymore. He didn't plan to leave the FBI, but undercover work was over.

Once he got Gabby out, he would make sure that "something different" included her. She would need therapy, as well, and time to heal. It would take time to find ways back to their old selves.

He could wait. He could do anything if it meant having a chance with her.

But their time here in this other world was running out. The Stallion would be expecting a full report from Rodriguez, and Jaime had put it off long enough.

He would do all the things he had to do to protect her. To free her.

"You have to go meet with him," she said, her tone void of any emotion.

He turned to face her on the bed. It was too narrow and they barely fit together, and yet he was grateful for the lack of space, for the excuse to always be this close. "How'd you figure that out?"

"You got all tense," she replied, rubbing at his shoulders as though this was something they could be. A couple. Who talked to each other, offered comfort to each other.

He couldn't think of anything he'd ever wanted more, including his position with the FBI.

"He's expecting a report from me."

Gabby frowned and didn't look at him when she asked her question. "Are you going to tell him I cried?"

He'd been planning on it. He knew it poked her pride, but it would be best if The Stallion thought her broken. It would be best if Jaime made himself look like a master torturer.

"Do you not want me to?"

"You would tell him you failed?"

He shrugged, trying to act as though it wasn't a big deal, though it was. "If you want me to. I don't think it would put me in any danger to make it look like I'd failed one thing considering everything else that's currently going down."

"You don't *think*?"

"He's not exactly the most predictable man in the world, no matter how scheduled and regimented he is."

"That's very true," she mused, looking somewhere beyond him.

"Gabby."

Her dark gaze met his, that warrior battle light in them. "Tell him I cried. Tell him I sobbed and begged. What does it matter? I didn't actually."

"If it matters something to you—"

"All that matters to me is you." She blinked as if surprised by the force of her words. "And getting out of here," she added somewhat after the fact.

He pressed a kiss to her mouth. Whatever tension he'd had was gone. Or perhaps not *gone*, but different somehow.

Screw The Stallion. Screw responsibility. She was all that mattered. He wanted to believe that as he fell into the kiss, wanted to hold on to that possibility, that new tenet of his life. Gabby and only Gabby.

But life was never quite that easy. Because Gabby, being the most important thing, the central thing for him, meant he had to keep her safe. It meant that responsibility *did* have a place here. It was his responsibility to get her out. His responsibility to get her *free*.

He started to pull away but she spoke before he could.

"Go have a meeting. Find out if there's any news about Nattie, and make sure you remember every last detail. And then, when you can…" She smoothed her hand over his chest and offered him a smile that was weak at best, but she was trying. For him, he knew.

"When you're done, when you can, come back to me," she said softly.

He brought her hand to his mouth and pressed a kiss to her palm. "Always," he said, holding her gaze. Hoping she understood and believed how much he meant that.

He slid out of bed, because the sooner he got this meeting with The Stallion over with, the sooner he could find a way to make sure that this was over. For Gabby and for him.

Jaime collected his weapons. He could feel Gabby's eyes on him though he couldn't read her expression. She had perfected the art of giving nothing away and as much as it sometimes frustrated him as a man, he was certainly glad she had built such effective protective layers for herself.

He put the knives back in his boots and then strapped on his cross-chest holster with all of his guns. He buckled it, still watching her expressionless face.

She slid off the bed and crossed to him. She flashed a smile Jaime didn't think had much happiness behind it, but she brushed her lips against his.

"Good luck," she said as though she were scared. For him.

"I have to lock the door," he said, regretting the words as they came out of his mouth. Regretting the way her expression shuttered.

"Yeah, I know." She gave a careless shrug.

Her knowing didn't make him feel any better about doing it, but he had to. There were certain things he still had to do. Things that would keep her safe in the end, and that was all that could matter.

He kissed her once more, knowing he was only delaying the inevitable. He steeled all that certainty and finally managed to back himself out of the room. Away from her smile, away from her sweet mouth.

Away from his heart and soul.

He closed the door and locked it from the outside. He regretted having to add the chain, but any regrets were a small price to pay to get her out. He would keep telling himself that over and over again until he believed it. This was all a small price to pay for getting her out.

He walked briskly down the hall, noting the house was eerily quiet. It wasn't unusual, but often in the afternoon there was a little bit of chatter from the common rooms as the girls worked on their projects or fixed dinner.

Jaime cursed and retraced his steps to check on them. The two calm ones from yesterday were sitting on the couch working on something The Stallion had undoubtedly given them to do. Alyssa was pacing the kitchen.

None of them looked at him, so he could only assume he'd been quiet enough. Satisfied that things seemed to be mostly normal, he backed out of the room. Alyssa's frenzied pacing bothered him a bit. Gabby was right, the girl was a loose cannon, and it was the last thing they needed. But what could he do about it?

There wasn't anything. Not now.

He walked back along the hallway, going through the hassle of unlocking and unchaining the door, stepping out, then redoing all the work. His thoughts were jumbled and he had to sort them out before he actually saw The Stallion.

He paused in the backyard, taking a deep breath, trying to focus his thoughts. He forced himself to hone in on all the strategies he'd been taught in his years as a police officer and FBI agent.

He had to put on the cloak of Rodriguez, get the information he was after, lie to The Stallion about Gabby, then go back to her. Once this was over, he could go back to her.

With a nod to himself, he stepped forward, but it was then he heard the noise. Something strange and faint. Almost a moan. He paused and studied the yard around him.

The next sound wasn't so much a moaning but almost like someone rasping "Rodriguez" and failing.

Jaime started moving toward the noise, listening hard as he walked around the backyard. He held his small handgun in one hand, leaving his other hand free should he need to fight off any attacker.

He rounded the front of the house, still listening to the sound and following the source. When he did, he nearly gasped.

Wallace and Layne were sprawled out in the yard. Layne was a little closer to the house than Wallace, but they were both caked with blood and dirt.

"Rodriguez. Rodriguez." Layne moved his arm wildly and stumbled to his feet. "I've been dragging this piece of shit for who knows how long. Go get The Stallion. And water. By God, I need water."

"Where is your vehicle?" Jaime asked, his tone dispassionate and unhurried.

"Only go so far…" Layne gasped for air, stumbling to the ground again. "Asshole shot our tires. Got as far as I could."

Jaime looked at both men in various states of blood-ied harm. "You don't have her."

Layne's dirty, bloody face curled into a scowl, but he gave brief shake of the head.

"I don't know if you want me to get The Stallion if you don't have her."

"He shot us," Layne said disgustedly. "That prick shot us. Wallace might die. We need The Stallion. We need *help*."

"You may wish you had died," Jaime said, affecting as much detached disinterest as he could.

On the inside he was reeling. Gabby's sister had es-caped these men with Ranger Cooper, which meant that it was time. It was time to move forward. It was time to get the hell out. Her sister was safe and now it was her turn.

"Go get The Stallion," Layne yelled, lunging at him. He had a bloody wound on his shoulder and he was pale. Still, he seemed to be in slightly better shape than Wallace who was lying on the ground moaning, a bul-let wound apparently in his thigh.

After a long study that had Layne growling at him as he tried to walk farther, Jaime inclined his head and then began striding purposefully back to The Stallion's shed. He knocked and only entered once The Stallion unlocked the door and bid him entrance.

"What took you so long?" The Stallion demanded and Jaime was more than a little happy that he had a decent enough excuse to explain his long absence in a way that didn't have anything to do with Gabby.

"*Senor*, Wallace and Layne are in the yard. Injured."

The Stallion had just sat in his desk chair, but immediately leaped to his feet. "They don't have her?" he bellowed.

"No."

"Imbeciles. Useless, worthless trash. Kill them. Kill them both immediately," he ordered with the flick of a wrist.

Jaime had to curb his initial reaction, which was to refuse. He might find Wallace and Layne disgusting excuses for human beings, he might even believe they deserved to die, but he was not comfortable with it being at his hand.

"*Senor*, if this is your wish, I will absolutely mete out your justice. But perhaps…"

"Perhaps what?" he snapped.

"You will want to go after the girl yourself, *si*?"

The Stallion frowned as he walked over and stood by his dolls, grabbing one hand as though he was holding the hand of a little girl.

Jaime had to ignore that and press his advantage. "Clearly the Ranger is smarter than your men. But certainly not smarter than you. If you go after him, you can do whatever you want with both of them. Surely you, of all people, could outsmart them."

The Stallion had begun to nod the more Jaime complimented him. "You're right. You're right."

He dropped the doll's hand and Jaime nearly sagged with relief.

"You'll have to go with me, Rodriguez."

Jaime stilled. That was not part of his plan. "Tell Layne and Wallace they're in charge of the girls. We'll leave immediately."

"Their injuries are severe. Shot. Both of them. Surely incapable of watching after anything. You must have other men you can take with you, and I'll stay—"

"No." The Stallion shook his head. "No, you're coming with me. Wallace and Layne, no matter how injured, can keep a door locked. I'll send for another man, and he can kill them and take over here. Yes, yes, that's the plan. I need you. I need you, Rodriguez." The Stallion took one of the dolls off the shelf. He petted the doll's dark hair as though it were a puppy. "If you prove your worth to me on this, there is nothing that I wouldn't give you, Rodriguez." He held out the doll between them.

Jaime was afraid he looked as horrified as he felt, but he kept his hands grasped lightly behind his back. He forced himself to smile languidly at the unseeing doll. "Then I am at your service, *senor.*"

"Go tell them the plan," The Stallion said, gesturing with the doll, thank God not making him take it. "Not the killing part, of course, just the watching-after-the-girls part. Pack all your weapons and all your ammunition. Pack up all the water in my supplies and put it in the Jeep. We'll leave as soon as you've gotten everything together. Do you understand?"

Jaime nodded, trying to steady the panic rising inside him. *"Sí, senor."*

It wasn't such a terrible thing. He'd be there to stop The Stallion from getting any kind of hold on Gabby's sister and Ranger Cooper. But it left Gabby here. Exposed.

And he only had limited time to figure out how to fix that.

Chapter Thirteen

Gabby tried to ignore how locked in she felt. She'd been a victim for eight years. A prisoner of this place. Being locked in her room and unable to leave was certainly no greater trial to bear.

But she hadn't been locked in her room for any stretch of time since the very beginning. Mostly she'd been able to go to the common room or the kitchen whenever she wanted.

She'd gotten used to that freedom, and it was clawing at her to have lost some of it. That made it a very effective punishment all in all.

She wondered what the girls were doing. Had Alyssa calmed down? Was she ranting? Was she bringing reality to her threat to kill everyone in an effort to get out of there?

Gabby buried her face in her pillow and tried to block it all out, but when she inhaled she could smell Jaime and something in her chest turned over.

Oh, Jaime. That was part of why this locked-up thing was harder to bear, too. She'd felt almost real for nearly twenty-four hours. She and Jaime had spent the night, and most of today, having sex and talking and enjoying each other's company. As though they lived in an outside world where they were themselves and not undercover agent and kidnapping victim.

It made it so much harder to be fully forced into what she really was. Victim. Captive. Not any closer to having any power than she'd been twenty-four hours ago.

Except she'd stolen a moment of it, and wasn't that something worth celebrating?

She heard someone unlocking her door from the outside and sat bolt upright in bed. Jaime hadn't been gone very long. If he was back already, it had to be bad news.

If it wasn't Jaime on the other side, so much the worse.

But it was the man she'd taken as a lover who stepped into her room, shutting the door behind him with more force than necessary. His face reminded her of that first day. Rodriguez. The mask, not the man.

"Do you have anything in here you'd want to take with you?" he demanded.

"What?" She couldn't follow him as he walked the perimeter of her room as if searching for something valuable.

"I don't have time to explain. I don't have time to do anything but get you out now."

"What happened?" she asked, jumping off the bed.

His hand curled around her forearm, tight and without any of its usual kindness. "Is there anything you need to take?" he repeated, glaring at her.

"What's happened?" she pleaded with him. Her heart

beat a heavy cadence against her chest and she couldn't think past the panic gripping her. "Is it Nattie? Is—"

He began pulling her to the door. "Your sister and the Ranger escaped."

"Escaped? Escaped!" Hope burst in her chest, bright and wonderful. "So we're…we're just running?"

He looked up and down the hallway. "You are. I'll get the other girls after."

That stopped Gabby in her tracks, no matter how he pulled on her arm. "What?" she demanded.

"Layne and Wallace are hurt. I can get one of you out now without raising any questions because you're supposed to be locked up, but I can't get you all out. Not right this second. I have to go with The Stallion to track down your sister. Which is good," he said before she could argue with him or ask him what the hell he was talking about. "Because I will obviously make sure that doesn't happen. I have—" he glanced at his watch "—maybe five seconds to contact my superiors to let them know to raid this place, and then to try to find one just like it in the south." He shoved her into the hallway, but she fought him.

"You can't take me and not them."

His gaze locked on hers. "Of course I can. And that's what we're doing."

"No. You can't. They'll fall apart without me."

"They won't. And they'll be saved in a day or two. Three tops."

"You really expect me to leave Tabitha and Jasmine here with Alyssa? Alyssa will instigate something. You know she will. They'll all be dead before…" She didn't want to say it out loud, no matter how much he wasn't being careful himself.

He grabbed her by the shoulders and gave her a little shake, his eyes fierce and stubborn. "But you won't be."

It was her turn to look up and down the hallway. She didn't know where the girls were, where Wallace and Layne or The Stallion were milling about. Jaime was losing his mind and it was her... Well, it was her responsibility to make him find it.

"You have to get it together," she snapped in a low, quiet voice. "You have to be sensible about this, and you have to calm down."

He thrust his fingers into his hair, looking more than a little wild. "Gabby, I do not have time. You have to do what I say, and you have to do it now."

"Take Alyssa," she said, though it pained her to offer that. A stabbing pain of fear, but it was the only option.

"Wh-what?" he spluttered.

"Take Alyssa. I can handle more days here. Tabitha and Jasmine... We can hack it, but Alyssa cannot take another day. You know that. Take her. Get her out, we'll cover it up, and when the raid comes, you will come and get me."

"Have you lost your mind?"

"No! You've lost yours." Part of her wanted to push him, or reverse their positions and shake him, but the bigger part of her wanted to reach something in him. She curled her fingers into his shirt. "You know it isn't safe to take me out. Why are you risking everything?"

"Because I love you," he blurted, clearly antagonized into the admission.

She only stared up at him. It wasn't… She…

Love.

"I do not have time to argue," he said, low and fierce.

That, she was sure, was absolutely true. He didn't have time to argue. He didn't have time to think. But she knew the girls better than he did. She knew…

She reached her hands up and cupped his face. She drew strength from that. From him. From love. "If you love me," she said, low and in her own kind of fierce, "then understand that I know what they can handle. What they can't. I couldn't live with myself if I got out and they didn't. Not like this."

She wasn't sure what changed in him. There was still an inhuman tenseness to his muscles and yet some of that fierceness in him had dimmed.

"What am I supposed to do if something happens to you?" he asked, his voice pained and gravelly.

"I can take care of myself." She knew it wasn't totally true. A million things could go wrong, but she had to trust him to leave and save Nattie, and he needed to trust her to stay and keep the girls alive.

That she'd have a much easier time of doing if he took Alyssa. No matter that it made her want to cry. No matter that she wanted to be selfish and take the spot. But she couldn't imagine living the rest of her life if their deaths were on her head.

If there was a chance to get them *all* out, alive and safe, she had to take it. Not the one that only saved her. "You know I'm right."

He looked away from her, though his tight grip on

her shoulders never loosened. "You understand that I have to go. I don't have a choice."

"I want you to go. To save my sister."

His gaze returned to hers, flat and hard. "I'm not taking Alyssa."

"What? You have to." She gripped his shirt harder in an attempt to shake him. "If you can get one of us—"

"Gabby, I could get you out. Because you're supposed to be locked up, but more because I know you could do it. I could trust you to handle anything that came our way. I can't trust Alyssa. I can't trust her to keep her mouth shut when it counts. I can't trust her to get home. Like you said, she can't hack it. If I can't leave her here, then I can't take her, either."

"Then take one of the other girls!"

"You said it yourself. Alyssa would blab someone was missing. She'd… You can't trust her not to get you all killed. Don't you understand? It's you or no one."

"Why are you doing this?" she demanded, tears flooding her eyes. It wasn't fair. It wasn't right. He should take someone. Someone had to survive this.

"I'm not doing anything. I saw a chance for you— you, Gabby, to escape. If you won't take it, there's no substitute here. There is only you or nothing."

"Why are you trying to manipulate me into this? If you love me—"

"Why are you trying to manipulate my love? I know what the hell I'm doing, too. I have been trained for this. I have—"

"Gabby?"

Gabby and Jaime both jerked, looking down the hallway to Jasmine standing wide-eyed at the end of it. "What's going on?"

Jaime shook his head. "I can't do this. I don't have time to do this." Completely ignoring Jasmine, he got all up in Gabby's face, pulling her even closer, his dark eyes blazing into her. "I can save you *now*, but you have to come with me now. This is your last chance."

"It's your last chance to think reasonably," she retorted.

He looked to the ceiling and inhaled before crushing his mouth to hers, as though Jasmine wasn't standing right there. He seemed to pour all his frustration and all his fear into the kiss, and all Gabby could do was accept it.

"Goodbye, Gabby," he said on a ragged whisper, releasing her. "I love you, and I will get you safe."

She started to say his name as he walked away, but stopped herself as she looked at Jasmine. She couldn't say his real name. Even if she trusted Jasmine, she couldn't... This was all too dangerous now.

She wanted to tell him to save her sister. She wanted to tell him she loved him. She wanted to tell him he was being unfair and wrong, and yet none of those words poured out as he started to walk away. She wanted to tell him to be safe. That it would kill her if he was hurt.

But Jasmine was watching and she had to let him walk away. To save her sister. To save them all.

"What's happening?" Jasmine asked in a shaky voice. "I don't understand anything that I just saw."

Gabby slumped against the wall. "I don't know. I don't..."

"Yes, you do," Jasmine snapped, her voice sharp and uncompromising.

Gabby felt the tears spill unbidden down her cheeks. What was happening? She didn't understand any of it. But she knew she had to be strong. If they were going to be saved, she had to be strong.

She reached out for Jasmine, gratified when the girl offered support.

"We need to make a plan," Gabby said, sounding a lot stronger than she felt.

JAIME WASN'T SURE he could hide his dark mood if he tried. He was furious. Furious with Gabby for not coming with him. Furious at The Stallion for being the kind of fool who needed him to be there to do all the dirty work. Furious at the world for giving him something beautiful and then taking it all away.

Or are you just terrified?

He ground his teeth together and slid a look at The Stallion. The man sat in the passenger seat of the Jeep, typing on his laptop, swearing every time his Wi-Fi hotspot lost any kind of signal. He had a tricked-out assault rifle sitting precariously on his lap.

Jaime drove fueled on fear and anger. He'd had to leave the compound before he'd been able to be certain his message to his superiors had gone through. For all he knew, he could be out there alone with no backup. Gabby could be alone with no backup.

He wanted to rage. Instead he drove.

They were in the Guadalupe Mountains now, having driven through the night. Apparently, Gabby's sister and Ranger Cooper had run this way. Jaime was skeptical, considering how isolated it was. How would they be surviving?

But it didn't really matter. If they were on the wrong track, all the better.

What would actually be all the better would be reaching down to his side piece and ending this once and for all. It would put an end to two years of suffering. Eight for Gabby. Who knew how much suffering for everyone else.

But no matter how much anger and fury pumped through his veins, he knew he couldn't do it. Those same people who had been victims deserved answers and they deserved justice. In an operation like The Stallion's, so big, so vast, taking the big man out would produce perhaps a confused few days, but someone would quickly and easily usurp that power. Taking over as if The Stallion had never existed. It would create even more victims than already existed.

He couldn't overlook that. His duty was his duty. Intractable no matter how unfair it seemed. No matter what Gabby would think of it.

Gabby had implored him to trust her and, in the moment, he hadn't. He'd been too blinded by his fear and his anger that she wouldn't go with him.

In the quiet of driving through these deserted mountains, Jaime could only relive that moment. Over and over again. Regret slicing through him. He'd ended things so badly, and there was such a chance—

No. He wouldn't let himself think that way. There was no chance he wouldn't see Gabby again. No good chance they didn't escape this. He would find a way and so would she.

"Drive up there." The Stallion pointing at, what seemed to Jaime, a random mountain.

"There is no road."

The Stallion gave him a doleful look. "Drive to the top of that mountain," he repeated.

Jaime inclined his head. *"Sí, senor."* He drove, adrenaline pumping too hard as the Jeep skidded and halted up the rocky incline. He gripped the wheel, tapping the brakes, doing everything he could to remain in control of the vehicle.

Finally, The Stallion instructed him to stop. The man pulled out a pair of high-tech binoculars and began to search the horizon.

Jaime watched the man. He looked like any man, hunting or perhaps watching birds. He appeared completely sane and normal, and yet Jaime had seen him fondle dolls like they were real people.

"Senor, may I ask you a question?" It was a dangerous road to take. If The Stallion read anything suspicious into his questioning, Jaime could end up dead in the middle of this mountainous desert.

But The Stallion nodded regally as if granting an audience with the peasants.

"If you believe women are diseased, so you say, why do you keep so many of them?"

The Stallion seemed to ponder the line of questioning. Eventually he shrugged. "Waste not, want not."

Jaime didn't have to feign a language barrier for that to not make sense at all. "I… Come again?"

"Waste not, want not," The Stallion repeated. "I find them hideous creatures myself, as the perfect woman remains elusive. But some men, like yourself, require certain payments. Why should I waste the work they can do for the possible insurance they can offer me? It only makes sense to keep them. To use them. In fact, it's what women were really meant for. To be used. Perhaps the perfect woman is just a myth. And my mother was a dirty liar." The Stallion's fingers tightened on his gun, though he still held the binoculars with his other hand.

Jaime said nothing more. It was best if he stopped asking for motives and started focusing on what he was going to do if they found Natalie and Ranger Cooper. Focus on thwarting The Stallion's plans without tipping him off to it.

Or you could just kill him.

It was so tempting, Jaime found his hand drifting down to the piece on his left side without really thinking about it.

"There!" The Stallion shouted, pointing.

Jaime blinked down at the bright desert and mountain before them.

"I saw something down there. Get out of the Jeep. Remember, I don't care what happens to the Ranger, but I want the girl alive."

The Stallion jumped out of the Jeep, scrambling over the loose rock, his gun cocked, laptop and binoculars forgotten in the passenger seat.

Though Jaime wanted nothing to do with this, he also jumped out of the car. He had to make sure The Stallion did nothing to Ranger Cooper or Gabby's sister.

Jaime grabbed a gun for each hand. It was easy to catch up with The Stallion given Jaime's legs were longer. Since The Stallion had his gun raised to his shoulder, Jaime pretended to accidentally skid into him as he fired his weapon.

"Damn it, Rodriguez. I had a shot!" The Stallion bellowed.

Jaime surveyed the ground below. He could see two figures standing like sitting ducks in the middle of the desert. They were too far away to make a shot a sure thing, but why weren't they moving after that first shot?

Jaime raised his gun. "Allow me, *senor.*"

Jaime was surprised that his arm very nearly shook as he took aim. He'd used his guns plenty in the past two years, though usually to disarm someone or to scare them, not to kill them.

This was no different. He aimed as close as he could without risking any harm and fired.

"You idiot!"

"They are too far away. We have to be closer."

"Like hell." The Stallion raised his gun again and since Jaime couldn't run into him again, he did the only other thing he could think of. He sneezed, loudly.

Again, The Stallion's shot went wide. He snapped his furious gaze on Jaime, and as his head and body turned toward him, so did the gun.

Jaime held himself unnaturally still, doing everything he could to show no fear or reaction to that gun pointed in his direction. He couldn't clear his throat to speak, and he could barely hear his own thoughts over the beating of his heart.

"*Perdón, senor*, but we need to be closer," Jaime said as if a gun that could blow him to pieces wasn't very nearly trained on him at close range. "If you want to ensure the Ranger is dead and the girl is yours, we need to be closer." Jaime pointed out over the desert below, where the couple was now running.

With no warning, The Stallion jerked the gun their way and shot. The woman scrambled behind the out-cropping, but Jaime watched as Ranger Cooper jerked. Jaime winced, but Cooper didn't fall. He kept running. Until he was behind the rock outcropping with Gabby's sister.

"Get in the Jeep," The Stallion ordered with calm and ruthless efficiency, making Jaime wonder if he was really crazy at all.

Jaime nodded, knowing he was on incredibly thin ice. The Stallion could shoot him at any time.

You could shoot him first.

He could. God, he could all but feel himself doing it, but Gabby was back in that compound, defenseless. And if the message hadn't gotten through to his superiors… Even if he shot The Stallion his cover would be blown. He'd have to take Ranger Cooper back, and the FBI would intercept all that. Then they'd make him follow their rules and regulations to get Gabby out.

As long as he remained Rodriguez, there was a chance to get Gabby, and the rest of the girls, out by any means necessary.

So he drove the Jeep like a madman down to where the couple had been hiding.

"They are gone by now," Jaime said, perhaps a little too hopefully.

"Keep driving. Find them." The Stallion clenched and unclenched his hand on the rifle.

Jaime did as he was told, driving around mountains until The Stallion told him to stop.

"Stay in the Jeep," The Stallion ordered. "Turn off the ignition. When I call for you, you run. Do you *comprende*?"

Jaime nodded and The Stallion got out of the Jeep, striding away. Jaime thought about staying put for all of five seconds and then he set out to follow his enemy.

Chapter Fourteen

Gabby sat in the common room with Jasmine, Tabitha and Alyssa. They were huddled on the couch, pretending to work on a project The Stallion had given them a few days ago. Layne and Wallace were groaning and limping around the house. Both clearly very injured and yet not seeking any medical attention.

"They're vulnerable. We have to press our advantage now. We have to hit them where it hurts," Alyssa whispered fiercely, staring daggers at the men who were currently groaning about in the kitchen.

Jasmine looked down at her lap, pale and clearly not wanting any part of this powwow, but...

"Unfortunately she's right," Gabby said. "It's our only chance. They've had time to call for backup. The longer we wait...the more chance someone else comes."

She felt guilty for not telling them about the possibility of an FBI raid. They deserved to know the full truth, and they deserved to know what possibilities lay ahead, but Gabby knew they had to get Alyssa out of there before she got killed or got them all killed. They couldn't wait for the FBI to come. They couldn't wait for Jaime to magically fix everything.

No, they had to act.

"We have to time it exactly and precisely. Two of us against one, the other two against the other. Same time. Same attack. Same plan."

Gabby took stock of the two men grousing in the kitchen then of the three women huddled around her. Alyssa practically jumped out of her seat, completely ready to go, Tabitha looked grim and certain, but Jasmine looked pale and scared.

Gabby didn't want to draw attention to that. Not with Alyssa as…well, whatever Alyssa was. Without looking at her, Gabby reached over and gave Jasmine's hand a squeeze.

"I'm just not strong like you, Gabby," she whispered. "What if I mess up?"

Alyssa started to say something harsh but Gabby stopped her with a look. "That's why we're doing it in pairs. We're a team. Me and Jasmine. Alyssa and Tabitha. Right?"

Alyssa mostly just swore and Gabby watched her carefully. Jaime's words about trusting her rang through her head. Because how could she trust a woman who'd clearly lost her mind? Who'd just as soon kill them all as anything else?

But Jaime had been too cautious. Too afraid for her safety. Gabby didn't have anyone's safety to be afraid for right now. She and the girls were getting to the now-or-never point. Alyssa was already there, and though Tabitha and Jasmine had been somewhat more resilient, they had to feel as she did. They had to be losing that perilous grip on who they were.

Jaime had given herself back to her. Hope, a possible future, but those women hadn't had that. So she had to get them free.

"We'll take Layne," Gabby said, nudging Jasmine with her shoulder. "You two will have Wallace."

"But he's the bigger one," Jasmine whispered.

"It'll be fine. He has a gunshot wound to the shoulder. Wallace has one to the leg. We're four healthy, capable women."

"B-but what do we do, exactly? After we attack them, what do we do? Run?" Tabitha asked, clearly forcing herself to be strong.

"Kill them. We want to kill them. They did this to us. They deserve to die," Alyssa all but chanted, a wild gleam to her eyes.

Gabby wasn't sure why she hesitated at that. She had indeed been stripped from her life by men like these two, and they surely deserved death. But she found she didn't want to be the one to give it to them.

"We're going to use their injuries to our advantage, hurt them, and then tie them up so we can get away without fear of being followed."

Alyssa scoffed. "I'm going to kill him."

Gabby reached over and grabbed Alyssa's hands, trying to catch her frenzied gaze. "Please. Understand. I don't want to be haunted by this for the rest of my life. I want to leave here and leave it *behind*. No killing unless we absolutely have to. If we have a hope of getting out of here as unharmed as we are in *this* moment, we don't kill them. We incapacitate them."

"And then what? We're just going to run? Run where?"

"I have a vague notion of where we are, and that will help get us out. We've survived this, we can survive walking until we find a town."

Alyssa shook her head in disgust, but Gabby squeezed her hands tighter.

"I need you with me on this. We need to all be together and on the same page. Don't you want to be able to go home and go back to your old life and not have that on your conscience?"

"Who said I have a conscience?" Alyssa retorted, and for a very quick second Gabby believed her, believed that coldness. She'd seen nothing but cold for eight years.

Until Jaime.

That made Gabby fight so much harder. "The four of us are in this together. The four of us. They can't take that away from us. We have survived together, and when we get out, we will still be indelibly linked by that. We're like sisters. They can't make us turn on each other. You can't let them. As long as we work together, as long as we're linked, they can't hurt us."

Gabby wasn't certain that was true. They had guns and weapons, after all. But they were hurt. She had to believe it gave her and the girls an advantage.

Alyssa was looking at her strangely. "Sisters," she whispered. "I don't... No one's ever fought with me before."

"We will," Tabitha said, adding her hand to Gabby's on top of Alyssa's. Then Jasmine added her hand.

"We don't get out of this without each other," Gabby said, glancing back at Wallace and Layne. Wallace was still moaning, but Layne was glancing their way.

"We'll slowly make excuses to go to our rooms, but you'll all come to mine," she whispered as she pulled her hand from the girls.

Jasmine brought her sewing back to her lap and Tabitha pretended to examine the next package they were supposed to hide in the stuffing of a toy dog.

Gabby got to her feet, but Layne was there and, with his good arm, he shoved her back down.

Well, crap. This wasn't going to go well.

"Problem?" she asked sweetly, looking up at his suspicious gaze. She probably should avert her gaze and show some sort of deference to the man with a gun in his waistband and a nasty expression on his face.

"Aren't you supposed to be locked up?"

"I was just going back to my room when you shoved me back to the couch so rudely."

"I'd watch how you talk to me, little girl," Layne seethed, getting his face into hers.

Gabby bit her tongue because what she really wanted to do was tell *him* to be careful how he talked to her, and then punch him in his bloody bandage as hard and painfully as she could.

Instead she slowly got to her feet, unfolding to her full height. Though he was still much taller than she was, she affected her most condescending stare, never breaking eye contact with him as she stood there, shoulders back.

She was more than a little gratified by the way he seemed to wilt just a teeny tiny bit. As if he knew he couldn't break her.

"I'll just be going to my room now. Feel free to lock my door behind me."

"You little—" He lifted his meaty hand, she supposed to backhand her, and she probably should have let him hit her. She probably should let this all go, but whatever instincts to defend herself she'd tried to eradicate surged to life. She grabbed his hand before it could land across her face, and then put all her force behind shoving him, trying to make contact with his injury.

He stumbled back, though he didn't fall. He let out a hideous moan as, with his bad arm, he pulled the gun from his waistband and trained it on Gabby.

She was certain she was dead. She stood there, waiting for the firearm to go off. Waiting for the piercing pain of a bullet. Or maybe she wouldn't feel it at all. Maybe she would simply die.

But before another breath could be taken, Alyssa was in front of her, and then Tabitha and Jasmine at her sides.

"You'll have to get through us to shoot her, and if you shoot all of us?" Alyssa pretended to ponder that. "I doubt The Stallion would be too pleased with you."

"I'll kill all of you without breaking a sweat, you miserable—"

"Isn't it cute?" Alyssa said, looking back at Gabby.

"He thinks *he's* in charge, not his exacting, demanding boss. Well, I guess it takes some balls to be that stupid."

Gabby closed her eyes, she didn't think goading him was really the road to take here, but he hadn't fired.

Yet.

There was a quiet standoff and Gabby tried to rein in the heavy overbeating of her heart. Jasmine's hand slid into hers and Tabitha's arm wound around her shoulders. Alyssa faced off with Layne as if she had no fear whatsoever.

Together, they couldn't be hurt. God, she very nearly believed it.

"If you aren't in your rooms in five seconds, I will shoot all of you," Layne said menacingly.

Gabby didn't believe him, but she didn't want to risk it, either. The girls in front of her hurried down the hall first, and Gabby tried to follow, but Layne grabbed her arm as she passed, digging his heavy fingers into her skin hard enough to leave bruises.

"Tonight you'll be screaming my name," he hissed.

Gabby smiled. It was either that or throw up. "Maybe you'll be screaming mine." She yanked her arm out of his grasp.

She was pretty sure the only thing that kept Layne from shooting her at this point was Wallace's sharp stand-down order.

When Gabby got to her room, she locked the door behind her. It wouldn't keep her safe from Layne since he undoubtedly had a key, but it at least gave her the illusion of safety.

When she turned back to face her room, the girls

were all there, Tabitha and Jasmine on her bed, Alyssa pacing the room.

"And now we plan," Alyssa said, that dark glint in her eyes comforting for the first time.

JAIME STALKED THE STALLION. It wasn't easy to carefully follow a man who was carefully following another man, especially through a weirdly arid desert landscape dotted by mountains and rock outcroppings. But then, when had any of this been *easy*?

The Stallion stopped as though he'd seen something, and Jaime waited a beat. He realized The Stallion was peering around a swell of earth, and when The Stallion didn't move forward in the swiftly calculating pace he'd been employing, Jaime sucked in a breath.

On a hunch and a prayer, Jaime snuck around the other side of it. He kept his footsteps slow and quiet.

And then a shot rang out.

Jaime took off in a run, skidding to a halt when he saw The Stallion and Ranger Cooper standing off.

Jaime couldn't hear their conversation, but both men were unharmed and The Stallion didn't fire. Jaime dropped the small handguns he'd been carrying for ease of movement and unholstered his largest and most accurate weapon.

He trained it on The Stallion, only occasionally letting his gaze dart around to try to catch sight of the woman who remained hidden somewhere. The Stallion and Ranger Cooper spoke, back and forth, guns pointed at each other, lawman and madman in the strangest showdown Jaime had ever witnessed.

That gave Jaime the presence of mind to *breathe*. To watch and bide his time. Without knowing where Natalie Torres was, he couldn't act rashly. He—

Something in The Stallion's posture changed and Jaime sighted his gun, ready to shoot, ready to stop The Stallion before anything happened to Ranger Cooper. But before he could line up his shot and pull the trigger without accidentally hitting Cooper, Cooper fired.

The gun flew from The Stallion's hand and he howled with rage. Why the hell hadn't Cooper shot the bastard in the heart? Jaime was about to do just that, but the woman appeared from a crevice in one of the rocks, holding her own weapon up and trained on The Stallion.

She reminded him so much of Gabby it physically hurt. There wasn't an identical resemblance, but it was that determined glint in Natalie's dark eyes that had him thinking about Gabby. If she was safe. If any of them would make it through this in one piece.

He shook that thought away. They would. They all damn well would.

And then Natalie pulled the trigger. She missed, but before Jaime could step out from the outcropping, she'd fired again. Even from Jaime's distance he could see the red bloom on The Stallion's stomach.

"Rodriguez!" he screamed, followed by The Stallion's sad attempt at Spanish. Jaime sighed. He could only hope Cooper recognized him, or that they wouldn't shoot on sight. He could stay there, of course, but it would be worse if he waited for Ranger Cooper to find him.

He stepped out from behind the land swell and walked slowly and calmly toward his writhing fake boss.

Ranger Cooper watched him with the dawning realization of recognition, but Natalie clearly didn't have a clue as she kept her gun trained on him.

Jaime thought maybe, maybe, there was a chance he could maintain his identity and get back to Gabby, so he nodded to Cooper. "Tell your woman to put down the gun," he said in Spanish.

Cooper looked over at the woman. "Put it down, Nat," he murmured, an interesting softness in the command. One Jaime thought he recognized.

Wasn't that odd?

"I won't let anyone kill us. Not now. Not when that man has my sister," Natalie said, her hands shaking, her dark eyes shiny with tears. The Torres women were truly a marvel.

The Stallion made a grab for Jaime's leg piece, but Jaime easily kicked him away. No, he wasn't Rodriguez anymore. He had to be the man he'd always been, and he had to do his duty.

He wasn't Rodriguez, a monster with a shady past. He was Jaime Alessandro, FBI agent, and regardless of *who* he was, he'd find a way to get Gabby to safety as soon as he got out of there.

"Ma'am, I need you to put your weapon down," Jaime said, steady and sure, making eye contact with Natalie. "I'm with the FBI. I've been working undercover for Callihan." Jaime ignored The Stallion's outraged cry, because he saw the way the information tumbled together in Natalie's head.

She didn't even have to ask about Gabby for him to

know that's what she needed to hear. "I know where your sister is. She's…safe."

Natalie didn't just lower her gun, she dropped it. She sank to the rocky ground and Jaime had to raise an eyebrow at Ranger Cooper sinking with her.

He couldn't hear what they said to each other, but it didn't matter. He turned to The Stallion. Victor Callihan. The man who'd made his life a living hell for two years.

He was still writhing on the ground, bloody and pale, shaking possibly with shock or with the loss of blood. He might make it. He might not. Jaime supposed it would depend on how quickly they worked.

Jaime slid into a crouch. "How does it feel, *senor*," Jaime mused aloud, "to be so completely outwitted by everyone around you?"

"You think this is over?" The Stallion rasped. "It'll never be over. As long as I *breathe,* you're mine, and it will never, *ever*, be over."

Jaime had been through too much for those words to have any impact. The Stallion thought he could intimidate him? Make him fear? Not in this lifetime or the next.

"There's already an FBI raid at all four of your compounds." He was gratified when the man's eyes bulged. "Oh, did you think I didn't put it together? The southern compound? You know who helped me figure out its location? Ah, no, I don't want to ruin the surprise. I'll let you worry about that. You'll have plenty of time to ruminate in a cell."

The Stallion lunged, but he was weakened and all

Jaime had to do was rock back on his heels to avoid the man's grasp.

"Everyone should be out by the time I get back, and you know what my first order of business will be? Burning every last doll in that place," he whispered in the man's ear, before standing.

Jaime turned to Cooper who'd gotten Natalie to her feet. He ignored The Stallion's sputtering and nodded in the direction of the Jeep. "I have rope in my vehicle. We'll tie him up and take him to the closest ranger station."

And then he'd find a way to get to Gabby.

Chapter Fifteen

Gabby stood at the door to her room, Jasmine slightly in front of her. Alyssa and Tabitha had already gone back into the common room, plan in place.

Gabby felt sick, but she pushed it away. The girls were counting on her and so was... Well, she herself. She was the architect of this plan, the leader, and if she wanted them all to survive, she had to be calm and strong.

Jaime was out protecting her sister, and no matter how mad he might be at her for not leaving, she knew he'd do everything to keep Natalie safe.

And she hadn't even told him...

She forced it all away as Alyssa's cue blasted through the house. Gabby exchanged a look with Jasmine. Alyssa was supposed to yell at Tabitha, not scream obscenities at her.

As Gabby and Jasmine slid into the room, Alyssa attacked, stabbing one of her butter knives into Wallace's leg with a brutal force Gabby had to look away from.

Jasmine threw the cords they'd gathered at Tabitha. Wallace screamed in a kind of agony that made Gabby's blood run cold, but she couldn't think about that now. Layne was her target.

His eyes gleamed with an unholy bloodlust and his gun was in his grasp far too fast. But somehow everything seemed to move in slow motion. Before Gabby could even flinch, Jasmine was throwing her body at Layne's legs.

The impact surprised Layne enough that he fell forward, on top of Jasmine, who cried out, mixing with Wallace's screams.

Gabby scrambled forward, pushing Layne off Jasmine so he hit the hard floor on his injured shoulder. He howled in pain, but he didn't let go of the gun as Gabby grabbed it.

She jerked and pulled, but Layne didn't let go. He screamed, but she couldn't wrestle the weapon from his grasp.

Until Jasmine got to her feet and started stomping on his bad shoulder, a wholly different girl than the woman who'd, pale-faced and wide-eyed, told Gabby she wasn't strong enough. Gabby finally wrested the gun free of his hand, trying to think past the high-pitched keening from both men.

"Rope," she gasped then yelled louder. She glanced at Alyssa and Tabitha. Wallace thrashed, groaning in pain as he swung his hands out, but Tabitha had tied his legs tightly to the chair and Alyssa had already wrestled the gun out of his hands.

Alyssa kicked one of the cords Gabby's way and Gabby grabbed it as Layne tried to scuttle away from Jasmine, cursing and, Gabby thought, maybe even sobbing.

Jasmine stomped another time on his wound, which had now bled completely through his bandage and shirt. His face went white and his eyes rolled back in his head, and it was only then that Gabby realized Jasmine was crying and that Wallace had gone completely silent.

Feeling a sob rise in her throat, Gabby knelt next to Layne and jerked his arms behind his back, doing her best to tie the cord around his thick forearms and wrists. She pulled it as tightly as she possibly could and tied as many knots as the length of cord would allow.

She breathed through her mouth, because something about the smell of Layne—him or his wound—nearly made her woozy.

"I've got his legs," Tabitha said, moving to the end of Layne's lifeless body. Gabby could see the rise and fall of his chest, so he wasn't dead.

She almost wished he was, which was enough to get her to her feet. She glanced back at Alyssa who had ripped off half her shirt and tied it around Wallace's face like a gag. The man still wiggled, but the cords and knots were holding and if he tried to escape too much longer, he'd likely knock the whole chair over.

Alyssa held the gun far too close to Wallace's head.

Gabby crossed to her, holding her hand out for the gun. "Tabitha is going to guard them."

Alyssa didn't spare Gabby a glance. "My suggestion of just killing them stands," she said, her hands tight on the gun, sweat dripping down her temple.

"I need your help to gather evidence."

"They can," Alyssa said, jerking her chin toward Jasmine, who stood with Layne's gun trained on his unmoving form and Tabitha finishing up the knots at his ankles. She never looked at them, just gestured toward them.

"No, I need you," Gabby said firmly.

Alyssa's gaze finally flickered to Gabby. "You need me?"

"Yes. You're the strongest next to me. We'll be able to break down the doors easiest and carry the most stuff. I need you."

Gabby didn't really know if Alyssa was stronger, but it was certainly the most plausible. Clearly it also got through to her since she'd looked away from Wallace.

Maybe it would be easier to kill the men, but Gabby... She didn't want to have to relive that for the rest of her life, and she didn't want the other girls to have to, either.

Alyssa waved the gun a bit. "We might need this to bust the lock off."

Gabby remained steadfast in holding her hand out, palm upward. "Give me the gun, Alyssa. We need to do this as a team."

The woman's mouth turned into a sneer and Gabby thought for sure she'd lost the battle. Any second now Alyssa would pull the trigger and—

She slapped the gun into Gabby's palm. "Let's go get those doors open," she muttered.

Gabby nodded, looking at Tabitha and Jasmine. Jasmine had Layne's gun and Tabitha had what looked to be a dagger of some kind that she must have taken off one of the men.

"Scream if you need anything," Gabby said sternly. "Once we have whatever evidence we can carry, we'll come get you and lock this place back up, and then we'll start out."

Jasmine and Tabitha nodded, and though they'd handled themselves like old pros, everyone seemed a little shaky now. Far too jumpy. She and Alyssa needed to hurry.

They raced down the hall to the door. "Give me one of those knives."

Alyssa pulled one out of her bra and if Gabby had time she might have marveled at it, but instead she used it to start picking the lock. Turned out Ricky and his ne'er-do-well friends *had* taught her something.

She got the locks free and pushed on the door. It creaked open only a fraction. Alyssa inspected the crack. "It's chained on the outside," she said flatly. "Give me the gun."

Gabby hesitated. "What if it ricochets?"

Alyssa raised an eyebrow. "It won't."

What choice did Gabby have? A butter knife wasn't cutting through chain any more than anything else, and Alyssa might be losing it, but she was sure. They had to be a team.

Gabby handed over the gun. Alyssa shoved the muzzle through the crack, barely managing to fit it, and then a loud shot rang out.

The chain clanked and then after another quick and overly loud shot, Alyssa was pushing the door open.

Both women stumbled into the bright light of day. It very nearly burned, the bright sunshine, the intense blue overhead. Gabby tried to step forward, but only tripped and fell to her knees in the grass.

"Oh, God. Oh, God," Alyssa whispered.

Gabby couldn't see her. Her eyes couldn't seem to adjust to the bright light, and her heart just imploded.

She could smell the grass. She could feel it under her knees and hands. Hot from the midday sun. Rocky soil underneath. It was real. Real and true. The actual earth. Fresh air. The sun. God, the sun.

The one time they'd been let out it had been a cloudy day, and The Stallion hadn't allowed for any reaction. Just digging. But today...today the sun beat down on her face as if it hadn't been missing from her life for eight years.

Gabby tried to hold back the sobs, she had a job to do, after all. A mission, and leaving Tabitha and Jasmine alone with dangerous men no matter how injured or tied up wasn't fair. She had to act.

But all she could seem to do was suck in air and cry.

Then Alyssa's arms were pulling her to her feet. "We have to keep moving, Gabby. We've got time to cry later. Now, we have to move."

Gabby finally managed to blink her eyes open. Alyssa's jaw was set determinedly and she pointed to a fancy shed in the corner of the yard.

Gabby took a deep breath of air—fresh and sun-laden—and looked down at her hands. She'd grasped some grass and pulled it out, and now it fluttered to the patchy ground below.

The Stallion had kept her from this, *all of this*, for eight long years. It was time to make sure it was his turn to not see daylight for a hell of a lot longer.

JAIME DROVE THE Jeep toward where Cooper's map said there'd be a ranger station. Once they had access to a phone—The Stallion's laptop had been too encrypted to be of use—Jaime would call his superiors and Ranger Cooper's.

Things would be real soon enough, and he still wasn't back to Gabby.

Still, he answered Cooper's questions and only occasionally glanced at the woman sandwiched between him and the Texas Ranger.

She was slighter than Gabby, certainly softer, and yet she'd been the one to shoot The Stallion as though it had been nothing at all.

Jaime glanced at Cooper's crudely bandaged arm wound. It was bleeding through, though he'd looked over it himself and knew, at most, Cooper would need stitches.

There was an awkward silence between every one of Ranger Cooper's curt questions and every one of Jaime's succinct answers. Tension and stress seemed to stretch between all of them, no matter that The Stallion was apprehended in the back and would likely survive his injuries.

Unless Jaime slowed down. But it wasn't an option, not without news on Gabby and the raid. Too many unknowns, too many possibilities.

He finally found a road after driving through mountains and desert, and soon enough a ranger station came into view. Jaime brought the Jeep to a stop, trying to remember himself and his duty.

He pushed the Jeep into Park and looked at Cooper. "If you stay put, I'll have them call for an ambulance, as well as call your precinct. We'll see if there's any word on the raid to Callihan's house, where your sister was."

Ranger Cooper nodded stoically, putting his hand on his weapon, his glance falling to the back of the Jeep where Victor Callihan, The Stallion, Jaime's tormenter, lay still and tied up.

Bleeding.

Hopefully miserable.

Jaime glanced at Gabby's sister, but she only stared at him. She'd asked no questions about her sister. She'd said almost nothing at all. Jaime figured she was in shock.

"I don't know what to ask," she said, her voice weak and thready.

Jaime gave a sharp nod. "Let me see if I can go find out some basics." He left the Jeep and strode into the station.

A woman behind the counter squeaked, but Jaime held up his hands.

"I'm with the FBI and I need to use your phone." He realized he didn't have his badge, and he still had far too many weapons strapped to his body.

He needed to get his crap together and fast. He kept his hands raised and recited his FBI information. The woman shoved a phone at him, but she backed into a corner of her office and Jaime had no doubt she was radioing for help.

It didn't matter. He called through to his superior, trying to rein in his impatience.

"I'm in a ranger station in the Guadalupe Mountains National Park. I have Texas Ranger Vaughn Cooper and civilian Natalie Torres with me. The Stallion is hurt and disarmed. We need an ambulance for Callihan and Cooper, and I need an immediate debriefing on what's happening at The Stallion's compound in the west."

"Immediate," Agent Lucroy repeated, and though it had been years since Jaime had seen the man in charge of his undercover investigation, he could imagine clearly the man's raised eyebrow. "That's quite the demand."

"Sir," Jaime said, biting back a million things he wanted to yell. "There are four women in that compound, whom I left with armed and dangerous men. It is my duty and my utmost concern that they are safe."

There was a long silence on the line.

"Sir?" Jaime repeated, fearing the worst.

"The raid has been initiated per your message. Our agents are on the ground at the compound…"

"And Ga—the women?"

"Well… Let me get off the phone and contact the necessary authorities to get you out of there. We'll do a proper debriefing when you're back in San Antonio."

Jaime nearly doubled over, fear turning into a nauseating sickness in his gut. Oh, God, he hadn't saved her. She wasn't safe at all.

"What happened to the women?" he demanded. "One of the captives… Natalie Torres, the woman Ranger Cooper has been protecting, she's the sister of one of the captives. She deserves to know…" She deserved to know how horribly he'd failed.

Agent Lucroy sighed. "Let's just say there's a slight… situation at the El Paso compound."

Chapter Sixteen

"Do you think we can carry a computer as far as we need to walk?" Gabby asked, looking dubiously down at the hard drive Alyssa was unhooking from a million monitors.

Alyssa shrugged. "We can get it as far as we need to. Then it's got just as much a chance of being found by whatever cops we can find as any Stallion idiots."

It was a good point. In fact, Alyssa had made quite a few. Though Gabby still didn't trust Alyssa not to go off and do something drastic or dangerous, the woman was very effective under pressure.

They hadn't found any bags or things they could haul evidence in, so they'd shoved any important-looking papers into their pockets. Gabby had come across a map with markings on it, and she thought with enough time she'd be able to figure it out. She'd taken a page out of Alyssa's book and shoved it into her bra.

Gabby went through a shelf of tech gadgets and picked up anything she thought might have memory on it. Anything that could make sure this was over for good.

It's not over until you're out of here.

She tried to ignore the panic beating in her chest and *focus*. "That should be good, don't you think?" When she turned to face Alyssa, the woman was staring at a shelf of dolls. They all looked like variations of the same. Dark hair, unseeing eyes, frilly dresses.

A heavy sense of unease settled over the adrenaline coursing through Gabby. She understood now, completely, why the dolls had weighed so heavily on Jaime. She tried to look away, but it felt as if the dolls were just...staring at—

The shot that rang out made Gabby scream, the doll's head exploding made her wince, but when she wildly looked over at Alyssa, the woman was simply holding the gun up, vaguely smiling.

"Think I have enough bullets to shoot all of them?" she asked conversationally.

"No," Gabby said emphatically. "Let's go. Let's get the hell out of here."

Alyssa nodded, grabbing the computer hard drive and hefting it underneath her arm. She kept the gun in her other hand, but before either of them could make another move, the door burst open.

Gabby dropped to the ground, trying to hide behind the desk that dominated the shed, but Alyssa only turned, gun aimed at the invasion of men.

Men in *uniform*.

"FBI. Put down your weapons," they yelled in chorus.

Gabby scrambled back to her feet, blinking a few times, just to make sure... But there it was in big bold letters.

FBI.

Oh, *God.* She searched the men's faces, but none of them was Jaime.

"Drop your weapon, ma'am," one of them intoned, his voice flat and commanding.

Alyssa stared at the man and most decidedly did *not* drop her weapon.

"Alyssa," Gabby hissed.

"I'm not going to be a prisoner for another second," Alyssa said, her voice deadly calm.

"It's the *FBI.* Look at his uniform, Alyssa. Do what he *says.*" Gabby held up her hands, hoping that with her cooperating the men wouldn't shoot.

But Alyssa didn't move. She eyed the FBI agent, both with their weapons raised at each other.

"Ma'am, if you do not lower the weapon, I will be forced to shoot. You have to the count of three. One, two—"

"Ugh, fine," Alyssa relented, lowering her arm. She didn't drop the weapon and she stared at the men with nothing but a scowl.

"They're here to save us," Gabby said, feeling a bubble of hysteria try to break free. She wanted to cry. She wanted to throw herself at these men's feet. She wanted Jaime and to know for sure…

"It's over, isn't it?" she asked, a tear slipping down her cheek.

"Ma'am, you have to drop your weapon. We cannot escort you out of here until you do," he said to Alyssa, ignoring Gabby completely.

"There are two other women inside the house. Did

you—?" Gabby had started to step forward, but one of the men held up his hand and she stopped on a dime.

"We will not be discussing anything until she drops her damn weapon," the man said through gritted teeth.

There were four of them, three with their weapons trained on Alyssa, a fourth one behind the three on a phone, maybe relaying information to someone.

Alyssa had her grip on the gun so tight her knuckles were white and Gabby didn't know how to fix this.

"What are you doing?" Gabby demanded. She wanted to go over and shake Alyssa till some sense got through that hard head of hers, but she was afraid to move. They were finally free and Alyssa was going to get them both killed.

That made her a different kind of angry. "Why are you treating us like the criminals?" she demanded of the four men, soldier-stiff and stoic.

"Why won't you drop your weapon?" the agent retorted.

Gabby didn't know how long they stood there. It seemed like forever. Alyssa neither dropped her weapon, nor did the men lower theirs. Seconds ticked on, dolls watching from above, and all Gabby could do was stand there.

Stand there in limbo between prison and freedom. Stand there with the threat of this woman who'd become an ally and a friend dying when they'd come this far.

"Please, Alyssa. Please," Gabby whispered after she didn't know how long. Gabby had spent eight years trying to be strong. Beating any emotion out of herself, but all strength did in this moment was make this standoff continue.

She looked at Alyssa, letting the tears fall from her eyes, letting the emotion shake her voice. "Please, put down the gun," she whispered. "I want you safe when we get out of here. I don't want to have to watch you get hurt. Please, Alyssa, put down the gun."

Alyssa swallowed. She didn't drop the gun, though her grip loosened incrementally.

"We all want this to be over," Gabby said, pushing her advantage as hard as she could. "We all want to go home."

"I don't," Alyssa muttered, but she dropped the gun all the same.

JAIME SUPPOSED THAT someday in the future it would be a point of pride that he'd yelled at his superior over the phone and had to be restrained by three fellow agents, and still retained his job.

But when Agent Lucroy had explained there'd been a standoff—a *standoff*—with two women who had been *captives*, no matter how dangerous he'd felt Alyssa could be, Jaime had lost it.

He'd sworn at his boss. He'd thrown the phone across the ranger station. The only thing that had kept his temper on a leash as they'd waited for the ambulance was the fact that Natalie was Gabby's sister.

She didn't need to be as sick with fear and as stuck as he was.

The being restrained by three fellow agents had come later. When they'd had to forcibly put him on a flight to the field office in San Antonio instead of to Austin with Ranger Cooper and Natalie.

There had been a *slight* altercation once getting off the plane when he'd demanded his car and been refused. In the end, a guy he'd once counted as a friend had had to pull a gun on him.

He'd gotten himself together after that. Mostly. He'd met with his boss and had agreed to go through the mandatory debriefing, psych eval and the like. Sure, maybe only after Agent Lucroy had threatened to have him admitted to a psych ward if he didn't comply.

Semantics.

He was held overnight in the hospital, being poked and prodded and mentally evaluated. When he'd been released, he was supposed to go home. He was supposed to meet his superiors at noon and inform them of everything.

Instead he'd gotten in his car and driven in the opposite direction. He very possibly was risking his job and he didn't give a damn. He should go see his parents, his sister. They were in California, but if he was really going to take a break with reality, shouldn't it be to have them in his sight?

When he'd spoken to Mom on the phone, she'd begged him to come home, and when he'd said he couldn't, she'd said she'd be heading to San Antonio as soon as she could. He'd begged her off. Work. Debriefing.

The truth was… He wasn't ready to be Jaime Alessandro quite yet. He'd neither cut his hair nor shaved his beard. He was neither FBI agent nor Stallion lackey, he was something in between, and no amount of FBI shrinks poking at him would give him the key to step back into his old life.

Not until he saw Gabby. So he drove to Austin. Thanks to Ranger Cooper apparently being unaware that he wasn't supposed to know, Jaime had the information that Gabby was still in the hospital and had yet to be reunited with her family.

When Ranger Cooper had relayed that information, Jaime may have broken a few traffic laws to get to the hospital.

All he needed was to see her, to maybe touch her. Then he could breathe again. Maybe then he could find himself again.

Maybe then he'd forgive her for not getting out when he'd wanted her to.

He did some fast talking, but either the hospital staff was exceptionally good or they'd been forewarned. No amount of flashing his badge or trying to sneak around corners worked.

Eventually security had been called. When one security guard appeared, Jaime laughed. Then another had appeared behind him and he figured they were probably serious.

He wasn't armed, but there were ways he could easily incapacitate these men. He could imagine breaking the one in front's nose, the one in back's arm. This middle-aged, not-in-the-best-of-shape security guard *and* his burly partner. Bam, bam, quick and easy.

It was that uncomfortable realization—that he was

pushing too hard, pressing against people who didn't deserve it—that had him softening.

So, when the guards grabbed him by the arms, he let them. He let them push him out the doors and into the waiting room.

"What the hell is your problem, man?" the one guy asked, clearly questioning the truth of his FBI claims.

That was a good enough question. He was acting like a lunatic. Not at all like the FBI agent who had been assigned and willfully taken on the deep undercover operation that had just aided in busting a crime organization that had been hurting the people of this state—and others—for over a decade.

"You come through these doors again, the police will be taking your ass to jail. FBI agent or not."

Jaime inclined his head, straightening his shoulders and then his shirt. "I apologize," he managed to rasp, turning away from the guards only to come face-to-face with two women frowning at him.

"Why are you trying to see my daughter?" the middle-aged woman demanded, her hands shaking, her eyes red as though she'd done nothing but cry for days.

If she was Gabby's mother, perhaps she had.

It was the thing that finally woke him up. Really and fully. Gabby's mother, and a woman who looked to be Gabby's grandmother. He'd assumed Natalie wasn't there, but then she walked in from the hallway carrying two paper cups of coffee.

"Agent Alessandro," she said, stopping short. "Did something hap—?"

"No, Ms. Torres. I merely came by to check on your

sister, and I was informed, uh..." He glanced at the women who'd likely seen him get tossed out on his ass. "She wasn't seeing visitors."

Natalie handed off the drinks to the other two women, offering a small and weak smile. "She's asked not to see anyone for a bit longer yet, from what the doctor told me."

"And her, uh, health? It's..."

"As good as can be expected. Maybe better. They've had a psychiatrist talking to her a bit. Are you here to question her? I'm not sure—"

"The case we're building against The Stallion will take time, but your sister's contributions... Well, we'll certainly work with her comfort as much as we can."

He looked at the three women who'd been through their own kind of hell. He didn't know them. Maybe they'd spent eight years certain Gabby was dead. Maybe they'd hoped for her return every night for however many nights she'd been gone.

Gabby would know. She'd be able to figure out the math in a heartbeat, or maybe it was her heartbeat, every second away from her family.

A family who had loved her and taken care of her for twenty years. A family who had far more claim to her than the man who'd spent a week with her and left her behind.

He straightened his shirt again, clearing his throat. He pulled out his wallet, a strange sight. It held his ID with his real name. His badge. Things that belonged to Jaime Alessandro, not Rodriguez.

He blinked for a few seconds, forgetting what he was doing.

"Do you want me to call some—?"

He thrust his business card at Natalie, effectively cutting off her too kind offer. "If you need anything, anything at all, any of you, please don't hesitate to contact me. I'll be back in San Antonio for at least another day or two, but it's an easy enough drive."

Natalie looked at him with big brown eyes that looked too much like Gabby's for his shaky control.

"I want all three of you to know how strong Gab— Gabriella was during this whole ordeal," he forced himself to say, feeling stronger and more sure with every word. FBI agent to the last. "She saved herself, and those women, and did an amazing amount of work in allowing us to confidently press charges against a very dangerous man."

She'd been a warrior, a goddess, an immeasurable asset and ally. She was a *survivor* in every iteration of the word, and he wasn't worthy of her. Not like this.

That meant he had to face his responsibilities and figure out how to come back as just that.

Worthy of Gabby.

Chapter Seventeen

Gabby sat in a sterile hospital room dreading the seconds that ticked by. Every second brought her closer to something she didn't know how to face.

Life.

Her family was in the waiting room. She'd been cleared by both the doctor and the psychiatrist to see them. To be released from the hospital. There'd be plenty of therapy and police interviews in the future, but for the most part she could go home.

What did that even mean? Eight years she'd been missing. Eight years for hcr family to change. Daddy was gone. Who knew where Mom and Grandma lived. Surely, Natalie had her own life.

Gabby sat on the hospital bed and tried not to hold on to it for dear life when the nurse arrived. Gabby didn't want to leave this room. She didn't want to face whatever waited for her out there.

She'd rather go back to the compound.

It was that thought, and the shuddering denial that went through her, that reminded her... Well, this would be hard, of course it would be. It would be painful, and a struggle, but it was better. So much better than being a prisoner.

"Your family is waiting," the nurse said kindly. "I've got your copy of the discharge papers and the referrals from the psychiatrist. Is there anything you'd like me to relay to your family for you?"

Gabby shook her head, forcing herself to climb off the bed and onto her own two feet. Her own two feet, which had gotten her this far.

She took a shaky breath and followed the nurse out of the safety of her hospital room. The corridor was quiet save for machine beeps and squeaky shoes on linoleum floors. Gabby thought she might throw up, and then they'd probably take her back to a room and she could...

But they reached the doors and the nurse paused, offering a comforting smile. "Whenever you're ready, sweetheart."

Gabby straightened. She'd never be ready, so taking a second was only delaying the inevitable. "Let's go."

The nurse opened the doors and stepped out, Gabby following by some sheer force of will that had gotten her through eight years of hell.

The nurse walked toward three women sitting huddled together. None of them looked *familiar* and yet Gabby knew exactly who they were. Grandma, Mom, Natalie. Older and different and yet *them*.

Natalie got to her feet, her face white and her eyes wide as though she were looking at a ghost.

Gabby felt like one. Natalie reached out, but it was almost blindly, as if she didn't know what she was reaching for. As if Gabby were really a vision Natalie's hand would simply move through.

Her little sister. A woman in her own right. Eight years lost between them, and she was reaching out for a ghost. But Gabby was no ghost.

"Nattie." It was out of her mouth before Gabby'd even thought it. She grabbed Natalie's hand and squeezed it. Real. Alive. Her sister. Flesh and bone and *soul.* They weren't the same women anymore, but they were still sisters. No matter what separated them.

Natalie didn't say anything, just gaped at her. Mom and Grandma were still sitting, sobbing openly and loudly. Two women she'd barely ever seen cry. The Torres family kept their *sadness* on the down low or hidden in anger, but never...

Never this.

"Say something," Gabby whispered to Natalie, desperate for something to break this tight bubble of pain inside her.

"I don't know..." Natalie sucked in a deep breath, looking up at Gabby who remained an inch or two taller. "I'm so sorr—"

Gabby shook her head and cupped Natalie's face with her hands. She would fall apart with apologies from innocent bystanders. "No, none of that."

Natalie let out a sob and her entire body leaned into Gabby. A hug. Tears over her. Gabby didn't sob, but her own tears slid down her cheeks as she held her sister back.

Real. Not a dream. Nothing but *real.* She glanced over Natalie's head at her mother and grandmother. She held an arm out to them. "Mama, Grandma." Her voice was little more than a rasp, but she used as commanding a tone as she could muster. "Come here."

It only took a second before they were on their feet, wrapping their arms around her, holding on too tightly, struggling to breathe through tears and hugs.

Gabby shook, something echoing all the way through her body so violently she couldn't fight it off. It was relief. It was fear. It was her mother's arms wrapped tight around her.

"Are you all right?" Natalie asked, clearly concerned over Gabby's shaking. "Do you need a doctor? I'll go get the nu—"

But Gabby held her close. "I'm all right, baby sister. I just can't believe it's real. You're all here."

"They…told you about… Daddy?"

Gabby swallowed, her chin coming up, and she did her best to harden her heart. She'd deal with the softer side of that grief some other time. "The Stallion made sure I knew."

"But…"

Gabby shook her head. She shouldn't have mentioned that man, that evil. She was free, and she wasn't going back to that place. "No. Not today. Maybe not ever."

"One of us needs to get it together so we can drive home," Mama said, her hand shaking as she mopped up tears. Her other hand was a death grip around Gabby's elbow. Gabby didn't even try to escape it. It was like an anchor. A truth.

"I'm all right," Natalie assured them. "I'll drive.

Right now. We're free to go. We're... Let's get out of here. And go home."

"Home," Gabby echoed. What was home? She supposed she'd find out soon enough. But as they turned to leave the waiting room, someone entered, blocking the way.

Gabby's heart felt as though it stopped beating for a good moment. She barely recognized him. He'd had a haircut and a shave and today looked every inch the FBI agent in his suit and sunglasses.

She stiffened, because she wasn't ready for this, because her first instinct was to throw herself at him.

Because an angry slash of hurt wound through her. He hadn't come to check on her, and no one had told her what had happened to him.

She'd been afraid to ask. Afraid he'd be dead. Afraid he'd been a figment of her imagination. So afraid of everything outside these walls.

Now he was just *here*, looking polished and perfect. Not Jaime, but the man he'd been before the compound. A man she didn't know and...

She didn't know how to do *all* of this today, so she threw her shoulders back and greeted him coolly, no matter how big a mess she must look from all the crying.

"Ms. Torres."

Even his voice was different, as though the man she'd known in the compound simply hadn't existed. That had been a beating fear inside her for days and now it was a reality.

She could only fight it with a strength she was faking.

His gaze took her in quickly then moved to her sister. "Ms... .well, Natalie, I've got a message for you."

Gabby's grip tightened on Natalie's arm, though she didn't dare show a hint of the fear beating against her chest.

"It's from the Texas Rangers' office."

It was Natalie's turn to grip, to stiffen. Jaime held out a piece of paper and Natalie frowned at it. "They couldn't have called me? Sent an email?" she muttered.

Jaime's gaze was on Gabby and she just...had to look away.

"Agent Alessandro, would you be able to escort Gabby and my family home while I see to this?"

Gabby whipped her head to her sister, whose expression was...angry, Gabby thought. She thought she recognized that stubborn anger on her sister's face.

"I'd love to be of service," Jaime said. "But I doubt your sister..."

He was trying to beg off because of *her*? Oh, no. Hell, no. "Oh, no, please escort us, Mr. *Alessandro*. *I* don't have a problem with it in the least," Gabby replied, linking arms with Mama and Grandma.

He didn't get to run away anymore.

Gabby saw the uncertainty on Natalie's face, but Gabby wanted to be done. Done with law enforcement and the past eight years. "Tie up loose ends, sissy. I want this over, once and for all," she said, not bothering to even look at Jaime.

"It will be," Natalie promised before she stalked past Jaime.

When Gabby finally looked at Jaime, his eyebrows

were drawn together, some emotion shuttered in his expression. She couldn't read it. She didn't want to.

He didn't want anything to do with her now. Couldn't even stand to be in her presence? Well, she'd prove that she didn't care about him at all, no matter that it was a lie.

DRIVING GABBY AND her mother and grandmother home was very much not on Jaime's list of things to do today. It, in fact, went against everything he was *trying* to do.

The FBI psychiatrist he'd been forced to talk to had insisted that any relationship with Gabby had been born of the situation and not actual feeling.

Jaime didn't buy it. He was too seasoned an officer, had been in too many horrible situations. He knew for a fact Gabby was just *different*.

But the problem was that Gabby wasn't a seasoned officer. She was a woman who'd been a kidnapping victim for eight years, and no matter what he felt or what he was sure of, she had a whole slew of things to work through that had nothing to do with him.

He'd only meant to relay the message from Ranger Cooper to Natalie. Not…see Gabby. With her family. The same woman he'd shared a bed with only a few days ago, before the strange world they'd been living in imploded.

She'd been crying, it was clear. He'd had to stand there, forcing himself not to take another step, for fear he would grab her away from all of them.

He glanced over at her sitting in his passenger seat.

She was in his car. *His* car. In the daylight. Real and breathing next to him.

Her eyes were on the road, her profile to him, chin raised as though the road before them was a sea of admirers she was deigning to acknowledge.

He wanted to stop the car and demand she tell him everything, forget the fact her mother and grandmother were in the back.

But those women remained a good reminder of what had knocked him out of the raging idiot who'd nearly gotten himself fired and ruined the rest of his life. Women who'd truly suffered, nearly as much as Gabby, in the loss of her.

She deserved the time and space to rebuild with her family first. He didn't have any place in that. He would drive her home and...

He had to grip the wheel tighter because if he thought about leaving her at her house and just driving away...

But he'd made his decision. He'd made the *right* choice. He would keep his distance. He would give her time to heal. If she... Well, if she eventually came to him... He had to give her the space to make the first move.

You know that's stupid.

He ground his teeth together. No matter how stupid he *thought* it was, he was trying to do the right thing for Gabby. That's what was important.

"Natalie tells us you were undercover with the evil man?" Gabby's grandmother asked from the back seat.

"Yes." He turned onto the street Gabby's mother had named when they'd started. He didn't realize he'd slowed down to almost a crawl until someone honked from behind.

"It's the blue one on the corner," the grandmother supplied.

Jaime nodded and hit the accelerator. No matter that he didn't want to let Gabby out of the car, it was his duty. More, it was what she needed. Her family. Her life.

It would be a difficult transition for her, and he didn't need to make that any more complicated for her. It was the right thing to do.

No matter how completely wrong it felt.

He pulled his car into the driveway of a small, squat, one-story home. It looked well kept, if a little sagging around the edges.

Gabby blinked at it and it took every last ounce of control he had not to reach over and brush his mouth across the soft curve of her cheek. Not to touch her and comfort her.

She looked young and lost, and he wanted to protect her from all that swamp of emotion she'd be struggling with.

"I got written up," he blurted into the silence of the car.

What the hell are you doing?

He didn't know. He needed to stop.

"You…" Gabby blinked at him, cocking her head.

"I think they gave me a little leeway what with just being out of undercover and all, but they don't take kindly to ignoring orders."

Shut your mouth and let her go, idiot.

"You…ignored orders," she repeated, as though she didn't quite believe it.

"They told me not to come to the hospital. Or try to see you. I may have…" He cleared his throat and turned his attention to the house in front of them. "I may have caused a bit of a scene."

"He got kicked out by security guards that first morning you were in the hospital," Grandma offered from the back. "A little rougher around the edges that day."

Jaime flicked a silencing glance in the rearview at the grandma. She smiled sweetly. "Natalie said you must have spent some time together when you were both in that place. Did you take care of our Gabriella?"

Gabby stiffened.

"I tried," Jaime said, perhaps a little too much of his still simmering irritation bleeding through. *If* she had come with him, she wouldn't have been in that standoff with Alyssa. They would have had… They could have…

"Mama, Grandma, will you…give me a few minutes alone with Agent Alessandro?" Gabby asked, her voice soft if commanding.

"Gabriella…" Her mother reached over the seat and put a hand to Gabby's shoulder.

"Gabby, please. Only Gabby from now on," Gabby whispered, eyes wide and haunted and not looking back at her mother.

"Come inside, baby. We'll—"

"I just need a few minutes alone. I promise. Only a few." She looked back at her mother and offered a smile.

But he was supposed to be giving her space. Not… alone time. "You should go—"

Gabby sent him a glare that would have silenced pretty much anyone, Jaime was pretty sure.

"Come now, Rosa," the grandmother said, patting the mother's arm. "Let's let these two talk. We'll go make some tea for our Gabri—Gabby."

Gabby's mother brushed a hand over Gabby's hair, but reluctantly agreed. The two women slid out of the back of his car and walked up to the house with a few nervous glances back.

Gabby's gaze followed them, an unaccountable hurt languishing in her dark brown eyes. He kept his hands on the wheel so he wouldn't be tempted to touch her.

"So…" Jaime said when Gabby just stared at him for long, ticking seconds. "How are you feeling?"

She didn't answer, just kept staring at him with that hauntingly unreadable gaze.

"Well, I, uh, have things to do," he forced himself to say, wrenching his gaze from searching her face for signs of things that were none of his business.

"Take off your sunglasses," she said in return.

"Gabby—"

She reached over and yanked them off his face with absolutely no finesse. "Hey!"

"You look different," she stated matter-of-factly.

"A haircut and a shave will do that to a man," he returned, still not meeting her shrewd gaze. He had a mission. A job. A duty. Not for him, but for her. For *her*.

"You look *scared*."

"Scared?" he scoffed, despite the overhard beating of his heart. "I hardly think—"

"Then look at me."

Scared? No. He wasn't scared. He was strong and capable of doing his duty. He was a reliable and excellent FBI agent. He could face down a man with guns and evil, he could certainly face a woman—

Aw, hell, the second he looked at her he had to touch. He had to pull her into his arms despite the console between them. He had to fit his mouth to hers and *feel* as much as know she was there, she was alive, she was safe.

He brushed his hands over her hair, her cheeks, her arms, assuring himself she was real. Her fingers traced his clean-shaved jaw, over the bristled ends of his hair, as she kissed him back with a sweetness and fervency he wasn't supposed to allow.

"I'm not supposed to be doing this," he murmured against her lips, managing to take his mouth from hers only to find his lips trailing down her neck.

"Why not?" she asked breathlessly, her hands smoothing across his back.

"Space and…healing stuff."

"I don't want space. And if I'm going to go through all the shit of healing, I at least want you."

He focused on the edge of the console currently digging into his thigh, because if he focused on that instead of kissing her in daylight, real and free, he might survive.

He managed to find her shoulders, pull her back enough that her hands rested on his forearms.

Flushed and tumbled. From him.

"I'm supposed to give you space," he said firmly, a reminder to himself far more than a response to her.

"I don't want it," she said, her fingers curling around his arms. "And I think I deserve what I want for a bit."

She deserved *everything*. But he wanted to make sure giving it to her was…right. Safe. "I've had to see a psychiatrist, and there's some…mandatory psychological things I'll have to do before I'm reinstated to active duty. I'm sure the doctor suggested the same thing to you."

"Therapy, yes."

"There's a chance…" He cleared his throat and smoothed his hands down her arms, eventually taking her hands in his.

That wasn't fair because how did he say anything he needed to when he was touching her? "You shouldn't feel *obligated* to continue what happened in there. You should have the space to find out if it's what you really want."

She cocked her head, some mix of irritation and uncertainty in the move. "Do *you* feel obligated by what happened?" she asked.

"No, but—"

"Then shut up." Then her mouth was on his again, hot and maybe a little wild. But it didn't matter, did it?

He didn't want it to matter. He wanted her. This strong, resilient woman.

She pulled back a little, always his warrior, facing whatever hard things were in her way. "I want you. The Jaime I met in there. And I want to get to know this you," she said, running her finger down the lapel of his suit. "The thing is, awful things happened in there, but it was eight years of my life. I can't…erase it. It's there. Forever. An indelible part of me. I don't need to pretend it never existed to heal. I don't think that's *how* you heal."

"But I have this whole life to go back to, Gabby. I know you aren't starting over, but people knew I was coming back. I'm coming back to a job. It isn't the same space we're in. I don't want you to feel as though you need to make space for me. That...you need to love me or any of it."

She studied him for the longest time, and the marvelous thing about Gabby was that she thought about things. Thought them through, and gave everything the kind of weight it deserved.

Who was he to tell her she needed space? Who was he to tell her much of anything?

"I will tell you when I need space. You'll tell me when you need some. It's not complicated." She traced a fingertip along his hairline, as though studying this new facet to him. Eventually her eyes met his.

"And I do love you," she said quietly, weighted. "If that changes, I'd hardly feel obligated to keep giving you something I didn't have."

"Such a pragmatist," he managed to say, his voice rusty in the face of her confession. "I was trying to be very noble, you know."

Her mouth curved and he wondered how many things he would file away in his memories as *first in daylight*. The first time he'd kissed her with the sun shining into the car. The first smile under a blue sky.

He wanted them to outnumber his memories of a cramped room more than he wanted his next breath.

"I don't want noble. I want Jaime." She swallowed. "That is, as long as you want me."

"I practically lost my life's work for wanting you, and I'd do it a million times over, if that's what you wanted. I'd give up anything. I'd fight anything. I hope you know, I'd do *anything*."

She rubbed her hands up and down his cheeks as if to make sure he was real, and hers, though he undoubtedly was. Always.

"Come inside. I want to tell my mother and grandmother about the man who saved me."

"I didn't—"

"You did. I'd stopped counting the days. I'd stopped hoping. You came in and gave me both."

His chest ached, a warm bloom of emotion. Touched that anything he'd done had mattered. Moved beyond measure. "We saved each other." Because he'd been falling, losing all those pieces of himself, and she'd brought it all back.

"A mutual saving. I like that." She smiled that beautiful sun-drenched smile and then she got out of his car, and so did he. They walked up the path to her home with a bright blue sky above them, free and ready for a future.

Together.

* * * * *

Join Britain's BIGGEST Romance Book Club

- **EXCLUSIVE offers every month**

- **FREE delivery direct to your door**

- **NEVER MISS a title**

- **EARN Bonus Book points**

Call Customer Services
0844 844 1358*
or visit
millsandboon.co.uk/subscriptions

* This call will cost you 7 pence per minute plus your
phone company's price per minute access charge.

KCB3

MILLS & BOON®

Why shop at millsandboon.co.uk?

Each year, thousands of romance readers
find their perfect read at millsandboon.co.uk.
That's because we're passionate about
bringing you the very best romantic fiction.
Here are some of the advantages of
shopping at www.millsandboon.co.uk:

* **Get new books first**—you'll be able to buy
  your favourite books one month before they
  hit the shops

* **Get exclusive discounts**—you'll also be
  able to buy our specially created monthly
  collections, with up to 50% off the RRP

* **Find your favourite authors**—latest news,
  interviews and new releases for all your
  favourite authors and series on our website,
  plus ideas for what to try next

* **Join in**—once you've bought your favourite
  books, don't forget to register with us to rate,
  review and join in the discussions

Visit **www.millsandboon.co.uk**
for all this and more today!